Jill Mansell loves nothing more than going to the gym, eating salad and telling lies. She is a natural blonde with an enviably slim figure and some very delusional ideas. The upside of this, she has discovered, is that when she tells lies about fictional characters rather than real people, it becomes a novel and is allowed. Which is great, because otherwise by now Jill would probably be in prison.

OK, apparently some boring facts are also required in an author biography. Jill lives in Bristol with her noisy family and used to work in the field of clinical neurophysiology back in the day when she had a proper job. Her top secret affair with an A-list Hollywood actor has never become public knowledge because she is so utterly discreet. (Oh, but the stories she could tell…)

By Jill Mansell and available from Headline Review

Jill Mansell

A WALK IN THE PARK

headline
review

First published in 2012
by HEADLINE REVIEW
An imprint of HEADLINE PUBLISHING GROUP

First published in paperback in 2012
by HEADLINE REVIEW
An imprint of HEADLINE PUBLISHING GROUP

1

ISBN (B-format) 978 0 7553 5585 3
ISBN (A-format) 978 0 7553 5586 0

Typeset in Bembo by Palimpsest Book Production Limited, Falkirk, Stirlingshire
Printed and bound in Great Britain by Clays Ltd, Elcograf S.p.A.

Headline's policy is to use papers that are natural, renewable and recyclable
products and made from wood grown in sustainable products. The logging and
manufacturing processes are expected to conform to the environmental
regulations of the country of origin.

HEADLINE PUBLISHING GROUP
An Hachette UK Company
338 Euston Road
London NW1 3BH

www.headline.co.uk
www.hachette.co.uk

To the lovely Elsewine.

A huge and genuine thank you to everyone on Twitter who has ever brightened my day, kept me company while I was writing, watched TV shows with me, recommended books and web links, made me laugh and cry and helped with research. Every time I asked a question, no matter how obscure, the answer was magically provided in an instant — how great is that? And you're so helpful, enthusiastic and generous with your time and knowledge too. Thanks so much to all of you — you made writing this book even more fun!

Chapter 1

'OK, we can see it from here.' Lara Carson pulled up at the side of the road, buzzed down the window and pointed into the valley below. 'See the L-shaped house with the white gates and the green car outside? That's the one.'

Home sweet home. Or maybe not. Eighteen years had passed since she'd last set foot over the threshold. Who knew what it was like inside now?

Gigi was leaning across from the passenger seat, breathing minty chewing-gum fumes over her as she peered down at the house. 'Does it feel funny, seeing it again?'

'No.' That wasn't true. 'A bit.' Lara gave her daughter's hand a squeeze.

'Are you going to cry?'

'What am I, some sort of *girl*? I'm definitely not going to cry.'

They sat in silence for a few seconds, looking at the old house with its ivy-strewn walls, blue-painted window frames and neatly tended garden.

'OK, come on then,' Gigi said at last. 'It's nearly time. You don't want to be late for your own father's funeral.'

★   ★   ★

Lara was one of the last into the church. It felt like being in a film. Her high heels click-clacked across the grey flagstones and people swivelled round to see who was making all the racket. Of the seventy or eighty mourners, most were strangers and didn't recognise her, which suited Lara just fine. But there were a few who clearly did. Eyebrows were raised and elbows nudged. She made a point of steadily meeting their gaze before looking away and slipping into an empty pew at the back.

What a weird situation to be in. People were spreading the word about her now; she could practically feel the mini Mexican wave of whispers rolling forwards. Finally it reached Janice in the front pew, flanked by her sisters and wearing an extraordinary feathered black hat. Together the three of them stiffened then turned their frosty glares upon her. With the feathers waving around her head, Janice resembled an angry crow with an acute case of bed hair.

Was it very wrong to think ill of the grieving widow during her husband's funeral? Obviously it was, but where Janice was concerned, it wasn't easy to think of anything nice.

The organ music started, everyone rose to their feet and the coffin was brought in.

Lara watched it being carried past her pew. The weirdness intensified. Charles Carson, her actual father, was inside that coffin.

He was dead.

And she genuinely didn't feel a thing.

Outside the church, Evie waited for the service to end. It was a long shot, but she hadn't been able to help herself. The moment she'd seen the notice in the local paper announcing the death of Charles Carson and the date of his funeral, she'd booked the time off work. The chances of Lara turning up at the funeral might be slim, but it could just happen. And if it did, Evie wasn't going to miss her.

They'd been best friends once. There were so many unanswered questions. Coming here today was an opportunity she simply couldn't pass up.

Not long now before the service was over. From this distance Evie heard the organ cranking up again, launching ponderously into 'Guide Me O Thou Great Redeemer'. It was hot out here; the sun was blazing down and her hair was sticking to the back of her neck. Pushing open the car door for extra ventilation, she swivelled sideways and swung her legs out, then tipped her left hand from side to side to admire the way the emeralds and diamonds flashed in the sunlight. Was Lara inside the church? Would she be seeing her again for the first time in eighteen years?

Oh well, soon find out.

The funeral ended. The genial vicar made the announcement that refreshments were available at Charles and Janice's home, and that everyone would be welcome back there, but Lara guessed she probably wasn't included in the invitation.

Luckily she didn't want to go anyway.

From her pew at the back, she watched Janice and her sisters lead the exit from the church. As they came down the aisle, the looks they gave her pretty much confirmed her suspicions. The black feathers shuddered with outrage and three sets of pale eyes ringed with black make-up bored through her. Since now wasn't the time for a confrontation, Lara averted her gaze and waited for the malevolent trio to pass.

The church emptied. She sat and waited a few minutes longer for the mourners to disperse. Soon came the sound of cars being started up and driven off. Finally, when all was quiet again, Lara rose and headed outside into the welcome heat and sunlight of a glorious summer's day.

Everyone had left, apart from a lone figure at the bottom of the driveway. Someone was sitting on the wall next to the open gates; someone with red hair, wearing a cobalt blue shirt and a white skirt. Which in turn meant she was likely to have moss and lichen stains on the back of it.

Lara attempted to focus but the distance was too great and her superpowers weren't that strong. She hadn't thought to bring her binoculars with her.

But . . . there was something familiar about the figure that was causing prickles of recognition down her spine. It couldn't be, could it . . . ?

Her pace quickened and the distance between them was reduced. The redhead slid down from the dry stone wall and began to move towards her. Moments later they both stretched their arms wide and broke into a run. It was like one of those slow motion Hollywood sequences that more traditionally featured two members of the opposite sex.

'It *is* you,' shouted Lara.

'I *know*.' Evie beamed as they collided and hugged each other until they were both panting for breath. 'Oh my God, I can't believe it, you're really *here*.' She pulled back to study Lara's face. 'Your dad . . . I'm sorry . . . are you upset?'

'No, no.' Vigorously Lara shook her head. 'Don't worry, you don't have to be polite. I only came back because of the solicitor. He phoned and said I needed to get myself down here. Anyway, let's not talk about that now.' She was so thrilled to see Evie she was burbling uncontrollably. 'How are you? You look fantastic! Oh, I've missed you so much. You have to tell me everything!'

4

It was true, she had missed her oldest friend more than words could say. But at the time she'd known it was the only way. And look at Evie now, eighteen years older and obviously looking older . . . but at the same time miraculously unchanged. Teasingly, she turned Evie sideways and peered at the back of her white skirt. Thirty-four years old and she still hadn't learned how to keep herself stain-free. 'You've got dirt on your skirt.'

'Have I? Oh no! How did that happen?' As she always had, Evie seemed genuinely surprised. For a couple of seconds she slapped ineffectually in the general area of her rounded bottom before giving up. 'Oh well, never mind, you're *here*. This is so brilliant! I'd almost given up hope, then I heard someone say on their way out, "Was that her? Was that the daughter who ran away?" So I knew you were in there. Everyone's gone back to the house for drinks. Is that where you're going now?'

'Urgh, no way.' Lara checked her watch; almost two o'clock. 'I'm meeting the solicitor in his office at three thirty. But I'm free till then. Do you have to be somewhere or can I buy you lunch?'

Fifteen minutes later they were sitting at a pavement café by the abbey, drinking Prosecco and catching up. Having spotted the emerald engagement ring, Lara now heard all about Joel and the imminent wedding. Less than six weeks from now, Evie was set to become Mrs Barber. Joel was the one she'd waited so long for, and she'd never been happier in her life.

By unspoken mutual consent they'd covered Evie's story first, getting it out of the way. Then it was Lara's turn. Evie said, 'Tell me what happened,' and Lara took a deep swallow of fizzy, ice-cold wine.

'The people at the church, you said they called me the one

5

who ran away. Is that what everyone thought?' She placed the glass carefully in the centre of the table. 'I didn't run away. They kicked me out.'

'I called round to your house to see where you were,' said Evie. 'Your dad answered the door. He just said you'd gone and wouldn't be coming back. Then Janice appeared next to him and you should have seen the look on *her* face. Like she'd finally got what she'd always wanted. Which I suppose she had. But I'm telling you, it gave me the shivers. I was so worried . . . you could have been *murdered*.'

'I was late home,' said Lara. 'I had to be back by eleven o'clock and I missed the last bus. By the time I got home it was almost half past. That was when it all kicked off.' She didn't go into detail; this wasn't the time or the place. 'It was the biggest row we'd ever had. Janice called me some vile names and told me she wished I'd never been born. Dad said I was ruining his life and he'd had enough, he wasn't going to put up with it any more. He gave me an hour to pack my things. Then he told me to get out.'

Evie was appalled. 'How could he do that? You were sixteen!'

'Didn't matter.' Lara shrugged and emptied her glass. 'He wasn't going to change his mind. On the bright side, looking back on it now, I'm glad it happened. Mind you, at the time it wasn't so great. I'd never been so scared in my life.'

'You should have come to our house!'

'I couldn't. It was three o'clock in the morning. And I was just desperate to get away. So that's what I did. I sat outside the train station for the rest of the night, then caught the first train out of Bath.'

'Where did you go?'

'I called my Aunt Nettie and asked if I could stay with her

6

for a couple of days.' Lara broke into a smile at the thought. 'That was it, basically. I turned up on her doorstep in Keswick and that's where I've been ever since.'

'Keswick? In Cumbria? We had no idea,' said Evie. 'None of us knew where you were. I kept waiting for you to call or write . . .'

'I know. I'm so sorry.' The guilt had haunted her all these years, but even now she wasn't able to tell Evie the rest of the story. 'I just knew I'd never come back to Bath as long as my father was alive. It was easier to make a clean break.'

The food arrived, they talked and drank some more, then it was time for Lara to head off for her appointment with the solicitor in nearby Harington Place.

'And I have to get back to work.' Before they left, Evie took out her diary and said, 'But we're not going to lose touch again. Give me everything you've got . . . address, email, phone numbers, I want the lot. And you have to have mine too.'

Once that was done, Lara walked back to Evie's car with her. They hugged each other again hard.

'You must come to the wedding,' Evie begged. 'It'll be fantastic. You will, won't you? On the twelfth of August.' She squeezed Lara's hands. 'Please say you'll be there!'

Chapter 2

The offices smelled exactly like solicitors' offices always did: dry, serious and papery with undertones of dust and Pledge. Arriving with five minutes to spare, Lara was directed to a seat in the waiting room and offered a selection of magazines only a solicitor could love.

Her mind was occupied anyway. So much had already happened. Seeing Evie again and retelling the story had stirred it all up again.

Well, retelling half the story. Lara closed her eyes, her stomach clenching as the old feelings came crashing back. In the days leading up to that fateful night, her life might not have been perfect but it had been manageable. On the downside, her mother's death from cancer three years earlier had been horrendous, leaving her with a father who'd never been much of a father in the traditional sense. Less than six months after the funeral, *allegedly*, he had met Janice. In no time at all she'd been installed in the house, filling it with the cloying scent of her perfume and a vast collection of china ornaments. In no time at all, Lara had become the gooseberry, the third wheel, the unwanted extra. When she overheard Janice talking on the phone, saying, 'She's just in the *way*, why can't she just join the army or something?' it hadn't come as a surprise. It wasn't as if Janice was pleasant to her face and moaned about her behind her back. From the word go, she hadn't bothered to pretend to be nice.

So life at home had been pretty grim, basically, but it hadn't mattered as much as it might have done, because at least she'd had Flynn. And when you were sixteen years old, with the best boyfriend in the world . . . well, that made up for a lot. At the time, it had meant pretty much everything. Having Flynn in her life had made the awful stuff bearable. As a couple they could get through anything; together they could cope.

Until the day of the argument.

Lara could recall every last second of that day, from the moment she'd been gripped with fear at the realisation that her period was late, all the way through to the following morning when she'd finally fallen into an exhausted sleep on the train.

It had been a Friday afternoon and she'd been in double maths, wrestling with trigonometry, when the date had nudged her with its significance. Normally as regular as clockwork, she was five days overdue. *Oh God, please no, they'd been so careful* . . .

After school, numb with terror, she had stood in Boots the Chemist, gazing at the pregnancy testing kits and discovering she couldn't afford to buy one.

Then meeting up with Flynn, actually voicing her fears aloud was easier said than done. The words twisted themselves into knots inside her chest and refused to come out. Flynn would be appalled. He was seventeen years old. This wasn't part of the plan.

By ten o'clock that evening she still hadn't been able to pluck up the courage to tell him. Maybe she'd wake up tomorrow and everything would be all right, the problem would be resolved. Leaving it for another twenty-four hours wouldn't hurt.

9

That was when the phone had rung and Flynn had taken the call inviting him to spend the next few days at a skiing tournament in Austria. It was also the moment Lara realised she was on her own. Thrilled by the opportunity to take part in the tournament, Flynn said yes without even checking first that she was fine with it.

He put the phone down, and that was when the argument had begun. At first he thought she was joking. Amazed by her reaction, he assumed she was upset because his parents could afford to pay for him to fly over to Austria and her father would never do that. The fight went on and on, spiralling beyond all reason because Lara now knew she couldn't tell him what might be wrong. He was Flynn Erskine, the boy all the other girls fancied, the gilded sports star with his life ahead of him and a genuine talent that was already getting him noticed in the world of downhill skiing.

She called him self-centred, he told her she was turning into a crazy person. She yelled that he only cared about himself, and Flynn, gazing at her as if she were a complete stranger, said, 'My God, I can't believe you actually think that.' She bellowed that she couldn't believe she'd wasted the last eight months with someone like him and he shouted back that if he'd known she was going to turn into a neurotic basket case he'd never have got involved in the first place.

The argument had culminated with her announcing that she never ever wanted to see him again and storming out of his parents' house. But having lost track of time, she'd already missed the last bus. Being late home had been a bone of contention for months, filling her father with rage and bringing with it the threat of, 'If you can't abide by our rules, you can get out.' She'd never imagined he'd actually see it through but it turned out she'd underestimated him. When she let herself into the house forty minutes later, her father and Janice had had plenty of time in which to plan their own line of attack.

Not to mention haul the suitcases down from the loft.

Lara jumped as her mobile phone rang, bringing her crashing back to the present.

'Hi, it's me. How's it going?'

'Everything's fine.' She relaxed at the sound of Gigi's voice. 'I'm just waiting to see the solicitor. Bought anything nice?'

'A scarf with vampires on it in New Look and a leopard-print bra from La Senza!'

'The perfect outfit for any job interview.' As Lara said it, the door to the solicitor's office opened and an elderly man came towards her. 'Looks like I'm going in now.' She picked up her bag and rose to her feet. 'OK, sweetie, won't be long. I'll call you as soon as I'm finished.'

What must it have been like for Aunt Nettie? At the age of forty-seven, never married and having devoted her life to her animals, how must she have felt when Lara arrived on her doorstep with two large battered suitcases and a small embryo by way of baggage?

In all probability her heart must have sunk all the way down to her sturdy dog-walking boots.

'I'm really sorry. I didn't know where else to go. Don't worry, I'll think of something.' Lara's voice was muffled by the thick scratchy wool of Nettie's bright purple hand-knitted sweater. Clothes were about on a par, priority-wise, with eyelash extensions and the latest developments in pentapeptides. The sweater smelled of soap and dog. Nettie's yellow corduroy trousers had probably been donated by an ancient farmer to the local charity shop. That she had been Lara's mum's older sister seemed impossible; Barbara had been as elegant as Audrey Hepburn, the delicate whippet to Nettie's galumphing wolfhound.

But Nettie was a good soul with a heart of gold beneath the bluff exterior. Hugging Lara, she said gruffly, 'You did the right thing, love. You're staying here with me.'

OK, get it over and done with. Say it now. 'And I think I might be going to have a baby.'

Nettie pulled away, held her at arm's length and gazed down at her stomach. 'What, right this minute?'

Lara heard herself make a strange half-sob, half-laugh. 'No, but maybe in about eight months.'

'Oh well. So we've got plenty of time to get used to the idea. Got a boyfriend?'

Her heart ached. 'Not any more.'

But Nettie's no-nonsense, can-do attitude was infectious. Over the course of the next day or two they walked the dogs and talked and talked about everything. Nettie went into the local chemist and bought a pregnancy testing kit: 'Ha, that'll get the locals excited!' The test proved positive and they talked some more, coming to the conclusion that of course Lara was far too young to become a mother but between them they'd cope, and *not* having the child might make more sense but it simply wasn't an option. Neither of them could bear to do that.

And that was it. From then on there was no going back. Lara shed her old life like a snake sloughing off its skin. Two days after leaving Bath, her father called. Nettie had answered the phone.

'It's Charles.' His tone was abrupt; the pair of them had never liked each other. 'Have you heard from Lara?'

'Yes, I have.' In turn, Nettie was cool. 'She's here. And this is where she's staying. This is her home from now on.'

'Fine by me.' He sounded relieved. 'You'd better let the police know she's still alive then. That boyfriend of hers is threatening to report her missing.'

'She doesn't want anything to do with him either,' said Nettie. 'Don't go telling him where she is.'

Charles replied curtly, 'Why would I?' and hung up.

'There, all done.' Nettie put down the phone. 'You know what? We should have done this three years ago. I thought about it, you know. But I·didn't want to drag you away from your home and all your friends.'

Lara gazed around the messy, informal kitchen with the dog bowls lined up in a row and the latest batch of puppies curled up asleep in their basket in front of the Aga. Currently deep in self-preservation mode, she wasn't allowing herself to even think about Evie and her other friends. She *certainly* wasn't allowing herself to think about Flynn.

Aloud, she said with a crack in her voice, 'I wish you had.'

Chapter 3

Lara waited on a bench in Victoria Park and watched a couple of teenagers heading her way along the path, arm in arm, heads bent together and hips touching. Just like she and Flynn used to do when they had come here all those years ago. The boy whispered something in the girl's ear and she burst out laughing, responding with a playful dig in the ribs. Oh yes, they used to do that too.

As they passed by, the girl said, '. . . Dad was asking if you'd like to go to the football with him on Saturday, because he's managed to get an extra ticket.'

The boy's face lit up. 'Cool!'

OK, *that* didn't used to happen.

Then her phone rang again.

'Mum, I'm in the park now, by the playground. Where are you?'

Lara spotted her and lifted her hand. 'Look higher and over to the right. See me waving? Come on up.'

She sat back and watched as Gigi made her way up the hill. With her long legs, straight, swingy brown hair and merry silver-grey eyes, she was a head-turner with killer cheekbones and a refreshing lack of vanity. Her beautiful wilful daughter, the love of her life, the happiest accident she'd ever had. And by the looks of things she'd been on a spree; her arms were weighed down with bags.

What happened next would be all down to Gigi. Was their world about to change? Who knew?

'Phew, I'm shattered!' Gigi flung herself on to the bench and produced a can of Diet Coke from one of the carriers. She opened the ring-pull – *tsssssttt* – and drank thirstily. 'Ah, that's better. The shops here are great.' She offered Lara the can. 'I found this little boutiquey place having the most brilliant sale. Anyway, how was it? What did the solicitor say? Have you got the jewellery?'

This had been the reason for coming down to Bath. When the solicitor had called to inform her of her father's death and had also suggested they meet to discuss his will, Lara had been mystified. She knew her father too well to expect him to leave her anything of value. The inevitable conclusion was that he was passing on the few items of jewellery that had belonged to her mum. Not much and nothing for Sotheby's to get excited about, but unbelievably precious nonetheless. All these years on, she could still picture her mum wearing each piece . . . the tiny daisy ring, the thin bangles and the three narrow gold chains she'd always worn around her neck. There'd also been a long coral necklace, a jade pendant and a bracelet of sheeny black pearls.

And it was just as well she could still picture the items of jewellery, seeing as there had been no mention of them this afternoon.

'No. But we're getting something else.' Lara realised she was still in shock; her hands were trembling. 'You're not going to believe this. It's the house.'

Gigi choked on her drink. 'Are you joking?'

15

'I wouldn't.'

'But why? My God, because he felt guilty about kicking you out? Oh wow, that's so—'

'No,' Lara leapt in before Gigi could start thinking sentimental thoughts about the grandfather she'd never known. 'It's nothing to do with that. The house was never his in the first place.'

'What? How can that happen?' Gigi was stunned. 'He's lived in it for the last thirty years!'

Thirty-two years, actually. When Lara had been born, her parents had been living in a flat in Bradford on Avon, just a few miles outside Bath. Then, when she was three, they had moved into the house she'd grown up in. Her father had worked in a bank. She had always assumed they'd bought it with the help of a mortgage. This afternoon's meeting with the solicitor had been a revelation in more ways than one.

'The house was bought in my mum's name. And it was paid for in cash. When she wrote her will she left it in trust for me. But if she died before my father, he was allowed to live there for as long as he needed to. And now he doesn't need it any more.' Lara sat back and puffed out her cheeks. 'Which means it's properly mine.'

'We've got a house. We've actually got a house!' Gigi kicked her legs in the air. 'Woo-hoo! We can sell it!'

'Yes.' How much would it fetch? Bearing in mind that this was a super-pricey city. Guessing wildly, Lara estimated four to five hundred thousand pounds.

'Or we could live in it!'

Lara's heart went thuddity-thud. 'You mean here in Bath?'

'I was thinking we could maybe attach it to five million multi-coloured helium balloons and float it to wherever takes our fancy.' Gigi rolled her eyes. 'Yes, Mum, *of course* here in Bath.'

'Why?' Did she already know the answer to that question?

'Why not? Because we can!' Her daughter's sweeping arm indicated the park, the trees, the Georgian houses of honey-coloured Bath stone, the rolling hills in the distance. 'You always said you'd never come back as long as your father was alive. But he's dead now, so that's that taken care of. Your mum's just given you a house. And I really love this city,' said Gigi. 'I know this is going to sound mad, but being here for the first time just feels . . . *right*. I liked the shops. I like the people. You know when you get that squeeze in your chest, like falling a little bit in love?' She pressed her clenched fist to her breastbone for emphasis. 'That's how I've been feeling all afternoon! It's like coming home.'

'But what about your friends? Wouldn't you miss them?'

'Mum, we're eighteen, everyone's heading off to different places now anyway. Unis . . . gap years . . . we're all moving on. Besides, there's phones and Facebook, and we can still meet up when we want to. It's not as if we'd lose touch.' She shrugged and said, 'Plus, moving to a new place means making new friends.'

For a moment Lara couldn't speak. Gigi's instincts were a huge part of her personality; when she fell in love, whether with a piece of art, a new recipe, unicycling or kayaking or diving, it was never a passing whim. It became a passion.

And in all honesty how could she disagree with this one? She felt exactly the same way. Keswick and the Lake District had been wonderful but she had always loved her home town, had missed it desperately for so many years.

They could do it. There was nothing to stop them.

Other than Flynn Erskine.

Chapter 4

Evie was lying in bed watching shards of bright sunlight sneaking in around the curtains. It was eight o'clock in the morning and the weather forecaster had promised wall-to-wall sunshine today. Fingers crossed he'd got it right.

Because she was superstitious, Evie crossed her fingers and listened to the birds singing outside her window. Then she heard another door along the landing being opened. Floorboards creaked.

There was a tap at her door and she called out, 'I'm awake.'

The door opened and Bonnie appeared; fair hair rumpled, she was wearing a white cotton dressing gown and looking puzzled.

'Morning, darling. I'm sure there's something we're meant to be doing today. Any ideas?'

'No.' Evie shook her head. 'I'm just going to have a lie-in. Maybe go shopping later. Any good films on at the cinema?'

Another door slammed, they heard footsteps in a hurry and Marina raced past her mother into the bedroom. Taking a flying leap on to the bed, she sang, 'You're getting married in the morning!'

'That's it.' Bonnie heaved a sigh of relief. 'I knew there was something.' She broke into a grin and came over to envelop Evie in a hug. 'Here we are, can you believe it? Happening at last. Now, you stay there and we'll bring you breakfast in bed.'

'Ooh yes, we're going to spoil you rotten.' Marina bounced off the bed in her pyjamas and flung back the curtains. 'Don't move a muscle! Well, unless you need to go for a wee.'

Evie lay back against her plumped-up pillows and listened to the two of them clattering downstairs.

Lucky, lucky me.

In just a few hours she would properly belong to the family she loved more than any other family in the world. Bonnie would become her mother-in-law, Marina her sister-in-law. Ray would become not only her father-in-law but the father she had never had.

And she would become Joel's wife.

It was like a dream come true. Her life was about to become officially perfect. Gazing out of the window, Evie wondered how different things might have been if she hadn't met the Barbers.

Her own family was about as small as it was possible to get. Growing up, it had just been herself and her mother, who couldn't have been more different from Bonnie Barber if she'd tried. Evie had never known her father. Nor had she known much fun. In order to provide a decent standard of living, her mother had sacrificed her social life for financial security. Every spare hour had been spent working. Evie had learned not to make a nuisance of herself, or to expect much in the way of attention. Her child-hood had been lonely, which was why getting to know Lara in her early teens had made such a difference. Because Lara's home life was pretty miserable too. Their respective problems had cemented their friendship. In many ways, she'd had it easier; at least her mother was still alive. Nor did she have a father and stepmother who ganged up on her and appeared to resent her

19

very existence. Evie knew her mother didn't hate her; she just wasn't her number one priority.

Like today. The wedding was due to start at twelve o'clock. And her mother, currently snowed under at the office, was driving down from Swindon for the ceremony. On the phone last night she'd explained that she could be a bit late getting there but that she'd definitely be at the church by twelve fifteen. 'So I might miss a couple of hymns, but I'll be there in time for the main bit.'

Evie hadn't even attempted to protest. I mean, what more could any daughter expect? If her mother managed to stay for the first half of the reception it would be a bonus.

Was it any wonder she loved Bonnie and Ray?

From the foot of the stairs, Bonnie yelled up, 'Toast and marmalade, darling? Or croissants and cherry jam?'

'Ooh, croissants please.'

'Bucks Fizz?' This from Marina. 'Or orange juice and champagne in separate glasses?'

'Separate glasses please.'

'Moët et Chandon or vintage Bollinger?' Marina paused. 'Or lovely sparkly cava from the supermarket?'

Evie knew the proper stuff was being saved for the toasts at the reception. She grinned. 'Cava.'

'Good girl, cor-rect answer! OK, just give us a few minutes . . .'

Imagine it, in a few hours she wouldn't be a Beresford any more. She'd become Evie Barber instead. One of the family. Oh my.

She'd first seen Joel in a nightclub in Bath, shortly after the Barbers had moved down from London. That had been fifteen years ago. She'd been nineteen, on the gawky side, never a member of the cool set. Whereas Joel, at twenty and without even trying, had been the epitome of cool. Handsome, charming, reckless and impulsive, everyone had fallen under his spell and Evie had been content to watch from the sidelines. She didn't mind that he didn't notice her; Joel Barber was way out of her league.

But as time went on, their paths had continued to cross. Bath wasn't a huge city and there were only so many clubs and bars. Eighteen months after that initial sighting, Joel was leaving a pub just as Evie was on her way in and he accidentally swung the glass door shut in her face. He'd apologised profusely, made sure she was OK and insisted on taking the blame even though it had been as much her fault as his.

Which had been nice.

Then, a couple of years later, she had been jostled carrying a couple of drinks across a crowded bar and accidentally spilled one of them down the back of Joel's shirt.

This time it had definitely been her fault and she had been the one to apologise but he'd been lovely about it, assuring her it didn't matter a bit.

Another year or so after that, a friend of hers had started seeing a friend of Joel's and their social circles had begun to intersect, then merge. He finally learned her name and treated her as a girl-who-was-a-friend. It felt fantastic, despite the fact that she'd far rather have been his girlfriend in the proper sense.

But Evie kept her true feelings hidden. That was her secret and hers alone. Joel was still out of her league. At least he wasn't breaking her heart and leaving her in bits, like he was doing to the stream of pretty girls who passed through his life and did get involved with him.

And ended up regretting it.

Then an astonishing thing happened. At the age of twenty-nine

Joel fell in love with an older woman who did the unthinkable and turned the tables on him in a spectacular fashion, losing interest and returning to her older richer lover.

Joel was devastated and hopelessly unprepared. For the first time in his entire charmed life he learned how it felt to be rejected. Many sniggered and revelled in his downfall but Evie's heart went out to him. Joel repaid her sympathy by confiding in her and sharing his pain.

A fortnight later they ended up in bed together. It was a toss-up which of them was more surprised. But Joel told her he loved her, that he was turning over a new leaf, that she was the one for him. He was done with drama and high-maintenance females. It was time for a change.

Time for a change for him, a dream come true for Evie. They became a couple and miraculously turned out to be better suited than either of them had thought. Their different characters complemented each other. Evie wasn't temperamental, attention-seeking and overly dramatic. In short, she wasn't hard work and Joel truly appreciated that. Their affection for each other was genuine.

And when he introduced her to his family, her joy was complete.

Ray and Bonnie were the most fabulous parents anyone could wish for, warm and welcoming and wonderful in every way. Meeting them had felt like skulking outside in the cold for years, then finally being invited into a gorgeous house with a fire roaring in the grate. For Evie it had been love at first sight. What more could she want?

And then, unbelievably, it got better.

Having made his money in London's square mile and worked his socks off for twenty-five years, Ray had decided life was too short not to enjoy the rest of it. Upon moving the family down to Bath, he had set up MadAboutParties, a company providing party goods and fancy dress items to buy or hire. With Ray and Bonnie at the helm, the business thrived and expanded. Then three years ago, a vacancy had arisen at just the right time. Evie, working as a secretary for a husband and wife team of relationship counsellors, discovered her bosses were about to divorce each other. The atmosphere in the office grew icier and more uncomfortable by the day. When Bonnie said, 'Sweetheart, why don't you come and work for us?' Evie had jumped at the chance.

And thanked her lucky stars ever since. She truly loved her new job, helping in all aspects of running the business, both in the shop itself and on the internet. Working with Ray and Bonnie had been a joy from day one.

The bedroom door swung open and Bonnie came in, a tray in her hands and a red rose held between her teeth.

'Right.' She laid the tray across Evie's lap, took a bottle of water out of her cardigan pocket, filled a narrow vase with the contents and placed the rose in it. 'Ta dah! Now, you enjoy your breakfast while we run you a lovely bath. What time's Kirsty getting here?'

'Ten fifteen.' Fabulously inept when it came to hair and make-up, Bonnie had hired a professional for the occasion; having Kirsty turn up to make the three of them look amazing was her treat.

For the next hour Evie relaxed, ate her breakfast, watched a bit of enjoyably trashy morning TV then had a long hot bath. This week she'd been staying here at the house, having given up her flatshare in Batheaston. Tonight she and Joel were booked into the Royal Crescent Hotel, then tomorrow she'd be moving into Joel's super-smart flat in Bannerdown. But Bonnie had insisted she spend the last few days of singledom with them and she'd been happy to do so.

23

Another tap on the door. Marina, wrapped in a towelling robe after her own shower, said, 'Do I put my bridesmaid's dress on now, or is that supposed to happen after we've been tarted up?'

Evie hesitated; this wasn't her field of expertise either. But the one thing she didn't want happening was eye shadow or lipstick being spilled on their beautiful dresses. She said, 'Let's put them on afterwards. Keep them nice.'

'You're right.' Marina grimaced at the cherry jam stain on the lapel of her robe. 'We don't want to mess anything up.'

By ten fifteen the three of them were gathered expectantly in the living room in their dressing gowns, waiting for Kirsty to arrive.

'Ha, look at you.' Having helped himself to a glass of cava, Ray eyed them cheerily from the doorway. 'See no evil, hear no evil, speak no evil.'

'Dad.' Marina pulled a face at him. 'Bugger off.'

He beamed. 'Well, I must say, that make-up girl was worth every penny. You all look sensational, like a bunch of beauty queens.'

'You should be a stand-up comedian.' Bonnie beckoned him over and took a sip from his glass.

'Kirsty's late,' said Evie. 'She should be here by now.'

'It's the traffic. She's just been a bit held up. Don't you worry.' Bonnie's tone was unruffled. 'She'll be on her way.'

Chapter 5

By ten twenty they were still waiting.

At ten twenty-five, Evie reached for her phone and called Kirsty's number. 'It's gone straight to the answering service.'

Ray said helpfully, 'That's because she's on a plane to Hong Kong.'

'Will you *stop* it?' Bonnie gave him a playful swipe with the *Radio Times*. 'Darling, it's all right.' She turned to Evie. 'It means she can't answer because she's in the car on the way here.'

Bonnie's voice was so lovely and soothing. Evie forced herself to relax. But surely if Kirsty was held up in traffic she could make a quick call to let them know?

At ten thirty she tried again. Still no reply. Evie left a message asking her to call back at once.

OK, by ten forty there had still been no word and it no longer mattered why. In just over an hour they had to leave for the church.

'Right then, no problem.' A born non-panicker, Bonnie clapped her hands and said gaily, 'It doesn't matter a bit! We'll just do it ourselves!'

Evie couldn't help herself; she loved Bonnie dearly but her

heart still sank. Bonnie's idea of glamour was keeping her fine blond hair out of her eyes with a stretchy Alice band and treating her mouth to a good old crayoning with lipstick. For extra-special occasions she might even dab on some powder-blue eye shadow and spit on the block of mascara that Marina complained was older than she was.

But since they didn't have any choice, they set to work with what little they had. Everyone pitched in. None of them knew how to create ringlets with hair-straighteners but Bonnie found a clip on YouTube showing how it was done.

Ray went next door and returned with the set of unused heated rollers eighty-year-old Elsie had been given last Christmas by her well-meaning but useless son.

Marina filled the plastic plant-sprayer from the kitchen tap and sprayed everyone's hair with water. Between them they blow-dried each other's hair and did their best to pin and spray the styles into place. It was safe to say they looked nothing like they had last week after the dress rehearsal, when Kirsty had woven her magic. When they were done, they looked like the before in a before-and-after makeover.

'Girls, you look sensational!' They didn't, but Ray was doing his best to keep the mood upbeat.

'Right, make-up now.' Having raced upstairs, Bonnie was back with her ancient eye shadow and mascara. 'If anyone wants to borrow mine, just help yourselves!'

It was eleven twenty; the hair had taken a while. Most of Evie's toiletries were at Joel's flat but she had a small cosmetics bag containing the basics. Hurriedly she attempted to reproduce the effect Kirsty had achieved last week. Where was the blusher stuff supposed to go anyway? She'd never got to grips with blusher. And now her hands were shaking, she was starting to really panic

. . . this was her wedding day and she was supposed to be looking wonderful . . . what was everyone going to think when she turned up with—

'Ow! OW!' The mascara wand had jabbed into her eye, which promptly started streaming. Oh God, why had she tried to separate her eyelashes? She should have just left them in clumps.

'OK, sweetheart, here you go.' Ray came to the rescue with a sheet of waterlogged kitchen towel. 'Don't you worry, it'll all be fine.'

'You know what?' Having made a brave but misguided attempt at eyeliner, Marina put down the mirror she'd been peering into. 'I look like Lily Savage the morning after a party. I'm better off with no make-up at all.'

'I'm starting to worry about Kirsty now.' Bonnie was gamely squeezing lipgloss from a tube on to her mouth, flinching at the unfamiliar gloopy texture. 'Do you think she's had an accident?'

Evie had given up trying to imagine what might have happened to Kirsty. Her right eye was now bloodshot and painful, she was still in her dressing gown and they had to leave the house in ten minutes.

Avoiding the sticky lipgloss, Ray gave his wife an affectionate kiss on the cheek. 'You all look so perfect already, she probably decided she didn't need to turn up.'

Twelve minutes later they were dressed and ready to go. At least, as ready as they'd ever be. Despite her own panic, Evie found herself reassured by the Barbers' refusal to get upset. A more image-conscious family might have had a nervous breakdown but they were still laughing and joking, making the best of a situation that really wasn't the end of the world.

And now the limo was waiting on the driveway to deliver them to the church.

'Come here.' Ray, in his morning suit, held out his arms. 'You all look absolutely beautiful. I'm so proud of you.'

He hugged each of them in turn then ushered them to the front door, breaking into song as they headed over to the sleek silver Bentley. 'Off we go, mind your skirts, girls . . . Get us to the church on time . . .'

It no longer mattered but Evie still needed to know. Sliding her phone out of her white silk bag – she'd have to remember to turn it off for the service – she gave Kirsty's number one last try.

Astonishingly, this time the call was answered.

'Right. Hello.' It was Kirsty's voice, sounding oddly jerky. 'Sorry I couldn't make it.'

'Oh my God, we thought you'd had an accident!' The chatter in the back of the limo abruptly stopped so everyone else could listen. Evie said, 'Are you all right? What happened? Your phone was switched off! Why didn't you call?'

There was a strange buzzy silence. At last Kirsty said stiffly, 'I'm all right. So who did your hair and make-up?'

Who did she think had done it, Vidal Sassoon? 'We did it ourselves.'

'But you said you were rubbish at all that sort of thing.'

'We *are* rubbish.'

'I'm sorry.'

'So you keep saying.' Evie's voice rose in frustration. 'But you still haven't said why you didn't turn up!'

'Sshh,' murmured Bonnie, taking her hand and giving it a reassuring pat. 'It doesn't matter now.'

Her words drowned out Kirsty's reply but something, some sixth sense, told Evie it did matter.

'Sorry, I missed that.' She pressed the phone harder against her ear.

But all she could hear now was the sound of sobbing. At the other end of the line, Kirsty was crying and gulping for breath.

'Say it again.' Evie's stomach clenched with fear and premonition. 'Say it.'

'I can't tell you.' Between sobs, Kirsty hiccupped, 'You'll have to ask your p-precious boyfriend, OK? Just ask Joel why I didn't turn up. He can probably hazard a guess.'

The call ended. Kirsty had severed the connection. As if from a great distance, Evie heard Bonnie say, 'Darling, what's going on?'

'Can we stop the car? I feel sick.'

The limousine purred to a halt and Evie stumbled out, waving the rest of them back. 'Don't come with me . . . please, just give me a minute.'

At the side of the road she turned away so they couldn't see her face. She wasn't going to be sick, she was just struggling to work out what to do next. Joel had first mentioned Kirsty's name a couple of months ago; she was someone he'd come into contact with through the bar he drank in across the road from his offices. Upon hearing about his forthcoming wedding, she had told him she was a hair and make-up artist looking to expand her client base. Did Joel happen to know anyone who might be interested in a free session? Touched by her generous offer, Joel had suggested his mother, and Kirsty had duly come to the house the following week. The results had been impressive; she undoubtedly knew her stuff. She'd been helpful and friendly too. Delighted with her makeover, Bonnie had promptly booked Kirsty for this morning so they could all look dazzling on the big day.

Evie wrapped her arms tightly around herself and concentrated on taking deep breaths. A car shot past and she glimpsed smiling faces through the windows, strangers wondering why a bride in

29

a full-length wedding dress would be standing on the grass verge behind a gleaming limo.

Why indeed? Kirsty was a pretty little thing in her mid-twenties. During their practice run she'd been chatty towards Bonnie and Marina, quieter with her. Evie hadn't thought anything of it at the time, had simply assumed Kirsty was concentrating harder because she was the bride.

Then again, being gullible and not paying attention to small signs was something she'd grown good at. Turning the other cheek without even consciously realising this was what she was doing was practically her speciality.

But seriously, there were limits. Even for her.

God, look at me, I'm shaking . . .

'Are you alright, darling? Do you want some more tissues?'

Poor Bonnie, poor Ray. Did they suspect what had happened? And what might be about to happen?

'I'm OK. No, I don't need any tissues.' Lifting the hem of her dress, Evie made her way over to the beribboned limo and climbed back in. 'Let's go.'

Everyone was waiting inside the church apart from Nick, who was Joel's best man, and the photographer.

'Actually, could you not do that?' Evie raised a hand to shield her face, fending off the photographer as he tried to snap her emerging from the car. 'Nick, where's Joel?'

Nick was grinning. 'He's waiting for you! You're late. He'll be starting to panic and think you've done a bunk.'

'I wouldn't do that. But I need to talk to him. Look, could you please *stop it?*' The photographer was having another go with his camera. 'I don't want any pictures taken.' Evie turned her attention back to Nick. 'Just get Joel out here, OK? Now.'

If she'd had any doubts before, they were decimated the moment Joel appeared on the steps of the church wearing his innocent face.

That handsome innocent face with the fractionally raised eyebrows, signalling utter bafflement, because what could possibly be wrong?

And that was the giveaway, because it was just that little bit overdone. And because she knew him well enough to be able to glimpse that faint shadow of panic in his beautiful eyes.

'Evie? Are you OK? What's going on?'

'Why don't you tell me?' Evie watched and waited and saw the unmistakable flicker of guilt. *Oh yes, he knew.*

'Sweetheart, come on. We're getting married, everyone's in there waiting for us . . .' He tried to reach out to her and Evie took a step back.

'Did she call you?'

'Who?'

The fear was clearly visible now. This wasn't fair on his family, out of the car now and lingering awkwardly a discreet distance away. But what else could she do? Go ahead with the wedding, simply because everyone was assembled here in their best clothes and the reception had been paid for? Should she ignore what had happened and marry Joel anyway, just because she loved his parents and sister so much?

'You've been seeing Kirsty.' Evie heard the words coming out of her mouth as if someone else were saying them. 'Just be a man and admit it. She phoned me.'

Joel lifted his gaze heavenwards and for a moment she thought he was going to cry. He did love her, she knew that. In his own way. But Joel was a charmer, feckless and fun-loving; he fell into situations, couldn't help himself. He found it almost impossible to say no, whether to the offer of another biscuit, another drink or another party.

Or another girl.

'What did she say to you?'

Evie shrugged. 'It wasn't always easy to tell. She was crying so much. Enough to get the gist, though.'

He exhaled audibly, raking his fingers through his dark-blond hair. 'OK, I'll tell you. There was a bit of a thing. It was never meant to happen, and I swear to God it didn't mean anything, OK? And it's over. That's why she was crying. I'm sorry, I'm sorry, I didn't *want* this to happen . . .'

'But it did.' Evie's disastrously blow-dried hair was wilting in the strong sunlight, sticking to the back of her neck. Perspiration was trickling down her spine. There were tissues in her bag but her bag was still in the car . . .

'I finished with her. I told her last week. It was just a stupid fling. Bloody hell, she knew I was getting married! She *promised* she wouldn't cause any trouble.'

'Oh dear,' said Evie. 'She lied.'

'I know.' Joel nodded miserably. 'I know. But we mustn't let her win.' He clutched her elbows. 'That's what she wants, isn't it? We can't let that happen! Evie, we have to do this. I love you so much. I want to marry you. *Please*,' he begged in desperation. 'This is our wedding. Everyone's *waiting* . . .'

Chapter 6

The whispers had started up the minute Nick and Joel left the church. For Lara, it was weirdly reminiscent of the last time she'd sat in an uncomfortable wooden pew, only this time she wasn't the focus of attention.

At first the remarks had been jokey, along the lines of, 'That's it, Evie's stood him up, she's found someone else and gone off with them instead.'

But as the minutes ticked by, laughter gave way to curiosity and puzzlement. Before long, a couple of Joel's friends sneaked down the aisle and slipped outside to see what was causing the delay. Moments later they reappeared in the doorway, shaking their heads with barely disguised elation. 'Something's up. Don't know what's happened, but it looks serious.'

After that there was no holding the rest of them back. The prospect of drama was too big a temptation to keep everyone in their seats. What could possibly be going on? It was no good, they had to know.

Oh well, if everyone else was doing it, she wasn't going to sit here like a lemon on her own. Following everyone else outside, Lara shielded her eyes from the dazzling sunlight and zoned in on Evie and the man she was presumably meant to be marrying. They were standing a short distance away from the church, among the Gothic headstones in the graveyard, and were locked in an intense discussion.

Oh dear. One thing was for sure, it didn't look to be a cheerful one. There wasn't a lot of laughter going on.

Things weren't looking good.

Nor, for that matter, was Evie. Her hair was bizarre, not remotely bridal, and appeared to have been styled by an enthusiastic chimpanzee. Was that the reason for the delay? Surely Evie wasn't so upset by the state of her hair that she was refusing to walk up the aisle?

The next moment a taxi came barrelling up the tree-lined drive. Like Wimbledon spectators, all eyes swivelled avidly from Evie and Joel to the black cab as it screeched to a halt. Had the taxi been ordered by Evie to whisk her away?

But no, it was here to deliver a late arrival rather than remove an unhappy bride. The back door of the cab was flung open and a tall figure emerged. Wouldn't it be brilliant if it could be Nicky Clarke, appearing like a hairdressing knight in shining armour, turning up in the nick of time to pluck triumph from disaster?

Then the late arrival finished paying the driver and turned to gaze at the congregation gathered around the entrance to the church.

And Lara felt as if a medicine ball had landed on her chest.

The thud was that unexpected, that intense.

It was Flynn. He was here.

It hadn't been hard to keep track of him over the years. At first, his skiing skills had kept him in the sports section of the newspapers and she had followed his exploits through their pages. Then as time passed, the internet grew up and took over the world and she'd done it that way instead. Flynn's looks and talent

34

had gained him plenty of attention, companies fell over themselves to sponsor him and he was tipped for a medal at the next winter Olympics. He might have won one too, if it hadn't been for an accident in training, causing him to fall and break an ankle.

The fracture turned out to be a complicated one requiring intricate surgery and signalling the end of Flynn's skiing days. At the age of twenty-four he returned to Bath and took a job with Grey's, the wine merchants. His new employers made no secret of the fact that they had selected him for his celebrity qualities; basically he was there to charm the socks off the buyers and raise the public profile of the company. Nobody, not even Flynn, could have guessed what an asset he would become. Three years later he became a partner. Grey and Erskine went from strength to strength, supplying new and old world wines to an expanding list of hotels, restaurants, festivals and private clubs. They sourced and imported direct from small family-run domains, and garnered attention from wine writers impressed by their selection skills. Internet sales, introduced by Flynn, caused profits to soar to the next level. Flynn's genuine enthusiasm for wine and his ability to relay that to the customers was what made a big difference. Entering the world of wine may have come about almost by accident, but it had turned out to be an amazingly happy one.

Over the years Lara wouldn't like to admit how many times she'd clicked on the Grey and Erskine Wine Merchants website.

It wasn't stalking. She'd been hundreds of miles away. It was just . . . keeping an eye on Flynn and seeing what he looked like.

OK, call it stalking-from-a-distance.

Anyway, she no longer needed to switch on a computer in order to see him. He was here. Oh God.

She'd begun mentally preparing herself for the fact that at some stage in the near future she would be seeing him again.

But not here, now, today, without any advance warning at all. This really wasn't fair.

The thin, elderly man standing in front of her turned and gave her a quizzical look. Lara realised she'd been hyperventilating, panting like a dog at the back of his wrinkled tortoisey neck.

'Sorry.' Hastily she pretended she'd been using her hand to fan herself. 'Hot.'

But . . . oh, oh, it was Flynn. Flynn Erskine, whom she hadn't seen for almost nineteen years, and he was heading her way.

Not that he'd noticed her, skulking at the back of the group behind an old man with a corrugated neck. Lara ducked down further still and surreptitiously cupped a hand over her mouth to keep her rapid breathing to herself. Flynn had reached the foot of the steps now and was talking to some people he knew. Asking them what was going on, no doubt. God, he still had it. For some people starting off as a beautiful teenager meant it was all downhill from there on, whilst others improved with age. Flynn, needless to say, was one of those. He had the kind of face you could just gaze at for ever. His bone structure had sharpened, matured. Those dark brown eyes were still utterly mesmerising, that mouth as perfect as she remembered. His dark hair was less spiky, more grown up. And he was wearing a well-cut grey suit, which definitely wasn't something she'd seen him in before. In the old days, T-shirts and jeans had been about as sophisticated as—

'Oh my goodness, everyone out of the way, this lady's GOING TO BE SICK!'

The woman next to Lara let out a shriek and leapt to the left. Startled, Lara looked round to see who was about to throw up. Embarrassingly, it appeared to be her. Everyone else was now shrinking back and gazing at her in horror. Honestly, a bit of

36

hyperventilation and a hand clapped to your mouth and people jumped to all the wrong conclusions.

'I'm all right—' She began to protest, but not convincingly enough to prevent a matronly lady grabbing and manhandling her down the stone steps whilst simultaneously whisking a supermarket bag-for-life from her capacious handbag.

'Don't worry, dear. I'm a nurse, I'll look after you. Just vomit into here and you'll feel better. It's the heat.'

'Really, I'm fine.' Lara was trying to make herself heard but the plastic carrier was crackling and the bossy woman was plunging her face-first into it, as if she were a horse being fitted with a nosebag. Someone else was holding her up in case she fainted. It took a while before she could twist her head free. 'You can let go, I don't need the bag, I'm not going to be sick!'

OK, she hadn't meant that to come out quite so loud. This time the woman heard her. 'Are you sure?'

'I'm sure.' Lifting her face, Lara saw that everyone had heard her. Instead of watching Evie and Joel over by the gravestones, they were now all fixated on her instead, in the wary manner of people who suspect there may still be a chance of being caught in the line of fire.

All of them, that is, except Flynn Erskine.

Who was staring at her in stunned disbelief.

The bossy nurse said, 'Fine then, if you're sure,' and stuffed the crackly bag-for-life back into her sensible handbag.

Flynn moved closer. 'Lara?'

Of all the situations she'd imagined in which they would meet again, having her head forcibly plunged into a plastic bag hadn't featured high on the list.

And she certainly hadn't expected to see him today. When Evie had emailed her shortly after their reunion, she had told her that Joel and Flynn were good friends, having got to know each other following Joel's move to Bath. She had gone on to explain that Flynn would have been Joel's best man today, had he not had an inescapable previous engagement in Australia preventing him from being here.

It had been startling news, but Australia was a long way away. Lara had digested the information and convinced herself there was no need to let it worry her. She could relax and enjoy the wedding.

Except now he *was* here . . .

'Oh my GOD,' squealed a girl in her twenties, 'what's happening now? Is the wedding *off*?'

Every head swivelled away from Lara. Having concluded the heated debate with Joel, Evie was now hurrying across the car park towards a middle-aged couple standing beside a sleek silver limousine with a girl in a pale green bridesmaid's dress. Joel, remaining where he was, shook his head at his best man and signalled that things weren't looking great by drawing an index finger across his own neck.

Lara jumped as Flynn materialised at her side. *Oh good grief . . .*

'I can't believe it's you.' He kept his voice low. 'This is amazing. Did Evie track you down?'

'Kind of.' Having thought she could cope, Lara now realised she couldn't. He was too close, it was too much and they were surrounded by too many people . . . overwhelmed by his prox-imity and by the faint but still familiar smell of his skin, she found herself unable to meet his gaze. She could feel it though. And the sight of his tanned hands gave her another jolt; Gigi's were a smaller, girlier carbon copy of them. Their knuckles were eerily alike. OK, this was agonising; they had a million things to talk about. But how could they possibly do it now?

38

And maybe Flynn had come to the same conclusion. He looked across at Joel, then at Evie. 'So what's going on?'

'No idea. But it's not looking good.' All around them people were whispering to each other, buzzing with anticipation and speculating as to what could have happened. Joel was dazed and shaken, the picture of a broken man. The bridesmaid was deep in conversation with him, talking rapidly and waving her arms like an Italian street seller. A short distance away from them, Evie was now hugging the couple Lara guessed must be Joel's parents. The inexpertly fastened silver combs were falling out of her hair. As she lifted the hem of her skirt off the ground and turned, making her way towards the guests assembled at the entrance to the church, she seemed calm.

'Um, hello, everyone.' She paused, cleared her throat then continued. 'Right, well, as you've probably noticed by now, this wedding isn't exactly going according to plan.' Behind her Joel was climbing into the passenger seat of the limo; glancing round, Evie saw him speaking to the chauffeur. Taking a deep breath, she went on. 'In fact, it isn't going ahead, full stop. *Sometimes*,' she raised her voice to be heard over the gasps of dismay, 'it's the only thing to do. So look, I'm really sorry but me and Joel won't be getting married today. Or any other day. But seeing as everything's laid out ready at the hotel, the reception is still on and you're all very welcome to head on over there for food, drink, dancing and, well, probably a fair amount of gossip. And I hope you'll have fun anyway, so it won't have been a completely wasted day.' At this point her voice began to wobble. 'You can all have a lovely party . . .' Briefly overcome, she searched the gathering then spotted Lara and beckoned her over.

'Me?' Lara pointed to her own chest to make sure. Why would Evie choose to single her out?

'Yes, please.' Evie nodded rapidly and beckoned again.

'Don't disappear,' said Flynn. 'We have to talk. My God, I just flew in from Australia . . . if I hadn't made it back, I'd have missed you . . .'

But Lara was already squeezing through the milling crowd at the foot of the church steps. She made her way over to Evie, who held out her arms to her.

'I'm so sorry. And you came all this way. Are you staying down here tonight or going back?'

Up close, Evie's make-up was weird, almost clown-like. And she was trembling like a baby bird; Lara could feel her racing pulse as they clasped hands. 'I was going to stay.' She'd got a bargain price on a last-minute booking at the five-star Ellison. 'But I won't now. Where do you want to go?'

Evie's face crumpled with gratitude. 'I don't know. Anywhere. I think it's my turn to disappear.'

'No problem. My car's just down the road. Come on, we'll leave now.'

Out of the corner of her eye, Lara glimpsed Flynn as together she and Evie made their way down the tree-lined drive.

Evie murmured, 'Is everyone watching us?'

'Oh yes. We're the centre of attention. It's like that last scene in *The Graduate*.'

'And they've no idea who you are.' A glimmer of a smile lifted the corners of Evie's mouth. 'They're going to think we're a couple of lesbians running off together.'

A hundred yards down the road they reached the car and jumped in. As Lara was manoeuvring them out of the tight parking space, a white Audi pulled up in the road with its indicator flashing, waiting for the space to become free.

'Just hang on a minute.' Evie put a restraining hand on Lara's once they'd snaked out into the road. She waited until the Audi had squeezed into the vacated space, then buzzed down the passenger window and stuck her head out. 'Mum, it's OK, you don't have to bother getting out of the car.'

'Eveline? What's going on?' Evie's mother's overly plucked eyebrows arched in astonishment. 'How could I have missed it? I'm not that late!'

'It's not happening. We called it off,' said Evie. 'Well, I did.'

'Don't be ridiculous, you can't have!'

'Why can't I?'

'You wouldn't do that. You're not the type!'

People didn't change, did they? Lara inwardly marvelled at Evie's mother's response.

Evie simply shrugged and didn't attempt to argue. 'Well, the wedding's cancelled.'

Exasperated, her mother said, 'And it didn't occur to you to tell me? For goodness sake, Eveline. I had to cut short an important meeting to get down here today!'

'I know you did.' Evie nodded wearily. 'You've told me a hundred times. But look on the bright side, now you can go back to work.'

In response to Evie's signal, Lara stuck her foot down and they shot off up the road. It was the kind of moment that would have looked great in a film. It would've been even better if they could have had a zippy red convertible, with Evie's white veil flying behind them and her wedding bouquet being dramatically flung into the air as they sped off into a spectacular sunset.

Instead, they were in a dusty blue Nissan and Evie didn't have a bouquet to fling. Nor, since it wasn't long past midday, was there any sunset.

Lara saw that Evie's fingernails were digging into her palms.

41

'You're doing great,' she reassured her. 'Now, we need to pick up some stuff for you. Then I'll have to collect my things from the hotel.'

'I've been staying with Joel's parents. I don't want to go back there.' Despite the heat of the day, Evie's teeth had started to chatter. 'Oh God, poor Bonnie and Ray. I can't face them again, not yet. I just want to get away.'

'No problem. We can do that.'

Chapter 7

Fifteen minutes later they drew into the car park of the Ellison and Evie's heart sank. Every parking space was taken and girls in stunning jewel-bright outfits were picking their way across the gravel on the arms of men in top hats and tails. Irony of ironies, Lara had booked into a hotel where another glamorous wedding was about to take place.

'Let's hope things turn out better for this lot. Oh *God* . . .' Her feeble attempt at light-heartedness was scuppered in an instant by the sight of a tall blonde in a dress that resembled an emerald satin bandage. 'That's Emily Morris, she'll wet herself laughing if she sees me.' Evie ducked down in the passenger seat. '*And* she's been after Joel for years.'

'Right, what do you want to do?' Lara parked in the last available space, away from the hotel entrance and marked Manager Only. 'Wait here or come in with me? I'll be five minutes, max.'

Evie glanced over her shoulder at the boisterous wedding party milling around the entrance. Accompanying Lara into the hotel would mean having to squeeze through them and would attract way too much unwanted attention.

'I'll stay here.'

Lara jumped out of the car. Evie did her best to calm down. She was facing a high stone wall; there was no reason why anyone should notice her all the way over here. Too agitated to sit doing nothing, Evie switched on the radio and turned up the volume. Then she opened the glove compartment and found a packet of wet-wipes. Pulling down the sun visor, she looked at the wreckage of her face; the foundation was all blotchy, her lipstick had melted in the heat and the ill-advised attempt at eyebrow pencilling looked as if it had been carried out in the dark. How stupid to have imagined she could do it herself.

Evie pulled out a wet-wipe and began scrubbing it vigorously, like a flannel, all over her face. *Don't think about Joel, don't think about the wedding you've walked out of, just sing along to the music on the radio and block everything else from your mind.*

Bellowing along to a Madonna track, she heard a sharp knocking noise and slid the wet-wipe down from her eyes. She jumped at the sight of an unamused male eyeing her through the glass.

Evie buzzed the window down. 'Yes?'

'You can't park here.' He looked faintly horrified when he saw her face, which would normally have been mortifying but today just made her irate.

Instead of launching into the usual grovelling apology – *dammit, would Madonna apologise and grovel?* – Evie said, 'There weren't any other spaces. We won't be long.'

Ooh, that felt quite liberating, actually. Channelling Madonna had its perks.

The man's eyes narrowed. 'You shouldn't have parked here in the first place.'

'I didn't. I wasn't driving the car.' Ha, out-frosted him.

'It can't stay here.'

'Are you the hotel manager?' In his late thirties, with his

uncombed hair, rugby shirt and ripped jeans, he looked more like the gardener. 'I don't think so.'

He looked even more annoyed. 'I can still ask you not to park in a reserved space.'

'For crying out loud, will you stop giving me grief? Look at me!' In disbelief, Evie gestured wildly at her dress, her veil, her pink shiny face. 'Do I look like I'm in the mood to be hassled by some petty jobsworth who thinks he's—'

'Right, all sorted, let's go.' The boot of the car swung up and Lara's case landed inside with a thud. She beamed at the stroppy man and said, 'Did I park in the wrong place? Sorry! We're off now.'

'Don't do it again.' He shook his head as Lara jumped into the driver's seat.

'I won't! Not while you're watching anyway.' Lara said this last bit under her breath, then smiled again and gave him a cheery wave as she reversed out of the space. 'Shame he's so grumpy. He's got a nice bum. Were you two having a ding-dong?'

'Some people need to get a life. I just ran away from my own wedding.' Evie slid down in her seat and shielded her face as they drove past Emily Morris and her glamorous friends being photographed. 'I'm *obviously* not having a good day. Yet he decides to have a go at me about a stupid parking space. While I'm wearing my wedding dress. What kind of a moron *does* that?'

'A miserable one.' Lara swung the car out through the gates. 'Never mind him now. Are you sure you want to do this?'

Ahead lay the road junction. Turning right would take them back into Bath. Turning left meant hitting the motorway. Evie experienced a fresh wave of panic; talk about empty-handed. She'd be leaving without so much as a spare pair of knickers and a toothbrush.

Sod it. What would Madonna do? Apart from sending out a minion to buy new *everything*?

'Let's go to Keswick.'

'Good girl.' Lara reached over and gave her knee a pat. 'You're going to get through this.'

'You haven't even asked me yet what happened.'

'Well, I'm sure you had a good reason. You didn't just wake up and decide you weren't happy with the way he squeezed the toothpaste. Anyway,' said Lara, 'we've got five hours before we get to Keswick. There's plenty of time to tell me everything.'

And that was it. As if some inner key had been turned, the whole story came pouring out. Without censoring anything, Evie voiced all the secret doubts and uncertainties she'd kept quiet about for so long. The fear that Joel was settling for her because she was no trouble, easygoing and grateful enough to have him as a partner to turn a blind eye to his failings. And the awful thing was, she *had*. Over the years there'd been slips and hints and whispers suggesting he may have been playing away, but she'd always given him the benefit of the doubt. If she challenged Joel, he denied it absolutely. And if she carried on accusing him, it just made an awkward situation worse. They were both happiest when they weren't arguing, so it stood to reason that it had become easier not to bring the subject up in the first place.

'I've never said any of this before.' When she eventually finished, Evie shifted in her seat and began to regret the many cups of tea she'd had since breakfast. 'Did we just pass a service station?'

'A couple of miles back. Why?'

'I need a wee.'

Lara left the motorway at the next exit and found a pub. 'I'm going to grab something to eat. Do you want anything?'

'No thanks. But I wouldn't say no to a glass of wine.'

46

'Here.' Having opened the boot of the car and rummaged in a bag, Lara passed her a change of clothes. 'You might be more comfortable in these.'

Ignoring the raised eyebrows of the pub's incumbents, Evie swished her way through the bar in her billowing wedding dress and paid a visit to the Ladies'. Five minutes later she was back, wearing the faded purple T-shirt and slightly-too-big black jeans, with the wedding dress draped over her arm.

'Much better.' Lara handed her a large glass of white with a flourish. 'Here you go. Cheers!'

Jilting was thirsty work, it turned out. The Frascati went down practically in one go. Not normally much of a drinker, today Evie found herself needing help quelling her jangled nerves.

'Can I have another? I feel terrible about not having any money.' She watched the barmaid pour her a refill and Lara pay for it. 'You'll have to keep a tab so I can pay everything back.'

Lara ate a ham and cheese toasted sandwich and drank a Coke while Evie finished her second glass of wine.

'You and your old man had a falling-out already, then?' One of the men at the bar asked the question everyone else had been thinking. 'What've you done with him?'

The alcohol felt fantastic, snaking its silky way through her bloodstream. Emptying the last of the Frascati down her throat and jumping off her bar stool, Evie eyed the row of regulars and tilted her head in the direction of the car park. 'He's in the boot.'

Back in the car she slept for the next couple of hours, eventually waking again to find they were making good progress up the M6.

'I keep expecting my phone to ring.' It felt odd, being without it.

Lara pointed to her handbag in the footwell. 'You can use mine if you want.'

'No thanks. I think I quite like being out of reach. I wonder what's going on back there now. Do you think they're having a wild party?'

'Haven't the foggiest.' Lara hesitated, then said, 'Can I ask you something?'

'Fire away.'

'You told me Flynn wouldn't be there. You said he was in Australia.'

Evie looked puzzled. 'Yes, that's right. That's where he is, on a business trip. Touring vineyards and buying stock.'

'He isn't. He was there.'

'Where?'

'At the church! He turned up in a taxi while we were all waiting outside.'

'Did he?' Bemused, Evie said, 'I didn't notice. He must have caught an early flight back specially.' She thought about it and let out a groan. 'Oh God, and all for nothing. He'll be pleased.'

'Stop that. It's not your fault. You aren't the one who shagged the make-up girl.'

'I know, but still.' If you were cursed with the take-the-blame gene, this was what it was like, always feeling guilty and responsible whenever things went wrong. Evie changed the subject. 'I didn't tell him I'd invited you to the wedding. So how did it feel to see him again?'

'Weird.'

'Did he see you?'

Lara nodded. 'Yes.'

'And recognised you? Duh, stupid question, of course he recognised you. God, then what happened? He was devastated before, when you left. Did he get a chance to speak to you?'

'Only for a minute. Not even that,' Lara amended. 'A few seconds.'

Evie clapped a hand to her mouth. 'Oh no, and then I dragged you away! And now you're here and he's there. I mess everything up.' She exhaled noisily. 'I'm a walking disaster.'

'It's fine, don't worry,' said Lara. 'I'll see him again. After this many years it won't kill us to wait a bit longer.'

There was an edge to her voice. Looking across, Evie saw her knuckles whitening as they gripped the steering wheel.

'So, do you think there could still be something between you?'

'No.' Lara shook her head. 'There couldn't.'

How could she be so sure? 'Not even a little bit?'

'No.'

'But there might be. You two were so brilliant together before. He's single, and you're single . . .'

'That was when we were at school. Anyway,' Lara flicked the indicator as they approached the next exit, 'nearly there now. When we get home there's someone I have to introduce you to.'

'I know. Aunt Nettie. I can't wait to meet her,' said Evie. 'She sounds fantastic.'

They were heading up the slip road now. 'She is, but I didn't mean Nettie.'

'Who, then?'

Lara was smiling. 'Someone else.'

Chapter 8

On a how-great-are-you-feeling scale, Flynn was currently scoring a two. Yesterday, thanks to Herculean efforts, he'd managed to arrive back from his wine-buying trip to Australia in the nick of time to attend Joel and Evie's wedding which then hadn't gone ahead. Joel's solution to the problem had been to drink vast quantities of Jack Daniel's and vintage Taittinger, and he'd felt obliged to keep the jilted bridegroom company. Which meant this morning he was suffering the killer combination of both full-on jetlag and a champagne hangover.

But yesterday something else had happened that was even more astonishing: he'd seen Lara again. Unbelievably. And for all of sixty seconds before – irony of ironies – she'd disappeared once more.

But the memory of it wasn't going to go away in a hurry. The image of her had burned itself into his brain, taken his breath away. There she'd been, with that glossy dark brown hair falling to her shoulders, some of it curling in and some out, just as it had always done. And those incredible silver-grey eyes were the same too, beneath defined dark brows. She was looking better than ever. The figure-hugging red silk dress wasn't something she would have worn in the old days, but she was thirty-five now and had carried it off with panache. She still had the best legs he'd ever seen, too.

Flynn knew he had to see her again. Definitely. And no, he wasn't expecting to find her here today, but all he needed was an address.

Flynn rang the doorbell and waited. He'd never been welcome at this house. The last time he'd done this, Lara's horrific father had told him to clear off and make sure he didn't come back. That had been eighteen years ago.

He heard movement inside the house, followed by the metallic jangle of locks being unfastened. Finally the door creaked open.

Janice Carson, older and greyer, met his gaze. If she recognised him she gave no sign of it.

'What do you want?'

'Hi there, I'm hoping you can help me.' Flynn flashed her a smile. 'I'm trying to contact Lara and—'

'I can't help you.' Her mouth pursed like a cat's bottom; she recognised him all right.

'Well, maybe I could speak to your husband?'

'He can't help you either.' Without warning, she slammed the door shut. More clanking ensued. That was that, then. Unequivocally locked out.

Flynn headed down the drive. This was crazy. Reaching the pavement, he turned back and surveyed the house. A downstairs curtain twitched, signalling that they were keeping an eye on him.

Talk about frustrating. *Where was Lara?*

'Hello! Problem?'

He swung round to see who'd spoken. It was the next-door neighbour, semi-obscured by greenery. Moving along the pavement until he was out of Janice's sight, he saw her properly; in her mid-forties, short and voluptuous with friendly brown eyes and hennaed hair, she was wearing gardening gloves and carrying secateurs.

'I was just hoping for a word with Mr Carson.'

'Oh dear.' The neighbour stopped deadheading roses. 'I'm afraid that's not going to happen.'

'Clearly. His wife just shut the door in my face.'

'Mr Carson died,' said the woman. 'Let me see, when was it? About six weeks ago now.'

'Oh.' God, *died*. He hadn't been expecting that.

'I would say that explains why she shut the door on you.' The woman leaned closer, her tone conspiratorial. 'But to be honest, she's never been the friendly type.'

Flynn nodded in agreement. 'I knew her before. Many years ago.'

'You're the skier chap, aren't you?' The neighbour was eyeing him curiously.

'I am.' Another nod. 'I'm just trying to contact Mr Carson's daughter. She hasn't lived here for a long time, but I bumped into her yesterday and—'

'Oh yes, I heard about her! I'm Jacqueline Ann Cumiskey, by the way.' Whisking off a glove, the woman reached across the hedge and offered a soft, elegantly manicured hand in greeting. 'She turned up at the funeral. I wasn't able to go to the service, but I popped next door to pay my respects afterwards. Everyone was talking about the daughter. I was dying to see her, but she didn't come back to the house. Bit of a family feud, by the sound of things. Well, you may know more about it than I do.' She was evidently intrigued, longing to uncover a few more salient details.

'Look, could I ask you to do me a favour?' It was a long shot but what other choice did he have? Flynn took a business card out of his wallet. 'Mrs Carson doesn't want to help me. But if you do happen to hear anything, or if Lara turns up again, could you give me a call and let me know?'

'Of course I can do that!' Jacqueline Ann Cumiskey's eyes sparkled as she reached for the card and slid it into her shirt pocket. 'No problem at all.'

So that was twice Lara had come back to Bath recently, the first time for her father's funeral and then again for Evie's wedding-that-never-was. Where were they now? Could they still be hiding out somewhere in the city? At the thought of seeing her again, *properly, this time*, Flynn felt a kick of adrenalin in his chest. This wasn't about Joel and Evie and yesterday's debacle. This was about Lara.

He unlocked his car and nodded at the next-door neighbour. 'Thanks.'

Derwentwater stretched out ahead of them, cobalt blue and glittering in the sunlight like a lavishly sequinned quilt. Evie stopped walking, collapsed on to the grass and filled her lungs with fresh clean air. How, *how* had she never visited the Lake District before? And now it was almost time to leave. She turned her head slowly to take in the spectacle of the view, the islands dotting the lake and the fells surrounding it. She'd learned their names now. Cat Bells and Black Crag to the west, Castlerigg Fell to the east. And over there, rising up beyond Keswick, Skiddow. What a stunning part of the world this was, even if exploring the fells and mountains was giving her body more of a workout than it had experienced in years.

'Muscles still aching?'

'Just a bit.' Evie stretched her legs and arched her back.

Next to her, Gigi grinned. 'That's because you're so old.'

53

'Mean girl.' She aimed a foot at Gigi's ankle.

'See those deer up on the fells over there?' Having become her tour guide over the course of the last week, Gigi pointed them out.

'Yes, *dear.*'

It was Gigi's turn to give her a playful nudge. Evie unfastened her water bottle and took a drink. 'You're going to miss all this, you know.'

'But it's not going anywhere. It'll still be here when I come back and visit.'

This was true. What a revelation Lara's daughter was turning out to be. Tilting her head sideways, Evie studied Gigi's profile, the intelligent eyes, Lara's nose, those high cheekbones dusted with freckles and that neat, determined chin. Meeting her had certainly taken her mind off last week's farcical events.

Not that it was so astonishing to discover that Lara had a daughter. But discovering her age and who her father was had hit Evie for six.

Lara had relayed the whole story to her in the car as they'd completed the last leg of the journey from Bath to Keswick. Finally her disappearance made complete sense. Almost nineteen years on, Evie's heart had gone out to her friend. Sixteen, pregnant and cast out by her family; for goodness sake, it was like something out of Dickens.

And then, in no time at all, she'd been meeting the end result. Gigi Carson, with her mad freckles, dancing silver-grey eyes and insatiable curiosity. This wasn't a girl to be brushed off or ignored; if she had a question, she liked it to be answered. She was tall and long-limbed, her straight toffee-brown hair swished from side to side as she talked and she had one of those laughs that every now and again ended in a comedy snort. Evie had been captivated

54

from the word go. Apart from the snorty thing, it was like having the teenage Lara back again.

Interspersed with spooky flashes of Flynn.

'What?' Gigi was watching her. 'What are you thinking about now?'

She was also scarily intuitive.

'I'm thinking about your father. In a couple of days he's going to find out you exist.'

'Lucky him.' Pulling a fat blade of grass out of the ground, Gigi stretched it between her thumbs. She blew against it, producing a long quacking sound like a lovelorn duck.

'Are you nervous?'

'No.'

Was that really true? Evie marvelled at such self-confidence. How must it feel to be so supremely comfortable in your own skin?

'Don't get me wrong, I want it to go well,' Gigi went on. 'But I can't change *me*, can I? If he decides he doesn't like me, there's nothing I can do about it. I'm not going to pretend to be someone different.'

'Of course he'll like you,' said Evie.

'He might not. He might only want the kind of daughter who's mad on physics and museums and trips to the theatre to see plays by Shakespeare. *Or*,' Gigi added as Evie opened her mouth to tell her just how unlikely *that* was, 'he might decide he doesn't want any kind of daughter at all.'

'Oh, I'm sure he wouldn't do that.'

'You don't know, though. Or he might pretend to be pleased, just to get over the embarrassing bit, then back off a couple of weeks later. That happens quite a lot.' Gigi nodded sagely. 'I've watched the Jeremy Kyle show.'

'I don't think that'll happen.' Evie watched a windsurfer scud across the surface of the lake, veering perilously close to a rowing boat.

Gigi shrugged. 'But if it does, it won't be my fault. So that's why I'm not going to waste time getting nervous. How about you?'

'Me? Oh, I'm definitely nervous.'

'About going back? Why?'

She sounded so genuinely puzzled. 'You're eighteen. I'm thirty-four. And you're brave,' said Evie. 'I'm not.'

'Come on,' Gigi protested. 'How can you say that, after what you did? That was an amazingly brave thing to do.'

'It was. But it was pretty much the first brave thing I've ever done in my life. And it's OK while I'm up here, but it's not going to be so easy once we're back. Everyone's going to know. I don't know what'll happen with my job. It's just . . . scary.'

'No, it isn't.' Gigi jumped up and held out a hand to pull her to her feet. 'Anyway, you'll have us. Even if no one else in the whole of Bath is speaking to you, we still will.' She paused then added mischievously, 'Well, so long as you pay us.'

Chapter 9

The kitchen was filled with the scent of baking bread. Lara wrestled with the heavy packing cases, pushing them up against the wall while Nettie took the loaves out of the oven.

The front door opened and banged shut, signalling the return of Evie and Gigi.

'Lovely, just in time. Hungry, girls? There's white and wholegrain, and I've made vegetable soup. Could someone fetch the butter from the fridge?'

Straightening up, Lara turned and watched as Nettie expertly tipped the loaves out of their tins and rapped their bases to make sure they were done. At sixty-five, her aunt was a powerhouse. Her hair was white and poker-straight, and had never been touched by a hairdresser; Nettie used the kitchen scissors and did it herself. Her year-round tan accentuated the blueness of eyes that had never experienced contact with any form of make-up; she wasn't remotely interested in her appearance. Aunt Nettie loved cooking, she loved her animals and she loved Gigi and Lara. She was also mad about heavy metal music and liked to play it at maximum volume because that, apparently, was how you were meant to listen to it. Last night when Lara had complained about

Metallica blaring out at midnight, Nettie had blithely replied, 'Yet all these years I've had to put up with you caterwauling along to Take That.'

Caterwauling. What a cheek.

'Right, who wants brown?' Her aunt was wielding a massive serrated knife.

'I do.' Never mind wondering what life was going to be like without Nettie, what was it going to be like without her bread? 'Oh, Nettie, I'm going to miss you so much. Are you sure you'll be all right without us?'

Nettie rolled her eyes but she was smiling. 'You do talk some nonsense. Has it occurred to you that you might not be indispensable?'

Lara gave up and sat down. When they'd returned six weeks earlier with the news that the house in Bath was theirs, Nettie's first words had been, 'You can move back and live in it!'

'Or sell it.' Having planned on broaching the subject rather more tentatively, Lara had been taken aback. 'Or rent it out . . .'

But in all honesty, when had Nettie ever been tentative about anything? She'd said, 'It's your home, love. I'm not forcing you to live there if you don't want to. But if you do, I say go for it. Whatever you do, don't go thinking you should stay here because of me.'

And that was it; she had assured Lara and Gigi she'd be fine on her own without them. Although she wouldn't be completely alone; she'd still have her chickens, her dozy sheep and tetchy goats, her beloved dogs. And this was her own home, she'd lived here for the last forty years. If she ever needed help, any of the other smallholders in the area would come to the rescue; there were more than enough friends to help out.

So that was it, the decision had been made. All that had remained was for Lara to hand in her notice at the jewellers and make the necessary arrangements for the move south. Having left school in June and with a gap year to kill before heading off to university, Gigi was easy.

And the house – *their house* – was standing waiting for them, empty now. Following the reading of the will, the solicitor had given Janice Carson two months' notice to leave. She had finally moved out this week, gone to live with her wealthy sister in nearby Frome. Lara's solicitor, paying a visit to the house following her departure, had reported back that it was indeed empty, of absolutely everything. Even the lightbulbs, the curtain rods and the toilet-roll holders had been removed.

But nothing was going to put Lara and Gigi off. The rental van had been hired, their belongings had been piled into packing cases and first thing tomorrow morning they were heading off down the motorway to begin their new life.

Or resume the old one.

Lara slathered butter on to a chunk of hot bread and pointed it at Nettie. 'You know what I'm starting to think?'

'No one ever knows that, pet. We couldn't begin to guess.'

'I'm thinking you're looking forward to getting rid of us.' She waggled the bread for emphasis. 'Because I'm *thinking* there's maybe a little secret something going on between you and Fred Milton.'

'Really?' Gigi made an *eek!* face. 'Aunt Nettie! Is this true?'

'Of course it isn't true.' Nettie patiently ladled the soup into bowls. 'He's a friend, that's all. Fred's got the farm at the end of Highpool Lane,' she explained to Evie. 'He looks like a bald eagle and his favourite singer's Des O'Connor.' Her tone was dry. 'We're a match made in heaven, obviously.'

'You could be, though. He's a nice man,' Lara protested. 'It's

59

been four years since Mary died. Mary was his wife,' she added for Evie's benefit.

'He's over seventy.'

'But you get on so well together. And he's lonely.'

'Maybe so.' Clearly bored with the clumsy attempts at match-making, Nettie handed Lara a full bowl. 'But I'm not.'

Harry Wells had never needed to work hard at school. GCSEs and A-levels hadn't been an issue for him because he had always known he'd be going into the family business. His grandfather had set up the tiny clothing company in Keswick sixty years ago, his parents had run it in their turn and it had always been a given that he would carry it on. It was a mark of his personality, then, that he *had* worked hard at school, obtaining excellent grades in his exams. That was just the way he was. He'd enjoyed getting high marks and making the teachers happy. It didn't matter that in the twenty years since leaving school the obscure knowledge he'd gained had never found a use in real life.

Anyway, he was happy where he was, part of the community and ticking along nicely. Their tiny company produced well-made high-quality shirts for country folk and it was good to be appreciated. Most of their clientele were past retirement age and had been customers for decades. The shirts were put together by Morag and Betty in the workshop across the yard and Harry's cramped office doubled as the shop for on-site purchases, although they were also stocked by a few stores in the north-west. In addition, before going on holiday a fortnight ago, Harry had finally got around to setting up a website so they could be bought online.

It was going pretty well so far. Back from his holiday late last night and logging in, Harry had been pleasantly surprised. The website had been up and running for sixteen days now and they'd already sold nine shirts.

Betty was off with blood pressure and swollen ankles – 'They're like balloons, pet!' – so Harry and Morag were on their own this morning. He'd just made her a mug of tea and carried it over to her in the workshop when a glossy black monster of a car pulled into the yard.

Harry had never seen a Maybach before, not in the flesh so to speak, but that's what this was. Followed by a Mercedes. But this was Keswick and it enjoyed its fair share of wealthy visitors. The windows of both vehicles were tinted black but he had a private bet with himself that a dozen or so diminutive, immaculately dressed Japanese tourists would pile out with their cameras, pausing on their whistle-stop tour of the Lakes . . .

OK, so he was wrong. Instead the doors had opened and a dozen or so black men emerged all wearing sunglasses. The last thing you could call them was diminutive.

'Hello.' Wondering where they might be heading for, Harry said, 'Are you lost? May I help you?'

'Yo, man. What is that?' The smallest of the visitors, at a shade under six foot and athletically built, nodded at the sign above the door.

'The Flying Ducks. It's the name of our company,' Harry explained. The green and gold sign, incorporating their logo of three flying ducks, had never borne the actual name. 'We sell shirts.'

'Shirts?' The man smiled, revealing very white teeth flanked by a couple of gold vampire-style incisors. He removed his mirrored shades. 'What kind of shirts?'

'Well, no offence,' said Harry, 'but I can't imagine they'd be your cup of tea.'

Some of the other men visibly bristled. They were American.

61

By their body language, he guessed that the one asking the questions was the one in charge.

'Not my . . . cup of tea? You don't say.' Evidently amused by this expression, Vampire Teeth tilted his shaven head to one side. 'How about you let me be the judge of that?' He paused and pointed. 'Is this your store?'

'It is. Kind of. But you can't all come in,' said Harry.

Everyone stared at him. Finally, Vampire Teeth said silkily, 'And why not?'

Harry performed a rapid head count; there were eleven of them in total. 'Because there isn't room. You'll have to take it in turns. But I still don't think our shirts will be up your street.'

He led the way into the dusty, un-air-conditioned office-cum-shop, slightly embarrassed by what was bound to happen next. This collection of blinged-up characters with their oversized jeans and crystal-encrusted sunglasses – yes, really – were going to laugh their heads off when they saw what was on offer.

'Hey, y'all stay outside. Maz and AJ come in with me.' Indicating who should stay and who should go, Vampire Teeth followed Harry into the shop. He surveyed the messy desk, the boxes of shirts stacked in haphazard piles and the samples adorning the plastic torsos against the far wall. 'Man, you're kidding me, right? This is it? *For real?*'

'You can't say I didn't warn you.' Harry waited for them to turn and leave in disgust. Instead he saw Maz and AJ produce a couple of fancy-looking camcorders and start recording.

'Hey, man, don't be so tetchy. Who d'ya sell these to? You OK with this, by the way?' Vampire Teeth indicated the camcorders with a languid wave of the hand.

'I suppose so.' It wasn't the first time they'd been used in the shop; tourists from overseas tended to be entranced by its quaintness and lack of glamour. Harry said patiently, 'These shirts last for years. They're nothing to do with fashion. Hill farmers buy them. I'm sorry to have to keep saying this, but they're not your thing at all.'

Outside the wide-open door, a menacing New York voice growled, 'He disrespectin' you, boss?'

'Cool it, Alvin. I don't think he is.' Vampire Teeth flashed an evil, pointy-toothed grin at Harry. 'Don't let him bother you. Safe, man. Show me what ya got.'

Good Lord. Harry blinked and wondered if this was a hold-up. His heart began to thud. Did they have guns?'

Aloud he said, 'We don't have a safe.'

This provoked a bark of laughter. 'Hey, relax. I'm asking you to show me your shirts. The whole range.'

Oh. That was a relief. But did he really not understand he'd already seen everything there was to see? Harry pointed to the headless plastic mannequins in their shirts. 'This is our range. We have a choice of short sleeves or, um, long sleeves. Colours are beige, cream, dark grey or khaki. Here at Flying Ducks we concentrate on quality, cloth and workmanship. These shirts are designed to last for—'

'I'm a sixteen-inch collar. Can I try one on?'

Try one on? His customers didn't usually bother; it was only a *shirt*. Harry said, 'Of course, you're very welcome to, but I'm afraid we don't have a changing room . . .'

But Vampire Teeth was already peeling off his dazzling white T-shirt. He was evidently a regular at the gym, muscles rippling and not an ounce of fat on him. He looked at the label on the one Harry had pulled from its crackly cellophane packaging and raised an eyebrow. 'Medium?'

'Small, medium or large. We don't do collar sizes.' Harry watched him try the shirt on. It didn't help that the man was wearing

63

baggy jeans slung so low his underpants were showing; it was as incongruous as a rugby top teamed with a tutu.

And still the minions – they were definitely minions – were busy filming away.

Vampire Teeth surveyed his reflection in the small mirror on the counter.

'I like it.' He carefully examined the cuffs, the collar, noting the double stitching and the neatly edged buttonholes. 'Quality. And I like the ducks.' He tapped the green and gold logo on the breast pocket. 'How many you got in the medium?'

'In which colour?'

'All the colours.'

'You mean in stock now?' Surprised by the question, Harry said, 'Five in each colour. So, twenty altogether.'

'Right, I'll have them.'

'One of each colour?'

'All of them.'

'What, all *twenty*?'

'Yes. Is that a problem?'

This was surreal.

'It could be. Look, I'm sorry, but you haven't even asked the price yet. These aren't cheap, I'm afraid.' Harry cleared his throat. 'They're seventy-five pounds each. But as I say,' he added hurriedly, 'they're *very* well made and last for years, so you really don't need so many. One in each colour would be plenty.'

'Hey.' Vampire Teeth pulled a wallet from the back pocket of his designer jeans and flipped out a black Amex card. 'I want all of them.'

'You can't have *all* of them.'

'Why can't I?'

'Because if you did, there wouldn't be any left for anyone else.'

'So? That's their problem, not mine.'

'But they're my customers. This is my shop. If one of them came in this afternoon wanting a new shirt in a medium, I wouldn't want to let them down.' Harry stood his ground, steadfastly ignoring the camcorders. 'You can have sixteen shirts. Let me keep one of each colour and you can buy the rest.'

Vampire Teeth surveyed him in silence for several seconds. Finally he said, 'OK.'

'But I'm afraid we don't take American Express.'

A sigh. The Amex was returned to the wallet. A great wad of notes was produced instead. Harry's eyes widened at the sight of so much cash. Then again, with so many people around him, Vampire Teeth was unlikely to get mugged.

'You don't have a clue who I am, do you?'

'No, I don't. Sorry. I'm afraid that's, um, twelve hundred pounds in total. Are you absolutely sure that's OK?'

'I'm ahbsolutely shore.' Vampire Teeth mimicked his oh-so-English accent. 'You know something, man? I like you.' He watched as Harry began parcelling the shirts up with brown paper and string. 'You ever hear of a hip-hop artist called EnjaySeven?'

'I haven't. I'm sorry. Is that you? Art isn't really my forte,' said Harry. 'I did see the ceiling of the Sistine Chapel a few years back . . .'

'Michelangelo had some talent, but I'm not talkin' about that kind of artist. Hey, Ronnie, volume.' Vampire Teeth made the turn-it-up signal to one of the massive men lurking in the doorway, who in turn gestured to whoever was still in the first car. Some form of noise that until now Harry had been only vaguely aware of in the background was cranked up to shudder level and blasted across the yard: thud thud THUD-CRASH, thud thud CRASH.

Good heavens.

'That's you?'

'Yeah, man. That's me.'

'It's very . . . loud.' Harry felt sorry for the pigeons on the roof. What a racket.

'OK, Ron.' The signal was made to reduce the volume. 'So tell me what kinda music you listen to.'

'Not your kind, no offence. I enjoy Michael Bublé. Um, do you want to take the shirt off now?'

'No, I'll wear it. Flying ducks.' The heavy gold watch flashed on his wrist as he patted the breast pocket once more. 'Know something? You're a pretty cool guy.'

'That's not true. I'm the very opposite of cool. Even I know that,' said Harry.

'But I like you for it. You're comfortable with being yourself.' It was the turn of the gold incisors to glint in the sunlight streaming through the dusty window. 'You happy to appear on my show, man?'

'What show?'

'*My* show. All about me. These two aren't filming us for the good of their health, ya know. You'll be on MTV. You cool with that?'

All this talk of cool. Harry thought back over the last few minutes and decided he hadn't said or done anything he regretted. 'Fine. I imagine I'll be portrayed as the comedy uptight Englishman.'

'There is that small possibility.' The grin broadened. 'But you never know, you might turn out to be one of those comedy uptight Englishmen people like to see.'

Hmm, or throw rocks at. Oh well. Harry handed over the neatly tied parcels of shirts and shook the man's hand, as he always did with his customers.

'It's been a pleasure to meet you, Mr . . . er . . . And I hope you enjoy the rest of your stay here in the Lake District.'

66

'Yo, you too, man. And you gotta check out my website some time, listen to my music, yeah? You might decide it's not so bad after all.'

'Absolutely.' Harry nodded. 'I'll do that.'

Another flash of the vampiric teeth. 'Is that the truth or are you just being polite?'

'I'm just being polite,' said Harry.

The camcorders were switched off, the shirts thrown into the trunk of the Maybach. Everyone piled back into the cars. Morag, having finished her tea and brought the empty 'World's Best Nan!' mug over to be washed in the sink, visibly flinched as the music began booming out once more.

She joined Harry in the office doorway. 'Everything OK, pet? Tourists, is it?'

He nodded. 'Americans.'

'Horrible noise.'

'He's a musician. That's him singing.'

'Singing, is that what you call it? Sounds like a bull in a microwave. It's the kind of horrible thing my grandson listens to.' A hand raised in farewell emerged from one of the lowered tinted windows of the first car. Harry and Morag smiled and nodded and politely waved back. 'What did he say his name was?'

What had it been? Something with a number in it that made no sense. 'He did tell me,' said Harry, 'but I've forgotten. How are you doing with the shirt for Tom Huxtable?'

'Finished it, pet. I'll drop it round to him on my way home. At least he'll look smart for his cousin's funeral.'

'That's good.' Harry took the empty mug from her. 'I'll wash that for you, shall I? Could you do some more long-sleeved mediums next? We're running low.'

Chapter 10

'Well, here we are.' Having set off in a mini-convoy shortly after six in the morning, they had reached Bath before midday. Lara jumped down from the rented van and joined Evie and Gigi beside the car.

'Home.' Gigi looped an arm around her waist. '*Our* home. Yours too,' she added, reaching for Evie with her free hand. 'Until you decide what you want to do.'

'And there's no hurry.' Lara took out the key the solicitor had sent her. 'You can stay as long as you like. Crikey, this feels weird.'

Evie gave her a sympathetic look. 'It's bound to.'

'No, I mean holding this key feels weird.' Lara held it up to show them. 'I can remember the shape of it *exactly*. Right, let's go.'

Together they headed across the driveway and Lara unlocked the front door. The smell of the house hit her instantly and the memories came flooding back, both from before and after her mother's death.

The smell of the house itself was from before. That counted as a good memory. The altogether more pungent scents of Janice's own perfume and the cheap lavender furniture polish she'd always used were less pleasant. Hopefully they would fade over time.

68

The living room seemed larger, probably because it was empty. The kitchen had been redesigned, fitted out with pale ash units and mottled grey worktops. The dining room was wallpapered in flowery pink and green paper with hideous matching borders. Upstairs, the bathroom was new, plain and white, with the loo-roll holder having been painstakingly removed. The master bedroom was beige and stripy, the guest bedroom magnolia and plain.

Lara hesitated before entering the third bedroom. Her own old room. Would it still be the same? She had painted the walls purple and covered them with posters and prints. The carpet had been blood-red to match the bedcovers and she'd had furry multicoloured cushions on the bed. Janice had always called it a monstrosity.

She opened the door.

More magnolia, everywhere. The room was sterile and empty. Apart from the view from the window, she wouldn't have recognised it as hers. It was as if every last sign of her existence had been eradicated.

Actually, no if about it. That was exactly what had happened.

'I'm guessing this isn't what it was like before,' said Gigi.

Lara smiled briefly. 'You'd be right.'

'All this nothing-colour, it's all so *bleurgh*. Oh well, we can redecorate, brighten it up. Anyway.' Gigi pulled a list from her jeans pocket; she was the undisputed queen of lists. 'Things to do. It's midday. The beds are being delivered between one and three. We need to unload this van then make a start on the unpacking. I think we should sort the kitchen out first. Oh, and the fridge should be here by four. Shall we get going now?'

'If you're wondering if she's always this bossy,' said Lara, 'the answer's yes. Look, if you want to shoot off and see Joel's parents, just go. We can manage without you.'

But Evie was already shaking her head. 'It's OK, I'm staying here. I want to wait until we're settled before facing everyone and getting hassle from Joel.' She paused. 'That's if he hasn't run off with his little make-up girl.'

'Sure?'

'Completely.' Evie pushed up her sleeves and headed for the stairs. 'Let's get everything done first, while nobody knows we're here.'

Six hours on, the house was beginning to come together. Well, kind of. The beds had been delivered on time, which was a bonus. Having just finished making up the last one, Lara stopped to stretch her aching shoulders. Half the packing cases had been emptied, clothes had been hung in the fitted wardrobes, the chests of drawers they'd brought them in had been installed. OK, so they had no curtains and no curtain rails as yet, but the bookcase on the landing was now brimming with books, the TV was set up in the living room and the bathroom was all done.

Evie and Gigi had driven off ten minutes ago to pick up a Chinese from the takeaway Evie insisted was the best in Bath. Lara finished piling the rest of the sheets and duvet covers into the airing cupboard. Her stomach was rumbling, she was hot and sticky and her hair was glued to her neck. All the windows in the house were flung open in an attempt to clear the artificial smells she hated so much.

OK, next box. Opening it on the landing, Lara saw that it contained saucepans and kitcheny things. So much for Gigi's brilliant labelling system. She bent down and gathered the box into her arms.

Halfway down the staircase, the weight of the contents overcame the strength of the tape securing the bottom of the box.

Lara yelled, 'Noooo . . . !' as the cardboard flaps gave way, trapdoor-style, then 'Ow-*OUCH!*' as the contents landed on her bare feet before clattering the rest of the way down the stairs. Bloody chopping board, bloody buggering saucepans, *bloody* cheese grater.

Yuk, *literally*.

Lara sank down on the bottom step and examined the damage. A couple of cuts, a graze, and several incipient blue bruises; her feet looked as if they'd gone out, got drunk and got into a fight.

God, and they really *hurt*.

Then she heard the sound of knocking and realised there was someone at the door. There was a doorbell but it didn't work, thanks to the lovely Janice having unscrewed the case and removed the battery before she'd left.

Well, it couldn't be Evie and Gigi; they had a key. Limping across the hall, Lara peeked through the window to see who was out there on the doorstep. The next moment she ducked down out of sight, scalp prickling in disbelief.

How, *how* could Flynn be here on the doorstep?

And now her heart had gone into overdrive; giant cymbals were crashing away inside her chest. It was like Tchaikovsky's 1812 Overture in there. Lara closed her eyes, struggling to think. Selfishly, seeing Flynn again without warning was hard enough anyway. Last time she'd been all dressed up and looking her best. Today was different; she was scruffy and smeared with dust, her face was shiny, her hair was damp and there were sweat patches on her T-shirt. *Oh, the glamour.*

This wasn't just about her, though, was it? There were other people to consider. For a start, if he knew she was here, did that mean he knew about Gigi too? Because if not, he was going to get a shock.

But importantly, far more importantly, what about Gigi? She

71

wanted to meet her father, but not without any warning at all. Let's face it, the three of them had been working like dogs today in ninety degree heat. Given the choice, Gigi would much rather make a good first impression with shiny just-washed hair and clean clothes.

Lara exhaled slowly. She was still crouching on the floor and her feet were throbbing. If she stayed like this, was it remotely likely that Flynn would give up and leave?

'Lara? It's me. I heard you just now. Open the door.'

OK, so that answered that question. Now, if she were to ask him to leave, would he go? But what if he didn't, what if he stayed and started arguing? He'd definitely see the sweat patches under her arms; she could feel them expanding practically by the second.

'If you don't come to the door, I'm going to assume you're either dead or unconscious. In which case I'd better call 999.'

This was so typical of Flynn; he'd never been one to mess around. Still trying to formulate a plan, Lara attempted to wriggle backwards on her hands and knees. The next moment there was a sharp knuckle-rap on the glass and she looked up to see him gazing down at her through the living-room window.

Lara rose to her feet – ow, *ow* – and gingerly made her way through to the hall. She opened the front door and said, 'This isn't a good time.'

'It is for me.' Flynn was surveying her with interest. 'Why didn't you want to come to the door?'

'Because I look a mess.' It was as good an excuse as any. 'How did you know I was here? Did you hire a private detective?'

A fractional shake of the head. 'I took the cheaper option, left my number with the woman next door.' He indicated which side. 'I came round last Sunday to try and find out where you were.

Janice didn't want to help me. Then I got chatting with the neighbour and she told me your father had died. Sorry to hear that.'

Lara shrugged; they were adults and it was the polite thing to say, even if they both knew it wasn't true.

'Anyway, she gave me a call a couple of hours ago, told me there was a hire van sitting on the drive and stuff being moved into the house.'

Lara envisaged the helpful neighbour's conversation: 'There were three of them; a dark-haired one called Lara, a blonde one called Evie and a younger girl who looked like a cross between the dark-haired one and . . . well, *you* actually!'

Aloud she said, 'So you didn't know it was me.'

'I didn't. But I came anyway. And it is you.' A glimmer of a smile. 'You're here. Moving in.'

Oh God, how long had Evie and Gigi been gone? Fifteen, twenty minutes? It was unlikely that they were about to reappear, but it could happen.

'I am. But I really can't talk now.'

'Don't be silly, you don't look that bad. Can I come in?'

Talk about a backhanded compliment. 'No.'

'Why not?'

'I'm busy.'

'I can help you. What happened just now, did you fall down the stairs?' He was glancing behind her at the saucepans scattered across the parquet.

Lara shook her head. 'I'm fine, everything just fell out of the box.'

'You're not fine. Your foot's bleeding.'

'I'll live. Sorry, this really isn't a good time for me. You have to go.'

He gave her a speculative look. 'OK, I will. Just let me ask a couple of quick questions. Is Evie all right? Is she here too?'

'Yes.' Lara nodded. 'And yes. But don't tell Joel. She just needs a couple more days.'

'No problem.' Flynn dipped his head in agreement. 'Now you. Are you married?'

'No.'

'Partner?'

'No.'

'Why did you never contact me?'

There it was, the killer question, delivered without so much as a flicker.

'Look, we have to stop this now.' Her mouth was so dry she could barely get the words out.

'I don't want to stop. You might disappear again.'

'I won't. Are you free tomorrow? We can talk then, have a proper catch-up.' In contrast to her mouth, her palms were slippery with sweat; she had to get rid of him fast.

Flynn looked sceptical. 'How do I know I can trust you?'

'Because I say you can. Pick me up tomorrow evening and we'll go for a drink. I'll tell you everything then,' said Lara. 'I promise.'

Chapter 11

'Looking better today.' Flynn's gaze missed nothing when Lara greeted him at the door just over twenty-four hours later.

He still thought that was why she'd put him off. 'Thanks.' She was wearing make-up, and clean jeans, a white shirt and crystal-studded flip-flops; done up, but not too done up. 'Shall we go?'

'Not inviting me in?'

'No.' Not yet, especially not with Gigi currently hiding out in the kitchen. Lara closed the front door behind her and said, 'Let's go somewhere quiet, shall we? Where we can talk.'

They drove to a pub down by the river and sat at a table in the garden away from the other drinkers. There were butterflies dancing around the flower-filled hanging baskets and more in Lara's stomach as she twiddled the stem of her wine glass. Giving Flynn the news in writing had seemed too much of a cop-out, but doing it face to face was going to be terrifying. She had no idea how he might react.

'By the way, I haven't spoken to Joel,' said Flynn.

'Good.'

'Are you OK?' He was watching her closely, which didn't help.

'Yes, thanks.'

'You're different today.'

'I know.' Lara attempted levity. 'I'm much cleaner. Less dusty. And my foot's stopped bleeding.'

'Not that kind of different. Yesterday you were in a panic. Tonight you're nervous.'

'Yes.' She nodded in agreement.

'I'm trying to work out why.'

Time to get this done. Prevaricating wasn't going to make it any easier. 'Right, brace yourself.' Could he hear her knees juddering beneath the table? 'I have a daughter.' She forced herself to look him straight in the eye. 'And so do you.'

Silence.

Silence.

More silence.

Finally Flynn said, 'You're serious.'

Lara stopped twirling the glass stem; what kind of person did he think she was? 'It isn't the sort of thing you say as a joke.'

He nodded slowly, then exhaled. 'Sorry. Just taking it in. And that's the reason you left?'

'I left because my father kicked me out.'

'Because you were pregnant.'

'No, he didn't know. I didn't tell him.'

'You didn't tell me either. Jesus.' Flynn picked up his drink then put it down again, untouched. 'I can't believe you didn't tell me.'

'I didn't even know for sure, not then. And I *wanted* to tell you,' said Lara. 'Do you remember that last night? We were talking for so long that I missed my bus home. I kept trying to say it but you were so excited about your skiing trip. You were going on about the competitions, stepping up the training in the Alps, maybe getting picked for the British team . . . it was all you could talk about.'

76

He spread his hands. 'Because I didn't *know*. You still should have told me.'

'I know, but that's easier said than done. And then there was the thing with Danny Cole.' Danny had been a couple of years older, a fellow skier and rising star whose plans for the future had been scuppered in similar fashion a matter of months earlier. 'Everyone acted as if it was his girlfriend's fault, d'you remember that? They said that she'd "got herself pregnant".' Lara emphasised the words that at the time had replayed themselves endlessly in her head. 'You said she'd wrecked his life and he should never have got involved with her in the first place. You also said she'd done it on purpose.'

'I didn't say that.'

'Oh yes you did. Believe me.'

Flynn shook his head. 'God. I shouldn't have. But you know something? About her doing it on purpose, it turned out I was right.'

'Well, I can promise you, I didn't.'

'Sorry. Of course not. Carry on.'

She took a steadying breath. 'Anyway, I got home late and my father and Janice went ballistic. They told me to get out. If I hadn't been pregnant I would have come to your house. But I thought I probably was, so I couldn't. And I was desperate, so desperate you can't begin to imagine. All I knew was that I had to get away. So I went up to Keswick and landed on Aunt Nettie's doorstep. She took me in,' said Lara. 'She was brilliant.'

'And you had our daughter.' Flynn's dark eyes flashed with indecipherable emotion. 'What's her name?'

'Gigi.' She silently dared him to make some disparaging comment; the moment Nettie had told her that Gigi had been her mum's nickname as a young girl, she'd known it was the name she'd choose.

He didn't. 'I'm assuming you didn't have her adopted.'

'The local GP suggested adoption, but I couldn't have done it. Luckily I had Nettie on my side.'

A muscle was flickering in Flynn's jaw. He rubbed the flat of his hand over it. 'And where is she now?'

'Back at the house. Waiting to find out if you'd like to meet her.'

After a moment, Flynn said, 'That was why you were so jumpy yesterday. I'd turned up without warning. Was she there then too?'

'Evie had taken her out to pick up a takeaway. But they were due back at any minute. It wouldn't have been fair.'

'What's she like?'

'Beautiful. Perfect.' Just saying it caused Lara to swell with pride; it never failed to astound her that she had managed to produce such an amazing human being. To be fair, she added, 'In a bossy kind of way. Your daughter's no shrinking violet.'

He smiled briefly. 'Why doesn't that surprise me?'

'And your hands are the same.' She indicated his long, tanned fingers. 'Well, hers are smaller. Look, I've got a couple of photos if you—'

'No, don't.' Flynn stopped her unfastening her bag. 'I've missed eighteen years; I think that's long enough. Why don't we go back there now, and I can see for myself?'

It took them less than ten minutes to drive back to the house. Lara called ahead and let them know they were on their way. When they pulled in through the gates, Gigi was waiting for them on the doorstep.

'Oh my God.' Flynn narrowly missed crashing into the yew hedge. 'Look at her. This is unbelievable.'

Lara suspected he wasn't the type to cry, but for a moment it

78

was close. He drank in the sight of his daughter, then took a deep breath and climbed out of the car.

'Hi,' said Gigi.

Flynn nodded fractionally. 'Hi.'

'Well, this is kind of exciting, isn't it? And kind of scary. In fact, I can't quite work out how it feels.' Gigi hesitated, then stretched out her hand to shake his. 'And you haven't had enough time to *begin* to work out how you feel. So I think we should just do this for now.'

Taken aback, Flynn said, 'OK.'

They shook hands. 'That's a good handshake,' Gigi said approvingly. 'I hate it when people do painful ones, don't you? When they, like, squeeze your knuckles really hard. And I hate dead-fish ones too. But yours is fine. Anyway, I've also decided we should only have half an hour tonight. So we don't run out of things to say. How does that sound?'

He hesitated. 'I'm not sure. But if that's what you want, I'll go along with it.'

'You don't mind me doing all this, being in charge?'

'Go ahead.' Flynn half-smiled. 'Your mother warned me you were bossy.'

'Mum!'

Lara shrugged. 'What did you want me to tell him? That you're incredibly shy?'

They went and sat in the back garden. 'If you'd rather be on your own,' Lara offered, 'I can leave you for a bit.'

'No, Mum, stay. It's fine. Anyway,' said Gigi, 'I think he's still in a state of shock. He's only been a father for about twenty minutes.'

Good. Lara wanted to stay. Seeing the two of them together for the first time was causing her heart to twist with emotion.

79

It was also fascinating being able to compare their physical differences and similarities in real life rather than in her mind. Their hairlines were the same, there were the hands too of course, and they were both lean, long-legged and athletic. Gigi had undoubtedly inherited her sporty genes from Flynn; last year she had run a marathon. She also played a mean game of tennis.

'So.' Gigi was gazing intently at her father; was she thinking the same thing? 'How shall we do this? Do you want to ask questions or shall I just start telling you about myself?'

'Asking questions sounds good,' said Flynn. 'We can take it in turns.'

'Great, because I've got loads. And I know they really should be in order but they won't be, because I'll get muddled up. I actually did make a list,' Gigi went on. 'I spent ages writing them all down. But Mum said if I sat there barking questions at you, it would be like a job interview.'

Although when you stopped to think about it, it kind of *was* a job interview. Lara kept quiet.

'I think we should just start,' said Flynn. 'And we'll see how we go, shall we? We've only got half an hour, after all.'

'OK.' Gigi cleared her throat. 'Do you love lists?'

If he was startled, he hid it well. 'Love? No.'

'Oh. That's a shame. But to be honest, I think they're more of a girl thing.'

'My turn,' said Flynn. 'Do you ski?'

'Do you know what? It's something I've never tried. But I can ice-skate.' Gigi's silver-grey eyes shone. 'I'm good at loads of different sports. I *could* ski, I'm sure of it. I bet I'd be brilliant.'

Flynn broke into a smile. 'And have you always been this cripplingly modest?'

'I'm just being honest. If I'm rubbish at something I'll tell you that too. My turn again,' said Gigi impatiently. 'OK, first impressions. How am I doing so far?'

'Pretty good. Are you fishing for compliments?'

She grinned. 'Probably. Have you got any other children?'

He shook his head. 'Evie's told you about me, hasn't she? No other children.'

'Just double-checking. Why not?'

'Never met the right person to have them with, I suppose.'

That hurt. *Never met the right person?* Lara knew he meant once he was old enough to contemplate having children, but it was still wounding to hear him say the words.

'How about you?' said Flynn. 'I've just found out I have a daughter. Are you about to tell me I'm a grandfather?'

'Noooo! Eurgh, no way.' Gigi shook her head emphatically. 'Babies smell. I've just done my A-levels. This is my gap year, then next year I'm off to uni. Anyway,' she added, 'I don't even have a boyfriend at the moment. I did, but we broke up.'

'Why?'

'Well, basically because he was a complete div who started telling me I shouldn't wear short skirts or talk to other boys even when they were just friends I'd been to school with for years. Getting all jealous and possessive, that's just crazy. It's such a loser thing to do. So I told him it was over.'

Flynn gave a nod of approval. 'Good for you.'

'I know. He's going out with someone else now. She does everything he tells her to do. Go on then, what was your last girlfriend like?'

Lara saw the flicker of a smile at Gigi's bluntness. 'Truthfully? She didn't last long. She was very nice. Intelligent, kind to small animals, knew how to use a knife and fork . . . close to perfect.'

'Except?'

'She thought she was perfect too. And she wasn't,' Flynn said drily. 'She had no sense of humour.'

'What, none at all?'

'Not an iota. I didn't know that was possible, kept waiting for it to appear.' He shrugged. 'But it couldn't because it didn't exist.'

'Good job you got rid of her then. Have you had many girl-friends?'

'I've had my share. I hope you aren't expecting me to count them,' said Flynn. 'Which A-levels did you take?'

'Psychology. Maths. French.'

'Well done.'

'You don't know if I passed them yet.'

'Did you pass them?'

'Yes.'

'What grades?'

Lara waited, secretly bursting with pride; they'd only received the results the other day. Thrilled to have done so well, Gigi had screamed and hugged her and she in turn had cried maternal tears of joy.

And now, for the first time, Gigi was able to share the news with her father. Pretending to be completely laid-back about it, she said casually, 'AAB,' then flushed with pleasure when Flynn, evidently impressed, said 'Bloody hell, that's brilliant. *Really* well done.'

'Thanks.' Gigi beamed, then leaned forward. 'So, can you ice-skate?'

Lara went inside and made cups of tea. In the living room, Evie was watching TV.

'How's it going?'

'Great. They don't need me at all. I feel like a spare part.'

'Stay here then. Leave them to it.'

82

'I think I will. Gigi's set a time limit, anyway. Another twenty minutes and then he's out of here.'

'Why?' said Evie.

'It's so they don't run out of things to say.'

Chapter 12

You could see by the sunlight streaming through the gap in the curtains that it was set to be another hot day. Lying in bed, with just a sheet covering her, Lara checked the time on her phone. Ten to seven. She'd come upstairs at eleven last night, exhausted by the move and all the settling in. When she'd said goodnight to them, Gigi and Flynn had still been sitting outside in the garden. What time had he left?

The next minute she heard a low murmur of voices coming from downstairs and realised he hadn't, he was still here.

Lara threw on jeans and a T-shirt, washed her face and brushed her teeth. On her way down she heard the kettle coming to the boil in the kitchen. In the living room, Gigi was sitting cross-legged on the sofa. Her eyes were huge and she looked simultaneously happy and shattered.

'Hey, Mum. Good sleep?'

'Yes, thanks. Have you been up all night?'

Gigi nodded and yawned widely. 'He's just making another cup of tea. We haven't stopped talking. I'm getting a bit tired now though.' She yawned again; all the excitement might have carried her this far but her body was now visibly craving sleep.

She broke into a slow smile as the door was pushed open by Flynn holding a mug in each hand. 'Mum, look. My dad's just made me a cup of tea. How cool is that?'

It was evidently very cool indeed, in Gigi's eyes. And already she was calling him Dad.

'So much for time limits,' said Lara.

'It would have been stupid. We've just had so much to say.' Another enormous yawn gripped Gigi before she could take the mug from Flynn.

'Give it to me.' Lara took it from him. 'Sweetie, you're dead on your feet. You need to go to bed.'

'But . . . I don't want to.' Gigi looked like a five-year-old hell-bent on waiting up for Father Christmas. 'I want to keep going. I don't want this night to be over.'

'I know, but Flynn has to go to work. And you have to sleep. Come along.' She reached out with her free hand to help Gigi to her feet. 'He'll still be here when you wake up.' OK, that hadn't come out right. 'I mean, he isn't going to disappear. You can see him again.'

'Promise?' Gigi looked to Flynn for confirmation. 'Is that a definite promise?'

'Absolutely. You get some sleep now. Give me a call when you wake up.'

'Can I see you tonight?'

He nodded. 'Whenever you want.'

Gigi smiled; this was the answer she'd wanted to hear. 'OK, I'll go. Night, Mum. Night, Dad. See you later.'

Lara got a quick kiss on the cheek. Then she watched and waited while Gigi and Flynn exchanged a hug. The formal hand-shakes had gone the way of the time limit. OK, it was actually quite emotional witnessing the embrace. Without thinking, she took a gulp of hot tea and almost gagged; *pleurgh*, when was Gigi going to give up on her three sugars habit?

The next moment it hit her; somehow she'd never made the connection before. As a teenager Flynn had always taken three sugars too.

Gigi left them and climbed the stairs to bed. Lara, about to head out to the kitchen to make a sugarless tea, was stopped in her tracks by Flynn closing the living-room door. She waited for him to turn, to break into a smile and tell her what she already knew, that the daughter they had created was amazing, incredible and unique, not to mention a complete credit to her. Unable to contain his amazement and delight at how perfectly she'd turned out, he would thank her for doing such a great job with raising Gigi and—

'I can't believe it.' He was shaking his head.

'I know.' Lara was already basking in pleasure. 'Told you she was fantastic.'

Then Flynn turned and she saw the expression on his face. Instead of joy and gratitude, his dark eyes narrowed with anger. 'I can't believe you've done this to me. How *dare* you?' His voice was low and vehement, vibrating with controlled fury. 'What gives you the right to mess with people's lives like this? My God, I don't know if I'll ever be able to forgive you for this.'

It was like a slap in the face when you were expecting a kiss. Not that she'd expected a kiss, but still. Adrenalin surged through Lara and the hairs prickled at the back of her neck. 'Excuse me? If you're doubting she's yours, we'll take a DNA test and prove it.'

'Don't be ridiculous, of course she's mine.'

'And now I'm messing up your life, am I? Oh dear, you poor thing, being a father wasn't part of your plan? Fine then, walk away, I'll tell Gigi you're not interested. You've met her once, it's out of your system, that's enough. No problem at all.' Lara rattled on, the words spraying out like bullets. 'You're not indispensable. We managed without you before, we'll do it again. If that's what you want, it's your loss. Trust me, we'll survive.'

'What are you saying now? For God's sake,' Flynn flashed back. 'Are you doing this deliberately? I'm not going to walk away. I'm talking about what you did. She's eighteen years old now, she's an adult. I've missed out on *eighteen years*. Thanks to you, I've missed out on *everything*.' He was shaking his head, angrier than she'd ever seen him before. 'That's what I can't get over, that's what I don't know if I can forgive. You should have told me. She was my child and I'll never know what she was like, growing up.'

'OK, *how dare you*?' Having expected praise and gratitude, Lara was outraged by the unfairness of this attack. 'It's fine for you to come over all indignant now, but you weren't in my position. I've already told you what happened. I was sixteen, you didn't want a baby and if you're going to try and tell me you did, you're a liar and a hypocrite!'

'Am I saying that? I am not saying that!' Flynn's jaw was rigid. 'I'm talking about eighteen years. I know how old you were, I know it was difficult at first, I *accept* that. But did it never occur to you that maybe, just maybe, your daughter might have quite liked to meet her father when she was three . . . or eight . . . or eleven . . . ? Did you not think I might want to meet my daughter while she was still a child . . . before she was old enough to vote?'

Unfair unfair UNFAIR. The only thing stopping Lara from hurling the mug of hideously sweet tea at him was the knowledge that she'd be the one left with a ruined carpet.

'So let me get this straight. You're calling me a bad mother now? Do you seriously think I didn't ask how she felt about this? If she missed having a father around? Because for your information she didn't, she was completely fine with everything the way it was. Her best friend didn't see her dad either. It's not unheard of, you know. If Gigi had *ever* said she wanted to meet you, I'd have got in touch. But she wasn't bothered. And how did I know you'd be interested anyway? You might not have been. Plenty of men aren't.'

'You didn't even *ask*.'

'And you don't get to dictate when you might want to meet your daughter.' Lara was on a roll; did he seriously expect her to back down? 'You've already admitted you wouldn't have been ready when she was born. You can't just say maybe when she's a few years old I might be able to handle it . . . oh, actually, I'm off to university now, can we leave it a bit longer? You aren't allowed to pick and choose and decide when it's convenient for you. This is a human being we're talking about, not a timeshare apartment.'

'You didn't give me a choice. I didn't know she existed!'

'Oh dear, poor you.' Below the belt maybe, but she was seriously losing it now. 'And there was me, swanning around Keswick, having such an *easy* life.'

'Has it occurred to you that Gigi might have wanted to know her father?'

'I've already told you she didn't!'

Flynn raised an index finger, signalling to her not to yell. Keeping his own voice deliberately low, he said, 'Or maybe she only said it because she knew that was what you wanted to hear.'

Lara stiffened; this was a blow far lower than the one she'd just delivered. Her mouth was dry, her palms slick with sweat. The look on Flynn's face signalled that he knew something she didn't.

Because he'd just spent eleven whole hours in the company of his newfound daughter, hadn't he? *Of course he knew better than she did.*

Now her heart was clattering away inside her ribcage like an alarm clock. Oh God, what had Gigi told him? Lara shook her head and said, 'Don't you dare try and make me feel guilty. I did what was best for my child.'

But he did have a right to be angry; deep down she knew that too.

'Our child. And I'm not trying to make you feel guilty. I'm telling you that maybe you could have shared her,' said Flynn. 'I'm not talking about just for my sake. For hers as well.'

'Oh right, so now you're the parenting expert. How did I guess you'd twist everything round so you'd be the hero? Let me tell you I worked my socks off for that girl, I spent sleepless nights looking after her when she was ill . . .' Lara's voice cracked with emotion borne out of fury. 'I was changing nappies and mopping up sick when you were doing your A-levels and I did it because I loved her. She was everything in the world to me and I made sure she never missed out because she didn't have a father. I didn't do it to hurt her or to spite you, I was just doing what I thought was right. And guess what? I think I made a pretty good job of it.' Madder than she'd ever been, Lara stalked past him to the door and flung it open. 'I also think you have a bloody nerve.'

'Hey, look, I'm not saying—'

'No, you're not saying anything. Shut up, I don't need this, you can go now.' She was buzzing with angry electricity; how grabbing the metal door handle hadn't just given her a colossal shock she had no idea.

'I've missed out,' said Flynn. 'On so many years.'

'You can make up for it now.'

89

He was shaking his head. 'I'd have been a good father.'

'You don't know that. You like to think you would.'

'Lara—'

'Out.' Her arm brushed against his as she marched past him to the front door and this time the contact made her shudder. 'Out, I've had enough.'

'Tell Gigi to call me later. She has my number.' Flynn eyed her coolly. 'I'll see her whenever she wants.'

He walked past her out of the house. Lara shut the door. Just before it closed, she murmured, 'Until the novelty wears off.'

Chapter 13

Low, low, as low as she'd thought she'd ever go. But, realistically, he was a virtual stranger. After a gap of almost nineteen years, how could she tell what he was really like now? He could be all talk and ruthless self-absorption for all she knew. Back in school he'd always been convinced he knew best, had hated conceding defeat in any aspect of life, whether in or out of the classroom or on the sports field. Tall, confident, the one with all the opinions and answers, that had been Flynn Erskine. He was the biggest achiever of their year. Of course, if he hadn't been so competitive by nature, he would never have made the British downhill team . . .

'Oh *God*.' Lara exhaled and realised from her tingling finger-tips that she'd been hyperventilating with frustration. She was still so mad she could throw something. In the kitchen she switched the kettle back on, by now desperate for tea. Gazing at her reflection in the shiny stainless steel side of the kettle, she saw a white smudge on her upper lip. Great, toothpaste, so she'd looked like an idiot too. Not that it mattered.

Bastard.

'Hi.' Evie came downstairs in her pyjamas as she was wiping the toothpaste off. 'Did I hear you talking to someone?'

'Flynn. He just left.'

'*Really?*' Evie's eyes widened. 'Wow, quick work!'

Talk about jumping to the wrongest conclusion imaginable. 'Not like that.'

'Oh, shame.'

'He and Gigi stayed up all night talking. She's asleep now. Flynn and I have just had a massive fight.' Lara's hands were still trembling; the mugs clattered as she took them out of the cupboard.

'Here, let me do that. Why did you fight?'

'He had a complete go at me because he's so sure he knows best.' It was the unexpectedness of the attack that had caught her off guard and left her so shaken. All the emotions stirred up by seeing Flynn again had been sent into a reverse tailspin. It was like the ultimate betrayal, mingled with her own inward guilt. Lara said, 'Everything's my fault, apparently. I've deprived Gigi of having a father, I've cheated him out of having a daughter, I'm a selfish spiteful cow . . .'

'Did he *call* you that?' Evie looked appalled.

'Yes!' Had he? When she was this wound up, it was hard to separate the actual words spoken from the ones implied. 'Well, kind of. That's pretty much what he was saying. And he's never going to forgive me for not telling him before now, because if he'd known, he'd have dropped everything and devoted his whole life to being the World's Best Dad. *Obviously.*' Lara exhaled noisily like a punctured spacehopper. 'I'm so mad I could explode. Thanks.' She took the tea from Evie and drank too much too quickly. To add insult to injury she now had a scalded mouth. 'Right, I'm going to paint the living room.' She may as well make good use of all this fired-up energy. 'What are you planning on doing today?'

'Um . . . I thought I'd go and fetch my stuff from Joel's later.'

92

Since returning to Bath, Evie had been gearing herself up for this task. 'And before I do that, I need to visit Bonnie and Ray, talk to them. Apologise, I suppose.'

Bloody men.

'You don't have to apologise. You did exactly the right thing,' said Lara. 'Everything'll be fine.'

Evie managed a smile. 'It'll be fine if I still have a job.'

It had been a weirdly dislocating experience, spending the last week and a half without her own things around her, not even her phone. But the time had come to get them back. And seeing as Joel would be at work and her key to his flat was in her handbag which was in turn at Bonnie and Ray's house, this was Evie's first port of call.

She'd been bracing herself all the way here on the bus. Now, heading up to the house at eight thirty, Evie double-braced and mentally prepared herself for the worst.

The last time she'd crunched across this gravel she'd been climbing into a limo, about to be whisked to the church . . .

Anyway, don't think about that now. Evie licked her lips nervously and rang the bell. Joel's parents had appeared to be understanding and supportive on the day of the wedding but who was to say they hadn't had a rethink since then? What if Bonnie opened the door and threw a bucket of ice-cold water over her for wrecking her precious boy's life?

'Oh my goodness, you're back! Ray? Ray! It's Evie, she's here! My darling, come along inside, how are you? I'm so sorry! Are you OK?'

Flooded with relief, Evie found herself crushed against Bonnie's front. Being back felt like coming home. Bonnie was wearing her sky-blue MadAboutParties polo shirt, ready to open up the

93

shop and start work at nine. She smelled of coffee and toast and Pears' soap and the warmth of her welcome caused Evie's throat to constrict.

'Morning, Evie. Lovely to see you.' And now they'd been joined by Ray, patting her on the back. 'Come along through, join us for breakfast. We've got toast.' His eyes twinkled with mischief. 'Or if you like, there's plenty of leftover wedding cake.'

They sat round the kitchen table and talked. Of course she could come back to work; why wouldn't they want her? She was welcome to return as soon as she liked. As for the wedding debacle, it had been the talk of Bath. Joel was in disgrace and everyone had told him in no uncertain terms that he'd brought it on himself. They all thought Evie had been very brave. Of course she couldn't have gone through with the ceremony under the circumstances.

'He's our son and we love him,' Ray announced, 'but he's been a prize idiot. And he knows it.'

Bonnie shook her head. 'He's certainly heard it enough times.'

Awash with emotion, Evie experienced the first twinges of sympathy for Joel. From the sound of things he hadn't had the easiest of times. While she'd escaped to the Lakes, he'd evidently been left to face the music, finding himself ganged up on and given a hard time by all and sundry. She glanced down at her ring-free hands. 'How is he?'

'Miserable.' Bonnie was blunt. 'Devastated.'

Oh.

Ray said, 'The thing is, he did wrong, but he does still love you.'

Oh God.

'Some people just can't resist temptation,' Bonnie went on. 'And they always hope they'll get away with it. Like those

Premiership footballers with lovely wives, but they cheat on them with girls who mean nothing at all. You'd think they'd learn, but they never do.'

The operative word being 'never'.

'Sorry,' said Ray. 'We're not defending him. Just trying to explain.'

'We care about you, darling. We don't want to lose you. If you need somewhere to stay,' Bonnie's eyes were bright, 'your room's still here. We'd love to have you with us.'

'Thanks, but I'm OK for now. I've moved in with a friend.' Touched by the offer, Evie said, 'It's really kind of you though. Actually, I'm planning to go over to the flat today and pick up my things. And I need to collect the stuff I left here too . . .'

Back at the house, Lara had already made a start on the living room. The furniture was swathed in sheets and she was energetically rolling the second coat of Vampire Red matt emulsion over walls that a couple of hours ago had been beige-with-a-hint-of-grey.

'Wow. Bit different.' Evie stood in the doorway, well away from the risk of roller spray.

'I know.' Stopping to survey her handiwork with satisfaction, Lara grinned. 'If my father's haunting the house, he's going to be really hating this. How did it go with Joel's parents?'

'They're brilliant. I start back at work tomorrow. And I've got my handbag and overnight case back.' Evie held them up to show her. 'Next stop, Joel's flat to pick up the rest.'

'Want me to come with you?'

'No, I'll be fine. OK if I take your car?'

'Help yourself.'

Evie collected the keys from the kitchen; she was in the mood to get everything sorted. Before leaving the house she called Joel's mobile and felt her heart flip at the sound of his voice.

'Hi, it's me. *Are you at work?*'

Was Joel's heart flipping over too? He hesitated for a moment before replying. 'Yes. Does this mean you're back?'

'I am. Look, I'm coming over to the flat to collect my things. Is that OK?'

'Er . . .'

Hastily she said, 'I'm not asking your permission, just being polite and giving you some warning. In case you have . . . visitors.'

'I don't have visitors.' He sounded hurt. 'I'm at work though.'

'No problem. I can manage. Right, I just wanted to let you know.'

'Evie, I'm sorry—'

'Bye.' Pressing the disconnect button felt fantastic. For years she'd been a pushover, the person who turned a blind eye to anything she didn't want to see. Well, no more. She'd reached her limit and from now on no one was going to make her look like a fool.

I am strong. *I am Madonna.*

'Are you OK?' Lara was watching her.

Evie collected herself. 'Yes, great.'

'Doing the Madonna thing again?' They'd talked about it.

'Yes.'

Lara approved of this method, despite never having done it herself. 'Good girl.'

Chapter 14

The flat she was no longer going to be living in was in Bannerdown, on the top floor of a modern complex. In truth, Evie had never loved it; having bought it brand new five years earlier, Joel had furnished and decorated the place in typical minimalist man-style. The grey suede sofa had never known cushions, electronic gadgets took priority and he had only bought items that were useful. Aesthetics simply weren't Joel's priority. When Evie had attempted to introduce candles and framed photos he'd reacted with actual bafflement.

It would always have been Joel's flat; she was able to admit that now. Even after moving in, she would never have been able to completely relax. Especially not on that hard, angular grey sofa.

The visitor feeling was strong as Evie fitted her key into the lock. The flat smelled faintly of curry, bleach and Joel's aftershave. She keyed in the code for the burglar alarm and made her way through to the kitchen. Everything was clean and tidy. Like a nosy burglar, she checked the bin. What was she expecting to see, a jaunty stash of empty champagne bottles? Or a pile of sad little baked bean tins? There were neither. Nor did the fridge give much away; a carton of milk, a couple of cans of lager, some dolcelatte cheese, a packet of bacon and a bottle of freshly squeezed orange juice that had been there for weeks. The use-by date was the end of July; prod it and it might explode.

OK, move on. The living room was tidy too. It looked as masculine and stark as it always had. Evie went on through to the bedroom and stood beside the neatly made bed. Had he brought the hair and make-up girl – Kirsty – back here? Had other heads lain on her pillow since the day of the wedding? Unable to help herself, she picked up the pillow and smelled it. But no, it had been freshly laundered. Joel employed a cleaning lady to take care of all the mundane chores.

They'd been changed yesterday, though. And his own pillowcase, the one on the right, smelled of him. Despite everything, the scent exerted an emotional pull. When you'd adored someone for so many years, you couldn't delete that ingrained Pavlovian reaction overnight. Evie buried her face in Joel's soft squashy pillow and inhaled deeply. Tears prickled at the back of her eyes. She'd done the brave thing but she still loved him. And if you believed his parents, he still loved her. If it hadn't been for bloody Kirsty she'd be Mrs Evie Barber by now. For better or for worse. And maybe he wouldn't have been the best husband in the world but you couldn't say he wasn't good-looking and charming—

Oh God, *door*.

Darting back in fright, Evie threw the pillow on to the bed so recklessly it cartwheeled and bounced off the other side. She raced round to grab it and cracked her shin on the bottom corner. *Ow*, that hurt. Gasping in pain she then launched herself at the pillow on the floor, threw it back on the bed and saw it completely overshoot again.

Basketball had never been her forte.

It was too late now anyway. Joel had found her.

'What are you doing?' He was gazing at the pillows.

OK, what would Madonna do? Tell the truth, presumably.

Then again, maybe she didn't always have to emulate Madonna.

'I was looking at the labels on the pillows. I want to buy some the same and I couldn't remember if they were goosedown or duckdown.'

Well, what was she supposed to say, that she'd been breathing in the smell of him and getting all emotional?

'And what are they?'

'I don't know. I didn't have a chance to look.' Evie reached for the pillow still on the bed and hastily rummaged around inside the pillowcase. 'Right, here's the label. White Hungarian goosedown . . . OK, got it.'

Joel hesitated. 'Were you . . . sniffing them?'

'What? No! God, why would I want to do that?'

'I don't know.' He gestured helplessly. 'I'm so sorry. About everything.'

'You've already told me that.' She tensed her stomach muscles, pulled them in. 'Anyway, I thought you were at work.'

'I cancelled my appointments and came straight over. I've missed you.'

What was he expecting her to do? Fall into his arms sobbing and tell him she'd missed him too?

OK, but this was proving harder than she'd thought. Now that he was actually standing before her, being apologetic and looking so wounded, she could feel herself start to weaken. Maybe it was the pheromones in the pillow.

Stop it, don't let it happen.

Evie forced herself to get a grip. 'How's Kirsty?'

'What? I have no idea.' Joel shook his head and looked pained. 'I told you, she didn't mean anything.'

'She obviously thought you did.'

'Well, she shouldn't have. She knew I was marrying you. I finished with her, that's what she couldn't handle. Because that's the thing,' Joel protested, 'it all happened before the wedding. Once we were married, I wouldn't have done anything behind your back. Don't you see? That would have been the cut-off point. I swear on my life, once we'd said our vows I'd have been completely faithful.'

'Well, that's very . . . generous of you. But it's kind of beside the point,' said Evie. 'We were together. The whole idea of being in a relationship is that you're faithful all the way through. Before you get married as well as after. Anyway, I don't know why I need to explain this. It's completely irrelevant now. We're not getting back together, so why are we even having this conversation?'

'We could get back together,' said Joel. 'If you wanted to.'

Evie was taken aback; this wasn't something she'd anticipated. 'Why would I want to? Why would *you*? Didn't I publicly humiliate you?'

'Yes, you did. And I deserved it. I'm taking the blame for everything.'

'Good! Glad to hear it! Because it was your fault!'

'But I know now. How much I love you. More than before.' Joel moved towards her. 'I love it that it mattered that much to you. OK, I'll say this now, I always thought you knew when things happened in the past, but you pretended you didn't.'

Her stomach did a little flip. 'You mean other girls?'

'Yes! But I never started it. They made all the running. I just went along with it . . . and I thought you were OK with that, because you never said anything. So if you weren't bothered anyway, what would be the point of turning them down? It was

100

like you were giving me permission, so long as I was discreet. I swear to God,' Joel raked his fingers through his hair, 'I thought you *didn't mind.*'

'Well, guess what?' said Evie. 'I did. I really did.'

'I know that now.' He paused. 'I wouldn't do it again. *Ever.*'

'I'm taking my things.'

'You don't have to.'

'I'm going to.' Did he seriously imagine she'd forgive him on the spot?

'Mum and Dad would be so pleased if we got back together, you know how much they love you.'

'They love me whether we're together or not. I'm starting back at work tomorrow.'

'You are? That's great.' He gave her a poor-me look. 'You can't imagine the hard time they've been giving me since the wedding.'

'I can imagine. They've told me.'

'And where are you staying?'

'With Lara.'

'The one you disappeared with? The one who went out with Flynn years ago? I thought she lived somewhere up north.'

You see, this was Joel all over. She'd told him before the wedding that Lara was going to be moving back to Bath, but it hadn't filtered through. Basically, the information hadn't been interesting enough for him to pay attention.

'She did. Now she's back.' Evie didn't add, 'With Flynn's daughter.' It was up to Flynn to make that item of news public.

'And this Lara, she's single? I don't want her being a bad influence on you, taking you out on the town . . .' Joel was actually looking worried now.

'It's not a matter of what you want.' It gave her a thrill to say it. Evie shook her head, relishing the sensation of being in control.

101

'We aren't together any more. I can go out and do whatever I like.'

'You won't though, will you?' He searched her face, surveying her intently. 'You're not the type.'

'Then again, you wouldn't have thought I was the type to call off the wedding.'

'True.' He smiled sadly, his gaze locked on her face. 'God, Evie, you've turned me into a laughing stock. I should really hate you for that. But I don't. I just can't make myself do it.'

'Maybe because you know you deserve it. Anyway, we don't have to hate each other. Seeing as I'm working for your parents, it's better if we don't.'

There was silence for a couple of seconds, then Joel nodded. 'You're right. Again. Come here.' He took a step towards her, opening his arms and using the tone of voice she knew well. It was his 'hey-I've-been-naughty-but-I've-said-I'm-sorry-and-now-it's-time-for-you-to-forgive-me' voice.

And it would have been so easy – and so lovely – to just relax and let it happen. Not doing it felt like forcing a cranky old gearbox into reverse.

'No thanks. I just want to collect my things and go.'

Joel's hands fell to his sides. He said with admiration, 'You're amazing. I deserved that. But we can be friends, can't we?'

'I don't see why not.'

'And don't forget, I still love you. More than ever now.'

'Just friends is enough.' Evie was being outwardly brave, but inside she was in turmoil.

'It's not enough for me. But it'll do for a start.' Joel conceded the point with one of his winning heart-melting smiles. 'Just so you know, though, I'm going to do everything I can to win you back.'

★   ★   ★

102

On his way back from a meeting with a major client in Kelston, Flynn encountered a backlog of traffic that had ground to a standstill on Newbridge Hill. Switching on the radio, he learned that there had been an accident on Windsor Bridge Road and central Bath was in a state of gridlock.

Luckily, it had been his last appointment of the day. On the down side, he wasn't going to get home any time soon. Instead, diverting to the left, he made his way to Victoria Park.

It was six o'clock in the evening, still sunny and warm. Families were queuing at the ice-cream van as Flynn left the car and made his way past them into the park. After last night he should be dropping with exhaustion but, if he were back at the flat now, he knew he wouldn't be able to sleep. All day, this morning's furious argument with Lara had been replaying itself on a loop in his head.

It was a situation that clearly needed to be sorted out. And he may as well do it here, in the park they'd spent so much time in as teenagers.

Hands in pockets, he followed the path leading towards the wooden bridge over the pond. This was where he and Lara had liked to come and watch the ducks.

Lara, Lara. God, the last couple of days had been utterly surreal. This morning he had said some things he probably shouldn't have said. And so had she. Their emotions had got the better of them and they had got carried away. Which hadn't been ideal, and he was regretting it now. It was like happy families being visited by tragedy; when a child died, instead of clinging together and supporting each other, the parents found themselves grieving alone, taking their anger out on each other and eventually breaking up. It was a statistical probability, he knew that.

But this was the opposite scenario. Lara was back and he had *gained* a daughter, which was unbelievably amazing. He was a father. And Gigi was amazing too. This was no tragedy, it was a good-news story. Pretty much the best news possible.

And yes, Lara had been wrong to deprive him of his daughter for the last eighteen years, but she hadn't done it to punish him, he knew that. She'd thought she was making a sensible decision. It hadn't been a malicious one.

He could appreciate that now. Resting his forearms on the bridge's wooden balustrade, Flynn gazed down at the water. Sunlight bounced off the ripples created by a surge of activity from the ducks as an overexcited small boy hurled an entire loaf's worth of bread slices into the water, all in one go.

He'd missed out on all those precious duck-feeding years with Gigi.

'Oh, Darren, you big *wally*,' wailed the small boy's older sister. 'You're supposed to do them one at a time!'

'Ow!' Darren howled, as she gave him a shove and knocked him over. Grabbing a handful of stones, he flung them at his sister, who let out a scream when one of them hit her in the face.

'OK, you two, that's enough.' Their exasperated mother dragged them apart. 'If you can't be nice, we're going home.'

'I want to go home! He's used up all the bread and now there's none left for me! Darren, you are a PIG!' bellowed his sister.

Flynn watched them leave. Maybe duck-feeding wasn't always as idyllic as it was cracked up to be.

Anyway, he and Lara had hopefully got the worst of the anger out of their systems now, for two reasons. Because, as Gigi's parents, it was going to help if they were on speaking terms.

As for the second reason . . . well, it was pretty simple. Lara was back in Bath, back in his life. And seeing her again had only proved what he'd always suspected.

He'd never got over her. Nor had anyone else ever managed

to match up. Crazy though it sounded, she appeared to have been the love of his life. God knows, he'd tried to replace her and, over the years, there'd been plenty of willing candidates, but the chemistry that had bound them together had never been equalled. When Lara had looked at him with those thickly lashed, gunmetal silver eyes, she just *knew* him, and vice versa. They had shared something he couldn't even begin to explain.

And, all these years later, that feeling was still there.

A pair of swans had sailed out from under the bridge now, to investigate the remains of the bread. As Flynn watched them, a small dog on a lead brushed against the back of his trouser leg.

'Alfie, stop it. I'm so sorry . . . oh, Flynn, I didn't realise it was you! Hello!'

Her name was Nerys and she was a retired piano teacher who had been friendly with his parents before they had both died. Still elegant in her late seventies, she was walking her Jack Russell.

'Nerys, how nice to see you again. You're looking very well.' He greeted her with a kiss. She and his mother had shared a passion for music and had often attended the opera together.

'Well enough, I suppose, dear. Touch of arthritis, but I can't complain. Better than being dead, I suppose.' She gave him a bright smile tinged with sympathy. 'I do miss your ma and pa. You must too.'

Flynn nodded; they had gone within weeks of each other, first his mother succumbing to cancer, then his father to a heart attack. It had happened four years ago now.

'It's a blessing they went as close together as they did. Like a pair of swans, they were.' Nerys matter-of-factly indicated the swans on the water. 'Find the right partner and that's it for life. Romantic.' She paused and surveyed him with interest. 'And how about you, dear? Settled down yet?'

'Not yet.' Flynn smiled briefly.

'Taking your time, eh? Nothing wrong with that, did the same myself. Don't worry, it'll happen.' Giving Alfie's lead a tug and preparing to move on, Nerys said cheerily, 'When you meet the right one, you'll know.'

When she'd gone, Flynn stayed where he was for a while longer and watched the activity on the pond as the last of the sodden bread disappeared.

Like it or not, Lara appeared to be his swan. The question now was, would he turn out to be hers?

At the moment, there was no way of knowing.

One thing was decided, though. He would forgive her, but he wouldn't grovel.

From now on, everything that had gone before was water under the bridge.

Chapter 15

When Harry switched on his computer on Wednesday morning his first thought was that the antivirus must have failed. His email inbox had been spammed, completely overrun with emails. The last time it had happened, offers of Viagra had poured in. This spamming virus, however, appeared to have attached itself to the order forms on the website account. Which might be less embarrassing than the Viagra episode but it was still a complete pain, because computers weren't his forte and now he was going to have to take it along to the expert at the repair shop to get it sorted out. Damn and blast.

He made himself a cup of tea then sat back down, gazing helplessly at the screen. Not all the emails were viruses. So long as he didn't click on any of the bad ones, would he be OK? Or was that the wrong thing to do? Would it cause the virus to spread like typhus? Maybe he shouldn't risk it.

Harry leaned back with a sigh and sipped his tea. It was half past eight; the local computer repair shop didn't open until nine. He heard the sound of a car pulling into the courtyard. Morag and Betty had arrived for work but they'd be no help either.

Two minutes later, they appeared in the office. Morag, pink-cheeked in a floral dress and clutching a fluorescent yellow Post-it note, said, 'That singer fellow who was here the other day. Did he have pointy gold teeth here and here?'

She was baring her gums, pointing to her yellowish incisors. Bemused, Harry said, 'Yes, he did.'

'Was his name EnjaySeven?' Betty chimed in eagerly.

'Something like that. Sounds familiar. It was like half a post-code.' Harry nodded, still mystified. 'Why?'

'Our Darren just called me! You're on his website!'

Darren was Morag's fifteen-year-old grandson. 'Your Darren's got a website?' If he were technically minded, maybe he could get rid of this wretched virus.

'Not him, you twit! EnjaySeven! Here, our Darren's given me the site. You just have to type this in and it'll take you to the right bit.' Morag triumphantly slapped the yellow Post-it on to the desk.

'I can't, there's something wrong with the computer. Look at all the messages.' Harry pointed to the screen. 'That means we've been infected with a virus.'

'They're orders,' said Betty. 'It says so.'

'But it can't be actual orders,' Harry patiently explained. 'There are too many of them.'

'Shift your backside, pet. Let me do it.' Betty took over the swivel chair and began tapping away at the keyboard like a pro. 'See? They're orders. Told you!'

'But how . . . ?' Harry rubbed the back of his head.

'You big numpty! I can't believe you've never heard of EnjaySeven,' Morag chided. 'I can't believe I was working away in the back room and you didn't even think to tell me he was here. EnjaySeven's right up there with Eminem and Kanye and Jay-Z. He's *massive.*'

For heaven's sake, would you listen to them? He was thirty-eight.

Betty and Morag were in their sixties. They'd be breakdancing next. Or whatever kind of fancy dancing it was called nowadays. On the few occasions he'd seen it on TV it had looked a lot like dislocating your hips.

And now Betty had brought the website up on to the screen, and it was an impressively glitzy and professional affair with flashing bits and music playing and . . . oh good grief, a still from the video taken right here in this very office . . .

'There you are! That's *you*,' said Morag. Just in case he hadn't recognised himself.

Betty pressed play and the scene sprang to life, causing Harry's neck to prickle with embarrassment. He'd always hated seeing and hearing himself on friends' videos.

In dumbstruck silence they watched the clip, reliving the episode where Vampire Teeth – OK, EnjaySeven – demanded to buy all the shirts and Harry refused to sell them. The recording had been edited; the next moment he was saying they didn't take American Express, then that he wouldn't be listening to EnjaySeven's music. After that, the filming resumed inside the Maybach, with EnjaySeven mimicking Harry's reluctance, his reserve and his English-butler accent. Finally, it cut to EnjaySeven in his hotel room, wearing a smart suit, super-shiny shoes and one of the cream shirts.

'So here I am,' he drawled, 'all ready to go out on the town tonight, and I gotta tell you, guys, this is my all-time favourite make of shirt. The Effing Ducks, this is them,' He leaned towards the camera and tapped the logo with a manicured fingernail. His tone conspiratorial, he said, 'It's supposed to be the Flying Ducks but we've renamed it now. So you go to the link on our website and head on over to *their* website, where an *orffully nice gentleman* will take your order. So that's it, y'all get yourself a cool shirt like mine, yeah? You won't regret it. The Effing Ducks. Quack quack!'

The clip ended, fading to black.

'Ah, isn't that lovely?' Morag clapped her hands.

'And doesn't it suit him?' said Betty happily. 'Mind you, he's got the body for it. Nice pecs. You can tell he works out.'

Harry stared at the pair of them in outrage. 'Excuse me, are you both out of your minds? Has it not occurred to you that there is something . . . *wrong* with this situation?'

Mystified, they gazed up at him. 'What's wrong, pet? It's brilliant!'

'How can it be brilliant when he's saying . . . what he said?' Bad language wasn't something that tripped naturally off Harry's tongue; he'd just never been the type to use it. 'The Effing Ducks.' He found himself stumbling over the words. 'That's just completely offensive.'

'Oh, you're such an old fuddy-duddy, pet. Young people say it all the time these days. Anyway,' Morag's tone was soothing, 'Eff stands for Flying, so that's all right.'

'It is not all right! It's outrageous. What if our customers got to hear about this?'

Wordlessly Betty clicked off the garish site and returned to the emails. She began scrolling down the list of new orders. And down. And dooooooooooown. At last, one hundred and seventy-six emails later, she came to the end and said, 'Well, these customers don't seem too bothered.'

'I don't care. That man's bringing our name into disrepute. We have a reputation to maintain and I won't let him sully it.'

'But he's not sullying it, pet, not really. He's saying it's his all-time favourite shirt! All these years,' said Morag, 'we've never had a celebrity wear one of our shirts, and now we've got EnjaySeven! This is like a dream come true . . .'

110

'It really isn't.' Harry shook his head. 'I don't mind people making fun of me, but I won't have them making fun of our good name. Right, leave this to me, I'll sort it out. You two can go and make a start on these shirts.'

Within ten minutes he had fired off an email to the contact address on the website. In a calm but firm manner, he made his feelings clear. Finally, having expressed his hope that the situation could be resolved in an amicable manner, he signed off with 'Yours most sincerely, Harry Wells', and pressed send.

By this time, yet more orders had come pouring into his inbox. Which was pleasing in one way, of course it was, but the standard of the grammar in some of the accompanying messages was frankly appalling:

'Yeh man, giv uz a gray 1 in meedum but y no pinck or beter cullrs eh?!!!'

Harry winced. Oh dear, oh dear, what were the young people of the world coming to? At this rate 'textspeak' was set to signal the downfall of civilisation. Still, at least this one hadn't mentioned the Effing Ducks, like the sender of the next order.

And the next. Who spelled it Efinn.

Another called it FN Ducks.

After thirty minutes he printed off the list of orders and realised they were going to have to get a couple of extra workers in. The recession had taken its toll on the company as it had with so many, and sales had halved over the last decade. They still had two machines standing idle; now they could be brought back into service. He'd ask Betty if her sister would like to join them for—

Bbbrrring bbbrrring. The phone burst into life on the desk and Harry reached for it.

'Good morning, Flying Ducks, how may I help you?'

'Yo, Harry, how ya doin', man? EnjaySevaaaan!'

It wasn't the kind of voice you could easily forget. Harry said sternly, 'Oh hello. I'm well, thank you. But not *too* happy. In fact I've just sent you an email voicing my concerns.'

'I know you did, man. That's why I'm calling you. The girl who passed it on to me thinks you're kinda cute, by the way.'

'Well, thank you, that's flattering to hear, but we really have to do something about this Effing Ducks business.' There, he'd said it.

'*We?*' EnjaySeven sounded amused.

'*You,*' Harry said firmly.

'It's just a bit of fun, man.'

'Maybe it is to you. But to me it's besmirching the good name of our company.'

'Besmirching, that's a helluva word. You know what? I think I like it.'

'I just feel it's disrespectful,' Harry reiterated.

'Oh man, I ain't dissin' you, I thought you'd be pleased. It's free publicity, yeah? I tell my fans something's good, they buy it. Big companies pay a fortune to be endorsed by me.'

'I'm sure they do. And I *am* grateful . . .'

'You had any orders since we put the video up on the site?'

'Yes, we have. Quite a few,' Harry admitted.

'How many?'

'Orders for two hundred and eighty-six shirts.'

'See? And it only went up a few hours ago. Brace yourselves, there'll be more.'

'I won't be filling any orders until you remove the offensive comments from the site,' said Harry.

'Man, are you serious?'

'Completely.'

'You'll lose out on a ton of money.'

'I know that. But I'd still have my dignity.'

'Oh my. Oh my, oh my.' Enjay was chuckling now. 'You know who you sound like, Harry? You sound like my mom.'

'I'll take that as a compliment. Although I don't suppose I sound *exactly* like her.'

'You're right. You're more English.'

'And I'm a man.'

More laughter. 'OK, Harry. I'll get my people on to it.'

'What does that mean?'

'We'll bleep out the offending words. I'll post another clip telling people it's Flying Ducks only and if they call it anything else you'll sue their sorry asses.'

Honestly, these Americans and their addiction to legal action. Harry said, 'I couldn't afford to do that.'

'I know. We just say it, that's all. It'll be cool.'

'OK.'

'Happy now?'

'I think so, yes.'

'You've got everything you could possibly want out of this and you only *think* so? Harry, you crack me up. You're a funny guy.'

Did he mean funny ha-ha or funny peculiar? Harry thought he could hazard a guess. Luckily it didn't bother him. He said, 'I wouldn't say I'd got *everything* I could want.'

'Oh really? An endorsement by a global superstar not good enough for you? What's better than that, man?'

'Well, no offence,' said Harry, 'but personally I'd have preferred it to be Prince Charles.'

Chapter 16

'Morning,' said Flynn, when Lara opened the door.

'Hi.' She may as well get it over and done with. 'Sorry about yesterday. You had every right to be angry.'

His expression softened. 'I know. But so did you. I'm sorry too.'

Wow, she hadn't expected *that*.

'Look at us.' Lara smiled slightly. 'Behaving like mature adults. Who'd have thought it?'

'Best way. For Gigi's sake. Maybe we needed to get it out of our systems. Anyway, now that's done, we can start again.'

Her skin prickled in alarm; what did that mean? If he knew how she felt about him he could start toying with her emotions, messing her around like Joel had messed Evie around for years.

'Start again as Gigi's parents. Being civil to each other. That's all.'

'Exactly what I meant,' Flynn countered. 'So, am I staying out here on the doorstep, or were you thinking of letting me in?'

'Right. Sorry.' Lara opened the door wide; today he was taking Gigi into work with him to show her how the business was run. 'You're early. She's still in the shower. I thought you were picking her up at nine.'

Flynn shrugged. 'The roads were clearer than usual. OK if I have a coffee?'

'Can you make it yourself? I'm busy.' She was painting the dining room now, apricot yellow and white to make the most of the sunlight pouring in through the south-facing windows.

Flynn made coffee and brought one through to her.

'Thanks.' Lara breathed in his aftershave as he passed her the cup. She was getting to know it now.

'Can I ask you a question?'

'I expect you're going to anyway.' If he was about to give her more hassle she wouldn't put up with it.

'Relax, it's not about Gigi. Well,' Flynn amended, 'it's something she mentioned. About this house. I assumed your father left it to you in his will. But Gigi told me yesterday it wasn't his to leave.' He was looking puzzled. 'She said this place belonged to your mother. Is that true?'

Lara had been about to reload the paintbrush. Instead she put it down.

'Yes.'

'Did you know that before?'

She shook her head. 'No, no idea. Aunt Nettie didn't know either.'

'So, how did it happen? Where did the money come from?'

'Not the foggiest.' She leaned against the windowsill; having known her father all those years ago, Flynn was one of the very few people as curious about this as she was.

He frowned. 'Haven't you wondered about it?'

For heaven's sake. Lara stared at him in disbelief. 'Of course I've wondered! I've spent *hours* wondering about it, but there's no way of finding out! If my mum didn't tell Nettie, who else is there? I've asked the solicitor, but he only handled my father's will. It was over thirty years ago. We know there was no mortgage. I've racked my brains but there's nothing else to go on. I mean, it's not as if she had any rich relatives who could leave her a fortune. And Nettie would have known if she'd won on the Premium Bonds. All I can think is that my father supplied the money and put the house into my mum's name for . . . I don't know, tax purposes or something.'

'He was a cashier in a bank.' Flynn looked dubious. 'Where would he have suddenly got that amount of money from?'

Mystified, Lara shrugged. 'You're asking me questions I don't have the answers to. I have *no* idea. Unless he embezzled it from work and couldn't buy the house in his name because it would mean them possibly finding out.'

He raised an eyebrow. 'And would you be interested in contacting the bank and asking them to investigate that?'

'No I wouldn't.' Was he serious?

'Because if it turned out to be true, they might want their house back?'

'Exactly,' said Lara. Was it wrong to be admitting this? Oh well.

Flynn smiled briefly and drank some coffee. 'For what it's worth, I don't think that's how it happened.'

'Oh?' They both heard the clunk upstairs of the shower being turned off. Despite their recent falling out, Lara was touched by the thought he was putting into this.

'If it was your father's money, he'd have made sure it went back to him. Sorry, but we both know what he was like. He wouldn't have allowed your mum to leave the house to you. This was something he had no control over. And my God, I bet he hated that.'

He was right. Her father had been the ultimate controlling character.

'Makes sense.' Lara nodded. 'But it doesn't tell us where the money came from.'

'No friends you could contact?'

'There were only a couple. And I don't know their names. It was all so long ago.' She'd been thirteen when her mum had died; it was only during the intervening years that she'd guessed the pattern of her parents' marriage. In retrospect it seemed obvious that her father had discouraged friendship with others. All part of the control. 'There was a blonde woman . . . I remember me and Mum meeting up with her in the park a few times when I was nine or ten. And another friend whose house we used to go to. Her name was Janey or Julie, something like that, and she used to give me Jaffa Cakes.'

'Do you remember where she lived?'

'No. But I think she moved away anyway, she was going to live abroad somewhere sunny. I never saw her again after the funeral.'

Flynn frowned. 'And you don't have any old address books or diaries?'

'Oh, that's an idea!' Did he think she was completely brainless? Lara said brightly, 'You mean the address books and diaries that I've got upstairs, with all the names and addresses of people I've been longing to contact for decades? How silly of me not to think of looking inside them . . .'

He raised his hands. 'Fine, sorry, just trying to help.'

Bugger, did that mean she had to apologise as well? Again? Too exasperated to want to, Lara made do with a me–too gesture with her free hand. 'I don't have anything. Nothing at all. I asked the solicitor to ask Janice to leave any of my mum's personal effects with him. She told him there weren't any.'

'They destroyed everything?'

Lara shrugged, determined not to get emotional at the thought of all traces of her mother's existence being erased like writing on a whiteboard.

'That's what she said.'

'But there must be ways of—'

'Ready!' Gigi burst into the room in a lime-green top and pink and green polka-dotted skirt. 'Am I smart enough?'

Lara saw the look of pride on Flynn's face as he surveyed his daughter. 'I don't know.' He paused. 'What's seven times eight?'

'Ha ha, very good. If we're going to be meeting customers I want to look nice.'

He gave an approving nod. 'You're fine. And speedy. Which is always good.'

'I'm really fast at getting ready to go out. One of my many talents.' Gigi eyed Flynn's car keys and said hopefully, 'Want me to drive?'

'Nope.'

'She's a good driver.' Lara leapt to her daughter's defence.

Flynn smiled. 'I'm sure she is. But I need to sort out the insurance first.'

'Come on then, what are we waiting for?' When he hesitated, Gigi hustled him out of the dining room. 'Let's get out of here, shall we? I want to learn about wine!'

By six o'clock, the dining room was finished. Happy with the result, Lara had showered the paint spatters out of her hair and was now busy in the kitchen being a domestic goddess.

Well, kind of. Stabbing a fork through the cellophane covering the pack of mushroom risotto – rat-tat-tat-tat-TATT – she stuck it in the microwave. In three minutes, when it was ready, she'd add a splash of double cream, a scattering of black pepper and masses of grated parmesan. That was goddessy enough, surely?

Although a real goddess would probably be drinking chilled white wine with it, not Irn-Bru.

Gigi and Flynn returned fifteen minutes later. Sitting outside in the back garden, Lara heard the car draw up outside. Doors banged, then came the sound of voices. Was Flynn dropping Gigi and heading off somewhere else, or was he coming in? The former, she hoped. This morning's conversation had left her unsettled and on edge, reminding her of all that was missing from her life.

'Mum? There you are!' Gigi paused in the doorway before coming to join her, and Lara felt the tension dissipate, her muscles relax. Good, no Flynn. She could do without seeing him tonight.

'Hi, sweetie, how'd it go? Was it fun?'

'No, it was *not*. It was boring and tedious and duller than you could ever imagine.' Gigi flopped down on to the grass next to her, in the manner of a teenager about to expire of boredom. 'It was the opposite of fun.'

'Oh.' Lara put down her can of Irn-Bru. Not that it was the end of the world, but Flynn would be disappointed; he'd been looking forward to teaching Gigi about the business he loved. 'I didn't think it'd be dull. Weren't you meeting lots of people?'

'No! None!'

'Why not?'

'Because we were just stuck in the stupid office trawling through hundreds of dusty old invoices. Not hundreds,' Gigi corrected herself. 'Thousands. In fact, probably millions. Honestly, Mum, you have no idea.'

The back door swung open once more and Flynn appeared in the garden. Lara's stomach did a quick up-and-down shimmy at the sight of him in his white shirt and well-cut black suit trousers. On the one hand, he had a body to die for. On the other, he was getting on her nerves all over again.

'What have you been making Gigi do?' She shielded her eyes against the sun, all the better to scowl at him accusingly. 'I thought you were going to show her how the company was run. She's not your slave, you know.'

The expression on Flynn's face was inscrutable. 'I do know.'

'Mu-um, stop it, I was *joking*.' Gigi jack-knifed into a sitting position and rolled her eyes like an embarrassed parent.

Teenagers, honestly. 'Thanks for telling me. How was I meant to know it was a joke? So you weren't stuck in an office trawling through *millions* of boring old invoices.' This was to let Flynn know she'd snapped for a reason.

'Oh yes, we were.' Her smile impish, Gigi said, 'Millions.'

There was some kind of in-joke going on here. Presumably there was also a point to it. Lara looked over at Flynn. 'So what's this about?'

He pulled out a chair, sat down opposite her and leaned forward, resting his tanned forearms on the table. 'OK, let me just say I don't have a definitive answer. Yet. But with a bit of luck we'll get there.'

Something about the way he was saying it caused Lara's blood to race that bit faster around her body. 'Get where?'

Chapter 17

Flynn said, 'What we were talking about this morning reminded me of something. I was going to mention it when Gigi came down and dragged me away. Plus, I needed to think it through.'

Lara blinked. 'Go on.'

'It was nine or ten years ago. I was working at Grey's.' He paused, 'A woman came in to buy some wine. We were running a tasting and she was trying a few different kinds. We got chatting, then all of a sudden she asked me if I was the skier. I told her I was, and then she said did I used to have a girlfriend called Lara.'

'Who was she?'

'I said yes I had,' Flynn continued steadily. 'And she said she thought so, that she'd known you when you were growing up; she'd moved away years ago, but during her last visit back to Bath she'd seen the two of us together. She recognised me from the TV and was so glad to see you looking so happy. She asked if I was still in touch with you and I told her I wasn't, that you'd left Bath and hadn't kept in touch with anyone here.'

Lara's heart was thudding away. 'What was her name?'

'I don't know. But she talked about you for a bit, told me she'd been a friend of your mum's and how awful it must have been for you when she died. She said she left Bath just after it happened, and that she'd written to you but never had any reply.'

'I didn't get any letter.' Her mind was racing ahead. 'She might have sent one, but I never saw it. Anyway, carry on. What else?'

But Flynn was already shaking his head. 'That's it, that's all there was. Bearing in mind that I didn't have any reason to remember her. But I'm sure she was more tanned than the other people in the shop, as if she'd been abroad on holiday . . .'

'Or if she *lived* somewhere hot,' Gigi put in helpfully, 'and had just come back to Bath.'

'But you don't have her name,' said Lara. 'So that means we still don't know who she is.'

'She bought some wine.' Flynn leaned to one side and drew a folded sheet of paper from his trouser pocket. 'It was before I got the business computerised.' The Greys had been famously anti-technology prior to his arrival. 'But we've been through all the old invoices today. I've made a list of every female whose name begins with a J.'

'So you see,' Gigi chimed in again, 'it *was* boring, but it was worth it!'

'Can I see?' Lara reached for the sheet of paper. The names were in Flynn's hand, instantly transporting her back to their teenage years together; that untidy, spiky writing style was spookily unchanged.

She scanned the names, so many of them . . . Jane Morgan . . . J. Lancaster . . . Julie Knight . . . Judith Childerley . . . Jennifer Fuge . . . Joanne Margason . . . Josephine Pride . . . J. Carter . . . Jean Drew . . .

There were more. She scrutinised them all, willing the right one to leap out at her, released like a tiger from the depths of her subconscious.

'It's no good, I can't tell.' Reaching the end, she put the list down and felt her throat tighten with disappointment. 'I don't think I ever knew her surname. We're never going to know which one's her. Even if we could find out, those invoices are years old . . .'

'Don't be such a pessimist. Keep thinking about that name beginning with J. It might come to you.' Flynn retrieved the list then rose to his feet. 'Right, I have work to do. Better be off.' The moment he said it, Gigi jumped up and gave him a hug. Still in a daze, Lara nevertheless experienced a twinge of envy that he'd managed to get her off the ground; if she'd been the one leaving, Gigi would have stayed where she was and said, 'Bye, Mum!'

'Mum?'

'What?'

'Dad's leaving now. Are you going to say anything?'

'Oh. Um, goodbye.'

'Mum!'

'What?' Gigi was giving her a don't-be-so-*rude* look.

'You could try saying thank you.'

'Right. Yes of course, sorry.' Lara looked up at Flynn, silhouetted against the sun with Gigi still clinging to his arm. 'Thanks. Very much.'

Thanks for raising my hopes and dashing them again, thanks for stirring up all the old feelings, thanks for making me feel like a failure for not being able to remember my mum's friend's name.

He smiled slightly, as if reading her mind. 'No problem. Just trying to help.'

Evie was stuck in traffic on her way to drop off an order before heading home. Well, not her own home. Lara's. But in just a few days they'd fallen into such an easy routine it felt as if they'd been there for weeks.

The traffic lights changed and she edged forward in the queue of cars. It had been both strange and nice being back at work today. Some of the customers had known about the wedding-that-never-was and had been astonished to see her there in the shop with Bonnie and Ray. Others, complete strangers, had no clue about any of it. And a regular customer called Kevin, just back from a month-long visit to Canada, had greeted her with a cheery, 'So how's married life treating the new Mrs Barber? Everything you wished for and more, I hope!'

Which had resulted in one of those *slightly* awkward pauses until Ray had put a supportive arm around Evie's shoulder and said, 'Whoops, do you want to tell him, pet? Or shall I?'

The eventual consensus had been that Joel was a plonker. Then, just as Kevin was leaving the shop, an Interflora delivery had arrived. The young girl handed Evie a lavish cellophane-wrapped bouquet of Asiatic lilies, alstroemeria and germini.

'Blimey.' Kevin looked impressed. 'New boyfriend? That's what I call quick work.'

Because that was *so* likely, wasn't it?

'Oh yes, I'm beating them off with a stick.' Evie tore open the mini-envelope and glanced at the card which said: *I'm sorry. I love you.* 'But these are from the old one.'

'Ah, don't you love it when that happens? He's seen the error of his ways and now he wants to win you back.' Kevin had three teenage daughters and was accustomed to the associated traumas. 'Am I right?'

'You're right. But it's not going to happen.' Out of the corner of her eye, Evie saw Bonnie's face fall. Oh dear, did that mean she hadn't completely believed her before?

Now the traffic was starting to move again. The smell of the lilies was strong inside the car. Evie had tried to leave them with Bonnie but had been forced to bring them home with her. She reached the junction and turned left; ironically the outfits she had in the boot of the car needed to be dropped off at the hotel Lara had been booked into for the night of the wedding.

Driving in through the gates, she was relieved to see plenty of free spaces today. No sea of cars, no glamorous nuptials in progress, no grumpy gardener types waiting to have a go at her for parking in the wrong spot.

Evie lugged everything out of the boot and crunched across the gravel to the Ellison's imposing entrance.

OK, spoke too soon. As she approached the steps, the grumpy gardener appeared at the top of them with a watering can, evidently about to start watering the flowers in the stone tubs on either side of the heavy double doors.

Spotting her, he put the watering can down and said, 'Hello there, hang on, let me give you a hand with those.'

'It's alright, I can manage—' As she said it, one of the slippery polythene dry-cleaning covers slithered from her grasp, probably just to spite her, and she had to catch it between elbow and hip.

'Don't worry, no problem. I'll get them.' He didn't appear to have recognised her, which was good. Evie let him take three of the polythene-covered outfits and one of the bags containing various accessories.

'I need to leave them at reception.'

'The receptionist's just gone upstairs to help one of the guests sort out his TV.' The gardener held the heavy door open and followed her inside. 'She'll be back in a minute. I've just realised what I'm carrying here.' Amused, he held up the nun's habit and the bishop's robe. 'Ha, look at these. What's in the bag?'

Cheeky sod, and now he was opening it up, seeing what was in there. 'Excuse me, can you not do that? Leave it alone, it's not yours.'

'I just wanted to—'

'Well, you can't. Get your dirty hands off it.' Dumping the outfits on the desk, Evie snatched the bag away from him; the irony of it being her turn to tell him off didn't escape her.

'My hands aren't dirty,' he protested.

'I don't care. I still don't want you poking around in there. It's none of your business.'

'Hang on, haven't I seen you before?' He was surveying her more closely now. 'Where do I know you from?'

Oh yes, because that was just the conversation she wanted to have. Like she was actually going to remind him. Evie said, 'I've no idea. Anyway, I'll wait here for the receptionist to come down. You can get back to your watering.'

Whoops, she'd meant to sound mildly dismissive, not downright derogatory.

Beneath his uncombed hair, the gardener raised an eyebrow and said, 'Watering plants is important. If you don't do it, they die.'

Feeling guilty and keen to get rid of him before he remembered when they'd last met, Evie said, 'I know, sorry. And thanks for all your help.' Never had she been so glad to see the brunette in her smart blue uniform come clip-clopping down the staircase. 'Ah, here's the receptionist . . . bye.'

And still he didn't move. Why wasn't he heading back outside? Oh no, he'd helped her carry everything up the steps and into reception. Mortified that it hadn't occurred to her before, Evie scrabbled around in her jacket pocket and found a couple of the coins she kept in there for parking meters. A fifty pence piece and a pound. Well, he wasn't having both.

'Sorry, there you go.' Hastily she pressed the pound coin into his hand, then made a point of turning her attention to the receptionist. 'Hello! I've got a delivery for some guests of yours . . . the Manning family . . .'

There were some things you accepted might happen in real life, and others that were less likely. Then there were the things you really couldn't *ever* imagine happening, like Prince Charles taking up breakdancing or Rod Stewart marrying a brunette.

When Gigi came bursting into the living room clutching her laptop and yelling, 'Oh my God, you are not going to *believe* this,' Lara said, 'Let me guess. Robbie Williams joined Westlife.'

'*Way* better than that. Wait till you see.' Gigi plonked herself down on the sofa between Evie and Lara and wriggled to make room for her elbows. 'God, I can't believe he didn't tell us himself. But that's Harry for you. Leave it to him and it might occur to him to mention it in his next Christmas card.'

This was about Harry? Lara said, 'He might mention what?'

Evie peered at the screen. 'Is this Harry who was away on holiday when I was up there?'

'The very one.' Gigi was busy clicking on links. 'If we've told you he's a fuddy-duddy, you have no idea just *how* fuddy and how duddy. OK, here it is, take a look at this . . .'

'Wow,' said Lara when they'd finished watching. 'Just . . . wow.'

This was what Harry, in his inimitable way, would have called a turn-up for the books. She smiled, remembering how Gigi, aged five, had thought it was a turnip for the books. Ever since, anything remotely surprising had always been described as a turnip.

And this was a turnip and a half.

'It's just mad.' Gigi was busy scrolling through the hundreds of comments on EnjaySeven's website. 'Talk about the odd couple. But everyone's buying the shirts! Sales must be going through the roof. And then guess what you see when you go to the Flying Ducks website.'

'I can't guess.' Lara envisaged the old-fashioned, utterly basic homepage splashed with Hollywood-style fanfare and giant photos of EnjaySeven.

'Nothing! Nothing at all!' Clicking on to it, Gigi showed them. 'Not a single mention. *Unbelievable.*'

To be fair, there was a tiny message in a box politely requesting customers to be patient while orders were filled, due to an unforeseen increase in demand.

'Typical Harry,' Lara said fondly.

'Typical of *my* luck.' Gigi rolled her eyes. 'Eighteen years I lived in that town, and how many superstar rappers turned up? Yet the minute I move down here, it all kicks off in Keswick.'

'Never mind,' said Evie. 'You got yourself a dad instead.'

'I know. It's OK, I'm not complaining about that. God, it's just so weird though. This time last week I bet Harry didn't even know what YouTube was. Now he's not only on it, he's gone and got himself a million hits and everyone's going crazy for the uptight English guy.'

'He looks nice.' Evie gave Gigi a nudge and pointed to the screen. 'Go on, play another clip.'

Chapter 18

Lara was in Superdrug, trying to choose a new roll-on deodorant and sniffing her way through all the different kinds, because how could you buy one without wanting to know what your underarms were going to smell like?

God, though, so much choice. *So* much. Waterlily and Mint. Silkflower and Mandarin. Passionfruit and Pink Pepper . . . that one sounded like an hors d'oeuvre . . .

Her phone was ringing. She fished it out of her bag and saw Flynn's name flash up. 'Hello?'

'Hi. I just called round to the house and no one's in. Where are you?'

His voice still had the ability to make her pulse quicken; the novelty hadn't worn off yet.

'What are you, our parole officer?' Assuming by 'you' he meant the two of them, Lara said, 'Gigi's gone to get her hair cut. She must have switched her phone off.'

'I wasn't asking about Gigi. It's you I'm after.' Oo-er, he definitely didn't mean *that* the way it sounded.

'I'm shopping.' She put the other deodorants back on the shelf and went for Passionfruit and Pepper, dropping it into her basket alongside the exfoliating scrub and razors. Oh, the glamour. Hopefully Flynn would be picturing her wafting through Jolly's buying glamorous underwear and designer shoes.

As if.

'In town? Can we meet up? How about at the Moon and Sixpence in fifteen minutes?'

Lara checked her watch; it was midday. 'OK, but I have to be somewhere by one. Why do you want to see me? Is it about Gigi?' As she said it, her stomach tightened with fear; was he tiring of his daughter already? Did he feel overwhelmed by her full-on enthusiasm? Had it seemed like a good idea at the time, but the actual reality of being landed with her was turning out to be too much of a responsibility for—

'Yes, I do need to talk to you about Gigi.' Flynn paused and fear spiralled into maternal outrage; if he dared to utter just *one word of criticism* . . . 'But this is mainly about you.'

Lara made her way up past the Roman baths, thronged with tourists. The Moon and Sixpence was on Milsom Place. She bagged the last empty table outside in the private courtyard and sat down to wait. Flynn would be here in a few minutes. Damn, her underarms felt a bit sticky, but if she were to pay a visit to the Ladies' someone else might come along and grab the table.

OK, no problem, she could do this. Just to be on the safe side, Lara waited for the waitress to disappear inside before sneaking the deodorant out of her bag and surreptitiously slipping it up under her top. Left arm, done. OK, now swap over. Right arm . . .

'Hello.'

Bugger, caught in the act. Trust Flynn to be early. She chucked the lid into her handbag and left the roll-on wedged under her arm. Not ideal, but better than him seeing what she'd been up to.

'Hi, you're here!' Now she could escape to the Ladies'; keeping her right arm clamped to her side, Lara rose to her feet. Awkwardly, Flynn thought she was doing it to greet him with a cheek kiss. She experienced an involuntary frisson as his mouth brushed the side of her face, then felt his hand on her shoulder, gently guiding her back into her seat.

'I am. There was a parking space right outside. You're looking smart.'

In honour of her upcoming interview she was wearing a white jersey top and a charcoal pencil skirt. He looked smart too, in his dark suit. Was Flynn the kind of man for whom parking spaces magically materialised wherever he went? Lara watched him as the waitress came rushing over.

'Drink?' said Flynn.

'No, thanks. Just coffee.'

'Two coffees, please.'

The waitress was visibly, *effortlessly* charmed by his smile.

'Go on then,' Lara prompted when she'd left them to it. 'What's this about Gigi?'

He heard the tension in her voice and looked surprised. 'My God, relax. What are you expecting me to say?'

'I don't know. I just want you to tell me.'

'I thought it was best to check with you first, in case you have other plans. But if you don't, I've spoken to the Greys and it's fine by them. We'd like to offer Gigi a job.'

'Oh.' She hadn't been expecting that. 'At the wine merchants?'

'No, at the circus.' Flynn nodded. 'Yes. Not full time. Probably thirty hours a week. How does that sound?'

'Um, good.'

He frowned. 'Are you OK? You look kind of . . . stiff. Have you done something to your neck?'

It was hard to relax with a roll-on deodorant clenched under your arm like an alternative version of pass-the-orange. Lara shifted in her seat. 'I'm fine. I thought you were going to say something else.'

'Like what?'

'Like would it be OK if you took a step back, you've done your stint with Gigi, she knows who you are now, can you just get on with your own life?'

'You seriously think I'd say that?'

'I don't know! How would I? All I know is this is my daughter we're talking about and it's my job to protect her,' said Lara. 'And that's something I'll do until the day I die.'

Flynn said, 'She's my daughter too.'

'Fathers walk away from their kids all the time.'

'Sometimes mothers do too.'

'Not me.'

'Nor me.' He shook his head before they went any further. 'This is crazy. We're on the same side here. Based on no grounds whatsoever, you thought I wanted to opt out of having anything more to do with Gigi. But that isn't true, so that means there's nothing to argue about.'

'OK.' He had a point. But he also had no idea how easy it was to fear the worst. Lara forced herself to relax, whilst still unobtrusively keeping her right arm clamped to her side. Actually, now would be a good time to nip inside and get rid of the roll-on . . .

'So that's that sorted,' said Flynn. 'If you're fine with it, I'll go ahead and talk to Gigi. Now, the other thing,' he announced just as she was about to push back her chair. 'The main reason I wanted to see you.'

'Is it good news or bad news?' Either way, she was on her way to the loo.

'Good news, I hope.'

When had she ever been able to resist good news? Lara stayed put. There was something about the way he was saying it. 'Go on.'

'I've found your mum's friend.'

She stared at him. 'You can't have.'

'Ah, but I have.' Flynn was smiling, evidently pleased with himself.

'How?'

'I'm quite clever.'

'You're not Derren Brown though. I don't see that it's possible. How do you *know* it's her?'

'I emailed her this morning. Twenty minutes ago she mailed me back. And I did have some help,' he added. 'That was a long list we had to work through. It took a while to narrow it down.'

'But . . . ?' Lara was stunned; she couldn't begin to imagine how he'd managed it. She sat back as the waitress returned with their tray of coffee.

Flynn waited until they were alone again before saying in a low voice, 'I have a friend in the police force. They can trace people through their credit card details.'

Lara's eyes widened. 'Isn't that illegal?'

'Probably. But it's all in a good cause.'

'And that's how you found her?'

'It's how we found a lot of people who *weren't* her.' Flynn took out his iPhone and began tapping away at it.

'Are you calling her now? Don't!' yelped Lara. 'It's too soon, I'm not ready!'

'Calm down, I'm just showing you the email. I Googled the name and found a blog. And the details seemed to fit, so I started reading, and then there was a mention of having once lived in

133

Bath, so I sent her a message asking if she'd ever known someone called Barbara Carson . . .'

'And she said yes?'

Flynn nodded and passed his phone over so she could see the reply for herself. 'Her name's Jo Finnegan. She lives up in the hills outside Barcelona.'

Jo Finnegan. Possibly Josie or Joanne. It still didn't ring a bell but that was because she'd never really known the name in the first place. And it no longer mattered because Flynn had found her anyway. Lara gazed at the email on the screen and saw that Jo Finnegan hadn't just said yes, she'd bellowed:

YES I DID KNOW BARBARA!!! And I remember who you are too – how amazing to hear from you after all this time! Longing to know why you're contacting me and assuming – hoping – it has something to do with Barbara's daughter. (Good news, preferably.) Please let me know at once. Sorry, my mobile is kaput but send another message and I will reply asap.

Very best wishes, Jo.

Lara exhaled. How amazing. Against all the odds, he'd found her mum's friend. Not that there was any guarantee that this woman would be able to answer any of the questions she had for her, but it would still be wonderful to contact another person who'd known her mother. As the years had gone by, she hated the sensation that her own memories were depleting, leaving her with a picture like a jigsaw with more and more pieces falling away . . .

'Want to see what she looks like?' Taking back the iPhone, Flynn found the blog and scrolled down. 'There you go.'

The photograph was small but it was recognisably her mother's friend, a head and shoulders snapshot of a woman in her sixties with a round tanned face. No make-up, but plenty of paler laughter lines fanning out from the corners of her wide-set brown eyes. A crooked nose. Wavy light-brown hair fastened up at the sides with barrettes. Big silver earrings and a generous double chin.

Did she look like the kind of person you'd want to confide your deepest, darkest secrets in? Studying her carefully, Lara thought she probably did.

God, I hope so.

She raised her gaze to Flynn and said, 'Yes, I remember her face. Those eyes. Thank you.'

'No problem.'

'Did it take ages?'

'Yes. But it was worth it.'

'One minute I want to kill you,' said Lara. 'The next minute, you go and do something nice.'

'Drink your coffee.' He pushed her saucer closer. 'You haven't touched it.'

'In a minute. Let me go to the loo first.' Her brain in a whirl, Lara remembered that this was what she had to do next and jumped to her feet. Sadly she'd forgotten why she was meant to be doing it and reaching for her handbag caused the glass bottle of roll-on deodorant to drop out of her top and land head first with a clatter and a splash in her coffee cup.

Noisy and messy. Plus, everyone was turning to stare. Terrific.

With admirable restraint, Flynn surveyed the scene of the accident. 'Is that a . . . roll-on deodorant?'

'Looks like it.'

He raised an eyebrow. 'Am I allowed to ask where you were keeping that thing?'

'It was under my arm, OK? I forgot it was there. What can I

say? You make me nervous.' Lara hastily mopped up the mess with a napkin and handed the cup with the upended deodorant in it to the waitress who was doing her best not to smirk.

Flynn said, 'Am I allowed to ask if there's another one under the other arm?'

'No there isn't. Because that would be ridiculous.'

He nodded gravely. 'You're right, it would.'

'Everyone's still looking at me. Maybe we can go now.'

His mouth began to twitch. 'If that's what you want.'

Chapter 19

Inside, Lara paid for the untouched coffees and they left the restaurant. There was Flynn's car, parked just across the road.

'What do you want to do now?' He indicated the car. 'Can I drop you anywhere? Or if you want to go home and get on to the computer, I could give you a lift.'

'I've got an appointment at one. A job interview. God, I wish I *didn't*. All I can think about is that woman, Jo. I can't concentrate on anything else.'

'Here, just sit in the car.' Guiding her across the street, he opened the passenger door. A Volvo drew up beside them, the driver keen to park in their space. Even in her agitated state Lara couldn't help secretly loving the way Flynn shook his head at the man, indicating with a minimal hand gesture that they wouldn't be leaving. There was just something about his capacity for being masterful and taking control.

The inside of the car smelled of leather and sunlight and aftershave and toast. Lara breathed it in and wished her own car could smell this nice. Maybe if her car seats weren't plastic and she took to wearing Acqua di Parma aftershave it might stand more of a chance.

'Here. Why don't you send her a message now?' Flynn was offering her his phone.

'I want to, but I don't think I can.'

'Why not?'

Lara held out her hands to show him how much they were shaking. 'She'd get an email saying Yabi orntstrib, kizzr prym slerky. And then she might think I'm weird.'

'I'm saying nothing.' His eyes glinted. 'But I can do the sending if you want to dictate.'

Grateful to him, Lara said, 'Sounds like a plan.' She closed her eyes, breathed in the toasty leathery smell and thought about what she'd like to say.

'Right, ready?'

'Fire away. Boss.'

'Hi, Jo, this is Lara, Barbara's daughter. I'll email you properly later but just wanted to say how fantastic it is to have found you. I'd really love to speak to you about my mum, I have so many questions. Thanks so much for replying to Flynn's message. He worked very hard to find you. OK, I have to go now. Speak later. Very best wishes, Lara Carson xx.'

'Send?'

'Send.'

The message was despatched. He said, 'It's ten to one. Where's your interview?'

'Not far from here. I can walk it. Thanks for everything.'

'No problem. Let me know what happens.'

See? He could be *so* nice sometimes. 'I will. Can I ask a question?'

'Go ahead.'

'Why does it smell of toast in here?'

Flynn looked mystified. He shrugged. 'Does it? I don't know why. No idea.'

Lara paused. There was such a thing as looking a little *too* mystified.

'Anyway,' said Flynn. 'You haven't told me yet about this job you're applying for.'

Hmm, a bit too mystified and a bit too keen to change the subject.

She leaned forward, sprang the catch on the glove compartment and watched it fall open.

Inside sat a blue china plate with a thick slice of buttered toast on it.

Flynn raised his hands in defeat. 'What are you, some kind of bloodhound?'

'You always did have a thing for toast.'

'I still do.'

'But it's cold!' She picked the slice off the plate and watched it droop. 'It's all soggy and bendy!'

'Don't criticise it. That's how I like my toast.'

'And when were you planning on eating this?'

'Whenever I want to. When I get hungry. It's handy when you're stuck in a traffic jam.'

It was time to leave. Lara opened the passenger door and said, 'That's a weird habit you have there.'

Flynn gave her a look. 'Says the woman who keeps spare roll-on deodorants lodged under her arm.'

She handed him the plate with the bendy toast on it. 'Here, you enjoy your gourmet lunch. Bye.'

Temple and Son, Fine Jewellers, was situated on York Street, the windows shielded from the elements by striped mulberry and blue awnings. Inside the shop, glass-fronted cases contained good-quality items, the walls were covered in mulberry and gold flocked wallpaper and there were photos of old Hollywood movie stars hung everywhere.

Don Temple resembled Mrs Tiggywinkle without the frilly cap. In his early sixties, he was small and round, with beady eyes, a pointy nose and short spiky Brylcreemed hair. He was wearing a grey shirt, immaculately pressed trousers, a red waistcoat and dainty black patent leather shoes.

'. . . so the thing is, I'm fine now, the tablets are keeping everything under control, but my doctors have told me I need to take things easier, cut down on the hours, give up the back-to-back triathlons.' His hedgehoggy eyes twinkled. 'That's a joke, by the way. Now, enough of me and my dicky heart. Your turn to tell me about you.'

He had to be gay. Did he really have a son?

'I grew up here in Bath.' Lara already knew she liked him. 'Moved up to the Lake District when I was sixteen, and now I'm back. I've spent the last seven years working in a jewellers in Keswick. If you want to give them a call they'll say nice things about me. I'm good with customers and easy to work with. I love the old Hollywood movies . . . Doris Day, Cary Grant, Rock Hudson, Sophia Loren—'

'Who starred in *An Affair To Remember*?' Don interrupted her.

Lara smiled, because he was testing her. 'Cary Grant and Deborah Kerr. He played Nickie Ferrante.'

'Good girl!' He clapped his small, well-tended hands. 'Sorry, but I had to check you weren't spinning me a line. Favourite film?'

'*Buona Sera, Mrs Campbell.*' She'd first watched it on TV with Nettie before Gigi had been born and had seen it countless times since.

140

'Ah, heaven! Gina!' His whole face lit up.

'And Phil Silvers and Telly Savalas.' Ironically the film had been about three American ex-servicemen all believing they were the father of Gina Lollobrigida's daughter. It had struck Lara at the time that some babies were born with a surplus of fathers and others with none at all. It could have upset her, but she'd been won over by its warmth and charm.

'And Shelley Winters. What a woman. What a *broad*.' Don shook his head, lost in admiration as he unlocked one of the cabinets. He chose three items of jewellery and laid them out on a strip of black velvet. 'Well then, let's see how well you do with these. Talk me through them, darling. Sell them to me.'

'OK. May I?' She nodded at the loupe in his other hand and he passed it to her. Holding it to her eye, Lara examined the first ring he'd chosen. 'Hmm, nice. Well, it's a brilliant-cut diamond, one carat, set in platinum. Second-hand, good condition.'

'Colour? Clarity?'

'G. And there are a few small inclusions. I'd say VS1.'

'Correct.' Don looked pleased. 'Next.'

She moved on to the second ring. 'Older. Art Deco. Eighteen-carat white gold, old transitional cut central diamond surrounded by square French-cut diamonds. G or H. Probably VVS2. Beautiful.'

'And finally . . .' He handed her the pendant.

'Victorian, eighteen-carat yellow gold setting. Five-carat natural blue opal surrounded by sapphires. The chain's very pretty but it has a weak link . . .'

'What?' Don took back the loupe and peered at the chain. 'Bloody hell, you're right. I didn't spot that.'

'They're all gorgeous,' said Lara, 'but that Art Deco ring is the one you should buy. It's a show-stopper, a real statement piece. People would notice you wearing that. And see how the shape of the ring suits your hand . . . it has *elegance* . . .'

'OK, you're good.'

'I know.'

'I have other people to see.'

'Of course.' *You can see them, just please don't give them the job.*

'But I like you.'

'I like you too.'

'I think we'd work well together.'

'We could talk movies,' said Lara. 'When there aren't any customers, of course.'

'Can you tap dance?'

'No.' He looked so hopeful she hated to disappoint, but it wasn't the kind of thing you could bluff your way through.

'Shame. Anyway, I'll let you know by the end of the week.' He led the way to the door.

'Can I just ask,' said Lara. 'The shop's called Temple and Son. Do you have a son?'

'No, no children. I was the son.' His currant eyes crinkled at the corners. 'I'm single.'

Of course.

'It's been lovely to meet you anyway. *Oh*,' Lara added as an afterthought, 'and I've done first aid. Just so you know. In case it makes any difference.'

Back at home, Lara changed out of her interview outfit into jeans and a T-shirt, ready to start wallpapering the bedroom. First, though, she sat down at the computer, found Jo Finnegan's blog and began to type.

An hour later one wall was finished. Lara made herself a cup of tea and went back to the computer. Miraculously, a reply was waiting in her inbox:

Hello, my darling girl, I may not have all the answers to your questions but hopefully I shall have one or two. How wonderful that you're back in Bath now. Here's a suggestion – I fly home every couple of months to see my elderly parents and was due to come over ten days from now, but I can easily bring the date forward to this week. Would you like me to do that? Let me know if you'd be free on Tuesday. If you are, we could meet up. Or leave it until next weekend if that's easier. Either way, it would be lovely to see you again. Let me know!

The answers. Not all of them, but hopefully one or two. One or two didn't sound like many, but it was better than none at all.

Hi again Jo.
   Yes please! This Tuesday would be perfect for me – the sooner the better. Can't wait!

Another hour, another wall. Another email. Jo Finnegan had booked her ticket and would be landing at Bristol Airport at midday on Tuesday. Lara typed:

Fantastic. I'll be there to pick you up. Xx

Chapter 20

The third wall was trickier and took an hour and a half. The phone rang as she was slathering paste on the final length of wallpaper.

'Lara? It's Don Temple. The job's yours if you want it.'

'Really? That's great!' She flushed with pleasure; this was turning into a proper good-news day.

'I called your last employer. He said you were a good girl. Full of praise.' Don paused, then said, 'Shall I tell you what the clincher was?'

'Go on.' Lara thought she probably knew.

'The bit about you knowing first aid.'

Bingo.

'I guessed. Our postman in Keswick had a heart attack last year while he was at work in the sorting office. He's fine now, but he told me how scared he was being on his own in case it ever happened again.'

'Same here.' Don sounded relieved. 'That's exactly how I feel. If the shop's empty and I don't have time to call for help . . . or if someone's there but they don't know what to do . . . you know what the traffic's like in Bath, an ambulance might get stuck . . .

I mean, I know the chances are it won't happen again, but it's the thought that it *could* . . .' Hopefully he added, 'Have you ever done any real-life CPR?'

It might make him feel better but it wouldn't be right to lie. Lara said, 'Not real-life, but the course tutor gave me top marks when I did it on the plastic dummy.'

'That's good to hear.' Don sounded as if he were smiling. 'Let's hope you never do need to try it in real life. Now, when can you start work?'

He suggested Tuesday. They agreed on Wednesday and Lara hung up hoping he wouldn't have another heart attack on the Tuesday while she was on her way to Bristol to meet Jo.

Then she celebrated by finishing off the task in hand, including the fiddly bits involving light switches and wall sockets. *Et voilà*, one bedroom papered in midnight blue and ivory freckled with silver. Ivory carpet. Silver and cream duvet cover and pillows. Not so much a bedroom, more a boudoir. Although it was unlikely that any man would be clapping eyes on it in the foreseeable future.

Satisfied with her handiwork, Lara stood back to admire the end result. If it was going to be a man-free zone, she might even go mad and get some silver sequinned cushions.

The front door opened downstairs and she heard Gigi call out, 'Mum, where are you?'

'Up here. Come and look at this!'

Lara leaned proudly against the doorframe, waiting for Gigi to join her and be suitably effusive. Then she turned and saw that the footsteps on the stairs belonged to Flynn.

Ach, a man! In her designated man-free zone!

'Sorry.' He saw the look on her face. 'I gave Gigi a lift home. She's just gone to the downstairs loo. She told me to come on up.'

More to the point, a man who had the power to make her heart race one minute and completely infuriate her the next.

'So this is the end result. You've done a good job.' Flynn surveyed her bedroom and gave a nod of approval. 'Better than it was before, anyway.'

'Before?'

'Gigi showed me over the house yesterday, while you were out.'

See? Just like that, he could both pay a compliment and be annoying in three seconds flat. Even if it had largely been Gigi's fault. When she'd left the house yesterday afternoon to buy wallpaper, her bed hadn't been made and a build-up of clothes in need of washing and sorting out had been strewn across the floor. Her manky hair-dye towel, the one that *looked* dirty but *wasn't* dirty, had been chucked over the back of the chair. Flynn must have viewed the scene with a shudder of revulsion . . .

Oh well, too bad. She wasn't going to make a point of defending herself. They both heard the sound of the downstairs loo being flushed and the taps running, then Gigi was galloping up the staircase to join them.

'You've done the whole room! Cool!' She admired the bedroom and said cheerily, 'Looks a bit better now. Where'd you hide all the clothes?'

'Nowhere. They've all been sorted out.'

Gigi nudged Flynn. 'I bet I know what she's done.'

'I've put them away,' said Lara. But it was too late; Gigi had already reached the fitted wardrobe and was flinging open the doors.

It was like lava exploding out of a volcano. Gigi had to jump back to avoid being buried.

'See what I have to put up with?' She raised her eyebrows at Flynn. 'The wicked lies my mother tells.'

146

Which, under the circumstances, wasn't what you'd call diplomatic.

'I just stuffed everything in there to get it out of the way.' Lara felt her face overheat. 'So I could put the pasting table up and get the wallpapering done. Tonight I'll sort through the whole lot properly.'

'Yes, Mum, of course you will.' Gigi mimed her nose extending, Pinocchio-style. 'Because you're the tidiest person *ever*.'

Out of the corner of her eye Lara could see the manky hairdye towel flaunting itself on top of the clothes mountain. Seriously, how much more humiliation could she be expected to endure in one day?

'Shall we go downstairs? Or do you want to stay here and help me with this lot?'

'Do you want us to help?' said Flynn.

'No, I do not!'

'Then we'll go downstairs. If you're hungry, we're planning to pick up some Mexican food.'

And bring it back, presumably. *Like he lived here.* Having earlier been afraid that Flynn was planning to ease back on his newfound relationship with Gigi, Lara now found herself fretting that he was becoming too full-on. Because what if it got Gigi's hopes up and *then* the novelty began to wear off?

'I'm fine. I'm busy. You two carry on.'

'Oh, I can't believe I forgot to ask,' Gigi exclaimed. 'How'd the interview go?'

'Great. I got the job. Start on Wednesday.'

'My clever mum. I knew you'd get it. And Dad already told you he was taking me on too. So that's both of us celebrating today.' Gigi beamed at them. 'With burritos and chimichangas, yay!'

Flynn finally left at ten o'clock. When it was just the two of them once more, Lara said, 'You shouldn't have done that thing earlier.' Several Mexican beers had loosened her tongue; she felt compelled to say it.

'Done what thing?' Gigi was busy licking guacamole off her fingers.

'The wardrobe thing. Opening the doors and showing him where I'd hidden the mess.'

Unable to leave food alone when it was in front of her, Gigi reached for another quesadilla and dipped it in sour cream. 'I didn't think you'd mind.'

'I don't *really* mind. It's just a bit . . . you know . . .'

'Just a bit interesting that it obviously does bother you quite a lot? Because you want to create a good impression and you don't want him thinking you live in squalor?'

'Excuse me!' Lara gestured around the living room. 'Does this look like squalor to you? I do *not* live in squalor.'

'OK, I know. I'm just saying.' Her tone playful, Gigi said, 'It's interesting, that's all. You keep telling me he doesn't mean anything to you . . .'

'And he *doesn't*. I suppose I just want him to think I'm a good mother. Being untidy can be . . . embarrassing.' Lara was struggling to make herself understood. 'I'd hate him to be secretly thinking, God, did she bring my daughter up in chaos? Did she send her off to school in rags? Because I *didn't*.'

'Oh, Mum, he doesn't think that! I'm sorry!'

'He criticised me before, though, that's the thing. He said stuff he had no right to say and he shouldn't have said it.' Lara had been secretly lacerated by Flynn's comments about Gigi wishing she'd had a father while she was growing up. 'I did what I thought was right and he should accept that. He's probably telling everyone

I did it to punish him and they're all going to think I'm a complete cow . . . anyway, never mind.'

'Do you quite like him, though?' Gigi looked interested. 'I mean, apart from that, do you fancy him?'

Lara was firm. 'No.'

'Not even a little bit?'

'No.' She would carry on saying it for as long as it took.

'Why not? You did once.'

'And do you remember how much you used to love your Spiderman pyjamas? When you were five? You wore them every day,' Lara reminded her. 'To the shops, to the park, to every party you were invited to. You made us call you Spidey.'

'That's different. I was five.'

Lara shook her head. 'It's not different at all. You changed your mind about those pyjamas, same as you did about Westlife and spaghetti hoops and Barbie.' She paused. 'I was sixteen then.'

'And you're ancient now,' Gigi said helpfully.

'Yes, I am ancient. And grumpy and pernickety. And guess what?' said Lara. 'I'm allowed to change my mind too.'

In bed and unable to sleep a couple of hours later, Lara gazed up at the ceiling and prayed this was a situation she could remain on top of. It was necessary to keep concentrating on the ceiling because every time she closed her eyes all she saw was Flynn. Would her life have been easier if she'd never known him? Sometimes she wondered if it was Flynn who'd succeeded in spoiling her for other men. Of course, there had been boyfriends since then . . . but none had ever come close to making her feel the way he had. They'd all seemed like second-best. She hadn't wanted it to be that way but it wasn't something you could consciously control. Saying no to Gigi earlier, insisting the interest

149

in Flynn was no longer there, had been a lie. Alongside the annoyance, the anger and the frustration she felt towards him, there was an inescapable physical draw. The chemistry still existed. On her side at least. Who knew if Flynn was feeling it too? He hadn't said anything, was playing his cards pretty close to his chest. Either way, whether the attraction was mutual or not, nothing was ever going to happen.

Lara gazed up at the faint crack in the ceiling to the left of the window. She had already made that executive decision and whatever happened she'd be sticking to it. Because there was too much to potentially lose now. This wasn't about her; it wasn't about what she may or may not want to happen in the future. Her number-one priority was her daughter. Gigi was the important one. Even if, ironically, she seemed quite taken by the idea of her parents getting back together . . .

The prospect of that happening was like closing your eyes, throwing a bunch of flaming torches over your shoulder and wondering if any of them might be about to land in the fireworks box.

Because that was how risky the potential situation would be. The thing about relationships was never knowing in advance how they might end up. And the unknowable answer to that question was what made any kind of involvement impossible. Some people lived together happily ever after. Some broke up and managed to remain friends . . . or at least friendly enough not to let it ruin their lives.

And then there were those who experienced the horror of the kind of break-up that caused fury and havoc and vengeance and retribution and was impossible for either partner to forgive.

Lara had seen it happen to people she knew. Previously loving couples were capable of descending into insult-trading, vicious name-calling and boiling no-holds-barred hatred. Years could pass and still they would be incapable of breathing the same air, even exchanging a couple of simple pleasantries in public. The bitterness intensified and once-happy families remained torn apart.

Which was why she was never going to risk that happening to Flynn and herself.

If the only way to prevent it was by making sure they didn't get involved in the first place . . . well, for Gigi's sake, that was what she'd do.

Chapter 21

In her head she'd been calling him the gardener but he had to be more of an odd-job man. From inside the shop, Evie watched as the blue van with Ellison's Hotel on the side pulled up in the yard. Odd-job, wearing a holey grey T-shirt and muddy khaki combats, lifted the bags out of the back and carried them in.

'Hi there.' He greeted her with the kind of cheery attitude that suggested his brain had been wiped clean since their last encounter. 'Bringing back everything the Mannings hired for their party. They had to leave early this morning but they said to say thanks and the costumes were great.'

'Good. OK, I just need to check them.' Evie emptied the first bag on to the counter and began giving the outfits a quick but thorough once-over.

'Making sure there's no damage?' said Odd-job. 'Does that often happen?'

'Not always accidentally. The other week a client tried to drop off a Marie Antoinette dress. All the buttons were missing.' Evie pulled a face. 'She thought they were pretty so she cut them all off and hoped we wouldn't notice.'

'Tell me about it. We once caught a couple of guests smuggling a chest of drawers down the staircase at three in the morning.'

Evie smiled slightly. 'Chest of drawers beats buttons.'

'Annoying all the same.' He had a direct gaze and an easy manner as if they were old friends. 'Don't worry, I promise I haven't snipped any rhinestones off the Elvis jumpsuit.'

'Glad to hear it.'

'I managed to figure out where I'd seen you before, by the way.'

'Oh?' Bugger. Evie kept her head down and concentrated on examining the nun's habit; please don't let him start asking questions.

'You were the one in the wedding dress. In the car that was parked where it shouldn't have been.'

'Right.' She nodded. *Don't ask, don't ask.*

'That's what fooled me, why I didn't make the connection. That big white flouncy wedding dress. Didn't recognise you in your normal clothes.'

'Mm.' Evie frowned at the left sleeve of the habit; subtlety clearly wasn't his strong point.

'So, can I ask you something?'

'Depends what it is.'

'Tell me to mind my own business if you want, but you aren't wearing any, you know, rings.' He nodded at her bare left hand. 'Does that mean you're single?'

Evie marvelled at his powers of diplomacy. What a cheek. She raised her head and stared at him. 'Yes, it means I'm single.' Was he trying to work out whether she'd run off and left her husband just before the wedding or immediately after it?

Odd-job looked pleased. 'Good. In that case I'm going to just come out and say it. How about dinner one night?'

153

For a split second the question made no sense at all. 'Who with?'

He didn't falter. 'With me.'

'But . . . why?' Honestly, some men were unbelievable. Evie was fairly sure she was gaping like a goldfish. The awkward silence was broken by Bonnie bursting into the shop carrying a tower of boxes and sporting a long black dangly moustache.

'Evie, look at these! They're the Fu Manchus I ordered last week!' She wiggled her nose like a rabbit and beamed at them both. 'And the Ozzy Osbourne glasses have arrived, thank goodness, just in time for the Taylors' party.' She dumped the boxes on a chair and peeled off the Fu Manchu moustache. 'These are very well made, you know. Only three pounds each!'

'I'll buy one.' Odd-job playfully addressed Evie. 'I could wear it when we go out on our date.'

'Yes, you must! How funny . . . oh . . .' Bonnie's voice trailed away as she gazed at Evie. Mystified, she said, 'Does he mean *you*? What's going on here that I don't know about?'

'I just asked Evie to have dinner with me. I'm hoping she's going to say yes.' His smile was wry. 'Fingers crossed. She hasn't said anything yet.'

Bonnie was agog. 'Goodness, I didn't realise, I had no idea! So sorry, I shouldn't have interrupted—'

'No, it's fine,' Evie blurted out. 'I'm not going.' She turned back to Odd-job. 'Thanks, but I really couldn't.'

'That's a shame.' He rubbed the back of his head resignedly. 'Well, never mind. Am I allowed to ask why not?'

'To be honest, I can't believe you asked me. After the first time we met,' said Evie. 'Considering the whole . . . you know, situation I was in.'

He looked baffled. So did Bonnie, who said, 'Darling, call me a nosy old bat, but I'd love to know what you two are talking about.'

Evie hesitated, struggling to marshal her thoughts.

Odd-job stepped in. 'It was a couple of weeks ago, there was a big photo shoot for an ad campaign over at the Ellison. Evie was one of the models and we chatted for a bit . . . oh God, have I said the wrong thing?' He glanced from Bonnie to Evie, taking in their stunned expressions. 'I'm really sorry, I just assumed she'd know about the modelling job.'

Bonnie said in astonishment, 'Evie? Modelling? I had no idea you'd been doing that!'

Odd-job was now shaking his head behind her, mouthing: *I'm so sorry.*

'But don't worry,' Bonnie exclaimed, 'there's no reason to be shy! I think it's *fantastic*, darling. Such a thrill! What kind of ad campaign is it?'

What indeed? Some clothing company, presumably, that sold the kind of glamorous dresses you'd wear on special occasions. Because it hadn't been a real wedding, it had been a photo shoot. And Emily Morris, the acquaintance she'd assumed to be a guest, was forever boasting that she was on the books of a modelling agency and had once appeared in a TV ad for Andrex.

Which went some way towards explaining why Odd-job didn't think it was weird to invite someone out to dinner just a fortnight after seeing them in a wedding dress.

She still wasn't going to go, though.

'These are all fine.' Evie opened the till and handed him back the deposit. 'OK, there you go. Thanks very much. Bye.'

He flashed her yet another look of apology and left the shop, just as his phone started to ring.

155

'Tell me everything!' demanded Bonnie the moment the door had swung shut behind him.

Outside, through the window, Odd-job was now facing away from them, talking into his mobile.

'I wasn't modelling. I was wearing my wedding dress. We just stopped off at the Ellison to pick up Lara's things before heading up to Keswick.'

'Ah, that's a shame. I did wonder why you hadn't happened to mention this fantastic new career.' Bonnie dismissed the reply with a flick of the hand, then said eagerly, 'But he invited you to dinner!'

'I know. How embarrassing.'

'Not embarrassing at all. I think you should go.'

Evie stared at her. 'Why?'

'Because — oh no, he's leaving, just say yes and I'll tell you afterwards! Hang on, I'll bring him back . . .'

Oh God, this was typical Bonnie, acting on impulse whether you wanted her to or not. Outside, having finished his phone call, Odd-job was about to get into the van. Rocketing outside, Bonnie stopped him and launched into an earnest conversation; with a bit of luck he'd just shake his head, tell her that he wasn't desperate and drive off.

But he evidently *was* that desperate, because he was now coming back into the shop. This time Bonnie waited outside.

'Look, I'm sorry,' Evie blurted out, 'she gets these mad ideas into her head, you don't have to take any notice of her—'

'Hey, she insisted. And I always do as I'm told. Besides,' Odd-job sounded amused, 'I like a challenge. Are you free tomorrow night?'

Bonnie was now watching her intently through the glass, nodding encouragement. Evie sighed and said, 'Well . . .'

'That'll be a yes, then. Your boss already told me tomorrow's fine. Where would you like me to pick you up?'

156

'Nowhere. I mean, I'll meet you in town.'

'OK. How about outside Brown's at eight o'clock?'

'Fine.' She shrugged.

'Cheer up. You never know, you might end up enjoying yourself.'

'I might.' Evie didn't hold out much hope; she already wanted to strangle Bonnie.

'Good. I'm Ethan, by the way.'

'Hello, Ethan. Can I just apologise in advance, because you probably won't have much fun. It's only fair to warn you.'

'Like I said, I'm up for the challenge.' As he headed for the door, Ethan added playfully, 'Just don't stand me up, will you?'

When he'd driven away, Evie said, 'OK, now tell me why you made me do that.'

'Be-*cause*,' Bonnie launched into her agony aunt voice, 'you know I want you and Joel to get back together. But he behaved like an idiot and cheated on you, and if you were to eventually forgive him and take him back, you'd always, deep down, resent what he did. But if you have a fling with someone else, you won't have to feel resentful any more. That would make you equal!'

Evie briefly closed her eyes; talk about moving the goalposts. 'You didn't say a fling, you said dinner. I really don't want a fling.'

'Dinner's a start. Honestly, it worked a treat for my friend Brenda. Her husband had an affair and she was in bits. She moved out of the house and they were heading for divorce. He was distraught and kicking himself, but she couldn't get over what he'd done – she just wanted to punish him and didn't know how. Then out of the blue she met this younger man at the gym and they had the most amazing affair . . . and it did the trick! She felt better, her husband felt worse, the balance was restored and they saved their marriage!'

'Bonnie—'

'That was nine years ago, they're still together and they're *happy*,' Bonnie emphasised. 'I don't know why I didn't think of it before. It just came to me in a flash when this one said he'd asked you out. It's perfect!'

'But not very fair on him. What happened to the guy your friend met at the gym?'

'Darling, who knows? But he was a personal trainer with the body of a Greek god. I'm sure he didn't pine for too long. Anyway, you're going out on a date – wait till Joel gets to hear!' Evidently thrilled with her new plan, Bonnie said, 'This is going to be just the kick up the backside he deserves.'

Evie frowned. 'If that's why I'm doing it, wouldn't it be easier for me to just pretend I'm seeing someone else?' OK, this was crazy, she wasn't at all sure she even wanted Joel back. Game-playing had never been her forte.

'Ah, but that's only a tiny bit of it.' Bonnie held her thumb and forefinger an inch apart. 'The main point is that *you'd* know you were seeing someone else. If you're just pretending, how can that make you feel equal? You have to give Joel a taste of his own medicine!'

'You mean you want me to sleep with this . . . stranger from the Ellison Hotel? Because that's not going to happen.'

'You don't have to sleep with him. It's not compulsory. Just have a night out with another man.' Bonnie beamed encouragingly. 'He seems nice enough. It could be fun, and it'll definitely teach Joel a lesson. What could be better than that?'

Honestly? A lazy evening in front of the TV with a bag of Lindor truffles and a box set of *The Wire* would be a thousand times better.

But it was a bit late to say so now.

Chapter 22

The flight from Barcelona had just landed on time. Bristol Airport was packed with travellers. Lara, having turned up early to be on the safe side, was drinking coffee and people-watching, one of her favourite pastimes. A married couple were getting emotional, preparing to be separated. The wife was hugely overweight, the husband superskinny and they kept giving each other one last hug-and-kiss before he headed upstairs to Departures. At least, they were both wearing wedding rings; maybe they weren't married to each other.

Next, Lara turned her attention to a gaggle of girls off on a hen weekend, exchanging saucy banter with a separate group of men setting out on a stag do. If they were all on the same flight it would be a rowdy one . . . and who knew which of them might end up sharing more than a plane.

Finally, a vignette that tugged at the heartstrings: a mother in her mid-fifties saying goodbye to her early-twenties backpacking son. Determinedly upbeat and cheerful, she stood at the foot of the escalator and waved as he called out, 'Bye, Mum, see you next year!' Only when he'd disappeared from view did she turn away and allow her composure to crumple, the tears spilling down her face.

Oh God, poor woman. Lara felt a lump expand in her own throat; saying goodbye to your children had to be the hardest thing in the world. It was going to be bad enough when Gigi left to go to university . . . OK, don't think about that now. She finished her coffee and headed over to Arrivals; it was time for the travellers from Barcelona to start filtering through the gate.

She didn't have long to wait. With only a carry-on bag and no reason to wait at baggage claim, Jo Finnegan was one of the first to appear. Lara recognised her at once from the photo on her blog and waved to attract her attention.

'My goodness, look at you!' Jo greeted her with a warm hug. 'Little Lara, all grown up!'

It was an oddly emotional moment. She didn't know many people who'd known her mum. Lara felt a surreal urge to plug Jo into a computer and download every last memory she had.

'It's lovely to see you. Thanks so much for changing your plans.'

'My pleasure. I've always been the impatient type. Now, let me take a proper look at you . . .'

Lara did the same. Jo Finnegan was browner and wrinklier in the flesh, and she was sporting bright coral lipstick today. Her earrings were again huge and dangly, her faded brown hair haphazardly pinned back. She was wearing a purple linen shirt and matching loose linen trousers, with dusty leather sandals on her feet.

'I can see your mum in you,' Jo pronounced with satisfaction.

'I know.' Lara loved being able to pick out the similarities in the few photographs she had of her mother; the tilt of the chin, the line of the eyebrows, the same legs.

'And your father. Is he . . . well?'

There had definitely been a moment of hesitation. 'He died a few weeks ago.'

'Oh, I'm sorry.'

'No need. I'm not.'

They exchanged a long look, signalling mutual understanding. Lara felt a swizzle of excitement in her stomach.

'Oh, my darling girl.' Jo reached for her hands and clasped them warmly. 'We have so much to talk about.'

The swizzles ramped up to the next level. This was so thrilling. *There was definitely something here to find out.*

Some conversations you simply couldn't have while you were driving a car. During the journey back to Bath they chatted instead about Jo's time in Spain. Happily divorced nowadays and working as a potter, she had made many friends and adapted well to life in a mountain village, although regular trips back to visit her aged parents meant she didn't miss out on such vital aspects of British life as Marks & Spencer and Marmite.

As they approached Bath, Jo said, 'Do me a favour, will you? Be a darling and pull in at the next lay-by. I just love the view from here over the city.'

Spooky coincidence or what? Lara did as she asked and switched off the ignition. 'It's my favourite place too. When I came back for the first time after eighteen years, I stopped at this exact spot to show my daughter where I used to live.'

'You have a daughter?' Jo looked pleased. 'That's lovely. How old?'

'Eighteen.'

'Oh my goodness! Really? But that means . . .'

Lara opened the driver's door and said, 'Yes, it does.'

They sat together on the grassy slope below the lay-by, drinking in the view. Lara told Jo the story of how she'd come to leave Bath. Jo listened without interrupting once.

'So that's it,' Lara concluded several minutes later. 'Everything worked out fine. It could have been a disaster but it wasn't. Gigi's perfect. And now she's getting to know Flynn . . . all in all, the last few weeks have been pretty eventful.' She paused, then tilted her head. 'But you can see why I said what I did about my father. It sounds awful to say I'm not sorry he died, but it's the truth. I don't think he ever liked me and I could never understand why. Then there was the will-reading in the solicitor's office and I found out the house had never been his, it had been bought in my mum's name. But how could that happen? Where did the money come from? And was this why he hated me, or was there some other reason . . . ?'

Jo had been watching her intently. 'If you're asking me if he was really your father, the answer is I don't know.'

'Right.' Lara was sitting with her arms wrapped around her knees. She was squeezing so hard her knuckles had turned white. *Damn.*

'But I do know there was a . . . friendship. With another man.'

Yes! *Yes yes yes!* Tears of joy sprang without warning into Lara's eyes. It had to be that, it explained everything. Her father had hated her because he knew he wasn't her father. It made perfect sense. Thank you, God.

'Who was he? Did you know him?' *Go on, say yes, tell me all about my mother's secret lover . . . no, stop it, don't shake your head . . .*

But Jo said with regret, 'Sorry, no I didn't. It was before I met your mum. She told me about him, though. I'll tell you as much as I know. His name was James.'

James. That was a nice name, a good name for a father to have. James? Are you my father? God, I really hope so.

'James who?' said Lara but Jo was already shaking her head again. Life was never that simple, was it?

162

'No idea. Your mum never mentioned his surname. Or showed me a photograph. She met him a couple of years before you were born.' Jo paused for a moment to gently bat away a hovering dragonfly. 'He was married.'

'Oh.'

'And he'd been married and divorced before that.'

'Ah.'

'Well, quite. Back in those days that was a pretty racy history. He was wealthy too. Some kind of successful businessman, but don't ask me what kind of business – I haven't a clue. The marriage wasn't a happy one, apparently. He was in love with your mother. Well, he told her he loved her.'

'What does that mean? She didn't believe him?'

'She wanted to. But from what she said, she didn't know if she could completely trust him. He'd been married, divorced, married again . . . I got the impression your mum was afraid he might be the type who just got bored easily.'

Lara's fingers were cramping. She unclenched her knuckles and gazed out over Bath, with its curving streets of higgledy-piggledy biscuit-shaded houses. There, just down there to the right, was her own home. Had James paid for it? If he had, surely that must mean he was her father?

'Are you OK?'

She nodded at Jo. 'I'm fine. This is all good news. Frustrating, but good. Anything that means my father might not be my father is brilliant. Look, I know you don't know, but do you think it could have been James?'

'Oh, darling, who can say? Your mum never said he was. It wasn't the kind of question I felt I could ask. This may sound unbelievably old-fashioned, but we didn't talk about sex so much in those days. It really wasn't the hot topic it is now. Maybe if we'd been friends since childhood I might have done, but we weren't, we just got to know each other because I worked in the café near your school and we hit it off from there. That was when you were nine or ten. Your mum used to come in for a cup of tea. She'd hear me moaning about my useless husband. Then when I had to take our dog for a walk after work, she'd join me. Maybe it was that neither of us had happy marriages. It can be a bonding thing, you know? Nice to have someone else going through a miserable time. Your father sounded like the domineering type.'

Jo glanced at her for confirmation and Lara nodded. 'Yes, he was.'

'I only went to your house once. He made it clear I wasn't welcome.'

'He hated visitors.' Theirs had been a silent home, singularly lacking in laughter whenever the three of them had been in it together. Lara felt sickened by the memory of it. Back then, she hadn't realised the extent of her father's controlling behaviour, simply because she'd had nothing to compare it with. Nowadays it made her shudder. And how proud she'd been when Gigi, without any prompting from her, had recognised the wrongness of her last boyfriend's attitude towards her. Good-looking he might have been, but as soon as he'd started criticising her choice of clothes and tried to stop her seeing her friends, Gigi had called him a loser and calmly ended the relationship.

Why couldn't her mum have done the same? Lara's jaw tightened. It was a question that had haunted her for years.

'What are you thinking?' said Jo.

'Just wondering why she didn't leave him. Our lives could have been so different.'

'Your mum knew that. The problem was, she was worried it

164

might turn out to be the wrong thing to do. Your lives could have turned out better, but what if they'd turned out worse?'

Lara exhaled. 'How could it have been worse?'

'In her eyes it was possible. She used to say, "At least he doesn't hit me, he's *never* hit me." And she was filled with guilt about James. I think she felt she deserved to be punished for that. Almost as if Charles was entitled to make her life miserable. Oh, who can say what it was like for her? Bullies undermine their partners' confidence. Who knows what he might have threatened her with?'

'I know.' Lara had been over it all in her head a million times. 'She did what she thought was best.'

'For the two of you.'

'Oh God, I want to find James.' She threw herself back on the grass and watched the tiny clouds scudding across the sky.

'I don't know how you can,' said Jo.

'I found you. Well, Flynn did. There must be a way.'

'Did she have any other friends you can ask?'

'No, I wondered if you'd know anyone.'

Jo shook her head. 'I don't, darling. I'm sorry.'

Lara gazed up at the vapour trails criss-crossing overhead. Where were those planes headed? Who were the passengers flying in them? They could contain anyone, be going anywhere. One of those passengers might know James. Or *be* him.

That was the thing, you just never knew.

'You've done well for yourself,' said Jo. 'You're living a good life. Your mum would be so proud if she could see you now.'

'Thanks.' It was lovely of Jo to say it and Lara was grateful to her. But she was only hearing half the story and it was no longer enough.

Chapter 23

The thing to do was to keep telling yourself it wasn't a real date.

Evie waited outside Brown's and realised without enthusiasm that she was going to have to insist on paying half the bill. Since it wasn't a proper date she couldn't land Ethan with the whole thing; it wouldn't be fair. Plus, add in a couple of decent bottles of wine and it might well come to more than he earned in a week.

OK, and relax. For the next couple of hours she and Ethan were going to chat together like two normal people who weren't out on a date. And as soon as the meal was over she could leave.

There wasn't going to be a goodbye kiss either.

Oh look at the people sitting at the tables outside, they were all so glamorous and stylishly dressed. Please don't let Ethan turn up in his manky old khaki combats and that faded T-shirt with the holes in it.

He didn't have her phone number but when her mobile began to ring, Evie experienced a rush of hope that it could somehow be Ethan calling to tell her he couldn't make it after all. Right now she'd positively welcome being stood up.

But the name flashing on the screen was an altogether more

familiar one. Unable to ignore it, she answered and said evenly, 'Hello, Joel.'

'Mum just called. She told me you're out with some bloke tonight.'

Thanks a lot, Bonnie.

'So?'

'So who is he?'

Evie checked her watch; if he wasn't going to do the decent thing and stand her up, Ethan would be here any minute now. 'Look, it doesn't matter who he is.'

'It matters to me.' Joel sounded hurt.

'We're having dinner, that's all.' It was secretly gratifying to hear his concern. 'I'm allowed to do that.'

'What's he like?'

Oh yes, another mini-frisson of power. Evie said, 'If he wasn't nice, I wouldn't be meeting him.'

Joel said, 'Where are you?

Like she was going to tell him that. 'I have to go now,' said Evie. 'He's here. Bye.'

And she ended the call.

Yay, just like Madonna.

Best of all, she wasn't even lying. Ethan was making his way down the road towards her. Sadly still scruffily dressed though less so than before. He was wearing crumpled navy chinos and an olive-green shirt worn unbuttoned over a faded purply-grey T-shirt. Oh well, these could be the best clothes he owned. Maybe he didn't possess an iron.

And he had made an effort, she noted as he reached her. His hair might be overlong and unstyled but it was freshly washed. He was wearing aftershave too; whatever it was, it smelled nice. Maybe his mum or sister had bought it for him for Christmas.

167

'Hey, you're here.' He didn't, thank goodness, attempt any form of hug or air-kiss by way of greeting. 'Thanks for turning up. I'm not late, am I? Have you been waiting long?'

'Just a couple of hours,' said Evie.

His eyes crinkled at the corners. 'That's good. And I'd tell you how nice you're looking if I thought you wouldn't mind. But I'm going to err on the side of caution and not say it.'

'Thanks.' He had a dry sense of humour, she'd give him that much.

'Hi there.' Ethan caught the attention of a passing waitress. 'We have a table booked for eight o'clock, name of McEnery. Is it OK if we sit outside?'

Evie opened her mouth to protest then shut it again. It was a stunning evening, perfect for eating al fresco; if she objected, he'd think she was embarrassed to be seen with him in public.

'Is that all right with you?' Ethan turned to check with her.

'Fine.' He was a gardener; it stood to reason he'd like fresh air. She smiled and nodded at him. It didn't matter if they were seen. They were shown to a table and Ethan pulled out a chair for her. He had nice manners; he'd definitely been well brought up.

'So tell me about working in a fancy dress shop.' Once the waitress had taken their drinks order and left them, he leaned forward and rested his elbows on the table between them. 'What's the weirdest outfit anyone's ever asked for?'

'That would be a fleet of lime-green Daleks. Not blue,' said Evie. 'Not silver, not pink. They only wanted lime green. Six Daleks. They were unbelievably annoyed when I told them we didn't have any.'

'What did you do?'

'I persuaded them they'd rather be Tellytubbies instead.'

'The mark of a good saleswoman.' Ethan gave her a nod of

approval. 'I'm really sorry about the modelling thing at the hotel, by the way. Didn't think it through at all. You were meant to be working in the shop that day, weren't you, that's why you couldn't tell your boss the truth.'

OK, she was going to have to explain. Evie sat back as the waitress returned with their drinks. If she was honest, being mistaken for a model had been something of an ego boost. She wasn't deluded about her appearance; on a scale of prettiness she was a notch, possibly two notches, above average. But no more than that. And figure-wise, she was average with a slightly big bum. She didn't wear make-up or model-type clothes. In her whole life, no one had ever before mistaken her for a model.

And it secretly felt . . . great.

'Something like that.' She smiled and dismissed his apology with a shake of the head; what the hell, did it really matter if she skimmed over the truth? 'Anyway, not a problem. Bonnie was fine about it.'

Ethan looked relieved. 'She seems nice.'

'She is.' Telling fibs, Evie discovered, made her mouth dry. 'What's it like working at the Ellison then? Have you always been a gardener?'

He hesitated. 'Well . . .'

'Sorry, gardener-handyman.' Hurriedly she made it sound more important. 'I bet you have to do all sorts to keep the place together! Always busy with a job like that . . . cutting the grass one minute, mending stuff the next, fixing anything that needs to be fixed . . . they couldn't manage without you!' Oh help, did that sound patronising? She hadn't meant it to come out quite so infant-schoolteacherish.

Luckily Ethan didn't appear to have taken offence. He sat back and said easily, 'That's true, I bet they couldn't.'

'And have you always been good with your hands?' *Ergh, no, accidental double entendre . . .*

But once again, thank goodness, he seemed not to notice. 'I like mending things,' said Ethan. 'Fixing stuff.'

Two girls at an adjacent table had overheard though. One of them stage-whispered, 'I *love* it when they're good with their hands,' and they dissolved into fits of giggles.

Thank God for a big menu. Evie hid her burning face and studied it intently. There was a cheese soufflé on the starter list and soufflés were her all-time favourite but it stated that they'd take twenty minutes to arrive so she went for the prawns instead. The sooner this non-date was over, the better.

Having given their orders they handed the menus back to the waitress. Evie reached for her drink, sat back and almost spilled the lot down her front. There, twenty yards away on the other side of the road, was Joel.

And he was standing there watching her.

'Whoops!' The cheery waitress handed her a napkin to dab at the splashes of rose wine on her top. 'Here you go, lucky it wasn't red!'

'Thanks.' Evie dabbed and dabbed. Then she glanced up again. Joel was still there, not looking as if he were planning on going anywhere. She pushed back her chair and said to Ethan, 'I'll just get myself cleaned up. Back in a minute.'

In the Ladies' she phoned Joel. He answered on the second ring.

'What are you doing?' Evie hissed. 'How did you know I was here?' OK, *that* was a stupid question.

'I asked Mum.'

And of course Bonnie had told him, because she wanted him to be jealous.

'Well, you can go now.'

'Who's that you're with?'

'Joel, just leave.'

'Why?' he protested. 'I'm not doing any harm.'

'You're stalking me!'

'I just wanted to know what I was up against. If you ask me,' said Joel, 'I win, hands down. I'm way better looking than he is.'

This was so true Evie didn't even bother arguing the point. She said, 'Maybe he's more faithful than you are.'

'You're doing this to teach me a lesson. That's the plan, isn't it?'

'It's really not.' This was true; it was actually Bonnie's plan. 'Just leave me alone, Joel. Please don't spoil my evening.'

Emerging from the restaurant, she stood and stared at him across the street. Joel stared back for several seconds. Finally he shrugged, turned away and headed off in the direction of Pulteney Bridge.

So long as he didn't throw himself off it, into the churning weir below.

'All better now?' Ethan smiled as she returned to him.

'Yes, thanks. Sorry to be so long.' What with talking to Joel then sponging and drying the front of her top under the hand-dryer, she'd been gone a while.

'No problem. I bumped into someone I know. We've been chatting.' He nodded across the terrace and Evie politely followed his gaze. Before she could work out which one was Ethan's friend, she spotted a familiar face she'd rather not have seen. Oh for heaven's sake, Emily Morris was here; talk about bad timing. What was this, some kind of cosmic conspiracy?

The next moment Emily glanced up and saw her. She did a cartoon double-take and clearly mouthed I-don't-believe-it.

Seriously, what were the chances? And now she was jumping up, heading towards them, completely overdoing the look of amazement as she insinuated her long legs and narrow hips between the tables.

Evie braced herself and waited, because subtlety had never been Emily Morris's strong point.

Bath might be a beautiful city but sometimes it wasn't nearly big enough.

'Oh wow, Evie, I don't believe it! I heard you were back!' Emily enveloped her in a hug so showbiz they barely made physical contact. 'You poor darling, how *are* you? And you've lost weight . . . well, that's hardly surprising. Oh dear, look at your face, it's so *gaunt*.'

Bitchiness masquerading as sympathy, that was Emily Morris's strong point.

'Hi, Emily. I lost a few pounds, that's all.'

'When Ethan said he was having dinner with someone I had no idea it was you!'

It was Evie's turn to be stunned. This was the friend Ethan had been talking to? She turned to look at him. 'I'm surprised too. How do you two know each other?'

'Just through the hotel.' Ethan gestured casually. 'How about you?'

'Oh, I've known Evie for *years*,' Emily jumped in. 'I'm just amazed to see her out and about so soon after what happened . . . I mean, God, jilting someone at the altar's a pretty major thing . . . when I heard about it I was like, *wow*. And so gutted I missed it! I've never been to one of those weddings where it gets called off at the very last minute. It's like something out of *Sex and the City*!'

Oh well, it was out there now. Good job it hadn't been a deep dark secret. Ha, and Ethan, bless him, was doing his best not to look shocked. Just as well they weren't out on a real date. Handily, across the terrace, a waiter was delivering plates to Emily's table. Evie pointed and said, 'Your food's arrived.'

'Ah, shame. Anyway, catch you later . . . we could join you for a drink after dinner! OK, ciao for now . . .'

Ciao for now? Did people really still say that? This one evidently did.

Emily left them, doing her wiggly model-walk all the way back to the table so that everyone would look at her.

Ethan murmured, 'We'll have to get out of here before that happens.'

'That's a terrible thing to say. She might be one of my closest friends.'

'Except she isn't.' He looked amused.

'How about you?' Evie countered. 'Is she one of yours?'

'Not at all. I just know her from the hotel. I get the impression she's what's known as a man's woman.'

'That's the polite way of putting it.' Evie pulled a face; Emily regarded other women as rivals and liked to bring them down at every opportunity.

'So shall we pretend she didn't mention the wedding?' Ethan paused. 'Or do you want to talk about it?'

'I'm fine. It's not a secret.'

'Now I understand why you weren't keen on coming out to dinner with me. Can I just say, though, anyone who jilts another person at the altar deserves to be miserable for the rest of their life. That's just a disgusting thing to do. *Evil.* And he certainly didn't deserve you.'

'Thanks, it's nice of you to say so.' Evie looked suitably grateful. 'Sadly, the disgusting evil jilter wasn't him. It was me.'

Chapter 24

Without missing a beat, Ethan said, 'In that case, brilliant. Good for you. You did exactly the right thing.'

Evie smiled, and liked him more. 'I know.'

'And he obviously deserved it.'

'Funnily enough, he did.'

'Are you glad you didn't marry him?'

'I think so. I mean, I know it was the right thing to do.' Ethan was easy to talk to, she was discovering. Some people just had that natural ability to be good listeners. 'But I was expecting to get married . . . we'd been together for a few years . . . it takes a while to get used to being single again. It's all a bit *urgh*, to be honest. Kind of confusing.'

'No wonder you didn't want to meet me tonight.'

'It's OK. At least I warned you I'd be boring.'

'You call this boring?'

'Well,' Evie picked up her wine glass and gave the stem a twirl, 'you know what I mean. If this was a proper date I wouldn't be telling you how I really feel, would I? I'd be putting on a front to impress you, pretending I was totally fine and over it. I'd be acting all confident . . .'

'Like Emily.'

'Exactly like Emily. She used to flirt with my fiancé.' A thought belatedly occurred to Evie. 'Oh God, he probably slept with her too.'

'Is that what happened? He had an affair?'

'Plural. It turns out he had many affairs. But yes, basically he felt sharing himself with just me was a bit of a waste. Why only sleep with one girl when you can have six?' She saw the look of puzzlement on his face. 'But I only properly found out on the way to the church. Not the greatest timing in the world. Still, like Emily said, it gave everyone something to talk about.'

Ethan was frowning now. 'And this happened when?'

'Three weeks ago.'

He blinked. 'But that was when I first saw you. In the car park at the hotel. You were . . . oh shit, you weren't part of the photo shoot, were you? You were in a wedding dress because . . .'

'Because I'd just run away from my wedding. I know,' Evie marvelled, 'what are the chances? And thanks for thinking I was a model, by the way. That was really an ego boost. But I'm not.'

Their food arrived and they carried on chatting about MadAboutParties, about unexpectedly not getting married at the last minute, even about gardening and how to keep temperamental house plants alive. Much to her surprise Evie found herself relaxing and enjoying the evening she really hadn't expected to enjoy. Thanks to his laid-back manner, Ethan was easy company. There was no need to try and impress him. Appearance-wise he was frankly a bit of a disaster, which helped a lot. He was so unassuming. For years she'd been accustomed to Joel being the centre of attention wherever they went. Being out with someone like Ethan was far easier; gone was the stress of knowing you were being covertly watched all the time.

Although . . . yes, across the terrace, Emily Morris was still keeping an eye on them. But that was only because she was an absolute fiend for gossip.

'Right,' Ethan declared when dinner was over, 'Emily and her friend are still on pudding, so how about we make a quick getaway before they try and join us?'

'Definitely.' Evie watched him signal to the waiter. 'And we're splitting the bill.'

'I invited you. Let me pay.'

'No, please, I can't.' She flushed slightly; it was like holding up a placard announcing I REALLY DON'T FANCY YOU, NOT EVEN A LITTLE BIT, SO DON'T GO THINKING ANYTHING'S GOING TO HAPPEN AT THE END OF THE NIGHT BECAUSE IT JUST WON'T.

'Fine then, no problem.' Ethan silently read the placard and backed down with good grace.

'It's just, we're not on a real date. I'm really not ready for anything like that. But I have had fun,' said Evie. 'It's been better than I expected.'

He smiled briefly. 'For me too.'

'I'll be back in a minute.' Evie excused herself and headed inside to the Ladies'.

She was washing her hands when the door swung open and Emily appeared reflected in the mirror behind her. 'Hiya! We were about to come and join you but I've just spoken to Ethan and he says you have to leave.'

'Yes we do.'

'That's such a *shame*, it's so nice to see you again. I'm just amazed you're out and about like this . . . after what happened, I thought you'd be in pieces for, like, months!'

'Life goes on,' said Evie, rinsing the soap off her hands.

'Well, *obviously*. And good for you. I had no idea you and Ethan were . . .' Emily bobbed her head from side to side and waited expectantly.

'Friends.' Evie plunged her hands into the supersonic hand-dryer, forcing Emily to wait for her to finish.

'Well, I have to say I'm impressed. So, are you sleeping with him?'

Honestly, what was this girl like? The eagerness in her eyes was positively *avid*.

'No, I am not,' said Evie.

'Sure?' An idea belatedly occurred to Emily and she gasped. 'Oh my *God*, is Ethan the real reason you didn't marry Joel?'

Poor Ethan. If he got to hear about this, hopefully he'd find it funny. Evie said, 'There's nothing going on. At all. I didn't even know him before the wedding. He's just the handyman from the Ellison, I bumped into him when I was dropping off some outfits, then yesterday he brought them back to the shop. That's all there is to it. We're just two people having a chat.'

While she'd been speaking, Emily had been lavishly applying creamy beige lipstick. Now, meeting Evie's gaze in the mirror, she raised an eyebrow and said, 'He's just the handyman at the Ellison?'

Oh no, not again. When you were being picked up for making a condescending remark by Emily Morris, you knew you'd put your foot in it big time.

'I don't mean it like that *at all*. He's the gardener-handyman, there's nothing wrong with that, it's a perfectly good job, I was just explaining that's how we met.'

Emily finished filling in her lips. She efficiently clicked the top back on the lipstick – Dior, what else? – and turned round. There was an expression on her face that Evie was familiar with, the one where Emily knew something the other person didn't and she couldn't be happier about it.

'Right, I see. So . . . is that what Ethan told you? That he's the gardener-handyman?'

'Yes. Why?' She'd seen him watering the tubs. He dressed like a gardener. They'd talked about his job, for heaven's sake. He hadn't said anything to contradict her. Evie frowned and said, 'Doesn't he work there?'

'Not really.' Emily was having trouble keeping a straight face. 'I mean, not properly. Ethan owns the hotel.'

He owned the hotel. Of course he did. Evie digested this piece of information. The Ellison belonged to Ethan. She'd decided he was the gardener and for whatever reason he'd carried on letting her think it.

Like a complete div.

Emily, visibly in her element, said with a mix of elation and mock concern, 'Oh my God, I can't believe you didn't know! You must be so embarrassed!'

'There you are. I was starting to think you'd jumped out of a back window.'

'I tried. It was too small. I'd have got stuck and had to be winched out with a crane.' The bill was on the table along with two twenty pound notes. Grateful that he was letting her pay her way, Evie opened her purse and put down the same amount. All the same, forty pounds. *Ouch.*

'Did you really want to escape?'

'I did a bit, yes.'

Ethan looked worried 'Why?'

'Humiliation. Awkwardness. Feeling like a prize idiot.' Out of the corner of her eye Evie saw Emily heading towards them once more. 'Let's get out of here, shall we, before she comes over to gloat?'

'Gloat about what?' Ethan followed her along the pavement.

'About me thinking you were the odd-job guy at the hotel and not realising you owned the place.'

'Ah.' Ethan caught up with her. 'Who told you, or is that a silly question?'

'Emily just came and found me, in the loo.'

'Of course she did.' His eyes narrowed with amusement. 'Look, I'm sorry. I thought you'd be embarrassed if I corrected you.'

'Fine. Except I'm embarrassed now instead.'

'Hey, stop for a minute.' They'd rounded the corner into Manvers Street; now that they were out of sight of the restaurant, Ethan reached for her arm and turned her to face him. 'I've really enjoyed this evening. It's been great. And maybe it was just my imagination but I thought you were having a good time too.'

'I was.'

'Glad to hear it. And that was when you thought I was the odd-job guy. It didn't bother you at all.'

'No.' Evie was forced to move closer to him as they were overtaken by a stream of Japanese tourists making their way to Pulteney Bridge.

'I liked it that you didn't know the truth. We just hit it off naturally. You know what usually happens when people figure out I own a big hotel?'

'You find yourself the centre of attention?'

'Exactly. From the kind of women I wouldn't want attaching themselves to me.' He paused. 'Women with . . . expensive tastes, shall we say.'

'Like Emily.'

'Exactly like Emily.' He rubbed his chin. 'It's bloody terrifying,

179

actually. That highlighted hair of hers, all swingy and perfect . . . she told me it took thirteen hours in the hairdressers to get it looking like that. I mean, can you imagine? If you added up all the time I've spent in the hairdressers in my whole *life* it probably wouldn't come to thirteen hours.'

Evie kept a straight face. 'Now why doesn't that surprise me?'

'She asked me out last month. Four times. I kept having to say no.' Ethan looked perplexed. 'She has her eyelashes individually glued on in a beauty salon. They stay on for six weeks. Did you know that was even physically possible?'

'Well, I've heard about it. Can't say it's something I've ever done myself.'

'Exactly. It's like science fiction.' Ethan exhaled in disbelief and Evie realised her own particular unique selling point was the fact that she was as disastrously un-savvy in the hi-tech beauty stakes as he was. Together, essentially, they were Aunt Sally and Worzel Gummidge.

'So what you're saying is, you like me because I'm almost as scruffy as you are. *Almost*,' Evie reiterated. 'You still take the gold medal.'

He grinned, unoffended. 'Hey, look at me. I'd be lying if I said it wasn't an advantage. I like you because of your smile, your personality and your honesty. But I also like the fact that you have your own fingernails, your eyelashes aren't covered in black gloop and you can actually move your forehead.'

Yet another crowd of tourists was in the process of disembarking from their coach; the air was filled with excited chatter and clicking camera shutters.

'If I'd known yesterday that you owned the hotel I wouldn't have come out with you tonight.'

'I guessed. That's the other reason I didn't tell you. Now, are we going to stand here on this pavement for the next three hours or shall we go somewhere for a drink and carry on getting to know each other?'

He might wear decrepit clothes but he did have a nice smile. 'Well, OK then. But this still isn't a date,' said Evie.

Ethan shuddered and took her arm. 'Eurgh, no way, definitely not. Perish the thought.'

'Oh God,' murmured Evie, 'we're the only ones left. I didn't realise.'

'No?' Ethan grinned across at her, the light from the burnt-down candle on the table between them reflected in his eyes. 'We've been the only ones in here for the last hour.'

'What?' She stared at her watch in disbelief. 'Are you serious? It's one thirty in the morning! I don't believe it.'

'If this is how observant you are, it's probably just as well you aren't an international spy.'

'OK, this is embarrassing.' Evie had no idea where the evening had gone. All she knew was that they'd talked non-stop. After leaving Brown's they'd gone on to a bar. When that had closed, they had come to this dear little Italian restaurant. Not for food, because they'd already eaten, but in order to stay they had asked for wine and a pizza between them – which they'd been unable to resist picking at in the end. 'I mean it,' she said, mortified. 'We have to go.'

'Does that mean you've had enough of me?'

'It means these poor people are waiting to go home!' Evie gestured with agitation at the last remaining staff, chatting desultorily as they polished wine glasses behind the bar.

'Hey, don't worry. All sorted.'

'What does that mean?'

181

'I had a quiet word with them after the last table left, said we'd like to stay on for a bit and that I'd pay them extra for their trouble. They were more than happy with that. We can stay here all night if we want.'

Evie exhaled with relief. 'But we can't really.'

'I suppose not. And you want to leave now, I can see that. You wait here,' said Ethan, 'and I'll sort them out.'

She sat back and watched him, amazed by the turn the evening had taken. Well, it just went to show what could happen when you weren't expecting it. In fact, her expectations had been completely confounded. What a fantastic time they'd ended up having. And if they didn't both have work in the morning she could easily have stayed here all night. Ethan had been a revelation. It was as if they had been fated to meet . . . OK, this sounded crazy and she wouldn't say it out loud to anyone, but being with him had almost felt like falling under a spell, as if some kind of magic dust had been sprinkled over them . . .

And she wasn't even drunk.

Oh God, whatever happened, she mustn't tell him that. And especially mustn't try to kiss him. Just play it cool, *play it cool* . . .

Chapter 25

It was raining and Lara was in the car on her way to Bradford on Avon. Funny how you could be dreading and looking forward to something at the same time.

Yesterday she had introduced Jo to Gigi, then Flynn had arrived and the four of them had enjoyed a barbecue in the sunny back garden, everyone getting on well together so effortlessly that the evening had been an absolute joy. From a distance they could have been mistaken for a proper family. If only that were true. How must it feel to be normal?

Oh well, maybe normality was overrated. Never having experienced it, she wouldn't know. Lara drove down the steep winding hill into Bradford on Avon and switched her wipers up to double-speed to keep the windscreen clear. Anyway, she had a job to do today and it was already making her feel sick with anticipation. Like those dreams where you walked into an exam room and suddenly realised you'd been studying the wrong syllabus . . .

It didn't take long to find Bingham Close; she'd learned the directions off by heart. The sky was charcoal grey. Number 32 was at the end of the street, suitably dark and gothic and wrapped in a cloak of dripping trees.

The good news was that, despite the fact that it was ten o'clock in the morning, there were lights on in the house and two cars on the driveway.

Pulling up, Lara switched off the engine and took a deep breath. Let her be in, let her be in. And please God let her talk.

The front door was opened by Joan, the elder of the two sisters, whose mouth snapped shut like a rat trap at the sight of Lara on the doorstep.

'Hi, I've come to see Janice. It's about something very important.'

'She's having breakfast.'

Janice had always liked her lie-ins; Lara had deliberately chosen this time because she'd be unlikely to be out.

'I can wait until she's finished. I really do need to see her though.'

'What about?'

'It's private.' She was going with the polite-but-firm approach, praying that curiosity would overcome Janice's instinctive reluctance to see her.

'Stay there,' Joan ordered, her dyed black hair quivering with disdain. 'Don't move.'

Within thirty seconds she was back from the kitchen.

'She'll see you in fifteen minutes. You'll have to wait outside until then.'

'In the rain?'

A beady glare and a cool response. 'What do you expect, turning up without warning?'

Touché.

'OK, no problem.' Since saying thank you would make her sound desperate, Lara said, 'See you in a bit.'

She waited in the car for exactly fifteen minutes then rang the

184

doorbell. Joan answered the door again and silently ushered her towards the sitting room. Lara's nostrils quivered; there was the smell of Janice's cloying, noxious perfume, the lingering dregs of which she'd had to work so hard to eradicate from her own house. The room itself was large and gloomy, with heavy dark furniture and hectically patterned carpet. And there, sitting in the centre of the ox-blood leather sofa, was Janice, toadlike and wearing her habitual navy blue; her bosom rested on her stomach and her pudgy feet were squashed into high-heeled court shoes.

'Sit there.' She pointed to an uncomfortable-looking chair before folding her bejewelled hands across her front. At least two of the many rings on her fat fingers, Lara was fairly sure, had once belonged to her mum. But if she were to query this, Janice would either deny it, or get shirty and insist they had been her husband's to do as he liked with.

OK, get your priorities straight, choose your battles. She wouldn't want jewellery that had been worn by her stepmother anyway; even the thought of it made her feel sick.

'How are you, Janice?' And she was going to be polite too.

'I'm all right. Considering.' Janice's eyelashes were black and spidery with blobs of mascara quivering on the ends. She blinked slowly and said, 'What are you doing here?'

'I need your help.' Lara kept her voice steady. 'We both know my father didn't love me. So there's a question I'm really hoping you can answer. Because what I'm wondering is, was he maybe not my father after all?'

Janice's chins wobbled. 'And it's taken you this long to work that out, has it?'

There it was, just like that, the answer she'd been waiting to hear for so many years. Lara felt her stomach disappear and her lungs expand, in desperate need of air.

185

'So he wasn't my father.' Thank God, thank *God*. 'And he knew that all along.'

'He knew it.' Janice's knuckles were clenching now. 'In his heart he knew the truth. But your mother told him lies, she said you were his child and he wanted to believe her so he stayed married. Because that's the kind of husband he was, you see. He did his best with the rotten hand he'd been dealt. Charles was a decent man, a good man.' Her eyes were filling with tears now; beneath the heavy layers of powder and foundation her cheeks were flushed with anger. 'Everyone's always talked about your mother as if she was some kind of saint because she died of cancer and wasn't-she-young and wasn't-it-tragic, but she was the one who had the grubby little affair. Not Charles. She might have played him for a fool but he was faithful to her. He brought up another man's child and how many husbands would do that? You've come here for the truth, have you? Fine, I'll give it to you straight. Your precious mother was nothing but a tart.'

Lara didn't trust herself to speak. More than anything she wanted to defend her mum, to scream at Janice and tell her to shut up, how dare she say such vile disgusting things, it wasn't fair.

On the other hand, she still needed to know more. It was a miracle that Janice had spilled out this much information. Getting angry with her now might cause her to clam up and she couldn't afford to take that risk.

'How did my . . . um, Charles find out about the affair?'

This time the beady gaze was unwavering. For a few seconds the only sound in the room was the sonorous ticking of the grandfather clock. Then Janice said, 'He found out when I told him.'

Lara felt herself actually shake her head because that just *so*

186

wasn't the answer she'd been expecting. She said, '*What?*' and saw the glint of triumph in Janice's kohl-rimmed eyes.

'Oh yes. That surprised you, didn't it?'

'Just a bit. So, hang on, does that mean you *knew* my mum?' More and more surreal. She'd always assumed her father hadn't met Janice until around the time of her mum's death. But this meant they'd met each other fourteen years before then . . . God, this was *unbelievable*.

'I knew the man she had an affair with.'

'You knew . . . him?' If Lara hadn't been sitting down, her legs might have given way; more information than she'd ever antici-pated was bombarding her hopelessly unprepared brain. There was a loud drumming in her ears. She knew she wasn't dreaming but it felt like a dream. She had literally *no* idea what Janice might be about to come out with next. Dry-mouthed, she said, 'How? Who was he?'

Janice was now relishing her position of power. All these years, Lara realised, she'd held the knowledge to her massive chest and been forbidden by her husband from saying anything. But now he was gone, he couldn't stop her. Janice no longer needed to keep the information to herself. By turning up here this morning, she'd succeeded in poking the first crucial hole in the dam and now all the answers were going to come gushing out.

They hadn't needed to track Jo down after all.

'I worked for him,' said Janice. 'I was his secretary.'

His secretary. Lara's jaw was clenched tight with anticipation. 'What was he like?'

Janice's lip curled. 'The kind of man who thought he could do everything. Anything he wanted, he could have. He was married but that didn't stop him. Mr Charm.'

OK, presumably that wasn't his real name.

187

'What happened?' said Lara. 'How did it start?' She wanted to hear every last detail.

'I don't know how they got together in the first place. But your mother started calling the office. She wasn't the first.' Janice's tone was disparaging. 'I was used to fielding calls from his fancy women. But they usually only lasted a few weeks. This time it carried on. She'd ring up, I'd put her through, then he'd leave the office for an hour or two. And I was expected to cover for him.' Her expression hardened. 'If his wife called, I'd have to fob her off, say he was in a meeting. I had to lie to her. It was part of my job.'

'Did you see him and my mum together?'

'Not for weeks. Then she called him one lunchtime and he went rushing off to meet her as usual. I had a dental appointment that day so I left the office twenty minutes later. I was taking a short cut through the back of the Botanical Gardens when I saw them together.' Janice's lip curled as she said it.

Oh heavens, what had they been doing? Lara inwardly panicked; please don't let it have been anything inappropriate.

'They were sitting on a bench,' Janice continued. 'Talking to each other and holding hands.'

'Right.' Thank goodness for that, holding hands was fine.

'The way he was looking at her . . . it was as if she was the only woman in the world. They didn't notice me watching them. And then he reached up and touched the side of her face.' Janice was shaking her head now, gazing out of the window as she recalled the event in her mind's eye. 'The next minute she was in his arms and he was holding her, kissing her. That was when I realised he could turn his head at any minute and see me. So I left, because I hadn't followed him there, but he'd think I had. I saw her face though, well enough. And the wedding ring on her left hand. That was the thing that really got me. Two married people not caring about the vows they'd made, breaking promises, sneaking around behind their partners' backs and taking stupid risks just for the thrill of it, because all they care about is themselves and their own happiness and why shouldn't they have a bit of fun?'

'So you didn't say anything to him,' said Lara. 'He didn't know you knew.'

'No, but he wasn't exactly discreet. Some men are like that, they just assume you'll go along with whatever they're doing. I'd put her calls through to him and he'd say, "Barbara! Darling, how are you? When am I going to see you?" and ten minutes later he'd be off. He just took it for granted I wouldn't tell his wife!'

Chapter 26

Lara said, 'Did you tell his wife?'

'Yes, I did. I felt she deserved to know.' The look of defiance on Janice's face said it all.

'And?'

'She didn't want to know.' The vermilion mouth pursed like a cat's bottom. 'Told me she wasn't interested. Try and do someone a favour and they're scared to face up to the truth. Too fond of her lifestyle, that's what it was. The big house, the fancy cars, trips to Ascot and Wimbledon and a holiday home in the south of France. She couldn't risk losing it all, could she? So she chose to turn a blind eye instead. He did whatever he wanted to do and she carried on with the shopping trips to London, the visits to Harrods' beauty hall, living the pampered life along with all her rich-wife friends.'

Lara said, 'What was his name?' If she slipped the question in unobtrusively enough, maybe Janice would be tricked into saying it.

'Anyway, everything did carry on.' Janice pointedly ignored her. 'Your mother would call the office. He'd disappear to visit her. Then a year later I overheard him on the phone saying something about when the baby was born. Well, I knew he wasn't talking about his own wife. So the next time he arranged to meet her, I followed him to the park and there they were, together again. That was when I saw she was expecting.'

'With me?' Lara's mouth was dry. 'Was it me?'

'Of course it was you. Your mother was a married woman carrying on with another man . . . and now she was having a child . . . call me old-fashioned, but I find that pretty distasteful . . .'

'So you told my father.' It didn't take a genius to work it out. Everything was starting to make sense now. Lara said, 'How did you track him down?'

'That was simple. I worked for a careless man.' Janice's tone brimmed with scorn. 'I already knew she was called Barbara from the phone calls. All I had to do was look in his diary and there it was, written down bold as brass. Barbara Carson and the number. Looked it up in the phone book – hardly anyone was ex-directory in those days – and had the address. Right here in Bradford on Avon, as it turned out.'

'And you paid my father a visit.' She hadn't succeeded with James's wife, so she'd felt compelled to tell the other woman's husband instead.

'Yes I did.' Janice was unrepentant. 'I didn't know if he'd even be there, but he was. It was a Sunday morning and he was outside the flat washing his car.'

This was a scenario Lara was familiar with; washing and painstakingly polishing the car on a Sunday morning had occurred without fail throughout her childhood. She'd never been allowed to help him either; he'd brusquely explained that she wouldn't do it well enough.

'So you just went up to him in the street and told him everything?'

'Don't be ridiculous. I didn't know if your mother was inside

191

the flat. I asked him if he was Charles Carson, then I said if he wanted to find out something interesting about his wife, he should give me a call. I handed him my number and walked away. He was the one who called me back and invited me into the flat. Barbara had gone to church, appropriately enough for a sinner.' Janice blinked slowly and refolded her hands in her lap. 'He said she wouldn't be back for an hour. And he really did want to know. So I told him. He didn't say much. Just took it all in.'

Lara pictured the scene: reserved, uptight Charles Carson, married to Barbara and imagining he was shortly to become a father, painstakingly polishing his car on a Sunday morning when along comes a complete stranger announcing that not only has his wife been seeing another man but that the child she's expecting may not be his.

Talk about a bolt from the blue.

But he'd stayed married to her mother, who had presumably denied the affair. And thirty-six years ago, divorce had been far more of a last resort than it was now; the stigma would have been hard for someone like her father to bear. Presumably remaining unhappily married was preferable to admitting that your wife had become involved with another man.

'And then he thanked me,' Janice continued, 'which was nice of him. He said he'd deal with the situation. He also asked me if he could call again in case he needed to find out any more information in the future.'

'You told him who your boss was?'

Janice shook her head. 'No, I couldn't take the risk, could I? Charles was a stranger, who knew what he might do or say? I didn't want to lose my job. I explained that to him and he understood. I left him to it, after that. It was months before I heard from him again.'

Lara wished they could open a window in this stuffy room; Janice's perfume was giving her a headache. But she couldn't stop now. 'So he challenged her when she got home?'

'He did. She was shocked, naturally. Denied everything, insisted she'd done nothing wrong. Then he told her she'd been seen in the park and she crumbled, admitted it was true but maintained he was a friend, nothing more. It's what people do, isn't it, when they've been caught out?' Janice shook her head dismissively. 'Fly into a panic and deny, deny.'

'And then what happened?'

'She promised she wouldn't see him any more. And for a while she stuck to it. The phone calls stopped. No more secret meetings, not for months. Then you were born. She rang the office a week later and they had a conversation lasting almost an hour.'

It was like listening to a radio play. Lara gazed at the wall and pictured everything in her head, her mother clutching a baby in one arm, awash with emotion as she whispered into the phone. And James, sitting at his desk at work, possibly her father, possibly not . . . oh God, what did he look like? She had no idea.

'Charles contacted me shortly afterwards and I told him. Anyway, there were no more phone calls after that, not to the office.' Janice paused before continuing. 'Then two years later, the company was sold and I was made redundant. My former employer finally divorced his wife, sold their house and announced that he was moving abroad. I did wonder if your mother would go with him. Charles wondered too. But we waited, and nothing happened. He left. Your mother stayed with Charles.'

'And that was when we moved from the flat in Bradford on Avon into the house in Bath,' said Lara. 'When I was two. And the house was bought in my mother's name.' She saw the flash of annoyance in Janice's eyes. 'Did he give her the money to buy it?'

193

'Evidently so. Not that I knew at the time. Charles kept that bit of information from me. The flat wasn't good enough for Barbara, you see. Too small, too damp, no garden. When he told me they were moving, I assumed he'd bought the place himself. It was a matter of pride, I imagine. He only admitted the truth after we were married. Barbara chose the house herself and announced that the two of you were moving into it. She presented him with an ultimatum, basically. Charles had no choice but to go with her. Pretty humiliating situation for a married man to find himself in.' Janice carefully wiped the corners of her mouth with a tissue. 'So you see, your mother wasn't always the angel she was painted.'

Lara felt as if she was in a small boat whose oars had slipped away. She didn't want to be hearing this bit. Equally, she was determined not to let Janice know how upsetting it was.

'Your boss.' She tried again. 'What was his name?'

Janice regarded her scornfully. 'If I was going to let you know his name, don't you think I'd have done it by now?'

'So you're not going to tell me?' It was agonising but hardly a surprise.

'No. Charles didn't want you to ever meet him.'

'I don't want to meet him, I just want to know who he is. Look,' Lara protested, 'all this stuff that happened . . . none of it was my fault. It's like I'm being punished for something I had no control over.'

Janice shrugged. 'As far as Charles was concerned, this man ruined his life.'

'But he might be my biological father.'

'And he might not be.'

'OK, is there any way of finding that out? If there is,' said Lara, 'could we at least do that?'

'It's too late.' Janice was adamant. 'I wanted it to happen years ago. I *said* he should find out, then he'd know for sure. But it would have meant contacting you in Keswick and Charles couldn't bring himself to do that. Anyway,' her mouth set in a vermilion downward curve and she spoke with an air of finality, 'there's no way of doing it now. He's dead.'

The rain had stopped by the time Lara left the house. Joan was now outside in the front garden, vigorously deadheading roses and hurling slugs over the wall into next door's carefully tended shrubbery. Turning at the sound of the front door being closed, she said, 'You'd better not have upset my sister.'

'I haven't upset her at all.'

Joan's eyes narrowed as she scooped another slug on to the end of her secateurs and lobbed it next door. 'Looking pleased with yourself.'

Lara beamed. 'I'm happy. We're pretty sure Charles wasn't my father. Janice has told me all about James.'

That startled her. 'She did?'

'I've just heard the whole story. I'm so grateful to Janice. It's the best news in the world.'

'You might think that, but you didn't know him.' Joan had her lemon-sucking face on as she snip-snip-snipped away at the roses. 'Men like him just take what they want and walk away when they've had their fun. Janice idolised him and he treated her like dirt, same as I expect he did with your mother.' Viciously she said, 'So good luck with finding him, if that's what you're planning on doing. Because I'm telling you now, that bastard Agnew broke my sister's heart.'

★   ★   ★

'You see, that was always the thing with Janice. Too much time watching *Keeping Up Appearances* and *Antiques Roadshow*,' said Lara. 'Not enough *CSI*.'

Everyone watched as she lifted the plastic carrier bag out of her shoulder bag. Inside it was Charles Carson's hairbrush. Not the loveliest item in the world, but containing enough strands of grey hair to enable a DNA test to be carried out.

'The moment I mentioned hair, she said she still had his sponge bag upstairs. She went and fetched it and there was the brush, still there from the last time he was in hospital. All I have to do is send it off with a bit of my hair and see if they match. Hopefully they won't. It's so exciting I'm actually feeling sick.'

'And you've got James's name too,' Jo marvelled.

Lara nodded. She had, she had, despite not imagining for a moment that the ploy would work. Underhand and cheeky it may have been, but she wasn't going to feel guilty about it.

James.

Agnew.

Together the two words made up the name she'd so badly needed to know. And at this very moment Flynn and Gigi were side by side at the computer, narrowing down the likely suspects with the help of 192.com.

Which not only gave you the address and phone number of all the James Agnews in the UK but their ages too. Who knew?

'He'll be in his mid-seventies, I'm guessing.' Jo was peering over Lara's shoulder. 'I'm sure he was a few years older than Barbara.'

'If he's living in the UK, he's either this one or this one.' Flynn brought up the two options. The amount of information available was staggering; how long each man had been living at their current address, details of the other occupants of the property, lists of the neighbour's details, aerial photographs of the address and recent house prices in the vicinity.

The first James lived with his family in a back-to-back terrace in a dodgy part of Birmingham. If this was the one, his lifestyle had undergone a dramatic downward slide.

'We can try him,' Jo said doubtfully, 'but I wouldn't bet money on it being that one.'

Flynn moved on to the second James Agnew, listed as the sole occupier of a rather more salubrious address in London. The house was situated in a leafy avenue in Wimbledon where the average selling price was over two million.

Was it him? Was this her father?

'I'm going to call the number.' Reaching for her mobile, Lara did it before she had a chance to start hyperventilating. It rang at the other end . . . and rang . . . and rang again . . .

Please, someone answer the phone, just pick up . . .

''Allo?'

A female voice, foreign and hesitant.

'Hi, could I speak to James Agnew, please?'

'No, no.'

Lara's palms grew damp as the silence lengthened. 'OK. Why not?'

'Meester Agnew 'oliday.'

Not dead then. That was good.

'Right. Um, does he have a mobile phone?'

'Eh?'

'Is there another number I can reach him on? Or an address?'

'No . . . I clean 'ouse.'

'Where is he? Meester Agnew?' This heavy accent was catching.

'On water. Beeg boat.'

'OK. When will he be back?'

197

'Yes, I 'ave bad back. Ver' bad, ow, hurt *ver' much.*'

They carried on like this for a couple more minutes. Lara finally hung up, frustrated and none the wiser. She'd left her number but who knew if the cleaner had even written it down, let alone understood that she was meant to pass it on?

And it might not be the right man anyway. Her James Agnew could be living anywhere in the world. Or he might not still be alive.

Well, she'd try the number again in a few days.

In the meantime, at least they could press ahead with the DNA test.

Chapter 27

Six days had passed and Lara had left two more messages with James Agnew's cleaning lady. She had also called the house an embarrassing number of times and failed to get any reply. Wherever he'd gone on holiday, he wasn't back yet. It didn't help either that Gigi had brightly suggested the woman at the other end of the phone might be James's current ladyfriend, fobbing off potential rivals by pretending to be his foreign I-know-nussing cleaner.

Anyway, she had her new job to keep her occupied. Don Temple was great company in the shop. Fond of gossip and as camp as Christmas, he was capable of keeping up the most scurrilous running commentaries on the people walking past the window, which would get him sued for slander if they ever heard him. He sang too, and encouraged Lara to join in. His regular customers loved him and he was hugely popular with the ladies, in that flirtatious way only truly non-threatening men could get away with.

In fact it was happening right now. The customer, a well-kept woman in her late sixties, had come in ostensibly to have the claws checked on her diamond bracelet. In reality she was doing her level best to convince Don to join her for a few days at her holiday apartment in the Algarve. 'Darling, you'd love it, you know you would! And we'd have such *fun* together. Oh, please say you'll come . . . I do so hate going on my own.'

By the time the woman eventually left, she'd persuaded him to at least consider the offer, before sweeping out of the shop in a cloud of Dior No. 19.

'Bless her heart, it's hard to say no.' Don raised his neat eyebrows and shook his head as the door clanged shut behind her. 'She's lonely since her husband died. I'm still not going, mind.'

'Why not?' said Lara. 'You might have a brilliant time. I can look after the shop for you.'

'That's not what I'm worried about. She invited me to a dinner party at her house last year. Wanted me to . . . *stay behind,* if you know what I mean, after all the other guests had left.' He shuddered fastidiously. 'Poor darling, completely desperate.'

'Oops.' Lara grinned, envisaging his horror. 'Thought she could turn you, did she?'

For a fraction of a second there was silence. Then Don frowned and said, 'Turn me into what?'

Help, backpedal, *backpedal.* 'Um, I mean she was trying to win you over, make you change your mind about her.'

But Don was giving her an odd look. 'No, you don't mean that. You said *turn.* Like you assumed I was gay. And now you're blushing. Is that what you really think?'

Well, this was awkward. 'No, not at all!' Lara felt her traitorous face turn the colour of ketchup. 'OK, maybe I did. Just . . . you know, the tiniest bit.'

'How strange. Why would you imagine I was gay?' He seemed genuinely surprised. Did that mean he didn't know? Was he actually oblivious to the impression he created with his fussy, gossipy persona, his great passion for show tunes and his pointy little patent-leather shoes?

'Sorry, I'm so sorry . . . it must have been when you said you'd never married or had children . . . I just jumped to the wrong conclusion.' Mortified, Lara said, 'Because I'm an idiot.'

'Oh, darling, don't worry about it, I'm not offended. To be honest, it's happened once or twice before. I just never expect people to think it, so it takes me by surprise every time.' Don tilted his head to one side like a quizzical blackbird. 'D' you know, I sometimes think I must come across as a bit camp.'

A *bit* camp? This from the man who kept a buffer about his person at all times so he could polish his fingernails to a mirror-bright shine?

Aloud she said, 'It doesn't matter to me either way.'

'I know, darling. But I'm not gay, never have been. I like the ladies,' Don confided happily. 'Maybe it does surprise people sometimes. Just because I dress nicely and take care of my appearance.' His eyes twinkled as he smoothed his immaculately pressed trousers. 'But we can't all be hulking great burping, beer-swilling rugby players, can we?'

Lara said with feeling, 'I'm extra glad you're not one of those.'

'. . . so he's completely hetero.' Lara chopped up the tomatoes and threw them into the salad bowl. 'I couldn't believe it. And the next thing I know, he's booking tickets for us to go and see *Les Mis* at the Bristol Hippodrome. He's the gayest straight man on the planet.'

'Good for him.' Flynn had called in on the way back from work to let her know that Gigi had gone to the gym but would be home in an hour. 'Maybe it's his way of getting women to relax in his company and trust him.' He paused. 'Maybe I should give it a go.'

'You could definitely try that.' Lara added sliced spring onions and reached for the olive oil and balsamic vinegar mixture she'd whizzed up earlier. Pouring it into the bowl, she began tossing the salad with her fingers, lifting the leaves high into the air as she'd seen Jamie Oliver doing on TV the other day because it helped to distribute the dressing more evenly, apparently, plus it was more cheffy and artistic and made you look like a pro in the kitchen.

'So you think acting gay might help me?' Flynn leaned against the worktop and pinched a crouton from the blue dish next to her.

'When you're as shy and retiring with the girls as you are, you need all the help you can get.'

'I do have a couple of pink shirts.' He thought for a moment. 'And I was dragged along to the ballet once.'

'Did you like it?'

Flynn gave her a look. 'No.'

'You need to get more in touch with your feminine side,' said Lara. 'Talk about your emotions and how you're feeling.'

'Right now I'm feeling hungry.' He was reaching for the croutons again. She nudged him away with her non-oily forearm and Flynn gave her a playful nudge back.

'Hey, leave them alone.' Lara whisked the blue dish out of reach, sadly misjudging the oiliness of her hands. The dish slipped from her grasp and went skidding across the worktop. Launching herself after it, she collided with Flynn and her elbow sent the salad bowl flying across the kitchen—

'Noooo,' yelped Lara.

'Oh dear.' Flynn pulled a face as they surveyed the mess; by some miracle the bowl hadn't broken but the floor was now strewn with glistening salad. 'That was careless of you.'

'Careless of *me*?' Lara gasped at the slur. 'It was your fault!'

He shook his head. 'Oh no, it was definitely your elbow.'

Lara picked a crouton out of the blue dish and threw it at him. Flynn deftly caught it in his left hand and placed it between his teeth. 'Thanks.'

'You made me knock the salad on the floor.' She threw more croutons at him; he caught and ate each one in turn.

'Only because you physically assaulted me. In fact,' Flynn rolled up his shirtsleeve, 'I think you might have broken my arm.'

Then he rolled up the other sleeve and together they began collecting up the oily lettuce leaves, the skittery cherry tomatoes, the chunks of avocado and the fiddly little slivers of spring onions.

'What's really annoying', said Lara, 'is I used my very best balsamic instead of the cheap one.'

'I'll buy you another bottle for your birthday.' Their heads were close together as they began wiping up the oil with kitchen paper. Flynn paused to glance across at her. 'You still have those long eyelashes.'

'It'd be pretty weird if I didn't.'

He was smiling slightly. 'True. You also have salad dressing on your cheek.'

'That would be your fault.' Lara was bare-legged, her skirt hitched up as she knelt – glamorously – on a square of kitchen paper. Inches away, crouching rather than kneeling in order to spare his black trousers, Flynn adjusted his balance and reached up to smooth the shininess away with the back of his index finger. The next moment he wiped it slowly and deliberately on the other cheek instead.

His eyes, oh those beautiful eyes. Lara picked up a dressing-coated leaf of lollo rosso and carefully stuck it to the side of his face.

Here they were, surrounded by bits of salad, and now it felt as though they were gazing into each other's souls. Lara was abruptly ambushed by lust. Flynn reached across and smudged the dressing across the bridge of her nose. It was like being sixteen again. He truly did have the most incredible mouth. She found herself extending a hand without meaning to and experimentally brushing her fingertips across his lips, so soft compared with the golden stubble on his jaw. There hadn't been as much of *that* when he was sixteen, but otherwise every line and angle was achingly familiar . . .

And now he was cradling the back of her head, drawing her towards him, and she was peeling the lettuce leaf off the side of his face. His breath was warm, her heart was cantering away and their mouths were meeting and all those years of trying to remember exactly how that had felt were melting away because it was all coming back to her . . . this was the mouth, this was the kiss . . . it was both the same and better, and she just wanted it to go on and on and never st—

'Dad? Dad!' The front door opened and slammed shut, sending them ricocheting apart like violently opposing magnets. 'You'll never guess what, there was a power cut at the gym and they sent us all home! I ran all the way! Eurrgh, what happened in *here*?'

What indeed?

'Your mum knocked the salad on to the floor.' Flynn recovered first. 'I was helping her clear up the mess.'

'It was his fault, not mine. He made me do it.' Lara grabbed a handful of kitchen roll and began spraying the floor wildly with the bottle of Cif she'd managed to kick over while they'd been otherwise occupied.

'Mum's always been accident-prone. Well, you probably know that. Anyway, guess who I just had a text from?'

Lara looked up, because Gigi was addressing her and sounding excited. 'Who?'

'Harry!'

'Don't be daft, Harry doesn't know how to text.' Harry did in fact own a cheap mobile but he used it as gingerly as if it were an unexploded grenade and spoke into it like someone from the nineteen fifties.

Gigi shrugged. 'Well, he does now. And he wanted to know if we're in tonight, because if we are he'll pop round.'

'How can he pop round?' Lara frowned; was Harry drunk? 'Has he bought a TARDIS? Are you sure it wasn't a joke text from one of your friends?'

'It came from his number. By the way, you've got a bit of lettuce in your hair.' Gigi helpfully picked it out. 'How did you manage that?'

Er . . .

'Who's Harry?' said Flynn.

'Oh, you remember, the one with the shirt factory and the rapper friend. You *do* remember,' Gigi insisted when he continued to look blank. 'I told you about him. The one that married Mum.'

Chapter 28

Flynn may have spent the last couple of weeks being bombarded with information, relevant or otherwise, by his newfound daughter, but his face was a picture now. This bit of information evidently took the biscuit. Her emotions in a fizz as it was, Lara spluttered with laughter and said, 'I'm not married to him *now*.'

Between them they cleaned up the mess, then Lara set about making another salad.

'So were you going to mention this husband at any stage,' Flynn said finally, 'or was it just not interesting enough to bother me with?'

Well, he was bound to ask.

'It didn't occur to me to tell you.' Lara was busy chopping up yet more tomatoes. 'It honestly wasn't that important. I suppose I thought Gigi might have mentioned it.'

'And I thought Mum had probably already said something,' Gigi chimed in. 'So in the end neither of us did. But it doesn't matter anyway. It's hardly relevant.'

'Not relevant that you had a stepfather?' Flynn raised his eyebrows in disbelief as he swung his gaze back to Lara. 'Not relevant that you married another man? When you told me you'd brought Gigi up as a single mother, that there hadn't been anyone else, that it had been such a terrible struggle, *just the two of you on your own* . . . ?'

'OK, let me explain.' Lara put down the knife. 'It was just one of those stupid mistakes. It didn't even last a year. All I wanted was to be a good mother and make Gigi happy. When she was four, she started infants' school. One day she came home and asked me where her daddy was. She said other children had daddies and she wanted one too.'

'I can't remember any of this, by the way,' Gigi put in helpfully. 'I don't remember saying it at all.'

'Well, you did.' Aware that Flynn might feel she should have used this as an opportunity to contact him and keen to avoid *that* argument again, Lara said, 'Anyway, I was twenty years old and there weren't many boys in the area interested in hooking up with someone in my situation. But Harry was there, and he was different from the rest of them. He was twenty-three and he liked me. We were good friends.'

'He felt sorry for you,' said Gigi. 'Harry always wants to do the right thing,' she explained to Flynn. 'He likes to be helpful, it's just the way he is. He's lovely.'

'So you told him you wanted to get married,' Flynn turned back to Lara, 'and he went along with it?'

Did this paint her in a really bad light? Well, there was nothing she could do about that. 'Yes he did. But I didn't force him,' said Lara. 'He offered. He'd known Gigi since she was born. He already loved her. And she adored him. At the time it just seemed perfect, the answer to everything.'

'Except you didn't love him. Or did you?'

She prevaricated. No, of course she hadn't loved Harry, not in that way. But as a friend you couldn't have asked for more. He

207

was thoughtful and unselfish, and had done her the biggest favour just when she most needed it.

'I wanted us to be a happy family. We tried to make it work. Harry's a good man.' Lara did her best to explain. 'I hoped we could, you know, grow into a couple. I thought the whole falling-in-love thing was probably massively overrated and we could get by as we were.'

'But you said it lasted less than a year.' Flynn was leaning against the fridge, watching her intently. 'What happened?'

'It just didn't work out.' Lara had no intention of telling him the real reason; it was none of his business. 'We were like two kids playing house, pretending to be a couple. It was wrong. We kept waiting for everything to click into place and start feeling normal . . . *real* . . . but it just didn't happen. We realised we'd made a mistake and cut our losses. Me and Gigi moved back in with Nettie. But there weren't any hard feelings. We've stayed friends ever since.'

'And how about you?' Flynn turned to Gigi. 'Did you like having him as a stepfather?'

'I don't remember any of it. I was a flower girl at the wedding,' Gigi spread her arms, 'and I can't even remember being there. But there are photos, so I definitely was!'

'We did it because she wanted a daddy. Ironically,' said Lara, 'she never did call him that. It was always Harry. Except she couldn't pronounce her r's back then.'

'I used to call him Hawwy.' Gigi beamed at Flynn. 'So don't worry, no need to get jealous. After all these years you're the first one I've ever called Dad.'

'And I'm the last one you're going to call Dad.'

'Anyway,' Lara hastily chimed in. 'Like I said, no harm done. Harry's been like an uncle to her.'

208

Gigi said fondly, 'The kind of uncle you can tease because he doesn't know who Ashton Kutcher is or he's never heard of N-Dubz. But if you're stuck on some really stinky history home-work he'll spend ages helping you out.'

'I'd have helped you too,' said Flynn.

'I know you would.' Gigi gave his arm a squeeze. 'It's OK, you don't have to get competitive. I'm just saying.'

Lara's phone rang and Harry's name flashed up. 'Speak of the devil. We were just talking about you.'

'Hi, yes, it's me.' Harry never failed to be amazed by caller ID. 'Um, you're at home, right?'

'Yes! Where are you? What's going on?'

'I'm in Bath. Is it all right if I come round?'

'Of course it's all right, but I still don't know what you're doing down here!'

'I'll tell you in a minute.' Music was playing in the background; Harry sounded weirdly as if he were in a nightclub. 'Look, you can say no if you want, that's perfectly fine.' He sounded tentative. 'But is it OK if I bring a friend?'

Gigi peered out of the window, saw the enormous car draw up outside and realised she was right. Oh wow, oh seriously wow.

'Mum, they're here. And it isn't a girlfriend. Oh my God, this is the maddest thing ever!' She flung open the front door, about to race across the gravel, then abruptly braked because racing would make her look like a groupie.

So Gigi sauntered instead, although it was hard to saunter with insouciance when you were walking barefoot over gravel. Too late she made the discovery that shoes might have been an idea.

Then people began jumping out of the huge car and there

was Harry, dwarfed by the size of his companions and looking very conservative in comparison.

'Harry! My feet hurt!' Gigi waved both her arms and he hurried over to her, enveloping her in a hug.

'Hello, Pud. Look, sorry about this, I've got Enjay and the boys with me, are you sure Lara won't mind?'

Harry had called her Pudding for as long as she could remember. Gigi hugged him back. 'Of course she won't mind. It's brilliant to see you again.'

'There's going to be a bit of filming too, I'm afraid. It's for his TV show. If it gets too much, just say and I'll make them stop.' Lara had joined them and Harry included her in the apologetic explanation whilst behind him the video camera was already whirring away.

'We saw the stuff on YouTube,' Gigi told him. 'You're so funny together.'

'I know, even though I don't mean to be.' Harry gave her a bemused look. 'Everyone's calling us the Odd Couple. It's been the most surreal couple of weeks you can imagine.'

Lara said, 'Why are you doing it then?'

'Because they're paying me a ludicrous amount of money.' He shrugged then said good-naturedly, 'And it's also quite good fun. We're staying in all the best hotels. I have my own *suite*, can you believe it? Right, let me introduce you now. He's as mad as a box of frogs but just pretend you haven't noticed. The trick is not to put up with any silly nonsense.'

Enjay approached them and the introductions were made. Gigi found it hard not to stare at him, simply because she'd never been this close to a properly famous person before. Until now her biggest claim to fame was once colliding with Keith Chegwin on a pavement because she'd been fiddling with her iPod.

And this was EnjaySeven. He smelled wonderful and his T-shirt was eyeblindingly white to match his pointy teeth. His skin was sheeny and poreless, the exact same colour as her favourite River Island handbag. He had cheekbones to die for and short curly eyelashes framing intelligent, almond-shaped eyes. As for the way he was looking at her . . . well, that was bordering on intimate. Gigi felt her heart do a bit of a skip. Crikey, she was in the presence of some serious charisma.

'Gigi. That's a beautiful name.' His gaze lingered on her face as he said it. If he added 'for a beautiful girl' it would be nauseating and such a let-down; Gigi held her breath and waited for him to spoil everything.

But he didn't. He shook her hand and flashed her a charming smile before moving on to Lara.

Wow again, EnjaySeven just said she had a beautiful name. Talk about cool. He had a pretty fit body too; with pecs like that he must spend hours in the gym.

Shame he was so old.

Only Harry, Enjay and Maz the cameraman came into the house. The others, reassured that their boss was in safe hands, headed back to the hotel for dinner. Gigi proudly introduced Flynn to Harry and experienced a rush of sheer joy when Harry said, 'She's a lovely girl,' and Flynn replied, 'Couldn't ask for more.' It was one of those moments. And then they had to update Harry on the whole James Agnew story. There was so much to catch up on. Back in Keswick Harry had needed to employ more machinists to keep up with the demand for shirts.

'It's bizarre,' said Harry. 'People keep wanting to interview me for magazines. I've told them there's no point, I'm too boring to be interviewed, but they won't give up.'

'So he's refusing to speak to them,' Enjay added with amusement. 'It's driving them wild. PR genius, man. The more he says no, the more desperate they are to get hold of him. But for the moment Harry's all ours.'

Lara said, 'How long are you here for?'

'A week, maybe more. Who knows? The tour starts next month, so we're doing this for the TV series . . . Enjay in the UK, being shown around by Harry, introduced to different people and places. And Bath's a picturesque city, right? Lots of tourists visit here. We're gonna do some filming at the thermal spa tomorrow, gonna get our man Harry into some cool swimming trunks.'

'You most certainly are not,' Harry retorted.

Gigi said, 'Oh, Harry, you should. Those spa pools are amazing.'

'Maybe you could come with me instead.' Enjay eyed her with a lazy smile. 'Harry's too chicken. I guess he's just afraid of the water or something.'

'I'm not afraid of the water, I just don't want to appear on TV in a bathing costume.' Harry shook his head with an air of finality. 'It's not dignified and it's not going to happen.'

'He means he's scared people will laugh at his little white legs. Whereas you,' Enjay returned his attention to Gigi, 'wouldn't have to worry about that. Nobody would laugh at your legs. So how about it? Would you like to come for a swim in the spa with me, Gigi?'

He was saying it softly, like lyrics, as if it were a line in a song. Gigi said, 'Yes, if you want. I don't mind!' Oh dear, did that sound too eager? 'But I've got work tomorrow, so it'll have to be after that. Unless . . . ?' She glanced across at Flynn, who had been keeping out of the way.

He shook his head fractionally. 'You're working tomorrow.'

'OK.' Tuh, he didn't want her to go. Gigi brightened and said,

'But we could do it tomorrow evening. There's a twilight package, you can go up and swim in the pools on the roof while the sun's setting and all the lights start going on in the city. That'll be even better!'

'Cool.' Enjay nodded to Maz, behind the camera, and said, 'Fix that up, man. Give them a call.'

Excitement bubbled up. Gigi said, 'I'll have to find my swimsuit!'

'What d'you mean, a swimsuit? Like an all-in-one thing?' Enjay looked taken aback.

'It's a nice one. Navy blue.'

'Can't you wear a bikini?'

'I haven't got a bikini. I had one last year but the chlorine made the material go all weird.'

'No problem.' Reaching into his back pocket, Enjay took out a wallet and peeled off several fifties. 'Get yourself one tomorrow.'

Oh good grief, three hundred pounds? For *a bikini*?

'That won't be necessary.' Flynn was shaking his head again. 'You don't have to pay for a bikini.'

Was he cross? Gigi chimed in hurriedly, 'It's fine, I can buy my own anyway, they're only a fiver in New Look.'

'Hey, let me do this. I don't want you appearing on my show in something that cost a fiver.'

Gigi looked across at the camera, then down at her short yellow and white striped vest-style dress. 'Well, I'm sorry, but I think it's far too late to say *that*.'

Chapter 29

Last night had been eventful in more ways than one. Lara had fallen asleep at midnight, thinking of Flynn and that Interrupted Kiss. She'd been hoping to dream about it in more detail but the inside of her head was never that obliging; instead she'd dreamed that the shop had been crammed with angry customers shouting at her because they'd wanted to buy jewellery and she'd sold them giant pork pies instead.

Neither Flynn nor the Interrupted Kiss had put in an appearance, but the memory of it had continued to occupy her thoughts on and off all day. Basically because it had been like being presented with the most sensational dessert in a top restaurant but only being allowed to taste the tiniest morsel before it was whisked away . . .

And now he was back again, ostensibly to drop Gigi home from work and to give her a lift to the spa but in reality with plans to spend the evening being her chaperone.

Which was amusing in its own way, but not what a twenty-first-century eighteen year old was likely to tolerate. Still, it was up to Gigi now to handle the situation. Lara had already had her say and been rebuffed.

Having Flynn here wasn't doing a great deal for her equilibrium, to be honest.

'Right, I'm ready!' Gigi came skipping downstairs in her black cotton sundress and silver ballet pumps, swinging a cream holdall. Unzipping the bag, she produced a lime-green and orange sequinned bikini with a flourish and waggled it at them. 'Look, I got it at lunchtime, isn't it fantastic? Super sparkly!'

'It's beautiful,' said Lara, because it was.

'It's . . . small.' Flynn's tone was disapproving.

'It was six pounds fifty.' Gigi was delighted with her sale bargain. 'I pushed the boat out. And yes, it is quite small. I tried to find a bikini bigger than a king-sized duvet but they didn't have any left in the shop. *Ooh.*' Her face lit up as a throaty roar reached their ears. 'That's them now.'

Lara glanced out of the window and saw the Maybach pull up at the gate. She also saw Flynn's jaw tighten.

'I said I'd take you down there.' He watched Gigi stuff the tiny bikini back into her bag.

'I know, but now you don't need to. Enjay said it was no trouble to pick me up. And he'll drop me home later too.'

'But I was going to come along with you. I think I should.'

'Dad, stop it! Mum, tell him I don't need a chaperon. We're not in Jane Austen's world now.'

'Enjay's certainly no Mr Darcy,' Flynn retorted.

'Hey, don't worry, she'll be fine.' Lara rested her hand in the small of Gigi's back and said, 'Have a good time, sweetheart. Got your front-door key?'

'Yep. Bye, Mum, see you later. Bye, Dad.'

'Just let me have a word with him first.'

'Oh God,' Gigi groaned as Flynn opened the front door and headed over to the car. 'How embarrassing.'

'He's your father,' said Lara, 'and he's new to the job. It's nice that he cares.'

Gigi grimaced. 'He really needs to be wearing L-plates.'

The Maybach purred off down the road with Gigi inside it and Lara watched from the front door as Flynn made his way back to her.

God, she loved the way he walked.

'What did you say to him?'

'What do you think I said? I told him to watch himself or he'd have me to answer to.'

'And what did he say?'

'He gave me the kind of look you'd expect. Which made me want to wring his neck. Then he said it was cool, she'd be OK. Which means nothing at all.' Flynn shook his head. 'Then Gigi jumped into the car and said she'd email me a photo of the spa.' With visible frustration he said, 'She also called me Mr Bennet.'

Lara did her best not to smile.

'It isn't funny.' Flynn's voice rose. 'He's booked one of the private pools.'

'Calm down. She'll be fine.'

'Are you mad? He's a rapper who gets everything he wants. I can't believe you're just letting this happen.' He followed her through to the kitchen. 'You should have told her she couldn't go.'

'Of course. Why didn't I think of that? Silly me,' said Lara.

'Are you really not bothered?'

'Flynn, she's eighteen. For one thing, I can't tell her not to go. For another thing, Gigi's my daughter and all I can do is trust her. She knows how I'd like her to behave. There's no point going on and on about it.'

'Even after what happened to you?'

OK, this was starting to get irritating now. Lara said, 'Especially after that. Because all my father ever did was lay down the law and threaten me, and look how well that worked out.'

'So now you let your daughter do whatever she wants.'

'Can we stop this now?' She held up her hands. 'You can double-check with the police if you like, but I'm fairly sure handcuffing children and locking them in a cupboard isn't actually legal.'

'I'm just saying you don't seem to be taking the situation seriously. This isn't some teenage boy we're talking about,' said Flynn. 'He's a grown man with a reputation.'

Pot. Kettle.

'If you're worried about him seducing her, don't,' said Lara. 'It won't happen.'

'You don't know that.'

'Gigi doesn't approve of people having sex on the first night. Says it's stupid and a waste of anticipation. She tells her friends off when they do it.'

'You can't be sure.'

'I know that too. And sometimes I don't want to know. But she's an adult and whatever she decides to do, you still can't stop her.' Lara checked her watch; it was six thirty and she was meeting up with Harry in an hour. 'Plus, I brought her up and I don't enjoy having my parenting skills criticised.'

'You don't say. I'd never have noticed.'

'Especially by people with far less experience than me.'

'Thanks to you,' Flynn pointed out. 'That was your decision, not mine.'

OK, blood pressure. Time to relax. Lara exhaled and said, 'Can we change the subject before we get into another argument?'

He was looking at her mouth, which wasn't helping. For a couple of seconds the only sound in the kitchen was that of a fly buzzing furiously as it flung itself against the glass, desperate to escape.

Flynn reached over, opened the window and let the fly out. Then he turned and said, 'What would you rather talk about?'

Had he been thinking about yesterday's Interrupted Kiss too? From the glint in his dark eyes it seemed like a distinct possibility. Lara swallowed; all the feelings were back in her stomach and now she couldn't stop looking at *his* mouth . . . right, that was it, just go for it . . .

'To be honest, I'm not that bothered about talking.' She closed the distance between them. 'There's something else I'd rather be doing. Any idea what that might be?'

A flicker of a smile. God, he just had one of those faces capable of melting you with a look. All kinds of havoc were going on inside her.

'I think I might have an inkling,' said Flynn and she was near enough to feel his warm breath on her cheek. OK, she was really going to do it now. Reaching up, Lara wound her arms around his neck and drew his mouth down to meet hers. He didn't object; she'd guessed he wouldn't. And here were all the magical sensations back again, those hopelessly addictive chemicals flooding her bloodstream. When it came to kissing, Flynn was in a class of his own . . . it was a kiss you could lose yourself in. Almost two decades on from the first ones they'd shared, this had stood the test of time.

And . . . finish, over, *done*. Lara ended the kiss and drew back. She smiled at him. 'God, you're good.'

'Not so bad yourself.' He broke into a slow smile of his own. 'So what happens now?'

'Nothing happens now. That was it.'

His breath audibly caught in his throat. 'Why?'

'Because we were interrupted yesterday. I hate it when something's interrupted and you don't get a chance to finish. You know, like when you just need to find out what the rest of it would have been like,' said Lara. 'The not-knowing just kills me. You must be the same.'

'And now I've satisfied your curiosity, is that what you're saying? This is as far as you want to go?'

'Yes it is.' She stood her ground.

'You know what?' Finn raised an eyebrow. 'I don't believe you.'

'Fine then, but it's as far as I'm going to go.' He was gazing at her intently and it was very off-putting. 'I told you before, nothing can happen that might make things awkward for Gigi. You and I have to stay on good terms, we can't hate each other.'

'I don't hate you. You don't hate me.'

'We don't now, because we're not together. That's why we're never going to start anything. As long as we aren't involved, we'll be OK.'

'And what you did just now.' Flynn waved his index finger between her chest and his own. 'That's not what you'd call starting anything?'

'It wasn't a start. It was a finish. We've done it now. And we're still friends.' Lara willed him to understand. 'For Gigi's sake it has to stay that way. We're not going to do anything to spoil it.'

'What, *never*?'

He really didn't understand. She shook her head. 'Never.'

'Not even if you were completely crazy about me?'

'I'm not completely crazy about you.'

'I know,' said Flynn. 'I'm just saying. Hypothetically. If you realised you'd fallen madly in love with me and I felt the same way about you, if we were in love with each other . . . would you change your mind then?'

'No. But that's the thing, it would never get to that stage. We aren't going to let it happen because there wouldn't be any point.'

'And there wouldn't be any point because . . . ?'

Lara said steadily, 'Because we both know there's never going to be any sex.'

'Right.' Pause. 'To be fair, I've only just found this out.' Apparently no longer sure what to do with his hands, Flynn stuck them in his trouser pockets.

'You haven't. I told you before.'

'I didn't realise you meant never. As in, *never ever*.'

'Oh. Well, I did. I wasn't just playing hard to get.' Lara shook her head impatiently; had he really thought that? 'If this whole co-parenting thing's going to work, it's the only way.'

'Right. And no way of changing your mind?'

'No!'

'Thought not.'

Lara relaxed; everything was going to be OK. 'Hey, cheer up. Want to hear the good news?'

Flynn exhaled. 'Go for it.'

'Like mother, like daughter. Once Gigi decides not to do something, she doesn't give in. That's how I know we don't have to worry about her tonight.'

'Hmm.'

'You should be pleased.'

'I'm pleased about that part of it.' His tone indicated that as far as the other aspect was concerned, not so much.

'Look, I'm right and you know I am. Anyway,' Lara glanced again at her watch, 'I'm meeting Harry and he hates it if I'm late. So I need to jump in the shower.' She led the way out to the hall and opened the front door. 'But thanks for everything.'

Flynn said drily, 'Don't mention it.'

Was she doing a good job? Lara thought she was. 'And no worrying about Gigi; she can look after herself.' Mischievously she added, 'Like I said, I taught her well.'

Chapter 30

'You're late,' said Harry when Lara arrived at the pub.

'Not by much though. Only ten minutes. Come here, Grumpy.' Lara gave him the monster hug she hadn't had the opportunity to bestow yesterday. 'I can't believe what's been happening to you. It's the weirdest thing ever.'

'Tell me about it.' Harry smiled his deprecating, lopsided smile. 'I'm spending a fortnight with someone whose music makes my ears bleed. Half the time I need subtitles to understand what he's saying. He's like a spoiled child who always has to get his own way and when he takes his socks off he throws them "in the trash" because he never wears the same pair twice.'

'Wow. Are they cheap socks?'

'What do you think? Cashmere.'

'But you're having an adventure. It's brilliant.' Last night at the house Enjay had been the centre of attention; it was nice to have the opportunity to talk properly now. 'And how's it going with Moira? She didn't mind you doing this?' Moira, who ran a health food shop in Keswick, was Harry's girlfriend, although you wouldn't call it the romance of the year. Moira was an earnest character with unfortunate ears and a tendency to bang on about healthy eating. For someone so obsessed with wholegrains, mineral supplements and leafy green vegetables, it was ironic that she looked as if she'd spent the last decade living underground.

'We decided to call it a day.' Harry didn't sound bothered. 'It wasn't working out. To be honest, it's a relief not to have to swallow all those horse pills any more.'

'So you aren't sad?'

'I'm not sad.'

'That's good then. She was a bit scary sometimes.' Lara had done her best to be friendly, but when she'd once eaten three chocolate digestives on the trot, Moira had fixed her with a beady, mascara-free gaze and said, 'If you clog your arteries up, you're just going to have a heart attack and die.'

Which was always nice to hear.

'She could be a bit intense.' Harry was a gentleman who would never say anything mean about a girlfriend. 'Anyway, not a problem now. And how's it going with Flynn?'

'Brilliant. You saw Gigi last night,' said Lara. 'She loves him.'

'How about you?'

'I don't love him. And I'm not going to love him. Because that would make things too complicated for words.'

Harry said, 'I saw the way he was looking at you. When he wasn't busy glaring at Enjay.'

OK, if even Harry had noticed, it had to be blindingly obvious.

'I'm being mature and sensible.' Lara employed her best mature-and-sensible face.

He nodded sympathetically. 'Good for you. Hard work?'

'Killing me.' Harry was the one person she could admit it to. 'But I'm going to stick with it.'

'You'll be fine.'

'Flynn's worried about Enjay trying it on with Gigi tonight.'

'Well, he will. He can't help himself, he tries it on with practically every female who crosses his path. But she can say no. I did have a few words with him myself.' Harry grimaced. 'But it's like trying to tell a wasp to keep away from the jam.'

'She'll be OK. Anyway,' said Lara, 'how's Nettie? She always tells me everything's fine when we're on the phone, but I hope she's not lonely. Do you think she misses us?'

'I saw her at the market last week and she was on top form. And there's been a bit of gossip going around,' said Harry. 'Betty told me about it. Apparently Nettie's been spending some time with Fred Milton.'

'Fred? She kept quiet about that! I told her she should get together with Fred and she pretended not to be interested! You know what?' Lara spread her arms. 'I'm brilliant. I should be one of those professional fixer-uppers. That's so good to hear, though. Such a relief. I was worried she might be miserable on her own.'

'I asked her if she was missing you,' said Harry. 'She thought that was hilarious and said she was having the time of her life. *Ow*, what was that for?'

'Because you're not being very diplomatic. I'm glad Nettie's happy,' said Lara, 'but it would be nice if you could pretend she's missing us a little bit at least.'

'You know something? You're quite a girl. I had fun tonight.'

The words, spoken in that intimate American drawl, were designed to seduce. Gigi knew it and he knew it too. The weird thing was, she was going to laugh at him and turn him down, but secretly it felt really nice. Enjay had the knack of concentrating all his attention on you and making you feel . . . special. She'd enjoyed herself this evening. Floating in the steaming spa baths on the roof overlooking the city had been an amazing experience, doing it in the company of EnjaySeven even more so. He'd been funny and charming, and the sight of him in his board shorts had been . . . well, spectacular, basically. Enjay had the kind of toned, muscular body you could just gaze and gaze at.

Not that she had, of course. She'd called him flabby and done handstands in the water and sung country and western songs deliberately off-key to make him wince.

'I had fun too.' Gigi began to sing in a quavering Tammy Wynette-style voice, 'Oh mah kids all have nits an' mah bikini's cheap, Next man Ah marry, Ah'll look 'fore Ah *leeeeeap. . .*'

'You're crazy. Cute but crazy.'

'Don't forget intelligent,' said Gigi.

They were standing on the pavement beside the Maybach. Enjay reached out and touched her cheek. 'D'you know what I hate about me?'

'Tell me.' His fingers were cool. She loved the way his skin gleamed in the dim light from the street lamp. And how were his teeth so white? Even Simon Cowell's teeth weren't as white as that.

'I have principles,' Enjay murmured. 'I'm a man of my word. I want to kiss you, but I promised your father I'd treat you with respect.' He exhaled regretfully. 'Man, I wish I hadn't now.'

'He's just being protective.' Gigi smiled; she'd teased Flynn about it earlier, but having him there defending her had actually felt fantastic.

'And Harry gave me a hard time about it too. Well, in his own way.'

Oh bless him. She loved Harry and his morals and his gentle manner; he would have said it so politely as well.

'What makes you think I'd want to kiss you anyway? I'm eighteen. You're twenty-eight. That's ancient.'

225

'Hey, girl.' The white teeth flashed. 'I'm EnjaySeven. All the girls want me.'

'But doesn't that feel kind of horrible? That means they don't care what you're really like, deep down. They'll chase after you anyway just because you're famous.'

Enjay shrugged. 'And why would that bother me?'

He was like Joey in *Friends*. He *had* no deep-down. As long as he was being chased by girls, Gigi realised, that was all that mattered. Their personalities were irrelevant.

'Well, I don't want you.'

'You're just saying that.'

'Because it's the truth,' Gigi said patiently. 'It's interesting talking to you because I've never met anyone like you before. But you're so old. All the boys I've kissed have been teenagers. It'd be like if you had to kiss a woman ten years older than you—'

'Evening!'

'Oh hi.' It was their neighbour, Jacqueline Cumiskey, pulling up in her lime-green Fiesta after a night out and greeting Gigi with a cheery wave through the driver's open window. Jacqueline's dark eyes widened as she saw Enjay and realised who he was.

'You mean like her?' Enjay murmured under his breath. 'I could kiss her right now. And I bet she wouldn't object.'

'She might,' said Gigi. 'She has a fiancé. Anyway, don't even think about it. You have to go back to the hotel.' Just to make sure, she pushed him into the car before he could race over to Jacqueline and give her the shock of her life. 'I need to be up early tomorrow. Night.'

Enjay winked at her as the ever-discreet Maz restarted the engine. 'OK, bossy girl. But can I just say something?' Reaching for her hand and raising it to his lips – the contact sent a tingle up her arm – he said, 'I bet you dream about me tonight.'

'Goodness. He's a bit flirty,' said Jacqueline when the Maybach had disappeared down the street.

'He is.'

'Sounds quite confident.'

'Or you could call it full of himself.'

'So what's he doing here, then? How do you know him?'

'He's just a friend of a friend,' said Gigi.

Jacqueline raked her scarlet manicured nails through her hair. 'He's very attractive.'

Oh crikey, had she overheard Enjay's comments? *This was what it was like to be him*. Gigi said, 'I think you're probably safer with the one you've already got.'

Chapter 31

Sometimes working in a jewellers broke your heart. Either in a good way or a bad way. Yesterday a young engaged couple had spent over an hour choosing a bracelet for the girl's mother; money was tight but they wanted to find her the perfect thank-you gift in return for all her help arranging their upcoming wedding. Torn between two, the couple had finally chosen the more expensive bracelet and decided to carry on cycling into work rather than buy a car. The boy said, 'She's worth it though. She's the best mother-in-law anyone could wish for.' Then his fiancée had confided in Don and Lara that her mum had had a riding accident ten years ago and was now confined to a wheel-chair. Lara had had to work hard to swallow the lump in her throat as, hand in hand, they left the shop.

And then there was the other kind of heartbreak, the kind that made her feel like a priest hearing confession from someone she wasn't allowed to punish.

'So you can do that, can you?' The man was in his late forties, red-faced and full of bluster. The diamond ring he'd brought in was an almost flawless four-carat solitaire.

'You want us to remove the diamond and replace it with

cubic zirconium.' Even if he hadn't looked like a pig in a too-tight suit, Lara knew she wouldn't have liked him. His temples were shiny with sweat, and his manner shifty beneath the brusque exterior. 'We'd need proof, I'm afraid, that this ring belongs to you.'

'It's an heirloom from my side of the family, so I don't have a receipt for it. My wife's worn it for the last twenty years. But Mr Temple's seen it before.' The man indicated Don, out in the back room. 'She brought it in here to get it resized not long ago.'

Don came through, examined the ring and nodded. 'Yes, yes. Mrs Barrowman, I remember. It's a beautiful ring.'

'I want you to sell the diamond for me. How much d'you reckon it'll fetch?'

'Thirty-five, possibly forty thousand,' said Don.

'Fine, do it.' The man pulled out a handkerchief and blotted his damp face. 'Quick as you like. And my wife doesn't need to know about any of this, you understand. I told her the stone was loose so she thinks you're replacing the claws.'

'But—'

'She'll get her ring back and she won't know any difference.'

'If that's what you want,' said Don, and the man's jaw tightened.

'If I didn't want it I wouldn't be here, would I? Just sort it out. I'll give you my bank details so you can transfer the money into my account as soon as it's done.'

'These things happen in this business,' said Don when the man had left. 'You know that.'

'But his poor wife. It's such a horrible thing to do to her.'

'It might not be. He might hate the fact that he's having to do it. She could have cancer and it's the only way he can raise the money for her treatment.'

Which would be preferable – to have cancer and a loving

husband prepared to do anything he could to help? Or no cancer and a husband who was a complete bastard?

'You're such an optimist,' said Lara.

'Or their son's in terrible trouble and he can't bear for his wife to find out, the shock would kill her, but this way maybe they can sort it out and she'll never need to know.'

'OK, optimism's one thing. Now you're deluded.'

'You mustn't automatically think the worst of a person.' Don pointed out of the window. 'For instance, some people might look at that fellow across the street there and assume he was some kind of drug-dealing gangster, but I'd like to think he's worked hard for that fancy car of his.'

Over the road, a skinny, pasty-skinned, tattooed man in jeans and a T-shirt was climbing out of a red Lamborghini parked on double yellows.

Lara said, 'He has a face for *Crimewatch*. Look at that scar on his cheek.'

As they watched, the man dived into the greengrocers, emerging thirty seconds later with a cauliflower and a bag of leeks.

'See? He's just normal.' Don nodded, satisfied with his judgement.

'Even drugs barons need their five a day,' said Lara as the Lamborghini roared back to life and went screeching off up the road, scattering tourists in its wake.

'Appearances can be deceptive.' The next moment Don paled visibly and gasped, 'Oh dear God, they've got guns, don't let them in, press the panic button . . . PRESS IT . . .'

The light through the glass door had been temporarily blocked out by the twin man-mountains that were Maz and AJ peering in. Maz was clutching something long and narrow, rolled up in a plastic bag. Behind him, waiting for the shop to be declared safe to enter, Enjay was wearing a beanie hat and mirrored shades.

'It's OK, don't worry, it's Enjay and his minders.' Lara hurriedly pulled out a chair and helped Don on to it before he could collapse in a grey heap on the floor. So much for first impressions. She buzzed the door open and they pushed their way in.

'Hi, this is Don. You frightened the living daylights out of him.'

'Oh sorry. Did you think we was gonna rob you?' Maz saw them looking at the wrapped-up shotgun clasped in his enormous hand and said apologetically, 'My momma always tells me off for lookin' scary. Don' worry, it ain't a gun.' He unwrapped the package to show them. 'Weather forecast was sayin' it might rain later so Enjay wanted to buy an umbrella. He don' like his hair gettin' all wet.'

'Doesn't he? Me neither. Nightmare!' Fanning himself and recovering from the shock, Don said slightly hysterically, 'Nightmare on York Street! Sorry, still a bit out of breath, I have a heart condition. Seeing all of you out there put the willies right up me!'

'*What?*' The camp manner and unfortunate choice of words caused Enjay to freeze.

'It's a British saying, means scaring someone.' Lara broke the stunned silence. 'Anyway, lovely to see you. Where's Harry?'

'Just picking something up in Beaches. He'll be along in a minute. OK if we film in here?' Enjay indicated the camcorder AJ was taking out of its case. 'We thought it would make a good piece for the show.'

'Oh, now that *does* sound like fun!' Don instantly perked up. 'Lara was telling me all about this TV series of yours.'

Lara said, 'Here's Harry now,' and buzzed open the door.

'Hello. Sure you're all right with this?' Harry greeted her with

231

a polite kiss on the cheek before turning to Don and holding out his arm for a handshake.

'Hello, good to meet you, I'm Harry. I see we're going to be filming.' As he said it, the camcorder began to whir. 'I know it's all a bit of a faff but we won't bother you for too long, I promise. Enjay wants an earring, that's all. As soon as he's got it we'll be out of your hair.'

'A bit of a *faff*,' Enjay repeated in the background, mimicking his *über*-British accent.

'I don't mind at all.' Don looked slightly taken aback. '*An* earring, you say?'

Harry shook his head. 'I know, can you believe it? And he's a grown man too. I've told him it's utterly ridiculous but what can you do? This is what he's like.'

'Hey, man, earrings are cool. Oh Jesus, what have you been buying? What is *this* place?' Whisking the lightweight carrier bag from Harry's grasp, Enjay peered at the lettering on the side. 'BHS?'

'I told you that was where I was going. You just don't pay attention, that's your trouble. You're like a three-year-old,' said Harry.

'Bee-aiche-ess. I figured it was your upper-class way of saying Beaches. I thought it must be some fancy designer store I hadn't heard of.'

'It is,' Harry objected. 'They're incredibly good value.'

'Trust me, Harry, this bag ain't from no designer store. Oh my, and look what you picked up for yourself.' Enjay had pulled the cellophane packets of underpants out of the carrier bag and was now gazing at them in utter bafflement. 'Are you serious?'

'There were holes in my old ones. I needed some new pairs. These are comfortable and they fit well. Plus they're very cheap.'

'You're telling me.' Enjay was now waving them in front of the camera. 'Look, look at them!'

'They're underpants,' Harry said patiently. 'They don't have to have the wow factor. No one's going to see them.' His gaze dropped to the waistband of the Calvin Kleins visible above Enjay's perilously low-slung jeans. 'Unlike you, I prefer not to parade my underwear to the nation.'

'I'm sure the nation will be very happy to hear that,' Enjay retaliated with a mock brow-wipe of relief.

This was the double act they had formed, ridiculing each other's differences without malice. Lara said, 'What kind of earring are you looking for?'

Enjay flashed his vampire-toothed grin. 'Hey, a diamond. Is there any other kind?'

'And size-wise?'

'The usual, I'd imagine.' Harry rolled his eyes. 'Easy to spot from outer space.'

Enjay said, 'If you're gonna have a diamond, have a big one. Right, Maz?'

Maz nodded in agreement; it was part of his job description. 'Right, boss.'

Chapter 32

'Show me what you got,' Enjay instructed Lara.

'Well, for a start, we only sell earrings in pairs. So if you want a single one we'll need to have it made.'

'No, no, no.' Being made to wait for anything was clearly out of the question, it simply didn't feature in a superstar's world. 'I want it straight away.'

'Then you'll have to go to another jewellers.' Next to her, Don let out a whimper of anxiety. Lara continued smoothly, 'But what our customers usually do is buy the pair, then they have a spare if they ever need it.'

'Why would I want a spare?'

'OK, or you could give the other one to a friend as a present.'

Aware of the camcorder trained on him, Enjay broke into a slow smile and turned to Harry. 'Now that's a cool idea. How about it, man?'

Harry looked as if he'd swallowed a wasp. 'Oh please, don't even think it. Earrings are for girls.'

'Hey, man, I wear an earring and I ain't no girl. Come on,' he wheedled, 'you might like it.'

'I'm not having my ear pierced. Ever,' Harry said with an emphatic shudder of revulsion.

'Not even if it gives you an air of glamour?'

'I think you'll find it would give me an air of idiocy. But it's AJ's birthday next week. Maybe he'd like an earring.'

Maz took over the camcorder and trained it on AJ, whose face had lit up. Despite Enjay calling him bro, Lara had only realised last night that the two of them were actually brothers.

'Hey, bro, you want an earring?'

'Yeah, man.' Seven inches taller, ninety pounds heavier and five years younger, AJ was a gentle giant with an engaging growly teddy-bear voice and a slight lisp.

'Perfect. Right.' Lara unlocked the case with a flourish. 'Let's show you what we have!'

'And crystal?'

'Sorry?' *Crystal? What, the Austrian kind?* Lara hesitated; was Enjay saying he didn't want actual diamonds after all?

'Or another kind if you don't have crystal.'

OK, awkward moment, especially as AJ was now looking forward to his birthday present . . .

'Got it,' Harry said suddenly. 'He means champagne.'

Cristal . . .

'Of course I mean champagne, man.' Mystified, Enjay said, 'What else would I be talking about? I always get offered a drink when I'm buying watches and jewellery.'

'I bet you do.' Lara envisaged the sales assistants in the stores on Rodeo Drive employing every trick in the book to part the super-rich from their millions. 'But we don't do that here.'

'Why not?'

'Because it's like cheating. We prefer to sell to customers

when they have a clear head. You could have a cup of tea if you like.'

'Oh, *super* idea.' Harry brightened. 'I'd love a cup of tea.'

'Me too,' said Maz.

'I'll pop the kettle on.' Don jumped up, eager to please. 'Sugar, boys, or are you sweet enough?'

Enjay raised a *he's-a-homosexual* eyebrow at Lara.

Maz the man-mountain said in his growly lisp, 'I'll have two Hermesetas please.'

The tea was made, the various earrings were examined, and Don, by this time thoroughly excited by his new celebrity client, came over all Shirley Bassey and launched into an enthusiastic chorus of 'Diamonds Are Forever'.

'Welcome to England,' said Enjay, directly to camera. 'And we thought people in California were weird. Let me tell you, they have nothing on the crazy folks over here.' He flashed a grin and adopted his Harry voice. 'This lot take the absolute biscuit.'

The brothers finally settled on a pair of brilliant cut studs totalling seven point four carats. Any larger, Lara explained, and the weight of the stone would pull the earring down at an angle; it might also stretch the lobe.

Plus, they didn't have any bigger earrings in stock.

Enjay paid the eye-watering amount with his Platinum Amex, only flinching when Don clasped his hand and gushed that it had been *heavenly* to meet him.

'Once you realised we weren't badass robbers, come to blast open the safe and clean out your store,' he drawled.

Don's spiky hair quivered. 'Sorry about that. And you've been so charming. I'm going to rush out and buy all your records, you know. And I'll be telling everyone how wonderful you are.' He stopped abruptly as Lara elbowed him in the side. 'Right, sorry. Let me wrap these for you.'

'No need, we'll wear 'em now.' Looking relieved to have his hand back, Enjay surreptitiously wiped the palm on the side of his jeans. He turned to Lara. 'So, did your daughter enjoy the spa baths with me last night? Did she tell you she had a good time?'

'She did. She also said you're too old for her.'

Enjay raised an eyebrow and he leaned across the counter towards her. 'Has it occurred to you that she might be too young for me? Maybe I prefer the older lady.'

Erk, was this a come-on? Lara said, 'You want to try the tea rooms over by the abbey. Plenty of old ladies for you there.'

The wicked, wolfish, all-conquering smile was back. 'Hey, you know perfectly well what I'm saying.' Moving closer, he murmured in her ear, 'What are you, thirty-five? If you ask me, that's just about perfect.'

This was a man with way too many hormones for his own good. He was unstoppable. 'You're not my type,' said Lara.

'Ah, she says that now.' Enjay straightened up and addressed his audience. 'But wait until later when the cameras are off. We all know what's going to happen.'

Maz had the camcorder trained on them. Lara gave him a good-natured eye-roll and said, 'Good luck with trying,' guessing as she did so that it would be edited out of the exchange. This was Enjay's show, he revelled in his reputation as a Lothario, rejections would be few and far between and he certainly wouldn't publicise them.

Harry was reading her mind. 'Just ignore him, he's like it with everyone.'

'I know.'

'Excuse me.' Enjay jerked his head in the direction of Don,

who was fussily polishing away the fingermarks on the glass-topped cabinet. 'Not *everyone*.'

Oblivious, Don launched back into, 'Diamonds are foreverrrrrrr . . .'

'Hey, AJ, call the club and make sure we got the VIP room.' With his new diamond earring installed and the mirrored shades back in place, Enjay was once again admiring his reflection in the mirror. 'Oh, man, I am in the mood for some serious action tonight.'

He'd already announced they were heading up to London to check out the newest, coolest nightclub. Lara looked at Harry and said, 'If he's doing that, d'you want to come over for something to eat? We could have a game of Scrabble.' She wasn't so wild about it herself but Harry loved Scrabble and so did Evie.

'Thanks, but I have to go with this crew. Enjay thinks it'll be just hilarious to film me in a nightclub.'

'Hey, man, I don't think. I *know*.'

'He also thinks I'm going to dance.' Harry suppressed a shudder. 'He couldn't be more wrong.'

Enjay said, 'I'll pay you extra to dance.'

'There isn't enough money in the world,' said Harry. 'I'm going to be taking a book along with me to pass the time.'

As they left the shop, Don shook everyone's hand again and Lara observed Enjay's discomfort. Following them out on to the pavement, she took him to one side and murmured, 'I saw that. If Don noticed, he'd find it quite hurtful.'

Unused to criticism, Enjay stiffened. 'I know, but I can't help it. Creeps me out, man.'

'I can see that. And please don't call me man.'

He raised his shades and fixed her with a playful gaze. 'Sorry. Lah-rah.'

His attempt at mimicking the British accent was as over-the-top as ever. Lara said, 'I'll tell you something else. You think Don's gay. But he isn't.'

'Don't give me that.'

'It's the truth. He told me.'

'He's lying.' Enjay was visibly losing interest in the conversation. The next moment, without warning, he snaked an arm around her shoulder and kissed her full on the mouth. Out on the pavement, for heaven's sake, where everyone could see them.

Lara pulled away and shook her head. 'You're a nightmare.'

'Just a bit of fun, babe. Doing my bit to brighten your day.'

'Those earrings we just sold you? Thanks to them, my day's already bright enough. And Don *isn't* gay.' She needed him to know. 'I thought he was too, but he's really not.'

Enjay's lip curled. 'Fine, if you say so. But he still creeps me out.'

Chapter 33

Twenty-four hours later, they pulled up in the Maybach outside Grey and Erskine, Wine Merchants. Harry said, 'Listen, don't flirt with Gigi, OK? You'll just annoy Flynn.'

'Oh my, I'm so scared.' Enjay was entertained. 'Trust you to worry about that, Harry.'

'It's just a matter of common decency, being polite. He's her father.' Sometimes dealing with Enjay was like having to steer a wayward toddler across a busy road; he knew no fear and was infinitely distractable.

'Hey, it's all cool. How do I look?' Enjay admired himself in the car window, preening and checking that the collar of his white Flying Ducks shirt was just so.

'Extremely vain. No change there. I'm just saying you should behave yourself,' said Harry. 'It's basic good manners, that's all.'

He breathed in as Maz and AJ followed them into the main building. The air was heavy with the aromas of wood and wine. Bottles were stacked in crates and in boxed shelving lining the roughened whitewashed stone walls.

'Cool.' Enjay checked that Maz had started recording then raised a languid hand, superstar style, as Gigi and the customer she was dealing with looked up and saw them. 'Hey, baby, I need a beautiful assistant to . . . assist me.'

A door opened and Flynn made his way across the shop floor. 'Hi there. Can I help?'

'Thanks, but I'll wait for the beautiful assistant.'

The air crackled with tension and Harry realised Enjay had never had any intention of behaving himself. This was two alpha males vying for the upper hand. Harry, who couldn't imagine anything more alarming than being an alpha male, said pointedly, 'If you're here to buy wine, Flynn's the one who knows about it. He's the expert.'

'I don't want wine,' said Enjay. 'I don't drink wine. Only champagne.'

Harry cleared his throat. 'Shall we order some then?'

'Hang on, she'll be free in a minute. We can take a look around while we're waiting. I've never been to a British wine merchant's before. Kinda nice.'

The elderly customer was soon dealt with and despatched. Gigi came over and said, 'How did it go last night in London?'

'Ha. Harry loved it.'

'I did not. It was pure torture. I wore earplugs,' said Harry.

'He did. Any time anyone tried to say anything to him he'd go, "I'm frightfully sorry, I'm afraid I can't hear you, I'm wearing earplugs."'

'Did you dance?' asked Gigi.

'No.' Enjay was shaking his head. 'He sat there drinking tomato juice and reading a book about Roman Britain.'

Gigi said, 'That sounds like Harry. How about you, then? Did you have fun?'

'Hey, I always have fun.' Enjay winked. 'And I wasn't spending my time reading about the Romans, I can tell you.'

241

Harry shrugged, unoffended. It didn't bother him in the least what other people chose to get up to in their spare time. When they'd left the club last night Enjay had been accompanied by two lithe girls wearing barely more than bra tops, the tiniest of skirts and heels so high it was a miracle they could remain upright. All the way back to the hotel they'd entwined themselves like snakes around him. And this, according to AJ and Maz, was par for the course. Enjay's chosen form of entertainment was sex, pure and simple, with no question of any emotional involvement. In the morning he would send the girls off and never spare them a second thought. As far as Harry was concerned, it was a miserable, soulless way to pass the time. Personally he'd far rather read a book.

'So is there any danger of you spending some money with us,' said Gigi, 'or are you just here for fun?'

'I'm here to spend a lot,' Enjay announced. 'On Cristal. How much ya got here?'

'None at all,' said Flynn.

Enjay looked appalled. 'Oh, man, are you *serious*? What's wrong with you guys?'

'Ignore him.' Harry shook his head. 'He's obsessed with designer labels. It's a form of insecurity.'

'Hey, cut it out!' said Enjay.

'OK, come over here.' Flynn led the way across the shop to the floor-to-ceiling glass-fronted fridges. He selected a bottle from the second shelf, deftly removed the foil and the wire, then expertly turned the bottle to remove the cork with a delicate *pft*. Gigi lined up a row of slender glasses along the wooden counter.

'There you go.' Having poured a scant inch into the bottom of each glass, Flynn handed the first one to Enjay.

'Hey, I want more than that, man.'

'You see?' Harry shook his head in disappointment. 'This is *precisely* what marks you out as a philistine.'

'Smell it first. No, like this.' Flynn showed them how. 'Stick your nose right in and breathe in deeply. Cristal's a fantastic cuvée but I truly believe this one's better. Right, now have the first taste and tell me what you're getting. Try to separate out the different elements . . .'

Having got to know him over the course of the last couple of weeks, Harry had discovered that beneath the brashly shallow exterior, Enjay liked to learn about new things. Despite making fun of Harry for reading books, he had actually borrowed and enjoyed his copy of Khaled Hosseini's latest. Yesterday he had been taught by Don about the clarity and cut of various diamonds. And now he was listening intently as Flynn described the qualities of different grapes and growing conditions, production methods and vintages. Far more intelligent than he let on, Enjay preferred to keep this aspect of his character hidden.

At this rate he'd soon be giving Stephen Fry a run for his money in the cleverclogs stakes.

And thirty minutes later the order had been placed. As well as the champagne, Flynn had persuaded Enjay to select a variety of high-quality wines from New Zealand, Italy and France. Pinot Gris, Sauvignon Blanc and burgundy all featured, along with a case of Pinot Meunier demi-sec champagne from a new producer destined for great things.

'So when are you going to be drinking all this?' said Gigi as the crates were stacked up. She looked disappointed. 'Back in London, I suppose.'

'Not so, baby.' Enjay playfully looped a stray strand of hair away from her face. 'In fact I'm hosting a party at the Ellison tomorrow night. My way of saying thank you.'

Harry said, 'It's actually his way of saying sorry for the living hell he's been putting the staff and guests through.'

'Hey, man, it ain't no living hell.'

'You've been a nightmare. Playing that hideous music. Singing at all hours. Spending half the night in the swimming pool. There are little old ladies', Harry went on, 'flattening themselves against the walls every time they see you.'

'And tomorrow I'm inviting them to my party,' said Enjay, 'where I shall charm the pants off them.' He paused. 'Not literally. That would be revolting.'

Maz put down the camcorder and said, 'Want me to carry these out to the car, boss?'

'Yeah, do that.' Enjay knocked back the last of the Chablis in his glass and nodded at Gigi to refill it. 'I may like the older ladies,' he added, 'but not that old.'

Then he grinned and glanced at Flynn and in a flash Harry guessed what he was about to say next. Leaping into the breach, he blurted out, 'So he's throwing this party to make up for all the misery, and then he'll blast them with *more* of that dreadful music . . .'

'Are we invited too?' Gigi had never been backwards at coming forwards.

'Sure, come along, the more the merrier.' Now resting his arm across her shoulders, Enjay drawled, 'Bring your mom too.'

Harry winced; was he doing it deliberately?

No question. Of course he was.

'Hey,' Enjay gave Gigi a friendly squeeze, 'did she tell you about what happened yesterday?'

'She did. You went into the shop and bought diamond earrings for, like, ten million pounds or something.'

'I meant after that.' Enjay winked at AJ and behind him Flynn stiffened.

'She didn't say.' Gigi's eyes were widening. 'What happened?'

'Oh, nothing major. Bit of kissing, that's all. But pretty nice.'

'No!' Gigi let out a squeal. 'I don't believe it!'

Enjay shrugged. 'It's all on camera. Or you can ask Harry. He was there.'

Oh great, drag me into it.

'Right, sorry, could you take your hands off my daughter?' Flynn reached out and for a moment looked as if he was about to forcibly remove Enjay's arm from Gigi's shoulder. He stopped short of physical contact but gazed levelly at him. 'Thank you.'

Enjay waited a couple of seconds then let go of her. 'Just being friendly, man. Not doing anything wrong.'

'Maybe not. But I'd be grateful if you didn't do it anyway.'

'My my.' Enjay half-smiled. 'Something's bothering you. And to think I just spent a fortune in this store of yours.'

'I can cancel that. Feel free to take your custom elsewhere.' Flynn stood his ground.

'Dad!'

'You must think you're pretty special,' Enjay continued silkily, 'if you're talking like this while my crew's here.'

Flynn's jaw tightened. 'You must think you're pretty useless if you'd stand back and let them fight your battles for you.'

Shit, thought Harry who never swore, not even inside his own head. Oh good grief, and now man–mountain Maz was lumbering back into the shop in search of the next case, and AJ was clenching his oversized knuckles . . .

'Hey, no problem. It's cool.' Enjay raised his hands and stepped away from Gigi. 'She's your daughter and I respect that. You can trust me, man. I give you my word.'

Harry waited. Everyone did. Finally Flynn exhaled and visibly relaxed.

245

'OK.'

'See?' Enjay winked at Gigi. 'Your daddy's still lookin' out for you. That's a good thing. Shows he cares.'

'Shows he's bossy, more like.' Gigi was torn between pride and teenage embarrassment.

'No hard feelings, man. Come along to the party tomorrow night. Right, we need to head off now. Three houses to look at and the realtor's waiting for us.'

'Realtor?' Gigi's eyes were bright. 'You mean estate agent? Oh wow, are you buying somewhere in Bath?'

'You never know. If the right place comes up.' Enjay signalled a genial goodbye to the two of them as the group made their way out of the shop. 'See ya, guys.'

'See you tomorrow,' Gigi said eagerly.

Harry waited until they were all ensconced in the car. Then he shook his head at Enjay. 'I thought he was going to hit you.'

'Honestly?' Enjay sat back and sprang open the ringpull on a chilled can of Coke. 'For a moment back there, so did I.'

'And you aren't looking to buy a property in Bath.' The viewings had been arranged purely in order to provide more material for the show; as the producer had explained, TV audiences like nothing better than to see footage of amazing homes they could never afford to live in themselves.

'Never say never.' Enjay ramped up the volume of the music. 'This is life, man. Anything can happen.'

'Codswallop,' said Harry. 'You only said it to wind up Flynn.'

The word codswallop amused Enjay no end. 'I like winding people up. It entertains me.'

'For goodness sake, *why*?'

Enjay raised his mirrored shades and regarded him with affection.

'Oh, Harry, don't tell me you ain't noticed. That guy made out he was bothered about me and Gigi, but it wasn't her at all. What really made him mad was when I mentioned the thing with Lara.'

Chapter 34

When Lara arrived home from work on Friday, there was a picnic hamper sitting on the doorstep. Lifting the lid – it was a beautiful wicker hamper and her stomach was rumbling – she folded back the white cloth to reveal amazing picnic food, asparagus quiche, assorted tiny sandwiches, chilled wine, mushroom frittata, mini Scotch eggs and individual pots of hulled strawberries with clotted cream.

It was like the best present ever. And really, *so* many sandwiches . . . chicken and bacon, rare roast beef, smoked salmon and cream cheese . . . surely one or two would never be missed?

OK, three. Skilfully peeling back the cellophane, Lara helped herself to one of each kind then covered the rest up again. She glanced longingly at the mini Scotch eggs but exercised iron control. Mustn't be greedy. Unless the hamper was a present for her, in which case she could go crazy.

The next moment she heard a male voice inside the house and hurriedly closed the wicker lid. Then the door was pulled open and she came face to face with Joel, looking more than ever like a fallen blond angel.

'Oh, it's you. Do me a favour and tell Evie to sort herself out.'

He looked upset and resentful, and was wearing a cream linen jacket and jeans. 'One day she might change her mind and discover she's left it too late.' As he said it, he picked up the hamper and marched off down the drive.

Lara grabbed the door before it swung shut and let herself into the house. Evie was pacing the living room like an ex-smoker desperate for a cigarette.

'Let me guess. He wanted to take you out for a romantic picnic, and you said no.'

Evie heaved a sigh. 'This isn't as easy as I thought it was going to be. I'm all up in the air. I think I'm sorted, then Joel comes along and it's like he puts my heart in a blender.'

'Are you hungry?'

'No.' Evie abruptly stopped pacing. 'Actually, yes, I am.'

'Damn, I should have stolen more.' Lara took the hand out from behind her back and said, 'They were calling out to me from inside the hamper. You have them.'

'We'll share. Thanks.' Evie took a bite of the chicken sandwich, chewed and swallowed. 'That's really nice.' She looked miserable. 'Oh God, why do I feel so crap?'

'Tell me what he said to you.'

'He said I think someone better's going to come along, but who knows if that will happen? What if it doesn't? Maybe I'll regret being like this and wish I hadn't been so stubborn because I could end up with some complete no-hoper like the guy he saw me with outside Brown's.'

'Well, that's rubbish, because you said Ethan was nice. You got on well together.' Lara was indignant. 'You liked him. Just because he's not as *pretty* as Joel, what does that matter? Honestly, what a bloody cheek.'

Evie flung herself down on the sofa and covered her face. 'OK, this is what makes it worse. I didn't say it before, but I more than liked Ethan. I wasn't expecting it, but I ended up *really* liking him. We had such a good time. It gave me confidence, you know? I didn't feel like such a failure. And I thought he'd be in touch. I really expected him to call.' She slid her hands away and shook her head in defeat. 'But guess what? He didn't. I've waited and waited all week and it hasn't happened, so now I feel like a complete failure, a hundred times worse, and maybe Joel's right, I can't expect to end up with anyone at all.'

'Oh, don't say that. You *will*. Men are just stupid sometimes.' Lara tore the final sandwich in half and said, 'Just keep telling yourself it's not you, it's them.'

'OK.' Unconvinced, Evie said, 'Although right now it definitely feels like it's me.'

Evie's mobile burst into life thirty minutes later while Evie was upstairs. Seeing Joel's name on the screen, Lara impulsively answered it.

'OK, before you say anything, this isn't Evie. She's in the shower. And you telling her she's never going to meet someone else as good as you isn't fair,' she told Joel. 'You can't browbeat her into taking you back. You need to leave her alone.'

'But I love her.' Joel sounded as desperate as Evie.

'You cheated on her!'

'Anyway, that's not why I'm calling. I just tried to return the hamper to the deli and they wouldn't take it back. There were three sandwiches missing. I suppose that was you.'

'OK, two things,' said Lara. 'One, you left the hamper on the doorstep. When I got home there was a teenage boy running out of our drive. When I asked him what he was doing I couldn't make out a word he said because his mouth was full. And two, you can't take fresh food back to a shop because you don't want it any more. That's just wrong.'

'Yes, they said that too. I didn't know. Bloody hamper cost a fortune.' He sounded crestfallen. 'Anyway, sorry about accusing you.'

'That's all right. What are the sandwiches like?'

'Nice. I just tried one. To be honest, I've lost my appetite now.'

'Oh, that's a shame.' Lara was sympathetic. 'Aren't there any other girls you could get to go on a picnic with you?'

'No there aren't. And stop having a go at me,' said Joel.

'I'm not having a go. It's just that Evie's really hungry. And it seems like such a shame for all that lovely food to go to waste.'

The opportunity to get back into Evie's good books did the trick. Within minutes Joel had dropped off the hamper.

Well, waste not, want not.

'What's this?' Half an hour later, Gigi arrived home.

'Picnic.' Evie was devouring strawberries and cream.

'Indoor picnic.' Lara patted the space next to her on the tartan rug spread out on the living-room floor. 'This way we can watch *Coronation Street*.'

'And *EastEnders*,' said Evie.

'Without having to fight off all the wasps and mosquitoes.' Lara pointed to the last segment of out-of-this-world asparagus quiche. 'Try that, you won't believe it.'

'Not the only thing I didn't believe today.' Collapsing down beside her, Gigi said, 'Enjay told us what happened yesterday!'

Oh bum. Lara had really hoped he wouldn't.

'And now you're going all red,' Gigi crowed. 'So it did happen. Mu-um!'

Honestly. If she could be reincarnated with just one improvement, it would be the ability to remain calm and not blush. 'It wasn't me.'

'It *was* you. You kissed him.'

'He kissed me. For about half a second. And I didn't join in,' said Lara. 'He was just playing a game.'

'Yeah, I guessed. Ha, it was funny though. Dad wasn't pleased either.'

'No?' That caused a jumble of emotions to stir themselves up.

'I thought for a moment he was going to hit him.'

'What?'

'Oh, not over you. That was because Enjay had his arm around me.' Gigi took a greedy bite of Scotch egg. 'You know what he's like. Mum, these are fantastic!'

Honestly, Enjay made Jack Nicholson look shy and withdrawn. Lara said, 'Oh well, another week and he'll be gone.'

'That reminds me. He's throwing a party at the Ellison tomorrow night.'

'Why?'

'Just more camera fodder. Basically it's his way of apologising to all the other guests he's managed to annoy. We're invited too.' Gigi's gesture encompassed the three of them. 'He wants all of us there, to dilute the old crones.'

Ooh, opportunity. Lara looked across at Evie and said, 'We'll definitely go. You might see Ethan.'

Then her phone rang and she jumped, as she always seemed to be doing at the moment. What with still not having heard from James Agnew and waiting for the DNA results from the laboratory, she was turning into a nervous wreck.

But it was only Don, calling to ask her to open up the shop tomorrow morning because one of his crowns had come loose and he needed to visit the emergency dentist first thing.

Lara hung up, then called James Agnew's number again. No answer. If the foreign woman was still there she was no longer even bothering to pick up the phone.

Where was he?

Was he ever coming back?

Had he died?

Chapter 35

As they headed over to the Ellison on Saturday evening, Lara said, 'Look, I can't help it, I know I keep going on about this, but you know how sometimes you have a dream and it just makes so much sense? Seriously, it's like this one was an actual *sign*.'

'You do keep going on about it. Mum, give it a rest,' Gigi scolded. 'Poor Evie, she won't be able to look at him.'

'OK. Sorry.' Lara mimed zipping her mouth shut. It had been amazing, though; last night she'd dreamed that Harry and Evie were married! To each other! And they'd been completely perfect together, despite having to live in a stripy circus tent and do their washing-up in a paddling pool. But none of that had mattered, Harry had been relaxed and laughing, they'd held hands and barely been able to leave each other alone, and as she'd knelt on the grass outside their tent, washing the dishes in the blue plastic paddling pool, Evie had merrily announced, 'Thank goodness I didn't marry Joel.' Prompting Harry to add with genuine relief, 'Thank goodness I divorced Lara!'

Oh, and there'd been a baby dolphin leaping around in the washing-up water too. Read into *that* what you will.

The party was being held in the ballroom. Both Maz and AJ were filming as hotel guests, staff on their evening off and other invitees from heaven knows where milled about. Music was playing, but not the bleeding-ears kind that had caused all the complaints in the first place. Tonight it was Frank Sinatra all the way. Enjay, having scrubbed up like nobody's business, was wearing an immaculate bespoke grey three-piece suit, dazzlingly white high-collared shirt and brogues you could see your reflection in. He was also sporting diamond cufflinks, and an eye-boggling diamond-encrusted fob watch on a chain. As you do. He was currently wielding a microphone and singing 'New York' to a terrified-looking woman in her seventies clutching a champagne flute of orange juice.

'Poor thing,' Gigi murmured.

Lara said, 'He'll probably try to kiss her in a minute.'

'Here's Harry.' Evie gave her a nudge. 'Don't mention your dream.'

OK, she wouldn't. But it was intensely frustrating when you suddenly realised something brilliant and weren't allowed to make it happen. Couldn't Evie see she was right?

'Hello. Having fun?' Unlike dressed-to-the-nines Enjay, Harry was wearing a pair of chinos and a beige Flying Ducks shirt.

'Not yet. I want to know what really expensive champagne tastes like.' Lara waylaid a passing waitress and helped herself to a glass from the tray. 'Hmm.' She took a glug and concentrated hard. 'Tastes like cava.'

Harry said, 'That's because it is. The cheap stuff's in the glasses on the trays that are being taken around. The real deal's still in the bottles, being poured out for the important guests so they can see the labels and be suitably impressed. Put that down,' he instructed Lara, 'and we'll get you some of the fancy stuff.'

'Here, you can have this one.' Lara handed the glass to Gigi. 'Your taste buds won't know the difference.'

'Don't do that,' Harry warned as Enjay launched into the next song and Gigi waved to him across the room. 'If you're not careful he'll come and serenade you. Everyone's scared it's going to be them next.'

'If he sings at me,' said Lara, 'I'll join in. That'll make him stop.'

Despite the decided weirdness of the occasion, over the course of the next hour the various guests began to relax. Alcohol loosened their inhibitions, some people began to dance and a hatchet-faced old man who looked like a tax inspector took everyone by surprise when he joined Enjay onstage and sang like Dean Martin.

Once the Rat Pack medley was over, Evie watched as Enjay resumed chatting to the guests, working the room. It was an exercise in PR and the power of charisma. The scantily dressed girls in their twenties were doing their best to attract his attention but Enjay was concentrating his efforts on the difficult guests. And winning. Give it a bit longer and he'd have them up dancing to a bit of hip hop.

'Everything OK?' Harry came over to join her. Thank goodness he didn't know about their adventures last night inside Lara's head. Lara might have decided they'd make a great couple and Harry was lovely – in lots of ways he was exactly the kind of man she should go for – but at the moment all she could think about was Ethan.

Ethan who hadn't contacted her since their kind-of date a whole week and a half ago. Having expected to feel nothing, the connection they'd made had been startling. She'd really thought it was mutual too. Why hadn't he been in touch?

Anyway, never mind that now. Evie said, 'I'm fine. And it looks like everyone's enjoying themselves. How about you?'

'Well, I'm not going to be singing, that's for sure. But I may venture on to the dance floor at some stage.' Harry paused. 'In a sedate fashion, of course. Nothing too wild.'

Evie smiled; his brand of understated charm really was captivating. 'You wouldn't want to be wild.'

'I know, I'd only end up doing my back in.' Harry glanced at her. 'Although Lara did say I should ask you to dance. How does that sound? Not right now, of course. But maybe later?'

He was only asking her because Lara hadn't been able to resist sticking her oar in. Evie pulled a face. 'It's OK, you don't have to be polite.'

'I'm not just being polite.'

Which was, self-evidently, the only possible response a genuinely polite person could make. Evie said, 'Fine then, maybe later when you're feeling brave enough. We'll try really hard not to step on each other's feet.'

The ballroom was situated in the west wing, bright, gilded and high-ceilinged and with full-length French windows opening out on to the sweeping terrace. The other end of the hotel was altogether darker and more enclosed, with narrow wood-panelled corridors and smaller rooms.

Evie emerged from the ladies' cloakroom and rather than head straight back to the party decided to do a bit of casual exploring first. There had been no sign of Ethan this evening but he could still be here. She hadn't asked a member of staff; the last thing he'd want to hear was he was being pursued by that desperate female he wasn't remotely interested in. There again, she was an invited guest at a party being held in the hotel, which meant she

257

had a valid reason for being on the premises. Which meant if she happened to bump into the owner of the hotel whilst exploring the facilities, it didn't make her a stalker.

And if she *did* encounter him, she would be casual and polite. She definitely wouldn't clutch at his shirt front and wail, 'I really liked you and I thought you liked me, so WHY HAVEN'T YOU CALLED ME, YOU UTTER BASTARD?'

Anyway. There was a sweeping staircase leading up to the first floor, with a minstrel's gallery at the top and a discreet sign indicating the way to the library. Evie climbed the stairs and followed the sign along the corridor. The library, when she reached it, contained shelves of books, a couple of computers for the guests' use, a slew of glossy magazines on the low marble-topped coffee table and a box of board games beneath the window. There was also an unknown couple in their twenties, wrapped around each other and kissing enthusiastically on one of the velvet-upholstered banquettes.

A floorboard creaked beneath her foot and the couple broke apart, turning to stare at her.

'Sorry!' Evie backed away and left them to it, heading back along the corridor to the staircase.

She'd reached the minstrel's gallery when she saw Ethan making his way across the hallway downstairs. Evie's heart did a rabbity skip at the sight of him, the intensity of the jolt taking her by surprise. Clearly he was never going to be the type to wear a suit; in his untucked check shirt and corduroys he still looked like a gardener, but there was more to the laws of attraction than the clothes people wore. He paused at the reception desk as his phone began to ring.

'No, no, I'll be ten minutes. There's something I need to do first. I'll take care of it when I get there, don't worry.' Ending the call and attracting the attention of the girl behind the desk, he added, 'Can you get hold of Tina, send her through?'

Would he look up and see her watching him? Leaning forward, resting her elbows on the polished wooden rail, Evie willed it to happen. But she was out of his field of vision; Ethan headed off along the corridor to the right of the reception area and disappeared through the third door along on the left.

Evie hesitated, considering her options. The next moment a dark-haired girl in a chambermaid's outfit came hurrying across the hall and down the same corridor. Reaching Ethan's door, she knocked and waited before entering.

OK, what now? From what he'd said on the phone he wouldn't be in there for long. And further down the corridor was the ladies' cloakroom she'd visited earlier. In order to casually bump into Ethan, the simplest plan of action would be to make sure she happened to be passing when he emerged from the room. But since the receptionist couldn't see her from that angle, it wouldn't matter if she loitered for a few minutes in the corridor.

Evie descended the stairs and the receptionist smiled at her for the second time in ten minutes. She was either going to think she had raging cystitis or that she'd been knocking back far too many pints.

Right, best not to stand directly outside the room itself. Halfway between it and the cloakroom would be preferable. And she could pretend to be looking for something in her handbag, or appear engrossed in her phone, as if reading a particularly riveting text . . .

'. . . I don't care how ill they are, I don't want to hear about your bloody kids!'

What? Evie jumped. That was Ethan's voice, raised in anger.

'Oh, but p-please, I need to b-be wiz zem.' The girl was upset, clearly begging for time off.

'Not my problem.'

'But zey are too szmall . . . Anya eez only four . . . I do *anyzing* . . .'

'Listen to me, we've already been there.' Ethan sounded bored. 'The only thing I want from you is a proper day's work. If you can't manage that, I'll find someone else who can.'

Chapter 36

Evie felt sick, actually physically sick. Ethan was an employer and it stood to reason he'd have problems with staff, but the way he was speaking to the eastern European chambermaid was just down-right unpleasant. It was like eavesdropping on Father Christmas and discovering he was a wife-beater. Yet again, she'd managed to get someone completely and utterly wrong; Ethan wasn't the—

'Hi there, everything OK?' The receptionist had come out from behind her desk and, en route to the office, spotted her lurking in the narrow corridor.

'Um, yes . . . yes thanks. Just trying to get a signal.' Evie held up her phone as proof.

'Ah, it can be tricky in here. You'd probably have more luck outside.' The girl beckoned to Evie to join her, then indicated the main doors across the hall. 'Over by the fountain's best.'

Outside, Evie fiddled with her phone and pretended to make a call . . . Heading back in again, she saw the receptionist busy photocopying documents in the back office. With the coast clear, she headed back up the staircase and watched from the gallery, no longer able to hear what was going on between Ethan and the chambermaid but needing to witness the conclusion.

Maybe if she'd been a different type of person she might have burst into the room where Ethan was berating his employee and demanded he stop it. But she wasn't, confrontation wasn't her style – wedding days notwithstanding – and apart from being incredibly rude and abrupt, Ethan wasn't actually doing anything wrong.

He'd inadvertently revealed his true colours, that was all. While she'd succeeded in proving once more what a shockingly poor judge of character she was when it came to members of the opposite sex.

Evie experienced a pang; Joel had had his faults but he would never be as mean as that to an employee. Let's face it, he was more likely to go too far in the opposite direction and end up sleeping with them.

And maybe, just maybe, that made him a nicer person than Ethan. Joel was a flirtatious charmer; what you saw was what you got. But he was never deliberately cruel.

The next moment the door opened and the young chamber-maid emerged. Shrinking back into the shadows, Evie watched as the girl paused outside the room, wiped her eyes and gathered herself, then smoothed her hair, tightened her dark ponytail and headed back to work. Resigned to the fact that her young children would have to be ill without her there to comfort and care for them.

A minute later, Ethan reappeared too. Once again he didn't glance up. Tempting though it was to call down and let him know what she thought of him, Evie stayed silent and watched him go. She would only make herself look foolish, come across as a spurned, jealous and possibly unbalanced harpy.

To be honest, she'd already had quite enough experience of that.

*　　*　　*

Flynn watched Lara from the other side of the room. Life would undoubtedly be easier if he didn't feel this way about her, but there wasn't a lot he could do about that. She was looking amazing tonight, in a high-necked silver and white sleeveless shift dress that offset her tanned arms and legs.

But it wasn't just the way she looked; there was so much more to Lara than that. She was helping to keep the party going by persuading man-mountain Maz on to the dance floor. Playfully, she took the camcorder off him and handed it, still running, to one of the older guests. Then as Enjay and his band launched into 'Do You Want To Know A Secret?' she seized Maz's hands and started dancing, teasing him until he gave up and good-naturedly joined in.

Together they twirled around the dance floor, performing an impromptu comedy waltz in order to entertain the guests. Lara was laughing and chatting away to Maz, who must weigh close to three hundred pounds, but was surprisingly light on his feet. And, when she threw back her head and laughed, Flynn smiled to himself and had to hide it by taking a drink. Lara might drive him to distraction but she brightened his world. Funny, bright and generous to those she loved, she was a true life-enhancer.

Dammit, she was still his swan.

The party had livened up to the next level during Evie's absence. Back in the ballroom, she discovered that Frank Sinatra had given way to the Beatles and a crowd had now gathered on the stage, crowding around a microphone and bellowing out 'With A Little Help From My Friends' while Enjay performed an accompanying impromptu rap.

Unexpectedly, Flynn had also turned up and was surveying the proceedings with an air of detachment. Making her way over to him, Evie said, 'Didn't expect to see you here tonight.'

'Me neither, but Enjay invited me. God knows why.' Flynn's tone was dry. 'But it means I can keep an eye on Gigi.' He looked down at her. 'Are you OK?'

He was perceptive, she'd give him that. 'I'm fine. Just getting used to being single again. I'd forgotten what it was like.' Evie tucked her hair behind her ear. 'Men seem nice, then they stop being on their best behaviour and you realise they're not so great after all.' Ruefully she added, 'And sometimes you discover they're complete bastards.'

'Not all of them.' Flynn half-smiled. 'But you're right, it's a learning curve. I'm only just seeing it from your perspective for the first time. Like now.' He indicated his daughter with a nod; at the far side of the room, slinky and beautiful in a short red dress and strappy sandals, Gigi was dancing with a tall, long-haired lad sporting bad-boy black jeans, a ripped Sex Pistols T-shirt and more tattoos than Ozzy Osbourne. 'See? That's a potential nightmare right there. It's terrifying. I've never had to be like this before.'

It was entertaining seeing Flynn's paternal side. Evie said, 'It's nice that she's making so many new friends. Anyway, they're only having a dance. That's harmless enough.'

He shook his head, not remotely reassured. 'It's what comes next that's the problem.'

She laughed at his expression. 'Gigi's eighteen. She's a popular girl. You can't lock her in the cellar.'

'I could.' Flynn knocked back the rest of his wine. 'If I had a cellar.'

'Anyway, he might be a lovely boy.'

'Don't try and make me feel better. Look at him. Hardly ideal boyfriend material.'

'You can't judge by appearances,' said Evie.

His tone was rueful. 'I've discovered I can.'

'You used to wear stuff like that when you were that age. You had long hair.'

'Exactly,' said Flynn. 'And I know what I was like.'

Evie conceded the point. What was interesting, though, was that when he wasn't keeping an eagle eye on Gigi his gaze was sliding over to the other side of the room to check out what Lara was up to. Beneath the dazzling light from the chandeliers she was currently deep in conversation with a man in his forties, presumably one of the hotel guests, portly in build and wearing a slightly too small tweed jacket and mustard-yellow trousers. Evidently deciding that the man wasn't a threat, Flynn's shoulders relaxed and he turned his attention back to Gigi.

Evie waited a couple of seconds then blurted out, 'Oh my God, look at the fat guy kissing Lara!'

'What?' Flynn's head snapped round to see Lara now being introduced to the portly man's wife.

'Sorry,' said Evie. 'Couldn't resist.'

'And to think I've been so nice to you.'

'Life's never simple, is it?' She leaned against the wall. 'How much do you like her?'

'I think you already know the answer to that question.' Flynn reached for another glass from a passing waitress. 'It's just a shame Lara doesn't.'

'Oh, she knows. She just doesn't trust you.'

'Like you and Joel. I saw him a couple of nights ago. He's desperate to win you back. But you don't trust him.'

Evie raised an eyebrow. 'I wonder why that could be.'

'Lara's driving me insane,' said Flynn. 'I'm not Joel, I haven't slept with loads of other women behind her back. She just flatly refuses to even give me a chance.'

'And you're not used to that.' She gave him a teasing look, because Flynn might not be a serial love rat like Joel, but there had been plenty of girlfriends over the years. He'd spent his time riding high on an awful lot of females' wish lists.

'I'm not used to it.' He shook his head in agreement. 'And I don't know what the answer is. Have you talked to her about it?'

'Of course I have, but you can't force someone else to change their mind. They have to want to do it for themselves,' Evie said helpfully. 'Like alcoholics going into rehab.'

'Thanks a lot.'

'Oh, you know what I mean. Sshh, here she comes.' Having escaped mustard-trousers and his wife, Lara was now on her way over with Harry. Up on the stage, Enjay had finished rapping his version of 'Yellow Submarine' and was now launching into a sexy, soulful version of 'Yesterday'. Relieved to hear something normal, people piled on to the dance floor.

'There you go,' said Lara. 'Isn't it amazing, he's a really good singer when he stops doing all that gangsta stuff. Oh God, listen to me, I sound like somebody's granny. Right,' she whisked Evie's glass from her hand, 'you said you'd dance with Harry.'

'You sound like somebody's *bossy* granny.' Digging her heels in would be pointless, Evie knew; they may as well get it over with. It helped that Harry was looking as faintly appalled by the prospect as she was, but good manners compelled him to summon a brave smile and hold out his hand.

'Come on, we'll show them how it's done, shall we?'

Harry was a good man, a nice man, and that wasn't just her

266

own incompetent opinion; Lara had known him for almost twenty years. Maybe they would dance together and magic would happen. Evie stepped forward and said gamely, 'Let's do it.' She eyed Lara and Flynn. 'And you two have to dance together as well.'

Lara nodded. 'Absolutely.'

'Well?' said Flynn.

'Well what?' Lara was busy watching Harry and Evie on the dance floor.

'Are we getting out there?'

'No.' She couldn't, she just couldn't.

'Why not?'

'I just said it to make Evie go.'

'So you lied.'

'I don't want to dance.' Her mouth was drying up; just standing here next to Flynn was hard enough. His head was bent close to hers, his voice was low and she could feel the vibration from his chest as he spoke. She was also hyper aware of her own skin tingling in response to his proximity. No way, *no way* could she dance with him right now.

'You don't want to, or you're not going to?'

He was aware of the connection between them; he felt it too. The thing was, he knew there was attraction on her side but he genuinely couldn't begin to imagine the extent of it, or how hard she was having to work to keep herself under control.

'Look at the difference between them.' Changing the subject, Lara pointed to Enjay and a slinky, skimpily dressed blonde now entwined together up on the stage, their lithe bodies moving like oiled silk as they danced to the music.

Then she indicated Harry and Evie, manfully attempting to get through the next few minutes. They were smiling and doing their best to look as if they were happy to be there, but the awkwardness radiated from them like phosphorescence. Evie's feet had lost their rhythm and Harry, never the best dancer, appeared to have had all his joints soldered.

'Evie isn't usually like that,' said Flynn.

'I know, poor thing. But if they could just relax, wouldn't they make a perfect couple?'

'So you do like seeing other people matched up?' He gave her a pointed look.

'Of course I do. And Harry and Evie would be brilliant together. I'm right,' said Lara. 'I'm always right.'

'OK, two things. One, you're not always right. Two, Evie looks as if she's trying to dance with a stepladder. And three . . .'

He stopped and waited.

The pause was unnerving. 'You said two things.'

'I changed my mind. It's allowed.' Flynn's voice was as steady as his gaze, causing far too many hormones to swoosh through her veins. 'And three, don't think for one minute I'm going to give up on you. Because I'm not.'

Chapter 37

It was Sunday lunchtime when Gigi arrived at the hotel. The receptionist called Enjay's suite and he came down to meet her.

'Hey, babe.' Fresh from the shower, his white T-shirt clung to his super-toned abs and he smelled fantastic. Aware of the blonde receptionist's discreet glances in his direction, he winked at Gigi but didn't touch her. 'What's up?'

In the safety of the hotel he didn't need Maz or AJ to shadow him. Gigi said, 'There's something I wanted to see you about. Kind of in private.' She hesitated, because the receptionist might not be watching but she was certainly listening. 'It's a business proposition. Maybe we could go to your room.'

Upstairs in the opulent cream and wedgwood-blue suite, Enjay closed the door and said, 'Let's hear it then. Fire away.'

'Right. Well, first of all, thanks for inviting us to the party last night. It was great. And you won over all the oldies, made them like you. I wasn't sure you'd manage it.'

'What can I say?' He spread his arms. 'It's my modesty and charm. Gets 'em every time.'

'I brought you a thank-you present.'

'Yeah?' His dark eyes gleamed. 'Sounds good to me. I don't get too many presents from other people.'

'Hold out your hand.'

'Better still. I hope it's a Rolex.' He extended his arm.

'Sshh, you've already got one of those. I'm giving you something you don't have.' Gigi reached into her jeans pocket. 'Close your eyes.'

'Yeah, right, and when I open them again you'll have made off with all my jewellery.' But Enjay did as she asked and waited patiently until she'd finished tying the loose threads in a knot.

'OK, you can open them now.'

He did so. The gift looked pretty incongruous next to the diamond-encrusted Rolex and ornate rings, but never mind. If you can't compete in the diamond stakes, go for something different. Gigi said, 'It's a friendship bracelet.'

'Hey.' Enjay's voice softened. 'I know it's a friendship bracelet. This is really cool.'

Gigi watched him examine the painstakingly plaited centimetre-wide strip composed of tightly woven pink, green and purple threads. 'I made it this morning.'

'I bet it took you a while.'

'Two and a half hours.'

'You're going to see me wearing this from now on. Thank you.' He came forward, rested a hand on her shoulder and gave her a semi-hug before stepping back. As if she were slightly contagious.

'Do you like it?'

'I like it a lot.' Enjay flashed her his lazy wolfish smile. 'I'm glad I met Harry, and I'm glad I met his friends.'

'Can I say something?' Gigi mentally braced herself.

'It's a free country.'

'OK, I've been thinking. Remember the other day at the thermal baths, when you were pretty keen on me and I turned you down, told you I'd never do anything like that with you?'

'I remember.'

'Well,' said Gigi, 'I've changed my mind.'

A beat of silence.

'Meaning what?'

'Meaning I've given it a *lot* of thought. And I didn't want to be one of your conquests, a pretty girl who's basically a nobody who gets slept with then forgotten about. But now I've looked at it from the other angle.' She was speaking faster and faster, the words tumbling out in an effort to make him understand. 'And this is an opportunity for *me*, one of those once-in-a-lifetime things. Because how often am I going to get the chance to sleep with a world-famous rapper? It's never going to happen again, is it? And you're not going to be here for much longer. So that's it, I've decided. We should definitely do this thing. And you won't have to worry about me following you around afterwards, pestering you and expecting more once it's over. We both know it's only going to be a one-off.'

More silence. Finally Enjay said, 'So as far as you're concerned, I'd be an experience you could tick off your to-do list.'

'Exactly. This way we both get what we want!'

'OK. You said this was an opportunity that was never going to happen again.' He shook his head slowly. 'I got news for you, babe. It ain't going to happen at all.'

'Why not?'

'You changed your mind. Well, I changed mine too.' He gazed steadily at her. 'Does your daddy know you're here?'

'No he doesn't. Anyway, what are you, scared of him? I wasn't planning on telling him about any of this, if that's what's bothering you.'

271

'How about your mom?'

He was scared. This was definitely what was putting him off. Gigi said, 'She doesn't know either. Look, a girl I met at the gym is having a barbecue this afternoon. She invited me along. That's where I was going to be spending the day and that's where everyone thinks I am, at a barbecue on a farm in Lansdown.' She took a step towards him, lowered her voice and added seductively, 'But I'd much rather be here with you.'

'OK, now listen to me.' Enjay placed his hands on her shoulders but stayed at arm's length. 'Thanks, but I do have some scruples. Not many, but a few. And I'm gonna keep that promise I made to your daddy.'

'Oh but—'

'No arguments. And I'm doing this for your benefit.' His voice softened. 'In a couple of days we'll be leaving for London. I'll be hitting the clubs and I'll be hit on by bad girls, y'know what I'm saying? They're the ones I'll be sleeping with. Believe me, it's better this way.'

He was looking genuinely regretful, which only made the rejection worse. Gigi said stubbornly, 'I don't see why.'

'Hey, you're a good girl. Bad girls are more my scene.'

'I could be a bad girl.' She wasn't going to beg, but being turned down was definitely a frustrating thing to happen.

Except Enjay was already shaking his head again, half-smiling and regarding her as if she were a small child robustly announcing that she was going to be an astronaut when she grew up.

'You're too nice to be a bad girl. I can't take you up on it, but I do appreciate the offer. And the friendship bracelet too. Look, you go off to your friend's barbecue and have a great time.' He gave her a brief hug, then led her to the door. 'Bye.'

Gigi said in a small voice, 'I feel a bit stupid now.'

'Hey, darlin', you mustn't. You're worth more than that.' The glint was back in his eyes as he flashed her that trademark wicked smile. 'Look on it as a lucky escape.'

Lara was ready and waiting when Flynn arrived at the house to pick her up. The plan had been for Gigi to go along with him to a wine-tasting demo at a harbourside event in Bristol. But when she'd mentioned on Friday about the invitation to the barbecue, Lara hadn't had the heart to let her miss it. If she was going to properly settle in Bath, Gigi needed to make more friends and extend her social circle. Lara had volunteered to take her place at the wine-tasting.

She could do it. It would be fine. Maybe the more time she spent with Flynn, the easier things would become; the novelty of those out-of-the-blue adrenalin rushes might wear off.

With any luck.

'All OK?' said Flynn as she jumped into the car.

'Perfect.'

'Did Gigi explain what you'll be doing?'

'Of course.' Lara smoothed down her skirt and fastened the seat belt. 'You're the one running the show, being the clever expert. All I have to do is waft around being nice to people and pouring little bits of wine into glasses. It's practically my two favourite hobbies.'

'Is Gigi still at home?'

'No, she left early to go to the barbecue. She was really looking forward to it,' said Lara. 'Couldn't wait.'

'And what's Evie doing today?'

'Ah well, I put my masterplan into action. I told Harry that Evie loved golf but didn't have anyone to play with. And I told Evie that Harry was *dying* for a game of golf but hated going on his own.' Lara tried not to look pleased with herself and failed. 'So basically I explained that they'd be doing each other a massive favour and having a brilliant day out at the same time. *Then*,' she played her trump card, 'they're going to come back to the house and Evie's going to cook a roast dinner, and if anything's going to impress Harry, it'll be her roast dinner.'

Flynn gave her a look. 'You really think that'll work?'

'Listen, the first time she cooked one for me I nearly married her myself.'

'But Evie lives in Bath. Harry lives in Keswick.'

'God, you're such a pessimist. If they're right for each other,' said Lara, 'they'll find a way. It's called moving house.'

'Simple as that?'

'Simple as that.'

'Joel called me this morning. He still wants Evie back.'

'So he can cheat on her again? *Please!* He had his chance and he blew it. She deserves better,' Lara announced. 'And I'm going to make sure she gets it.'

As they headed out of the city, Flynn said drily, 'Whether she wants you to or not.'

Chapter 38

It had taken Harry and Evie all of three minutes to discover they'd been on the receiving end of one of Lara's oh-so-subtle set-ups. Thankfully, Evie had discovered, it hadn't mattered at all. Playing a round of golf, unlike dancing, didn't involve physical contact. They both genuinely loved the game. The course at Castle Combe, ten miles outside Bath and belonging to the Manor House Hotel, was brilliantly designed and set in stunning rolling countryside. And the sun had stayed out; who could ask for more?

Well, apart from coming in under par and birdying the eighteenth to win the game, obviously.

'That was great,' said Harry as they headed back into Bath.

'It was.' Chatting to him had been effortless; they'd had a truly enjoyable afternoon. There wasn't an iota of physical attraction between them and that hadn't mattered either. Lara would be disappointed, but that wasn't their problem. You could want it to happen but you couldn't make it happen; if the connection didn't exist, you couldn't magic it up out of thin air.

At least now, though, they could joke about it.

'When Lara comes home,' said Harry, 'we should tell her we've got engaged.'

'And give each other nicknames. Binky and Squeaky,' said Evie.

'Bunny and Booboo.'

'Putter and Hacker.'

'That's so unromantic. Wiggle and Fluffy.'

Evie said, 'OK, but I want to be Wiggle.'

When they arrived back at the house Harry said, 'We could go out for something to eat. You don't have to cook.'

The joint of beef had already been marinating overnight. 'I like doing it. Here.' Evie tore open a bag of King Edwards. 'And here's a peeler. You can help.'

'Lara says you do the best roast dinners.'

'She's right. They're my speciality.' Evie began finely chopping red onions for the gravy. 'Actually, I'm rubbish at everything else.'

Harry was efficient with a peeler, which was good to see. She grimaced as the house phone began to ring. 'Could you get that? I've got onion juice on my hands. It's probably Lara reminding me to do extra parsnips.'

'Hello?' Harry had such a lovely polite manner on the phone. Evie smiled and watched him listening to the caller. 'Oh yes, she's just here. Who shall I say is calling, please?'

See? So sweet. He really was like a character from the nineteen fifties. And now he was covering the receiver, turning to her and saying, 'It's for you. Ethan.'

The blade of the vegetable knife missed Evie's thumb by a whisker.

'Could you just hold on,' Harry continued into the receiver. 'She'll be with you in a moment.' He reached for the roll of kitchen towel and passed her a couple of sheets so she could clean her oniony hands.

'Hello, Ethan.' Her voice had gone all stiff; she hadn't meant to sound quite so much like a disapproving head teacher. But how ironic that he should finally be calling her now.

'Hi . . . um, hello.' He sounded wrong-footed too. 'How are you? Sorry I didn't phone before. I've been pretty busy, you know how things are . . .'

Pretty busy shouting at hapless foreign employees, you mean.

Evie didn't say it out loud. Lara might have launched into a vitriolic attack but she wasn't the type. Instead she said, 'Yes, busy. Me too.'

Evidently unnerved by her cool tone, Ethan cleared his throat and said, 'So I was, erm, wondering if you'd like to meet up again . . . ?'

She'd liked him so much. The chemistry that was so singularly lacking between her and Harry had, against all odds, blossomed during the course of that first evening with Ethan. On that *only* evening.

And how amazingly perfect it had seemed . . .

Until last night when he'd revealed his true colours.

'I don't think so,' Evie said curtly. 'In fact, no.'

'Oh.' Bizarrely, Ethan sounded disappointed. 'Well, OK.' As if attempting to make conversation, he went on, 'I saw you at the hotel yesterday, at the party in the ballroom. Went in to see how things were going, and there you were. I would've come over and said hello but you were dancing with some guy . . .'

'I was. He's here now. That was him answering the phone.'

'Ah. Right. I see.' Now he sounded resigned. 'Well, maybe see you around then. Good luck with everything.'

Evie swallowed; if she hadn't discovered what he was really like last night, she would've been thrilled he'd called now. It just went to show, you might think you knew what someone was like, but you really didn't. Silently congratulating herself on a lucky escape, she said, 'Thanks. Goodbye.'

There, done. She ended the call and went back to the onions. It was sad in one way, empowering in another.

'Was that the ex-boyfriend?' said Harry. 'Joel?'

'No, someone else. Seemed nice, but it turned out he wasn't after all. Surprise surprise.' Evie chopped and diced at a rate of knots. 'Shame, but there you go.'

'Ah well, his loss. Right, I've done the potatoes. Are we parboiling them before roasting?'

Harry, bless him, was already reaching for the kettle. Why oh why couldn't she fancy the pants off him? Filled with admiration, Evie said, 'There's something about a man who knows his way around a kitchen. You're practically perfect.'

'I know.' He looked modest, then pulled a face. 'But I'd be more perfect if I didn't dance like a giraffe.'

Dinner was almost ready, everything smelled fantastic and Harry was frying courgettes in butter, flipping them in the pan like an expert. Evie took the sizzling beef joint out of the oven, leaving it to rest on the side while she got on with making the gravy.

The doorbell went and Harry said, 'Expecting visitors?'

'No, it's probably just Lara being discreet. Warning us she's back, in case we need to make ourselves presentable.'

He looked amused. 'Maybe we should go upstairs and open the bedroom window, yell down at her to come back in an hour.'

'She'd be so happy.' Evie went to answer the door as the bell shrilled again. 'And we'd never hear the end of it; she'd demand *all* the credit.'

'Hurry back, Wiggle,' Harry called after her.

Evie trilled back, 'Will do, Fluffy. Missing you already!'

Then she opened the door and found Joel on the doorstep. Frowning.

'Who's Fluffy?'

Which might have been quite funny in theory, but was less so when it was actually happening.

'No one. It was just a joke.' Evie couldn't help it; her breath still caught in her throat at the sight of her ex-fiancé; compared with Ethan and Harry, he was a Greek god. 'Joel, what are you doing here?'

Joel shook his head and swayed slightly, and she realised he'd been Sunday-afternoon drinking. 'I had to come and see you, because I love you. Evie, Evie, I told you before I won't do any of that bad stuff again. That's a promise.' He paused to sniff the air. 'Are you cooking?'

'Yes.'

'Smells fantastic. Can I come in?'

'No.' Evie shook her head for added emphasis.

'Why not? Because you've got your new boyfriend in there? Ha, I knew it.' Joel smiled his rueful crooked smile when she hesitated. 'And I know who it is too. Ethan McEnery, the one who owns the Ellison. Emily told me that's the one who you were having dinner with at Brown's. I'm right, aren't I? So he's here and you're cooking a romantic dinner for him, and that's why you don't want me to come in.'

'And again,' said Evie, 'no. Ethan isn't here.'

'So let me into the house then! I need to talk to you!'

She could smell the alcohol on his breath, knew he'd spent the last few hours drowning his sorrows in his favourite wine bar. 'Still no.'

'I think he's in there and you're trying to protect him.' As Joel said it, they both heard the creak of the kitchen door. He opened his mouth to say something then closed it again as Harry appeared at Evie's side.

279

'He's really not here,' Harry said pleasantly. 'I am.'

'Who are you? Another boyfriend? *Oh*.' Joel looked shocked. 'You're . . . *Fluffy*.'

Harry inclined his head in polite agreement. 'And you must be Joel. Nice to meet you.'

'Look, no offence, but can I just say something?' Evidently more drunk than Evie'd thought, Joel turned to her and stage-whispered, 'We're not exactly talking oil paintings here, are we? You might be putting yourself out there and getting some attention, but so far neither of them's been as good-looking as me.'

Other men might have chosen to take offence at this remark. Harry simply said, 'I prefer to get by on personality.'

'Evie, Evie, I love you, you can do better than him,' Joel begged. 'You could have *me*.'

She heaved a sigh. 'This is crazy. How did you get here?'

'Taxi. It's gone now,' he added as Evie peered past him in the vain hope that the cab might still be lurking somewhere in the street.

'OK, so we'll just have to call you another one.' She spun round, went back into the hall, grabbed the cordless house phone and returned.

'. . . but you don't love her as much as I do,' Joel was insisting to Harry. 'You *can't*.'

'Look, shush, stop saying stuff like that. I don't want to hear it.' Evie held up a hand for silence and found the first taxi company in her address book. 'Hello, yes, how quickly can you get a car to Arlington Road . . . ?'

Who knew that Sunday afternoons were such a tricky time to find a cab? Thirty minutes was too long to wait. So was forty minutes. The third taxi firm wasn't even bothering to pick up its phone. And all the time she was trying, Joel was rattling on about how miserable he'd been without her and how he'd learned his lesson and would never ever be naughty again.

If only she could have shut the front door and left him to it, but Evie knew Joel well enough to know he'd just keep on ringing the doorbell. Nor, thanks to the Merlot they'd cracked open an hour ago, could she give him a lift home herself.

'This is so *stupid*.' She hung up again, exasperated. 'Why aren't they answering? Bloody taxi companies.'

'I'm quite hungry,' Joel said helpfully. 'Why don't you just invite me to dinner?'

'You're not having dinner with us!' Evie's voice rose. 'I just want you to go!'

There was a rustling in the bushes, then Jacqueline from next door popped her head over the wall dividing her garden from theirs.

'Hello? Only me! Look, I'm really not being a nosy neighbour but I couldn't help overhearing what's going on.'

Everyone had turned to stare at her. Joel frowned and said, 'Who are you?'

'Jacqueline Cumiskey.' Her dark eyes were bright, her manner friendly. 'And you are . . . ?'

'I'm Joel.' He gestured to indicate the others. 'This is Evie, the love of my life. And Harry somebody-or-other, who definitely isn't.'

'So I gathered. Anyway, I'm just off out to visit my mother and I wondered if you'd like a lift somewhere? So long as it's not too far out of my way.' Jacqueline pulled a face. 'I mean, not Manchester or anything.'

'That would be perfect.' Evie exhaled with relief. 'Thanks so much, you're a star. He just needs dropping off at his flat in Bannerdown . . .'

'No problem,' Jacqueline said cheerfully. She waved her car keys at Joel. 'Come on then, let's go.'

'What if I want to go to Manchester?' Joel protested.

'You don't.' Evie was firm. 'Bye.'

They stood together on the doorstep and watched Joel climb into the passenger seat of Jacqueline's lime-green Fiesta. When it had pulled away, they headed back inside the house.

'You're popular,' said Harry.

'Not really.' Evie sighed. 'It's not that much fun being popular with the wrong people.'

'Hey, cheer up. You're doing really well.'

He was so nice. 'I'm not. I'm a walking disaster. Still, at least we have roast potatoes.'

'Followed by Scrabble,' Harry reminded her.

'Let's see if Lara's on her way back.' Evie sent a quick text: 'Dinner's ready – how soon will you be home?'

By the time the plates were lined up, her mobile buzzed with Lara's reply: 'Not before ten, we're still in Bristol. Save some for me? Have fun! xxx'

It was only six thirty. Evie held up the phone to show him. 'She's not going to be back until ten.'

'Fine by me,' Harry said easily. 'Lara doesn't like Scrabble. That means more games for us.'

'Don't expect to win,' Evie warned him. 'I'm good, you know.'

There was a glint in Harry's eye as he surveyed her. 'I'm better.'

Chapter 39

'*Ha.*' Lara gazed in triumph at her phone. 'Knew it!'

'Knew what?'

They were just leaving Bristol on their way back to Bath. She waited until Flynn had pulled up at the traffic lights at the bottom of Park Street and showed him the texts. The second one from Evie said: 'OK, will do! See you later xx.'

'I am brilliant,' Lara said smugly.

'You're talking in tongues again. I need a translator.'

'Come on, it's obvious! Evie wasn't texting me because she needed to find out what time I'd be back for dinner. She's at the house with Harry and she wanted to know how much longer they had alone together!'

Flynn frowned. 'Because she was bored?'

'No! Because they don't want to be interrupted!'

He looked bemused. 'Are you sure?'

'Of course I'm sure.' She marvelled at his inability to understand. 'It's obvious. And when I told her to have fun, she said, "I will!"'

'But you asked her to save you some food. Are you sure that wasn't why she said it?'

283

'Look, you're just a man. I'm the expert.' Delighted with her matchmaking prowess, Lara said, 'Trust me, I'm right.'

'Except you told her you were staying in Bristol.' They were passing Cabot Circus now, about to hit the motorway. 'You can't go home until ten.'

He had a point; she hadn't thought this through. Okaaay . . .

'I'll go to the cinema,' said Lara. That was a good decision, wasn't it? 'Just drop me by the Odeon.'

Forty minutes later they were in Bath.

'What are you going to see?' Flynn pulled up on double yellows outside the cinema.

Lara pointed to a poster. 'That spy film with Rupert Everett.'

'Really? It's had terrible reviews.'

'OK then, the comedy with Jack Black and the other fat one.'

'That's supposed to be even worse.'

Lara already knew this; she'd Googled them on her phone as they'd been speeding along the M4. 'Fine, I'll watch the sci-fi horror thingy with the bald guy and Paris Hilton.'

Flynn smiled slightly, not even bothering to state the obvious. 'You can't stand sci-fi.'

'Maybe I'll just head over to the Ellison instead, then. See what Enjay's up to.'

He gave her a long look and pulled away from the kerb.

'Where are we going?'

'Home.'

'No,' Lara protested. 'Evie and Harry aren't expecting me. I don't want to be a gooseberry.'

'Not your home,' said Flynn. 'Mine.'

Ooh, that sounded masterful . . .

★   ★   ★

284

The flat, on the top floor of a smart Georgian terrace close to the Royal Crescent, was in what estate agents would describe as a prime location with stunning views over the city. Gigi had been here before but it was Lara's first time. The kitchen was pretty small but the sitting room was huge and airy, with faded-aubergine walls and a purply-grey carpet. There were interesting paintings on the walls, a typically massive TV and a fantastically comfortable dark blue velvet sofa. Switching on the TV while Flynn was in the kitchen making coffee, Lara moved a couple of copies of *SKI* magazine off the sofa and on to the floor, then kicked off her shoes and tucked her bare feet under her. It had started to rain outside; the sound of raindrops pattering against the windows was oddly hypnotic. There was nothing good on TV though; honestly, why were early Sunday evenings always so rubbish? Flynn's DVDs were over there but she'd got herself all comfortable now, couldn't be bothered to move . . . mmm . . . *mmm . . .*

Swimming back to consciousness with her eyes still closed, the first thing Lara became aware of was the warmth of the pillow her head was resting on. Followed by the realisation that it wasn't remotely pillowy.

Plus, it appeared to be breathing . . .

Her brain clicked into gear and began to race. She'd fallen asleep. Flynn had brought the coffee through from the kitchen and joined her on the sofa. At some stage she'd slid sideways from her upright position and ended up with her head against his chest.

It felt fantastic.

Next, she discovered his right hand was resting on her tucked-up knee; she could feel the warmth and the weight of it. To be fair, the way she'd ended up curled against him, there hadn't really been anywhere else for it to go. *Oh God, though, that felt brilliant too*.

Keeping her breathing slow and even, Lara half-opened her eyes. This was dangerous territory; she already knew she shouldn't be doing this. But it wasn't her fault, you really couldn't help what you got up to while you were fast asleep.

Like resting your own arm across the chest of the person you'd accidentally ended up snuggling against. Whoops, and there it was, draped over him. There was Flynn's white shirt, now crumpled as a result of the snuggling. And his dark grey trousers, his tanned forearm, his beautiful body, the delicious oh-so-familiar smell of him . . .

'Are you awake?'

She jumped slightly and felt him tilt his head to look at her.

'Just woke up. Didn't mean to fall asleep. Sorry.'

'No problem.'

Her own weakness terrified her. Lara struggled into a sitting position, raked her fingers through her hair and said, 'I should go.'

'You don't have to.'

She didn't *have* to, obviously. But she definitely *should* leave. And Flynn wasn't going to be any help, that was blatantly obvious. His hand was still resting on her leg, his thumb idly stroking her knee. He had that look in his eyes and it was having its usual chaotic effect. Lara found herself transfixed by his mouth.

'Stay,' Flynn murmured. 'I don't want you to go.'

The buzzing, when it came, felt like an actual electric shock. In her dazed state it took Lara a second to realise it was the phone in her shirt pocket, pressed between them and exerting a mini-jolt against both their chests, like being resuscitated in A&E.

She pulled back and eased the phone out of her pocket.

Flynn said, 'You could always not answer it.'

'It could be Gigi, she might need me.' Shamed by her earlier weakness, Lara intimated he didn't understand; when you were a parent, ignoring a ringing phone simply wasn't an option.

She knew the moment she'd said hello, even before hearing the voice at the other end of the line. The moment of hesitation was what gave it away. Her heart did an abrupt swoop-and-dive inside her ribcage and she could no longer meet Flynn's gaze – his presence was too much of a distraction.

'Ah, hello, you left your number a while back and I'm returning your call. My name's James Agnew.'

I know, I know, I KNOW. It was the voice she'd been waiting to hear. Propelled to her feet, Lara jumped up and moved over to the window. He even sounded right, somehow. As if he could be her father.

'Yes. Hi.' Her pulse was galloping. 'OK, um, this might be a bit of a bolt from the blue, but did you once know someone called Barbara Carson?'

This time she heard the surprise, the brief intake of breath. Followed by, 'Oh my goodness. Yes I did. Barbara. Yes. Sorry, wasn't expecting you to say that.'

Dimly aware that Flynn had disappeared into the kitchen to give her some privacy, Lara said, 'I'm sorry. I didn't know how else to do it.'

'And now you're contacting me. Can I ask . . . I mean, I'm listening to your voice. Is that . . . Lara?'

An enormous lump had sprung up in her throat. 'Yes.'

Silence. Then, his own voice softening, James Agnew said, 'Well, well, this is just amazing. I never thought I'd hear from you. How . . . absolutely *wonderful*.'

Hearing him was no longer enough. She wanted to see him, meet him in the flesh, know what he looked like. Nor could she ask him that all-important question, not over the phone. It wouldn't be right.

'I've called quite a few times,' said Lara. 'The woman who answered the phone couldn't seem to understand me . . . you've been away for ages.'

'World cruise. Just got back this morning. Yes, sorry about my housekeeper. She's great at vacuuming carpets and watering plants but I'm afraid speaking English isn't her forte.'

'Could we meet up?' Lara blurted the words out. 'Would that be OK?'

'Yes. Yes of course.' She heard him exhale. 'Oh dear, this is such unfortunate timing. Just back from the cruise, and on Tuesday morning I have to fly to New York on business, then on to Toronto after that. I'm away for three weeks . . . should we fix a date for the weekend after I get back?'

No, no, a whole *month* away? Lara's heart plummeted; that was far too long to wait. She couldn't bear it. But he clearly wouldn't be able to cancel such an important business trip.

'Unless . . . there's tomorrow,' James Agnew ventured. 'I mean, I have a lot of catching up to do, stuff to sort out . . . I don't know if there's any way you could meet me here in London, maybe come to the house—'

'Yes! Let's do that!' Oops, bit loud. 'Sorry, did I just burst your eardrum? I'll come to London.' Lara was babbling, overcome with relief. The shop was closed on Mondays. 'I've got your address, I know where you are. What time shall I get there? Whenever you like.'

'Tomorrow then. Perfect. Shall we say midday? I can't wait.' He sounded as if he meant it. 'Can I just ask one question?'

Oh God, did he *know*? Was he about to ask her if *she* knew he was her father? Lara said breathlessly, 'Go on.'

'How did you find me? How did you know my name?'

Lara exhaled. 'Luck and subterfuge.'

He laughed. 'Excellent. Good girl. I'll see you tomorrow.'

She smiled, completely loving the sound, the elegant timbre of his voice. 'I can't wait.'

'Well?' said Flynn when she burst into the kitchen.

'I'm meeting him tomorrow, going to his house. We'll talk about everything then. Oh God, I'm *shaking*.' She showed him her hands. 'It's really happening at last.'

'How will you get up to London? Drive?'

He knew about her car, that there was an ominous rattling noise in the engine and she'd booked it into a local garage to get the rattle checked out. Lara pulled a face and said, 'Can't risk it. I'll catch the train.'

But Flynn was already shaking his head. 'They're working on the line all week. Serious delays. Monday morning, it'll be chaos.'

'Hang on, I can't concentrate. Everything's in a whirl. I'll get a taxi.'

'You can't get a taxi.'

'Fine then, I'll ask Enjay, maybe he's going up.' For goodness sake, she'd walk there if she had to.

'Calm down, it's OK. I'll take you,' said Flynn.

Ooh, that would be nice.

'But you have to work.'

'Gigi can hold the fort. I'll take the day off.'

'You don't need to.' Was it the mention of Enjay that had prompted the offer? 'You could lend me your car.'

Flynn's dark eyes flashed. 'I'll drive you. God knows, it'll be safer that way.'

He was right; especially if she was going to be all of a jitter on the way there. Lara felt the tension ease from her shoulders.

'OK, thanks.'

'Hey, I'm happy for you. It's great news. How does he sound?'

Would he understand? Lara said, 'He sounds . . . *right*.'

'Good.' Flynn gave her a hug that five minutes ago would have played havoc with her body. Now she couldn't even concentrate on Flynn; her mind was in a complete spin.

Luckily for her, unluckily for him.

'Who are you calling now?' He watched her fumbling with her phone.

'Sorry? Hang on. Hi, it's me,' said Lara as Evie answered the phone. 'Look, is it OK if I come home?'

'Of course it's OK. Just give us enough time to get our clothes back on.'

'Really?'

'No, not really. We put them back on ages ago.'

'Oh my God, *really*?'

'That was another joke,' said Evie. 'It's fine to come home. Why are you sounding so weird? Are you all right?'

'James Agnew just called. I'm meeting him tomorrow.' Her voice trembled with happiness; she'd begun to think it would never happen.

'Yay, brilliant! What does he sound like?'

Lara took a deep breath and experienced a rush of pure happiness. 'I *think* he sounds . . . like my father.'

Chapter 40

'Here it is,' said Flynn. 'This is the one.'

For a moment Lara couldn't speak. How many times had she studied this house, this street, every last detail on Google Earth? But now she was actually here in Belvedere Grove, seeing it with her own eyes. A large property set back from the road, a nice garden that had presumably been kept that way by a gardener while James Agnew was off on his world cruise. Variegated ivy climbed the walls of the white stucco-fronted villa and the wooden shutters were painted a deeper shade of green. The house was clearly well cared for, its polished windows gleaming in the sunshine.

'Thanks for bringing me.' He'd been right about her being in too much of a state to drive; she'd never been more jumpy in her life. 'Do I look OK?'

Flynn smiled. 'You'll do.'

The irony of the situation hadn't escaped her. Lara said, 'This is exactly how Gigi felt before she met you for the first time.'

'I know. And that hasn't turned out too badly, has it?' He reached over and gave her hand a brief reassuring squeeze. 'Off you go. I'll see you later. Good luck.'

Once he'd driven off, Lara straightened her collar and smoothed her fingers over her hair. Last night she'd spent ages agonising over what to wear today. In the end she'd gone for nice jeans and her favourite white shirt, because it wasn't a job interview. She'd kept the make-up simple too, knowing from experience that the more important the event, the more likely she was to keep slathering it on. Plus, she might cry and the clown look was never a good one.

The front door was dark green and glossy with a heavy brass knocker shaped like a lion's head.

Right, here goes.

As she raised her hand to lift the knocker, the door opened.

And there he was, James Agnew, hopefully her father.

It was like being punched in the stomach, but in a good way.

He was tall, imposing, handsome, with silver-grey hair swept back from a tanned face and faded blue eyes surrounded by laughter lines. If she'd met him during those first few years of her life, she had no memory of it. Did he look like her? She couldn't tell. There was no deep-down thud of recognition, but it somehow didn't matter.

'I watched you getting out of the car. Look at you.' He shook his head, genial and marvelling at her. 'Baby Lara. I never thought the day would come. This is just . . . incredible.' He held out his hands, then hesitated. 'May I?'

He was actually asking permission to give her a hug. Lara nodded, unable to speak, and allowed him to envelop her in his arms. He smelled of cigars and coffee and expensive cologne.

How soon could she ask him?

Then he was ushering her into the house, across the hall, through a stunning pale yellow living room and out into an airy conservatory overlooking the garden. A tiny woman with a face like a wizened sultana followed them in and placed a laden tray on the gleaming glass-topped table, then noiselessly retreated and left them in peace.

'So. I want to know everything,' James announced. 'Did your mother tell you about me?'

'No. Never. I don't know if you know, she died when I was thirteen.'

He sighed. 'I did, I did. I came back to Bath, must have been a year or two after that, and asked one of the neighbours if the Carsons were still living in the house. That's when the woman told me about Barbara, that she'd died. I was devastated. As you must have been. I'm so sorry.'

Lara nodded. She still couldn't ask him; the words were trapped inside her chest. But if he had been her father, wouldn't he have hammered on the door, irrespective of Charles Carson's outrage, and demanded custody of his child?

Or would that only have happened if custody had been something he'd actually wanted?

'So tell me how you found me,' said James.

He was being wary, she realised, because he wasn't sure how much she knew. As far as he was concerned, she might not be aware that he could be her father.

'I left home when I was sixteen. Charles Carson kicked me out and I never saw him again. He died a few months ago,' Lara hurried on, 'and I came back for the funeral. Well, because the solicitor wanted to see me. That's when I found out the house had belonged to my mum.'

'Right, yes.' James nodded slowly, taking this in. 'So all those years he'd been living in it on his own . . .'

'I'm living there now.' She would tell him about Janice later. 'With my daughter.'

293

'You have a daughter?' His expression cleared. 'Wonderful!'

'Did you buy the house for my mum?'

There was a pause before he nodded again. 'Yes. Yes, I did. Well, for both of you really. Look, I don't know how much you know, or how you found out about me.'

OK, just say it, Lara took a deep breath. 'Charles Carson didn't love me. Basically, he never thought I was his. So I was wondering if you were my father . . .'

She raised her gaze and saw that James was already shaking his head.

'I'm so sorry, no, I wish I was. But I'm not.'

'Oh.' And that was it, just like that the dream was over. 'Right.' The sense of disappointment was crushing.

'That's why you came here. Oh dear. Sorry.'

'Not your fault.' Lara managed a weak smile. 'I suppose . . . I mean, are you absolutely sure?'

'Absolutely sure. Nothing like that ever happened between your mother and me. She was never unfaithful to Charles. Your father was your father.'

'Right. OK. So you were just . . . friends.'

'Thanks to your mum, yes. If it had been up to me, it would have been far more.' James's voice softened. 'But it was more than just a friendship. I loved her very much. And she loved me.'

Lara swallowed; her chest felt squashed tight with sadness. 'Why did she stay with my father? She should have left him. You could have been together . . .'

We could have been a happy family.

'Honestly? Barbara didn't regard me as a safe bet.' James looked at her with genuine regret. 'Sorry, but there it is. I was married and that wasn't working out. I'd also been married and divorced before that. I told Barbara it would be different

294

with us but she was terrified I might change my mind, go off her, let her down.'

Just as Jo had said.

'And was she right?' said Lara. 'Would that have happened?'

'You want more honesty? We'll never know. I obviously had the history, the dodgy track record. I adored your mother, she was the love of my life and I couldn't imagine ever feeling any differently about her. But our relationship was never consummated. Maybe that's what made it different. If we'd lived together, who can say if we'd have lasted? I like to think so, of course I do, but I can't put my hand on my heart and guarantee it. I've been married and divorced four times now.' James's grimace was apologetic. 'Maybe your mother was right about me. Most of my wives probably wish they'd never walked up that aisle with me in the first place.'

So many questions. *So* many. Lara said, 'I don't understand the thing with the house, though. Why did you give her the money to buy it?'

James smiled fleetingly. 'That was for your benefit, believe it or not.'

'But I wasn't your child.'

'I know, but you were Barbara's. And she was worried sick about you. That flat you were all living in, the one in Bradford on Avon, was full of damp. You weren't well at all, you had a weak chest and kept getting infections. Then, when you were two, you were admitted to the hospital with pneumonia. Your mum thought you were going to die. And Charles flatly refused to move out of that bloody flat, where there was mould growing on the walls, because he said the rent was all he could afford. That's when I did it. Because I could. And I wanted to help your mother.'

295

'God.' Lara exhaled. 'Well, thank you.' Which was hopelessly inadequate, but what else could she say?

'My pleasure.'

'She could have left him in the flat. Why didn't she do that?'

'She didn't want to split you up from your father. Keeping the family together was all that mattered as far as Barbara was concerned. For your sake.'

For my sake.

'I really wish she hadn't.' Lara spoke with feeling.

James said drily, 'You and me both. But she did. And I knew I had to get away. That's when I sold the company, divorced my wife and moved abroad. It was the only way.' He paused again, then reached forward and poured the coffee into their cups. 'So, was it your father who told you about me?'

'No. Actually, his second wife did, just the other week.'

'He remarried then? So you had a stepmother. What was she like? Nice, I hope.'

'You tell me,' said Lara. 'She used to be your secretary.'

For a moment he looked blank. Then the coffee jug tilted sideways in his hand and coffee poured out on to the silver tray.

'Oh my God, do you mean *Janice*?'

Chapter 41

The hours had flown by. Lara felt as if they'd known each other for years. James might not be her father, but if she could have chosen one from a long list, he would have been it. He was honest, self-deprecating and irreverent. There was no possibility of the two of them running out of things to say. They'd eaten lunch outside on the terrace and talked about his ex-wives and assorted children. She'd told him about Gigi and Flynn, her years growing up in Keswick with Nettie and now her new life in Bath.

'I still can't get over the Janice connection,' James marvelled as he topped up her wine glass with icy Sancerre. 'She had a crush on me, you know. Or a fixation, maybe call it that. Everyone at work was aware of the situation but obviously it was never referred to. Janice wasn't the type to have friends in the office. She was like a super-efficient toad.'

'She still looks like a toad.' The secret crush made so much sense to Lara now; on the surface Janice had disapproved intensely of James's wicked philandering ways but deep down she'd been burning with jealousy, desperate to be on the receiving end of the philandering.

'And she was jealous of your mum. Ending up marrying your father must have felt like some kind of payback. But then to take it out on you . . .' He grimaced again at the thought of it. 'That's just unforgivable.'

'It's all OK now though.' Being bitter about the past wasn't going to help; she'd made that decision years ago. 'The worst part was thinking if my own father could be like that with me, what was to stop Flynn behaving the same way towards Gigi. But I know now that he never would have done. They couldn't be more different.' Lara's smile was rueful. 'Thank God.'

Lunch was cleared away by Esther, the hard-working Filipino housekeeper whose grasp of English might be tenuous but whose cooking skills were sublime.

'Listen, I didn't know if you'd want to see them so I didn't dig them out, but I do have a couple of photographs of your mum. If you're interested,' said James.

'You do? Really? Oh please show me!' Lara jumped to her feet; he had no idea. 'I've got hardly any photos of her. Let's get them now!'

It took a while to sift through the contents of the boxes in the spare room upstairs; one of his young grandchildren had spent an afternoon last year helpfully taking all the photographs out of their albums and putting them back in random order. Terrified the ones she was desperate to see might no longer be here, Lara flipped through album after album, gaining a crash course in the life of James Agnew and his extended family. Finally, between a wedding snap and a picture of a Greek taverna, she glimpsed a familiar face and her heart did a leap of joy.

'There she is,' said James, his voice softening.

There she was. Lara took in every detail. The photograph, yellowed at the edges, taken all those years ago. Her mum was sitting on a bright red picnic rug, wearing a green and white shift dress and smiling up at the camera. She looked young, happy and utterly relaxed, as if she hadn't a care in the world. Her eyes shone and there was a dimple at the corner of her mouth that Lara had almost forgotten existed. *How could she have forgotten about the dimple?*

'And here's the other one, taken a few months later.' James had found the second photo in the album he'd been going through. 'We wanted a picture of the two of us together. I asked a stranger to take it.'

The stranger had done a good job. There was James, rakishly handsome in a shirt and tie, standing next to her mum with his arm resting across her shoulders. Her head was tilted towards his and she was holding her flared yellow skirt down at her side as if a sudden breeze might send it flying up. Her cardigan was fluffy and cream and fastened with mother-of-pearl buttons; with a jolt, Lara realised she remembered that cardigan from her own child-hood, no longer worn but folded up and put away in her mum's chest of drawers. The little buttons had been heart-shaped and delicious-looking and once she'd secretly tried to bite one, expecting it to taste like a sweet.

It had been, frankly, something of a disappointment.

'That angora cardigan was my favourite,' said James. 'I loved to see her in it.'

'She kept it for years.'

'My beautiful Barbara.' He ran an index finger lightly over the photo. 'If she'd only trusted me, our lives could have been so different.'

All our lives. Definitely different, hopefully better.

Lara's eyes prickled. 'I wish she had.'

'I know,' said James. 'Me too.'

★   ★   ★

He had plenty to organise ahead of tomorrow's departure for the States. Lara arranged for Flynn to pick her up at four o'clock.

'But we're not going to lose touch,' James promised. 'I mean that. As soon as I'm back from my trip I'm coming down to Bath to see you.'

'I can't wait.' Lara meant it too.

'And if it's still standing, there's a tree in Victoria Park with our initials carved into the trunk. I'll have to show you that.'

'Can you remember where it is?'

James's eyes crinkled at the corners. 'How dare you? Of course I remember. BC and JA.' He paused. 'In a heart.'

'Wow. That's really . . .'

'Naff. Corny. Ridiculous.' He shrugged. 'All those things, I know. But at the time it didn't feel corny and ridiculous. When you love someone that much, you just want to . . . commemorate the occasion. Especially when it has to be a secret and you can't tell anyone else. Leaving your initials in a tree is like proving the relationship exists.'

Flynn arrived to pick her up. Lara introduced him to James Agnew. James said, 'Look after this girl, she's special,' and Flynn said drily, 'I've tried, believe me, but Lara doesn't like being looked after.'

Was that what he thought? It was more a matter of needing to completely trust the person doing it. But Lara didn't argue the point. Instead she gave James a proper hug and said, 'Considering I didn't get to hear what I wanted to hear today, this has still been one of the best days of my life.'

'Mine too.' He embraced her in return. 'And I'll be coming to Bath as soon as I get back. Now, you've got the photos?'

'All safe.' She patted her bag. 'I'll scan them and send you copies. Thanks so much.'

'And don't forget, we've got something else to look forward to,' James reminded her.

'What's that?' said Flynn.

Lara's eyes danced. 'We thought it might be fun to pay a surprise visit to Janice.'

After having waited on tenterhooks for a week and a half, the envelope fell through the letterbox the morning after her trip to London to meet James Agnew. Lara, about to leave for work, tore it open and read the results from the lab, belatedly confirming that her father was indeed her father.

Oh well, couldn't be helped.

Chapter 42

It was the beginning of October; summer was behind them now and autumn had arrived, turning the leaves flame-red on the trees and ushering in misty mornings, a chill wind and the annual, always-welcome influx of customers in search of Halloween outfits.

Not to mention a bit of a guilty secret . . .

Anyway, don't think about that now, work to do. Evie concentrated on ringing up her customers' purchases and packing them into bags; not for a Halloween party this time, but one to celebrate their silver wedding.

The couple, having come into the shop together, were still bickering amicably about the number of helium balloons they needed and which photographs of themselves should feature on the giant banner that was going to be hung across the front of their house.

'It should be a picture of us *now*,' the husband insisted.

'Oh, Tommy, don't even say that, I couldn't bear it.' An elaborate shudder. 'Imagine a giant photo of me with all my bags and wrinkles . . . nobody'd turn up for the party! The sight of it would terrify the guests, send them running for the hills. Let's have a nice pic of the two of us on our wedding day when we were young and lovely.'

'My darling girl, you'll always be young and lovely to me.' Tommy winked as he said it, but with genuine affection.

'Will you listen to him?' His wife was laughing now. 'What an old smoothie.'

'Ah, but it's true.' He pretended to be affronted. 'Even if you did just call me old. You're my Maureen, more beautiful now than the day we were married. But if it's really what you want, we'll use the wedding photo.'

They were so visibly, tangibly happy. Their togetherness was captivating. Evie filled the next bag with packets of table confetti, silver paper plates, silver and white striped tablecloths, swirling ceiling decorations and metallic streamers.

'Leave that.' Tommy stopped his wife from reaching to pick up the helium canister. 'Too heavy. Let me do it. If we'd been more organised we'd have cleared out the boot of the car.' Hoisting the box containing the canister into his arms, he said, 'I'll go and sort it now.'

They watched him head outside, open the boot of the grey Audi and begin making room for everything they'd just bought.

'Look at him,' Maureen said fondly. 'I still can't believe it's been twenty-five years. When we first got together no one thought we'd last twenty-five weeks.'

'Really? Why not?' Evie slotted the Amex card into the machine.

'Ah well, Tommy was a bit of a lad in his early days. You know the type, good-looking, buckets of charm and all the chat that goes with it . . . my parents and sisters said I shouldn't give him the time of day, they told me he'd break my heart.' Maureen glanced out of the window once more. 'But you know what? He settled down, we had five wonderful children and it's been the best twenty-five years anyone could have wished for. We're the happiest married couple I know.'

'That's . . . so lovely.' It actually made Evie well up. You see? Leopards *could* change their spots and other people didn't always know best.

'Thanks, love.' Maureen took the credit card and receipt. 'Ah, he's losing his hair now and putting on a bit of weight, but he's still the one for me.' As Tommy came back into the shop to pick up the rest of the bags, she added cheerily, 'And my sisters who married so-called perfect men? Divorced, the lot of them! Turned out their husbands weren't so perfect after all.'

Yes . . .

Freddy Krueger came into the shop just before closing time. One minute his long pointy fingers were clawing open the door, the next he was advancing menacingly towards her, his fedora tilted over one sinister eye.

Evie said, 'The real Freddy would be wearing a red and black striped sweater.'

'Even mass murderers have to wear a suit to work sometimes. It's the opposite of dress-down Friday.' His eyes glinted at her from behind the rubber mask. 'Dress-up Freddy.'

She tried not to smile. 'And what are you doing here?'

'I brought you something.' Careful not to stab her with his plastic knife-blade fingers, he uncurled his hand and passed over a small scrumpled-up paper bag.

'What is it?' Evie opened the bag and found it full of wiry-looking strands of chocolate-powder-coated coconut. 'Oh *wow* . . .'

'Is that the stuff? You said it was your favourite when you were little.'

'Yes, yes! Sweet tobacco, it was called . . . or Spanish Gold . . . I haven't seen any for *years*.' She put some into her mouth. 'Oh, and it tastes exactly the same!'

'I had a meeting in Bristol. There was a shop in St Nicholas's Market selling retro-style sweets. I saw the Spanish Gold and thought of you.'

'Freddy, thank you. If you like,' said Evie, 'you can take your mask off.'

'Good idea. Before I suffocate.'

She watched Joel pull off the knife-hands before removing his hat and peeling the mask off over his head. His blond hair stuck up at angles and he carelessly smoothed it back with the old familiar gesture she'd always found so endearing.

'Ta-daaa,' said Joel. 'It's me.'

Evie smiled. 'So it is.'

This was her guilty secret, the one she hadn't yet been able to bring herself to share with Lara. Not that anything had happened between her and Joel, not in *that* way, but relations between them had definitely improved. He'd stopped making over-the-top declarations and extravagant gestures. Instead it was like going back to the early years when friendship had first tipped over into flirtation. And it was nice, it was fun, she looked forward to seeing him when he turned up after work, ostensibly to have dinner with his family but actually – they both knew – to see her.

Evie was enjoying his visits. Joel enjoyed them too. So did Bonnie, who was still longing for them to get back together. And it wasn't a foregone conclusion that this would happen, but a bit of gentle flirting was harmless enough, wasn't it? It brightened up her days no end. Lara and Gigi would doubtless tell her she was mad if they knew, but they didn't have to live her life and they couldn't begin to understand how it felt to be her. Finding out just how wrong she'd been about Ethan had knocked her confidence far more than they knew. Lara's keenness for her and

Harry to get together had only served to emphasise how impossible it was to conjure up a physical attraction when it didn't exist.

But when it came to Joel . . . oh, all those old feelings were still there.

And the thing was, if he didn't really like her, why would he still be making this much effort? Surely he would have moved on by now? It wasn't as if he didn't have a choice; it would be far easier for Joel to play the field with all the girls who made their interest in him so obvious. Or to fall into a new relationship with someone who didn't always give him such a hard time.

But Joel hadn't taken either of those options. He wanted her back and was going all out to win her round. Which was unbelievably flattering. And although he didn't know this, she was weakening. Not in a weak way, Evie hastily reminded herself, but with . . . maybe . . . newfound maturity and powers of forgiveness.

Because there was an undeniable connection between them, and she did still love him, even if she didn't love some of the things he'd got up to in the past.

But then you met happily married couples like Tommy and Maureen and wanted a relationship like theirs. And from the sound of it, Tommy had definitely played away before their wedding.

Basically, some men did just need to get their naughtiness out of their system before settling down.

Maybe it was their way of fully appreciating monogamy.

'Anyway,' said Joel, 'Mum says why don't you join us for dinner? She's made enough chicken casserole to feed a rugby team.'

'Chicken casserole?' It was Evie's favourite. There was also a good chance this was why Bonnie had made it.

'Go on. Stay.' Joel was giving her his no-pressure smile. 'They'd love you to. I'll drive you home later.'

Evie hesitated. 'I don't know . . .'

'I can drop you off round the corner so Lara doesn't see you in my car.' He didn't say it sarcastically, but with self-deprecation, acknowledging that he'd done wrong in the past and fully deserved Lara's mistrust.

And he wouldn't have done that before, Evie reminded herself. See? He really was changing, learning from his mistakes.

It was raining when Joel drove her home at ten o'clock. She still made him park round the corner.

'That was fun tonight.' He left his hand resting lightly on the gearstick. 'Just like old times.'

The five of them had spent the evening sitting companionably around the kitchen table, chatting and laughing as if nothing had ever happened. That whole happy-family feeling of belonging was what she'd so loved about their years together. Evie nodded in agreement and said, 'It was.'

'Sorry about the Spanish Gold.' After dinner Bonnie had served coffee and Evie had brought out the paper bag; within minutes the chocolate-dusted coconut strands had been demolished. Joel said, 'Next time I'm in Bristol I'll buy a massive box of the stuff.'

'I had two helpings of plum crumble,' Evie pointed out. 'It's a fair swap.'

'Anyway, thanks for staying.'

'And now I have to go.' She curled her fingers around the door handle.

Joel said hopefully, 'I wish I could kiss you. But I suppose you wouldn't want me to.'

Evie's heart did a little shimmy of pride; this was what having the upper hand felt like. As the rain spattered on to the windscreen she said, 'No I wouldn't. Let's leave things as they are, shall we?'

'You're right.' Joel's smile was sad but accepting. 'Dammit, you're always right.'

'Thanks for the lift.' Evie opened the passenger door and climbed out. 'Bye.'

In the kitchen, Lara and Gigi were doing the dishes and singing and dancing along to Enjay's new single as it blared out of Gigi's laptop. Since returning to the States to start his world tour, Enjay had been keeping them updated through emails and via his website diary. The actual TV show was due to air on MTV straight after Christmas. Harry, now back in Keswick, was doing his best to get back to living a normal life but was being asked for his autograph on a daily basis by the fans who'd been following Enjay's video blog. Harry still found the entire experience utterly surreal and baffling, but there was no escaping the fact that it had broadened his horizons. Sales of Flying Ducks were still on the up. More staff had needed to be taken on. And next week his shirts were due to feature in a photo shoot for *Vogue*.

Evie smiled at the memory of his phone call to them the other evening. Only Harry could wonder if there was really any point in having men's clothing featured in a women's fashion magazine.

Lara turned to greet her. 'There you are! Have you been at Bonnie and Ray's all this time?'

'And Marina was there too.' No need to mention Joel. 'We had chicken casserole and plum crumble with custard.'

'How did you get home?'

'Ray gave me a lift.' *Only a tiny fib.*

'Oh right. It's just that your eyes are all sparkly and your cheeks are pink. I thought maybe you'd run the whole way.'

Evie said, 'If I'd run, I'd be purple and crawling on my hands and knees. No, Ray dropped me off.'

'Ah well, that's good. There's still wine in the fridge if you want some, just help yourself . . . BABY, YO IS MIIIIINE,' Lara and Gigi simultaneously burst back into song, bellowing along to the chorus of Enjay's insanely catchy new single. 'ALL MINE, ALL MINE, AN' DON'T YOU FORGET IT. . .'

See? Evie reached into the cupboard for a glass. And it didn't count as lying, exactly.

It was just a matter of leaving certain bits out.

Chapter 43

'I can't help thinking this isn't doing you any good. Wouldn't you say it was kind of counter-productive?'

'Stop nagging me,' said Don. 'Just get on with it.'

Lara sighed and set about untangling the leads and wires; honestly, his fingers were trembling even as he struggled to remove the silver cufflink from his crisp white cuff. But Don was on an anxiety-generated health kick and there was no stopping him. He'd bought himself a DIY blood-pressure monitoring machine and he was determined to use it. Twice a day, every day. Even though the prospect of having his blood pressure measured caused him to hyperventilate with fear and trepidation.

He'd also bought a cholesterol-testing kit and had to hype himself up each morning in order to jab the tiny needle into his thumb and measure the levels in the resultant bead of blood.

The first three times they'd done it, he'd almost fainted.

'Right.' Don had managed to roll up his sleeve. 'Put the thing round my arm.'

They were in the office behind the shop. Lara did the honours and began pumping air into the blood pressure cuff. 'OK, don't breathe so fast. Think calming thoughts. Just close your eyes and relax . . .'

Not that it helped. Don failed to do so and the result was the same as yesterday. As was the cholesterol test, although on the plus side at least this time he didn't turn pale green.

'I listened to my Paul McKenna tape twice last night,' he complained. 'All the way through. Why does it work for everyone else but me?'

It was a vicious circle. Having succumbed to anxiety attacks, each failed attempt to reduce the anxiety just made the situation worse. Nor did Don's diet help. He loved butter and cream and couldn't get to grips with salad at all. His attempts at healthy eating were pitiful; in his mind, listening to Paul McKenna's soothing tones would counteract the diabolical eating habits.

Needless to say, it wasn't having the desired effect.

'Did you have your bran flakes for breakfast?' said Lara.

Don looked petulant. 'What are you, my nursemaid?'

Which meant he'd had bacon and eggs.

'Just trying to help.' It was tempting to remind him that if he had a cardiac arrest and keeled over in the shop, she was the one who'd have to give him mouth to mouth. But that probably wouldn't contribute much towards his state of serenity.

'If you want to help,' Don said glumly, 'you could come over to my place, break into next door and steal their drumsticks.'

'Oh dear. Still bad?'

'Worse.'

Poor Don. Until a few months ago his neighbour had been a sweet little old lady in her eighties. Peace had reigned and he'd taken it entirely for granted. Then she'd died and the house had been sold to a family who'd moved in six weeks ago.

They were charming people, friendly people, two parents, three teenagers and a dog. Unfortunately for Don, they were also the noisiest neighbours on the planet and blithely unaware of it. From six in the morning there was door-slamming, stair-stomping, music-playing, TV-blaring, dog-barking and banter. The teenage son had a drum kit, the daughters dreamed of *X Factor* stardom and liked to sing at the top of their voices, and between them they were driving Don insane. He'd tried a few times now to reason with them and they'd been hugely apologetic, promising to keep the noise down. But within hours the level had slid back up, simply because they genuinely didn't realise how much of a racket they made during the course of their normal daily life.

'If you really can't stand it,' said Lara, 'you'll have to move.'

'I know.' He was mournful. 'But it's my house, it's where I grew up. I've always been happy there.'

The doorbell rang while Don finished fitting the silver cufflink back into his shirt cuff. Lara went through to the shop and buzzed open the door to let the customer in.

'Morning!' The woman was middle-aged, slender, lightly tanned and wearing a pale blue raincoat over a grey wool dress. 'Brrr, it's chilly out there! Now, where's my ticket?' She began rummaging in the side pockets of her shoulder bag. 'I'm here to pick up my ring. My name's Betsy Barrowman . . . oh hello, Mr Temple, there you are! Haven't seen you for a while!'

Barrowman. Oh God, this was the wife of the sweating man in the too-tight suit. Mr Cubic Zirconium Bastard-Barrowman.

'Mrs Barrowman,' said Don. 'You're looking *very* well. Been away?'

'I have, I have! I took my darling mum to the west coast of Ireland . . . we stayed in a wonderful cottage in Galway and had the best time. Even the weather was perfect. I just got back last night,' Betsy explained. 'That's why I haven't been in sooner to collect the ring.' She waggled her thin fingers at them. 'My hand's felt so naked without it!'

'It must have done. Lara, could you get Mrs Barrowman's ring out of the safe?'

'Ah, that's better.' Betsy Barrowman actually heaved a sigh of relief as she slipped the ring back on to her finger. 'I don't feel naked any more!'

The truth was begging to come out. But Don had already issued a stern warning. Lara visualised her mouth being sealed with gaffer tape, metres of it being wrapped round and round her head. It was like being a doctor or a priest, he'd explained; you might discover unpalatable facts about a person but your job entailed keeping quiet about them.

'And it's been cleaned up too. Lovely!' Betsy was admiring the way the ring flashed, catching the light. Ironically, if the original stone had contained flaws, flecks of carbon, she would have known this wasn't her diamond. But the very fact that it had been close to flawless made it virtually impossible to tell.

'Thanks so much.' Betsy reached for her purse. 'Now, how much do I owe you?'

Don waved the credit card away. 'Nothing. Your husband paid when he brought it in.'

'Did he? Ah, that's so thoughtful.' Betsy's smile was fond. 'He's wonderful like that. It was Gerald who saw that the claws were getting worn and needed fixing . . . I wouldn't have even noticed.'

'*Zheeeeeeeessssssshhh*.' The moment the door closed behind Betsy Barrowman, Lara let out a noise like the valve being released on a pressure cooker. The smell of Betsy's light flowery perfume still hung in the air; it was *exactly* the kind of innocent scent worn by a wife blithely unaware that her husband was up to no good.

313

'I know, I know.' Evidently no longer giving Gerald the benefit of the doubt, Don sat down heavily on one of the mulberry and blue striped velvet chairs.

'I wanted to tell her!'

'But you can't. It isn't our place.'

'She should know the truth,' Lara wailed.

'You don't know that she wants to. How would you feel if you told her and she was so distraught she committed suicide?' Don's hair quivered as he shook his head. 'Either way, she's not going to be delighted.'

Which was true enough. Lara said, 'Are you OK?' because he was looking pale and dabbing at his forehead with a handkerchief.

'It's all the stress. Take my pulse.' Don held out his hand like a dog wanting to shake a paw. 'It's all over the place, going like the clappers. Look, I know you want to interfere but promise me you won't. Otherwise I'll have that to worry about too.'

'Oh but—'

'And if I die, you'll be out of a job.' This time he was kind of joking, kind of not.

His pulse was horribly rapid, like an old-fashioned train rattling over tracks. Also, he had a point. Lara gave up and patted the back of his hand. 'OK, I promise.'

Chapter 44

Lara wanted to burst with the thrill of it all. After a month away in New York and Toronto, James Agnew had been as good as his word. He'd booked a room at the Ellison and driven down to Bath for the weekend. And now it was Saturday lunchtime and here they all were, together in the house he'd bought for her mother because he loved her so much.

Gigi and James had hit it off from the word go. It was fascinating to watch them together, interacting as easily as if they'd always known each other, just as a grandfather and grandchild should interact. She was proud of Gigi, so sparky and funny and bright, and oddly proud too that her mother had been adored by someone as charming and urbane as James Agnew.

The clock chimed out in the hall and Gigi, on the sofa, unfolded her legs from under her.

'I feel like Cinderella. I have to go to work now.'

'Hey, doesn't matter.' James rose to his feet too. 'We'll see you later. I've booked a table for eight o'clock in the hotel restaurant. You, me and your mum and dad.'

'Yay, can't wait. Did I tell you Dad's bringing along some

special wine? From the year I was born.' Gigi wrinkled her nose. 'So let's hope it isn't all gross and manky.'

'And we still have tomorrow as well. By Sunday night you'll be sick of me.' He gave her a goodbye hug.

'No we won't. Mum, if you two are off out now anyway, can I have a lift to the bus stop?'

Once Gigi had been dropped, they headed over to Bradford on Avon in James's midnight-blue Mercedes. The sun came out and white clouds scudded across an autumn-blue sky.

'This is bringing back memories,' said James as they drove down the narrow winding street that led into the centre of town. 'The shops are different but the rest's exactly the same.'

'Oh look!' Lara pointed, entranced, to a pair of swans gliding down the river.

'And see over there?' Having crossed the Town bridge, James slowed and indicated a tiny row of shops. 'There used to be a bakery where that hair salon is now. Your mum loved fresh cream éclairs with coffee icing so I'd buy her one as a treat.'

Lara smiled. 'I remember coffee éclairs. They were her favourites.'

James turned left, then right, then left again. He pulled up in a narrow street and nodded at a tall house divided into flats. 'And that's where you lived before you moved to Arlington Road. The top flat with the narrow rickety stairs and all the mould and damp. It's been smartened up now. There used to be holes in the roof and a big crack going down the side of the house.'

'Until you rescued us.' There was a lump in Lara's throat; life was full of what-ifs. It was weird to think that if he hadn't, she might have carried on getting ill. Who was to say the next bout of pneumonia wouldn't have been fatal?

'Hey, cheer up.' James clicked the indicator and drew away from the kerb; when they reached the end of the street he turned left. 'Fun bit next.'

He was right. The last time she'd paid a visit to Bingham Close had been six weeks ago and it had been a wet gloomy day. This one was brighter, sunnier, happier all round. Would they get a welcome to match?

Luckily, she hadn't set her heart on it.

'Who are you? What do you want?' As before, the unwelcoming older sister answered the door of number 32.

'Hello there, I'm looking for Janice.' James flashed her his most charming smile. 'Are you Joan? Janice used to work for me years ago. She talked about you all the time! How do you do? My name's James Agnew.'

Was Joan stunned? Lurking to the left of James, just out of sight, Lara watched him seize Joan's hand, warmly shake it and say, 'Is Janice here?'

'Um, yes, she is. Do come in . . .'

'Thank you so much. It's been a long time.' Reaching out, he pulled Lara into view. 'Come along, darling, let's say hello to Janice.'

'*You* again.' Joan stiffened, her eyes instantly flinty.

'Oh now don't be like that, Joan.' James's tone was soothing as he entered the house with Lara at his side.

'But—'

'Janice wanted the hairbrush back.' Lara patted her handbag. 'And guess what?' she added brightly, suddenly channelling Jeremy Kyle. 'We've got those all-important DNA results!'

Ensconced in her armchair in the sitting room, Janice's pale eyes bulged at the sight of them. She'd never looked more toadlike.

Except most toads didn't wear gloopy mascara and tended not to flush a dull shade of maroon.

'Hello, Janice,' James said cheerily. 'Just a flying visit. How are you?'

'I . . . I . . .' It was like watching a toad go *ribbett-ribbett*.

'Excellent. Anyway, Lara has something for you.'

'I do.' Unzipping her shoulder bag, Lara pulled out the old-fashioned man's hairbrush, wrapped up in transparent plastic. 'There you go.'

'Lara came to visit me before the DNA results came back from the lab,' James continued. 'I was able to explain to her that she couldn't possibly be my daughter because nothing of that nature ever happened between Barbara and myself. Barbara was never unfaithful to Charles.'

'The results arrived the next day.' Lara produced an envelope from her bag and handed it, along with the wrapped-up hairbrush, over to Janice. 'Charles was my father all along.'

Janice's upper lip was slick with perspiration as she opened the envelope and scanned the letter inside.

'Anyway, thought you'd like to know. And meeting Lara has been a delight.' Turning to include Joan in the conversation, James said, 'I gather we have you to thank for that, even if you didn't mean to let the cat out of the bag.'

'She tricked me into saying it,' Joan stonily replied.

'Well, we're truly grateful.' He rested his arm around Lara's shoulders. 'It's a real shame we can't be related but we're going to make do with being the best of friends instead.'

'Sometimes,' said Lara, 'friends are better than relatives.'

'So that's it.' James addressed his silent ex-secretary. 'We just wanted to drop by and let you know the results, so now we'll be off. Don't worry, we won't be back.' Turning to leave he said genially, 'Bye,' then winked at prune-faced Joan. 'And thanks again, you were a tremendous help. Lara would never have been able to find me without you.'

'I think you've forgotten where it is,' said Lara.

They'd been walking arm in arm through mounds of dry fallen leaves, meandering this way and that along the pathways of Royal Victoria Park. She turned to look at James. 'You can't remember which tree you carved those initials in.'

'I can, I know exactly where it is. I'm just enjoying the walk and the sunshine. Not to mention the company.' His eyes twinkled. 'Can I ask you a question?'

'Fire away.'

'You and Flynn. What's going to happen?'

Sometimes, like now, unexpectedly hearing Flynn's name made her skin go zingy. All the more reason to keep herself under control. 'We're just going to stay friends,' said Lara.

'Really? Nothing more?'

'He's Gigi's dad. I don't want to risk spoiling anything. It's better if we don't get involved.'

'You could be fantastically happy together.'

'Or we might not.' Surely he was able to understand? 'It could all go horribly wrong.'

'And you aren't prepared to take that chance.' He gave her one of those annoying that's-fascinating looks.

'No, I'm not.' Lara felt herself getting defensive. 'What's wrong with that?'

'It just interests me that you're going for the safe option. I've heard this kind of argument before, remember.' His expression softened. 'You're more like your mother than you think.'

Lara hesitated; normally such a comparison would be a huge

thrill. In this instance though, she wasn't so sure. Changing the subject, she exclaimed, 'Ooh, conkers!'

And there they were, dozens of them, nestled inside their split-open cases beneath the horse chestnut trees. Within minutes they'd collected up some of the best specimens.

'Aren't they just wonderful?' James took the one she handed him, glossy and fat and with a waxen feel to its skin. 'They never stop being amazing.'

'When a man is tired of conkers, he's tired of life,' said Lara, breaking open another case. 'And this one's got twins inside! Look at them, how sweet is that? They're nestled together like puppies . . . ooh, careful . . .'

Had he spotted an even more perfect conker on the ground? But why was he trying to drag her down with him? The next moment she heard a guttural sound and realised he wasn't reaching, he was falling. Bracing herself, she did her best to hold him up and discovered it was impossible. James was too big, too heavy . . .

'*Ggrrrhhhggghh* . . .' He groaned again and clutched his head, scattering leaves and conkers as he crumpled to the ground. His face was grey and contorted with pain; was that why he couldn't speak?

'Oh God, it's OK, don't worry, I'll get an ambulance . . . you'll be fine . . . HELP!' Glancing up for a terror-stricken split second, Lara saw a jogger in the distance, heading towards her. 'HELP US PLEASE. Can someone dial 999?'

'Gnhnnurggh . . .' James was gazing helplessly up at her but his eyelids were starting to close. Oh God, please don't let this be happening. She loosened his tie and rolled him on his side into the recovery position.

'What's wrong with him?' A blonde woman in her twenties with a toddler in a pushchair had reached them.

'I don't know . . . maybe a stroke . . . can you help me?'

The blonde looked alarmed. 'Oh Lord, but I wouldn't know what to do. Shall I call 999?'

'Yes!' Lara's voice rose as terror launched her into overdrive. 'James, can you hear me? It's all right, we'll get you to the hospital . . . oh please, can you tell me what hurts . . . ?'

But James wasn't able to reply. His eyes were closed now, he was unconscious. Fumbling for a pulse, she was – horror of horrors – unable to find one. His chest was utterly still.

Oh please, no no no.

'Hello, we need an ambulance please . . . um, this old guy's kind of fallen down in the park . . . oh, um, Victoria Park in Bath, I don't know which bit, we're not too far from one of those monument thingys . . .'

The jogger reached them as Lara finished hauling James over on to his back and pushing his jacket clear of his chest. 'Need a hand? I'm a doctor.'

'Oh, thank God. He just collapsed, he's not b-breathing, I can't find a pulse,' stammered Lara. 'Can you check?'

Within seconds the jogger nodded to confirm she was right. 'Let's get going. If you're OK with the chest compressions, I'll do the mouth to mouth.'

'Yes . . . tell them it's the Marlborough Lane entrance,' Lara shouted at the blonde on the phone.

'Is he dead, miss?' Two young boys on skateboards had arrived.

'No he's not dead. Could you go to the Marlborough Lane entrance and tell the ambulance driver where to find us? Thanks.' As the boys scooted off to do as she asked, Lara knelt beside James. Keeping her arms straight and her fingers laced together, she press-press-pressed down on to his sternum then leaned back on her heels while the doctor tipped James's head back to ensure a clear airway and breathed air into his lungs.

'Good. You're doing well.' His voice was reassuring. 'Done this before?'

'Only on plastic dummies.' *Press press press.*

'Is this your father?'

There was that question again. Lara shook her head. 'No, he's not my dad.'

They carried on working away. It was like being trapped in a disaster movie with no director around to call Cut. How could it be happening? This was meant to be one of the best days of her life. When was James going to open his eyes, sit himself up and say, 'Dear me, so sorry about that, how embarrassing . . .'

'We told the ambulance people where you are.' The skateboarding boys were back, out of breath and exhilarated by their involvement in the drama. 'They're coming now!'

Chapter 45

Flynn saw her sitting on the steps outside A&E, white-faced and immobile with her arms wrapped tightly around her knees. When he'd taken her call, she'd asked him to come, saying only in a voice that was barely recognisable, 'It's James, something awful's happened.'

He pulled up away from the ambulances, and jumped out of the car. Lara rose to her feet and made her way woodenly across the tarmac towards him.

'He's dead.' She was dry-eyed, too shocked to cry. 'Oh God, I can't believe it. James is gone. He just . . . *died*.'

Flynn took her in his arms. James might have turned out not to be her father but getting to know him had meant the world to Lara. The connection between the two of them had been instantaneous. His heart went out to her.

'Come on, let's get you home.' He gently led Lara back to the car; she was walking like an automaton.

'The table's booked at the restaurant.' Her teeth were chattering. 'We're all supposed to be meeting there at eight.'

'Don't worry, I'll sort that out.' Flynn helped her into the passenger seat. 'I'll take care of everything.'

'Sorry. Being a nuisance again.'

Only someone in such a state of shock could come out with a statement like that. Bending down, he kissed the top of her head. 'Put your seat belt on.'

'Oh God, and James's car. It's still there outside the park. We only paid for two hours.' Lara turned to him, her tone fretful. 'He'll have got a ticket by now. What happens if it's towed away?'

'It's all right. Leave it to me. Have his next of kin been informed?'

'The police are doing that now.' She was twisting her fingers together in her lap. 'We were having such a nice time. We went to see Janice and Joan, gave them the DNA results. Then in the park afterwards we were just walking and talking about . . . well, loads of different things. I'd been making him laugh, telling him about the time Gigi thought her new Spiderman pyjamas gave her superpowers and she jumped out of a tree. Then, a minute or so later, he collapsed. Without even any warning. He was just lying in the leaves and I couldn't find a pulse and this jogger came along who was a doctor, so we were trying to get his heart going again, keep him alive . . . then the ambulance arrived and they used defibrillators and injections and everything they could. It went on for ages but nothing worked. He'd gone.' Lara took a couple of deep shuddery breaths. 'And we hadn't been walking up steep hills or anything, so it wasn't that. I just keep thinking it must have been me that caused it, making him laugh.'

It hadn't been her fault, needless to say. Lara knew that now. The post-mortem had revealed a catastrophic brain haemorrhage as a result of an aneurysm, a weakened blood vessel, bursting inside his head. The berry-shaped aneurysm had been there for years evidently, lurking like a time bomb; it could have happened at any moment. Telling James funny stories, the doctor had assured her, definitely hadn't caused the haemorrhage.

'Making people laugh is a good thing,' he'd added. 'I can't think of a nicer way to go.'

Chapter 46

Looking up as Don returned from his trip to the post office, Lara saw him let himself back into the shop unaware of the two lads directly behind him. The next moment they jostled him through the doorway, pulled Halloween masks out of their pockets and crammed them on to their faces.

'OK, don't move, this is a stick-up, right?' slurred Dracula.

'Give us all your stuff!' yelled Zombie Head.

'Oh Jesus, oh God, *no*. . .' Don clutched his chest and tottered over to one of the mulberry upholstered chairs.

'Make up your mind then.' Lara pressed the panic button beneath the counter and gave the boys a hard stare; she'd seen them earlier, hanging around outside the shop and swigging Stella from cans. They couldn't be more than sixteen and from the sound of it weren't accustomed to strong drink.

'What's that mean?' Dracula, the taller of the two, swayed on his feet.

'You told me not to move,' said Lara. 'But you also want me to give you all our stuff. I can't do both, can I?'

'OK.' Zombie Head nodded in bleary agreement. 'Give us all your stuff. But do it slowly, yeah? No funny business.'

'Fine. Do you have a bag?'

'What?'

'To put all the stuff in,' Lara patiently explained.

'Haven't you got one?'

'Well, no, because why would I need one? Look, let me just check he's OK.' She went over to Don, who was hyperventilating and trembling, and checked his pulse. 'It's all right, they won't hurt you.' Turning back to Zombie Head, Lara added, 'He has heart problems, you know. I can't believe you'd do this to a man who isn't well. What kind of weapon do you have, anyway? A knife? A gun?'

'Both.' As if belatedly realising it was meant to be an armed robbery, Zombie Head stuck his hand in his jacket pocket and made pistol fingers at her through the thin material. 'I got a . . . gun. He's got a knife.'

Dracula swayed and said, 'Yeah, I have.'

'Well, look, why don't you give me your hat and we can put everything in that? I'll start with some gold bracelets, shall I? The masks are great, by the way. Where did you get them from?'

'Phil bought them from that party shop place.' Dracula took off his beanie hat and handed it to her, revealing spikily gelled blond hair. 'You know, the one that does all the fancy dress and stuff.'

'Ah yes, I've been there. It's a brilliant shop. Now, let's get this cabinet unlocked . . . oops, better just make sure we aren't disturbed by any other customers . . .' Lara crossed to the door, opened it and said, 'It's OK, just boys, they're unarmed.'

'Eh?' Dracula looked bemused.

'What's going on?' slurred Zombie Head.

Lara stood aside and let the police in to arrest them. Honestly, some people, they didn't have a clue. She said to Don, 'OK now? I'll put the kettle on and make us a nice cup of tea.'

Having sobered up fast, Dracula started to sob as the two policemen handcuffed him, whisked off his mask and patted him down. 'Oh no, my mum's gonna go mental when she hears about this.'

The police took statements from Lara and Don, then carted the boys away for a fun-free afternoon down at the station.

'You treated the whole thing like a joke.' Don was fretful, refusing to calm down.

'That's because it was a joke. They were schoolboys on half-term break, so drunk they didn't know what they were doing.'

'They could have had guns!'

Lara said patiently, 'Don, stop worrying about it. They didn't.'

'But what if it happens again tomorrow with robbers who *do*?' He mopped his brow and shook his head. 'I'm going to keep thinking that now.'

'You won't. You'll be fine. Go home and get some rest. You'll feel better in the morning.'

'Rest? With my neighbours? *Ha.*'

He looked so upset. The racket next door had shown no sign of abating and the family had now acquired a cat that liked to sit on the wall each night yowling at the moon. When he'd attempted to protest, the charming mother had said, 'Oh but Don, how can we stop them? They're cats, bless them. It's what they do!'

Lara's heart went out to him. To add insult to injury they had already cheerily informed Don that on Sunday afternoon and evening they'd be holding a party.

'Look, come over to us on Sunday. I'm going to do a big lunch. How about that?'

'Really?' Don, whose idea of a Sunday roast was the kind you bought frozen on a cardboard plate and cooked in the microwave, looked tempted but wary. 'Didn't you say your aunt's coming down for the weekend?'

'Nettie? She is. That's why we're having a proper lunch.'

'I don't know. She sounds a bit scary.' He'd heard the stories from Lara about no-nonsense salt-of-the-earth Nettie.

'But in a nice way.'

'Hmm.' Don was still looking doubtful; he'd been intimidated by the tale of the escaped bull Nettie had once stopped in its tracks when it had gone on the rampage outside the local infants' school in Keswick.

'Stop it, she's great. You'll like her,' said Lara. 'I promise.'

Lara, lifting the blackberry crumble out of the oven, listened to the chatter and laughter carrying on in the living room. It was both strange and wonderful having Nettie back amongst them. Finally persuaded to leave her beloved animals in the care of Fred Milton, she had driven down yesterday morning and would be heading back up to Keswick tonight. Keeping in touch via phone calls over the past couple of months had been fine in its own way, but actually having her here was so much better. For the first time she had seen the house. Even more significantly, she'd met Flynn and they'd hit it off instantly.

'Come on then, tell us,' Lara heard Gigi saying now, 'what's been the thing you've missed about us the most?'

'Goodness me, how can I choose? Your singing, perhaps?' Nettie sounded amused. 'The splurts of toothpaste in the bathroom sink? The not-quite-empty Coke cans left in unexpected places?'

'Oh no, you haven't missed us at all! I bet you're loving having the place to yourself! *Hmm.*' Gigi's tone turned speculative. 'So how are things going between you and Fred?'

Smiling to herself, Lara returned to the living room with the crumble just in time to witness the give-nothing-away expression on Nettie's face. It was the kind of look you'd see on a politician being ruthlessly interrogated on *Question Time*.

'Fred's very well. Finished harvesting his potatoes. I gave him a hand with his ewes last week. All dipped and clipped, they are, ready for tupping.'

Don frowned. 'Tupping? What's that?'

'Mating.' Nettie, who always enjoyed shocking townies, kept a straight face. 'That's why the tail area needs to be clipped.'

'Ah.'

'No need to blush, darling. All perfectly normal. It's just sex.'

His flush deepening, Don swallowed and said, 'Right.'

After a long lunch, during which the story of Don's neighbours came out, Nettie said, 'Come on then, shall we get this thing sorted out?'

'Excuse me?' Don glanced up, belatedly realising she was addressing him.

'That noisy crew next door to you, the ones making your life a misery. I reckon they need a good talking-to.'

'I've already spoken to them.' He looked alarmed.

'And how much of an effect did that have?'

Lara watched, enthralled.

'But the thing is, they're really nice people,' Don protested.

'Excellent,' said Nettie. 'I shall be really nice too. I'll be an official from the council investigating noise pollution. I'll explain that unless they get their act together I shall be forced to serve a Noise Abatement Notice on them.'

'They'll know it's me who complained!'

'And so they should!'

'Oh God, they'll hate me.'

'And you'd rather suffer in silence?' Nettie raised her eyebrows at him in disbelief. 'Let your blood pressure climb until your heart explodes like a bomb? That, my darling, is called dying of politeness. Come on, let's go.'

As Nettie rose to her feet, Lara said, 'Do council officials wear checked shirts and jeans?'

Nettie said, 'This one does.'

Don was surveying her as if she were a rogue firework that might be about to go off. 'Are you always like this?'

'Only when it matters.' She reached for her keys and jangled them at him. 'Right, hop to it. The sooner we leave, the quicker we'll be back.'

Which didn't exactly happen, it had to be said. Dusk fell, the lights of Bath came on, the hours passed and Lara was on the verge of heading over to Don's house herself when they finally returned at nine thirty.

'Where the bloody hell have you two been?' She eyed them in disbelief. 'Why didn't you answer your phones?'

Nettie said reasonably, 'Mine's in Keswick.'

'And mine's right here.' Don patted the inside pocket of his smart cashmere jacket. 'It didn't ring. Oh, sorry, battery's flat.'

'We were worried about you! I thought maybe the noisy neighbours had drugged and buried the pair of you under their patio.'

'She's always been like this.' Nettie shook her head apologetically at Don. 'Over-dramatic.'

'You've been gone for four hours!'

'The neighbours invited us to their party,' Don explained.

'And you *went*?'

'He's right, they're lovely people.' Patiently Nettie said, 'I did have a chat with them about the noise and they promised to keep it down in future.'

331

'They've done that before,' said Gigi.

'Well, maybe this time they'll take notice. Anyway,' said Don, 'we had a good time. There was karaoke.'

'You mean you *sang*?' squeaked Lara.

'"I Dreamed A Dream".' He looked proud. 'From *Les Misérables*.'

'And you?' She turned to Nettie, whose grey-blonde hair was escaping from its clips.

'She did "Born To Be Wild",' said Don.

Oh good God. 'Seriously?'

Gigi said, 'Wow.'

Nettie said, 'Can you two stop looking at me like that? I got a standing ovation.'

'She did,' Don marvelled.

'And was drink involved?'

'Of course not.' Nettie was brisk. 'I'm driving home tonight. In fact it's time I made a move now. I need to be up again at six to milk the goats.'

Chapter 47

Harry gazed out at the twinkling lights of the harbour and marvelled that he was here. EnjaySeven's tour had criss-crossed the continents, moving from Japan to Australia, from New Zealand to Singapore. Finally back in Europe to promote the upcoming TV series, he had called and persuaded Harry to join him in Monaco for the weekend so they could perform their odd-couple double act for the press due to interview them tomorrow. The photographers, at a guess, would joyfully play up the juxtaposition of fuddy-duddy Harry exploring this, the flashiest of billionaires' playgrounds. He would be pictured on sleek yachts. There would be scantily clad girls with even sleeker curves and the kind of breasts money *could* buy.

Oh well. Harry, now comfortably settled on the wrought-iron balcony on to which his hotel room opened, sat back and sipped his coffee. Back at home the skies were leaden and the air temperature in single figures, yet here in Monte Carlo's balmy microclimate the sky was inky blue, the stars were huge and bright and he was out here at ten in the evening in just his shirtsleeves.

Dinner downstairs earlier had been delicious. The hotel – a

five star, naturally – was spectacular. And he'd started reading a book on the flight down here that was proving to be unput-downable. Checking how many pages he still had left to read, Harry saw to his satisfaction that there were three hundred. Excellent.

Other than the faint buzz of traffic and nightlife in the distance, peace reigned. Perfect coffee, fresh fruit in the bowl on the table beside him and maybe a cognac later. Harry opened his book and began to read. Ah yes, there were definitely worse ways to spend a weekend.

'That's good . . . oh yes, great . . . now just turn over on to your front, darling, and let Enjay run his finger down your spine.'

Harry, sitting in the shade while the photographer danced around Enjay and the two bikini-clad models, watched as Enjay gave the blonde model's bikini tie a playful tug.

'Hey, naughty.' She giggled and pouted up at him over her shoulder.

'Sorry, babe, can't help myself. Kind of just happens.' Enjay rested his hand lightly in the curve of her spine and winked at the second model as he said it. In turn, she blew him a kiss.

'Perfect,' yelled the photographer, snapping away. 'Harry, I want you in the background, peering at them over the top of your glasses and looking disapproving.'

Enjay's pointed teeth flashed. 'Harry can do that, he's had plenty of practice.'

It was midday and they were on one of the yachts moored in the harbour, bright sunlight bouncing off the polished steel, the white paintwork and the varnished wood of the upper deck. As the photographer finished up, the journalist put his phone away and prepared to begin the interview. In his mid-forties and sporting a slicked-back ponytail, he said good-humouredly, 'Is he always like this?'

'Oh yes.' Harry nodded.

'Hey, man, what you see is what you get.' Enjay was standing up now, his hand briefly cupping the blonde's pert bottom as she sashayed past him. 'It's just the way I'm made, take it or leave it.'

The journalist switched on the voice recorder, placing it on the table between them as Enjay pulled up a chair. 'And I'm guessing they don't often leave it.'

'Why would they, man? I keep myself in shape. I know how to treat a lady. Just ask the one I met in the casino and brought back to the hotel last night.'

'And Marina doesn't mind you sharing yourself around?'

Enjay shrugged. Marina was one of the backing singers he'd been seeing recently during the course of the tour. 'I haven't asked her. If she minds that much, no one's forcing her to put up with it. But let's be fair, she's thousands of miles away and I'm here.'

'Cool, cool.' The journalist nodded with approval. 'Their choice.'

'Exactly.' Adjusting the sleeves of his pistachio-green suit, Enjay paused to admire his reflection in the side of the silver ice bucket. 'If they decide they don't want me, they can always say no.'

'And has anyone ever done that?'

Enjay's light brown eyes gleamed as he paused for effect then broke into a wolfish, self-satisfied grin. 'Uh . . . *no*.'

The day had been filled with back-to-back interviews. When Enjay's immaculate pale green suit creased in the heat, it was replaced with an identical white one, then an hour or so later with a silver tuxedo.

Finally the last TV crew left, the empty champagne bottles

were carried off the yacht and a limo took them back up the narrow winding road to the hotel.

'Can I ask you something?' said Harry as they rode up in the mirror-lined elevator to the fourth floor.

'Fire away, old chap.' Enjay still loved to practise his over-the-top British accent.

Harry waited until he'd stopped admiring his profile in the double-angled mirrors. 'Why did you lie to that journalist?'

'Say what?'

'The one with the ponytail. You spun him a story about the girl you spent the night with last night. But it wasn't true, was it?'

Enjay's jaw tightened; he was no longer studying his reflection. 'It was.'

'No, it wasn't.' They'd reached their floor. The doors slid silently open and they stepped out.

'I don't know what you're gettin' at, man.'

Harry paused at his door then watched as Enjay used his key card to open his own. His hand wasn't trembling but nor was it entirely steady.

'I'm not having a go at you, I'm just curious.' Following Enjay into his suite, Harry added, 'I don't understand why you'd say all that stuff in the first place. You seem to think there's something admirable about sleeping with girls you don't even know, but I promise you there isn't.'

'OK, what makes you think I'm lying about last night?' There was an odd look on Enjay's face.

Should he back off? No, he jolly well wasn't going to. 'I just know,' said Harry.

'Bullshit, man. You said you were having an early night. You'd have been asleep way before we even left the casino.'

336

'Normally, yes, I would.' Harry stood his ground. 'But I was reading a good book. I heard you come back at midnight,' he went on. 'I was sitting out on my balcony and your window was open. I wasn't eavesdropping,' he added, because Enjay had now begun pacing the room like a panther. 'I just heard you flick through the TV channels. You called your mother and chatted to her for a bit. Then you had a shower and watched an old episode of *Star Trek*. After that you must have fallen asleep. I was outside until gone three and you *definitely* didn't have anyone else in that room with you.'

'Fine.' After a pause, Enjay's shoulders slumped. 'You're right. I was on my own last night.'

'So why—?'

'Hey, it's just something to say. That's the way people expect me to behave. All part of the job description.'

'Well, that's where I think you're wrong,' said Harry. 'A lot of people would be far more impressed if you were just honest with them.'

At this, Enjay emitted a brief bark of laughter. Turning his back on Harry, he gazed for several seconds through the full-length glass doors leading out on to his own balcony. Then his shoulders began to shake.

Watching him, Harry was puzzled. Surely it hadn't been that funny? After a moment he said, 'I don't get it.'

'Don't you? Really?' Slowly Enjay turned to face him and Harry, to his horror, saw that there were tears glistening in his eyes. He hadn't been laughing at all. 'You think my fans would want me to be honest? Well, let me tell you, they would not. No way, man. They'd be repulsed. My career would . . . I don't know, disappear into some bottomless pit. I wouldn't have no career, that's for sure.'

Harry was bemused. 'But, but . . . why would that happen? Pop stars don't have to behave like you do.' Blindly casting around for a suitable role model, he exclaimed, 'Look at Sir Cliff Richard. He doesn't sleep around and everyone loves him!'

'They do? Funnily enough, that doesn't make me feel better.' Enjay stopped and cleared his throat, then gazed directly at Harry. 'You still don't have the faintest idea what I'm sayin', do you?'

And up until that moment, Harry genuinely hadn't known or even suspected. But Enjay's manner was resigned and his eyes were still swimming; he blinked and a single tear rolled down his left cheek.

'Um . . . I'm not sure . . .'

'OK, but I think you've got it now. So I'm just gonna come right out and say it, because if I don't talk to someone I'm going to lose my mind. And I trust you, man. I'm trusting you with this and I hope I can rely on you to keep it to yourself because I swear to God I can't tell any other person on this earth.' Enjay's voice cracked as he reached the end and roughly brushed his hand over his face. 'Oh shit, I can't believe I'm doing this.'

Harry watched him cross the room, remove a miniature of vodka from the fridge and knock it back in one go. Something else he'd noticed in the past was that for all the conspicuous champagne consumption Enjay urged on those around him, he actually drank very little himself.

Presumably because he couldn't afford to lose control, to let his guard down, for so much as a single second.

'You're gay.' Harry said it and saw him flinch.

Enjay nodded. 'Yes. Yes, I am. Oh God.' He was hyperventilating now. 'And this is the first time I've ever said it aloud. I'm gay. I'm a liar, I'm a fraud, I'm a homosexual and I'm never going to be able to live a normal life. I'm never going to be happy. My family would disown me if they knew. And I'd never sell music again because who wants to follow a freak?'

'You're not a freak.'

'Trust me, in my world it's not what you dream of. If my family ever found out, they'd die of shame. If I ever left my house I'd be yelled at in the street.'

'It can't be that bad,' Harry persisted. 'People might be surprised at first, but they'd get used to it. You'd still be you.' He felt himself flush because talking like this wasn't exactly something that came naturally.

'I would still be me.' Enjay rubbed a hand wearily over his jaw. 'In their eyes I'd still be a faggot. Trust me, in my job no one's going to forgive me for that. Which is why no one's ever going to find out.'

He was serious. He meant it. Thinking it through, Harry realised he was right. In Enjay's world, homosexuality was something you didn't admit to; amongst his peers it simply wasn't an acceptable state of affairs. He would become an object of ridicule and his fans would desert him in their droves.

'I won't breathe a word. Ever,' said Harry. 'You can trust me.'

Enjay nodded. 'Thanks, man. I know. That's the only reason I told you.'

Following his confession, he was looking emotionally drained. Harry could only imagine the extent of the pressure he must have been under for years.

'So all those girls . . . the groping, the come-ons, the flirting . . .'

'I didn't want to do it. I had to.' Enjay grimaced. 'I know I act like a complete sleazebag, but it's what the world expects you to do.'

'You kissed Lara.'

'Sorry. I shouldn't have done that. Don't tell her about me, man. Please.'

'I won't. Everything was for show,' Harry marvelled. 'Did you sleep with any of them? Girls, I mean.'

'Just a few.' He pulled another face. 'Carefully chosen. Only the ones I knew would brag about it to the press. With the rest of them I just made out I was too tired. No one wants to admit to being the girl who wasn't exciting enough to keep EnjaySeven awake.'

'What about Marina?' said Harry.

'She's just a friend. We play computer games together.'

'OK, but one thing's bothering me. You're so adamant no one's going to discover the truth . . .'

'They aren't. It can't happen. If word ever gets out,' said Enjay, 'it won't have come from me. So I'll know it was you.'

Had he seriously not considered the risks? 'What about . . . if *they* say something?'

'They who?'

'You know.' Harry cleared his throat; just choosing the right words was awkward enough. 'The men you . . . are friendly with.'

'You mean the ones I have sex with?' Enjay regarded him frankly. 'Is that what you're trying to say?'

'OK, yes. But doesn't that worry you? Any of them could go to the papers, blackmail you . . .'

'Believe it or not, I do know that. And yes, it's something that concerns me. But it's never going to happen.'

Exasperated on his friend's behalf, Harry burst out, 'How can you be so sure?'

Enjay turned away, clasping both hands behind his head and tilting it from side to side as if to ease the accumulated muscle tension in his neck. Finally, addressing the wall, he said tonelessly,

'Because there aren't any men I have sex with. For precisely that reason. It's a risk I can't afford to take.' He paused and swung back round to face Harry. 'So I don't take it. End of.'

'What? Never?' Truly shocked now, Harry said, 'Never *ever*?'

'Not since I was eighteen. Hidden cameras, getting stuff recorded on mobile phones . . . how can I take that chance?' Those light brown eyes were brimming once more. 'Better safe than sorry.'

'It's no way to live.'

'It's the only way to live. I don't have any other choice.'

'What happened when you were eighteen?' Harry sensed that this was what had triggered the return of the tears.

'Oh, nothing much. I got friendly with a boy in our town. We used to go fishing every weekend. He was . . . the same as me. We ended up spending the summer together. It was our secret and no one ever found out. But Shaun couldn't handle the guilt, you know? He hated the way he was, just wanted to be normal. It really got to him, he couldn't see a way out.' Enjay paused, swallowing hard as he struggled to compose himself. 'Anyhow, he got more and more desperate and depressed. I tried my best to help him through it but there was nothing I could do to help. Shaun was something he didn't want to be and he just couldn't handle it. The shame was too much to bear . . .'

Harry broke the silence, although he already knew the answer. 'What happened?'

'He threw himself off a bridge into the river. They found him the next day, a few miles downstream. He left a note for his family.' Enjay's voice was devoid of emotion now. 'Told them he was in love with a girl who didn't love him back, and he couldn't bear to live without her.' A muscle began to jump in his jaw. 'His poor mother tried for years to find out who the girl was. Not

341

knowing almost drove her demented. She never found out the truth, that the person her son couldn't b-bear to live without was m-m-me.'

The next moment he broke down completely, years of suppressed grief and guilt bursting out like a disintegrated dam. For Harry, veteran of a lifetime of awkward moments, this was the most awkward by far. Paralysed with indecision, he didn't know what to do. If he were Lara, he would have already rushed over to Enjay, murmuring soothing words of comfort whilst enveloping him in a hug. It had never been his forte. Moreover, this was Enjay, who wouldn't want to be pitied and comforted by another man. He was the proudest of the proud.

So Harry just stood there feeling helpless, listening to the racking sobs, increasingly torn. Finally he went through to the bathroom and returned with a silver box of tissues. Pulling out a handful, he passed them to Enjay and gingerly patted him on the arm.

'Here. Sorry. It's OK.'

Enjay shook his head. 'I suppose you're disgusted with me.'

'Don't even say that.' *If only he knew.*

'You just touched me like I've got some infectious disease, man.'

Harry looked at him. 'That's because I thought you wouldn't want to be touched.'

'Oh God, my life is a nightmare.' Wiping his eyes, Enjay said, 'You can't begin to understand how this feels.'

Harry exhaled, steadying himself. Finally he heard himself utter the words he'd never thought he'd say. 'Actually, I think I can.'

Chapter 48

Running the shop on her own had been keeping Lara busy. But how could she complain when it had been her idea that Don should take a holiday? He was stressed and unhappy, in need of a break. She'd suggested he get away for a few days and to her surprise he had agreed. On Monday morning he'd flown out to the Algarve to join Wilhelmina, his ardent admirer, at her villa overlooking the sea in Albufeira.

'She'll be after you,' Lara had warned. 'She'll have designs on your body.'

Don had shaken his head. 'I've already told her I'm too ill for any of that malarkey. I'm there for rest and recuperation, that's all.'

And much as she loved him, Lara had found the first half of his week away oddly restful. Don's absence allowed her to relax and feel guilt-free. They both knew it was illogical and Don would never dream of saying as much out loud, but she was aware all the same that he felt she'd let him down. His faith in her had been irretrievably shaken. Before, she'd always been his insurance, his lucky charm. If the unthinkable were to happen, he had her there to save the day and keep him alive.

But since James, all that had changed. Don felt, she knew, that she could no longer be trusted to do whatever needed to be done. She'd failed in her mission and he no longer had confidence in her. Which in turn caused her to feel insidious creeping waves of guilt. As if it hadn't been bad enough berating herself for not being able to save James's life, she now had to feel not good enough in her boss's critical eyes too.

No wonder the last week, while he'd been over in Portugal, had felt like a holiday for them both.

Oh dear, poor Don, that was hardly fair, was it?

At three o'clock her heart did its habitual leap as the buzzer went and she saw Flynn on the other side of the glass. She'd tried so hard to get it under control but like an overexcited puppy, it refused to be sensible and calm down.

Flynn went to open the door and Lara buzzed him in. She knew he'd just got back from visiting a family who owned a vineyard in Languedoc-Roussillon.

'Hey, did you have a good trip?'

'I did.' He was gazing into her eyes, clearly eager to share some plan or other. 'Listen, I've had an idea and I wanted to run it by you before saying anything to Gigi. She's never been skiing.'

'I know.' *Duh*. 'Me neither.'

'So I was wondering about the first week in January, once all the chaos of Christmas and New Year is out of the way. A week, maybe ten days if we can swing it, in Val-d'Isère. What d'you think? Would she enjoy that?'

'I think she'd love it.' Lara beamed; how fantastic. 'And she'd be unstoppable too. You'd have your work cut out keeping her off the black runs.'

'I can imagine.' He was smiling too. 'So anyway, you're OK with that, are you? Me and Gigi taking off on a skiing holiday?'

Just for a moment, when he'd started talking about the first week in January, Lara had thought she was included, that the three of them might all be heading off together. But he hadn't meant that at all. Anyway, it was probably just as well.

'Of course I'm OK with it. Why would I mind? You'll have an amazing time throwing yourselves down mountains. Really, she'll be thrilled.'

'Good. I'll book a chalet and get the flights organised.' Flynn paused for a moment then said, 'You know what would make it even better? If you came along with us.'

Snow, après-ski, magnificent mountains! A gingerbread-house chalet, fabulous restaurants and vin chaud!

And more temptation than she could reasonably be expected to handle, in the form of Flynn Erskine.

Lara conjured up a series of mental images, each more adrenalin-pumping than the last. Basically, it was hard enough resisting him here in Bath. Being on holiday in Val-d'Isère would only make things a thousand times worse.

She knew her limits.

'Well, this is encouraging.' Flynn raised a playful eyebrow at the hesitation. 'Does this mean you're actually considering saying yes?'

Do the right thing.

Ooh no, go on, do the wrong thing!

And what would it lead to, hmm? Don't pretend you don't know the answer to that question.

'You two go.' Lara shook her head; it was the only way. 'Skiing's not my thing. I'd only end up breaking my legs.'

'But you don't have to—'

'And Don needs me here,' she went on firmly. 'Really, thanks for the offer, but you and Gigi'll have a brilliant time without me.'

'Lara.' His expression was unreadable. 'You know why I want you to come too. You and me . . . are you *ever* going to give us a chance?' As Flynn said it, he reached for her hand; instinctively, heart hammering, she flinched and pulled it away.

'No.' *There, said it.* Shaking her head, Lara murmured, 'No, it's never going to happen.'

'OK.' Another pause. 'And you're not going to change your mind?'

Oh God, oh God. 'No.'

'Right.' Flynn moved back a fraction. 'In that case you can relax, I won't be asking you again. So you don't need to worry. From now on, I'll leave you alone.'

Wow, where had *that* come from? Lara nodded, inwardly taken aback, externally cool. 'OK. Fine. Well, thanks for that.'

'No problem. I'm sure you're relieved to hear it. Hopefully it'll be easier for both of us.' Flynn gave her another long enigmatic look, then turned to leave. 'Anyway, good news about the skiing. I'll let Gigi know.'

It was Saturday, bonfire night, and the crowds had poured into the Rec, home of Bath Rugby Club, for the city's biggest firework display. And it truly was a spectacular sight; everyone was gazing up, enthralled, as explosions of colour like giant chrysanthemums burst out of nowhere to fill the night sky.

Next to her Gigi was rapt, but Lara was finding it hard to concentrate on the fireworks. On the way into the Rec she'd seen something that made no sense at all. Two small boys wrapped up against the cold in stripy bobble hats and puffed-up coats had been play-fighting with each other, using glowsticks as their weapons of choice. Inevitably one of them ended up getting jabbed in the head and, letting out a howl of protest, launched

346

himself at his brother. The tussle had been broken up by an elegant lady in a fur Cossack hat, presumably their grandmother. The next moment, getting a clearer look at the woman's face, Lara had done a double-take and realised it was in fact Wilhelmina.

As in, Wilhelmina the glamorous widow with whom Don was meant to be holidaying in the Algarve . . .

Then the crowds shifted and Wilhelmina and her small charges disappeared from view, leaving Lara to puzzle over what she could possibly be doing here in Bath.

Once the fireworks reached their dazzling, noisy crescendo and concluded with an ear-splitting finale, everyone applauded then began to move towards the exits.

'I'm hungry.' Lara linked her arm through Gigi's and said, 'Can you smell sausages? Shall we find out where they're selling hot dogs or give that new Mexican place a try?'

Gigi's nose was pink with cold, her breath clouding in front of her as she rubbed her hands together. 'Brrr, I can't feel my fingers. The thing is, Mum, I'm meeting Dad at Aqua in twenty minutes, so we're going to be eating there. Sorry.'

'Oh right, I didn't realise. Darling, that's fine, no problem at all. I'll grab a hot dog on the way home.'

'You're sure you don't mind?'

'Why would I mind you having dinner with your dad?'

Gigi hesitated and blew on her hands again. Avoiding Lara's gaze she said, 'Well, it's not *just* me and Dad . . .'

Clannnngggggg went the penny as it dropped.

As they left the rugby ground, Lara spotted Wilhelmina again ahead of them, and insinuated her way through the crowds until she caught up with her.

'Hello!'

347

With a grandson clutched in each leather-gloved hand, Wilhelmina recognised her and said cheerily, 'Oh hi, darling. How's Don? Is he here too?'

Hmm.

'No, he isn't, he's gone on holiday for a few days,' Lara said casually. 'For some reason I thought you were away this week too, staying at your villa in Portugal.'

'Me? No, my daughter's expecting her third child soon, so I'm not going anywhere. Staying right here doing Granny duty, eh boys?' She swung their arms cheerfully. 'While Mummy stays at home and gets some rest.'

'Mummy's having a baby.' The younger grandson looked mournful. 'She's really fat.'

'We wanted a meerkat,' grumbled his brother. 'But we've got to have a sister instead.'

'Babies are really *boring*.'

'And *stinky*.'

'Stop it, you two, she won't be boring for long and you're going to love her to bits.' Rolling her eyes, Wilhelmina said, 'Come along then, boys, let's get you home.' She smiled a little wistfully at Lara. 'Give my love to Don when you see him. Who's he gone on holiday with, do you know?'

Poor lonely widowed Wilhelmina. Poor *allegedly* lonely Don.

Lara said, 'No idea, he didn't tell me.'

'Oh well.' Another brave shrug. 'So long as he has a nice time. Bye.'

Together Lara and Gigi made their way across Pulteney Bridge, up Northgate Street and along the Walcot Loop Road.

'Mum, you don't need to walk with me. It's out of your way.'

'No problem, it's fine. I'm in the mood for a walk and I'd rather know you're safe. So . . . tell me about this new girlfriend of your dad's, then.' The subject had been buzzing around inside Lara's head like an angry wasp since Gigi had first mentioned it. Now, broaching it aloud for the first time, Lara kept her tone super-casual. 'How long's it been going on?'

'Only a couple of weeks, I think. He was running a private wine-tasting at a house on the Royal Crescent and she was one of the guests.'

'What's her name?'

'Annabel.'

'*Annabel.*' Lara didn't know what kind of name she'd been expecting, but it hadn't been that. What did an Annabel look like? Was she a cool blonde? Or did she have smouldering gypsy eyes and wild curly hair? What kind of clothes would she wear? 'And he just . . . asked her out, did he? At the wine-tasting?'

'No idea,' Gigi said patiently. 'He's my dad, I'm not going to ask for all the gory details, am I?'

They reached Aqua on Walcot Street and Gigi gave her a kiss. 'Bye then. They'll be waiting for me at the bar. I'll see you later, Mum.'

'You know what? It's going to look really unfriendly if I leave you here without even popping in.' Lara heard the words come tumbling out; the timing might not be great but she couldn't *not* do it. 'I'd hate Flynn to think I was being rude.'

'Oh but—'

'No, I should.' She nodded vigorously at Gigi. 'I'll just come in and say hello, then whiz off again. It's only polite.'

The restaurant was busy, buzzy and full of life but Lara spotted them instantly. There they were, waiting over at the bar. Flynn was saying something to Annabel, who burst out laughing so it must have been funny.

Unless they're laughing about *me* . . .

OK, of course they weren't doing that. Anyway, no time for a crisis of confidence, Gigi was already leading her over.

'Hey, sweetheart.' Flynn greeted Gigi with a kiss on the cheek. 'This is Annabel. Annabel, meet my beautiful daughter.' He paused while they shook hands before adding, 'And this is Lara, Gigi's mum.'

'Hello!' Keen to show how friendly she was, Lara heard herself using too many exclamation marks. 'Don't worry, not gatecrashing! Just wanted to make sure Gigi wasn't going to be stood up!'

'She knew we'd be here,' said Flynn. 'I wouldn't stand her up.'

'Anyway, hi.' Annabel, who appeared to be in her mid-twenties, beamed and shook Lara's hand. 'I'm Annabel. Lovely to meet you. Are you joining us for dinner?'

'Ooh, well . . .'

'No,' said Flynn and Gigi simultaneously.

Oh.

'OK, well at least stay for a drink.' Signalling to one of the barmen, Annabel claimed two more glasses and reached for the already opened bottle on ice. 'This is delicious, you must try it.'

Goodness, she was pretty. Her hair, black and straight and cut in a geometric bob, was as shiny as glass. Her eyes were brown, her mouth a perfect pink rosebud and she had the neatest little nose Lara had ever seen. Plus, she was wearing a dove-grey body-con dress that screamed *class*. It also screamed, 'Look at me, I'm a size eight, aren't I chic, aren't I fabulous, aren't I *dinky*?'

She was also right about the wine, which tasted amazing. Lara nodded in appreciation and said, 'So you're a wine connoisseur too?'

'Hardly.' Annabel pulled a face. 'Just putting on a show to impress Mr Expert here. I'm more of a pint-of-lager girl, to be honest.'

Oh Lord, pretty *and* nice.

'*Lager?*' Gigi looked impressed.

'When you're a med student,' Annabel confided, 'it's pretty much a rite of passage.'

Lara did an inner double-take. 'You're a medical student?'

'Was, years ago. I'm working as a neurosurgical registrar now. At Frenchay Hospital, in Bristol.'

'Cool,' said Gigi. 'So basically you're, like, a brain surgeon.'

'I am.' Annabel's eyes sparkled.

'You don't look old enough though.'

'I promise you I am. I'm absolutely ancient.' Clutching Gigi's arm she leaned towards her and stage-whispered, '*Thirty-three.*'

'Wow.' Gigi boggled. 'Mum's only thirty-five and you look *loads* younger than her.'

Shin-kicking would probably be regarded as out of order. Which was a shame. Maybe she'd do it later when they were at home.

'Hello.' The charming maitre d' approached them. 'Just to let you know, your table's ready if you'd like to come through.' He added inquiringly, 'We had you down as a three, but if you want us to add an extra place . . . ?'

The ensuing expectant pause was broken by the sound of Lara's stomach rumbling. Like a begging dog.

'I don't think so.' Flynn was shaking his head.

'No,' Gigi chimed in. 'She has to go now, don't you, Mum?'

Apparently so. 'Yes I do. But thanks anyway.' Lara smiled at the maitre d', the only person there who apparently wanted her to stay.

'It was lovely to meet you.' Annabel's glossy hair swung as she said cheerily, 'See you again soon!'

Flynn and Annabel headed off with the maitre d' and Gigi accompanied Lara to the door.

'I could have stayed,' Lara protested.

'I know, but then it'd be like a tennis match. You and me versus the two of them. That's how it would feel, anyway. And Annabel seems really nice. I just want to get to know her.'

'Why? Because she's a brain surgeon and looks so much younger than me?' The dig slipped out but Lara needn't have worried; Gigi didn't even notice.

'Well, sort of. But it's an interesting job, isn't it? Plus, I've never seen Dad with a girlfriend before. And if she ends up marrying him, she'll be my stepmother!' Gigi pulled an *oh-wow* face, blithely oblivious to the clenching in the pit of Lara's stomach. 'Imagine that!'

Chapter 49

Lara had already opened up the shop on Tuesday morning when Don appeared, as smartly dressed and with his hair as carefully gelled as ever, but with a surprising lack of suntan to show for his holiday in the Algarve.

Alleged holiday.

'Hi,' she greeted him. 'Fab time?'

'Wonderful.' Don beamed.

'You should have called me last night. I could have come and picked you and Wilhelmina up from the airport.'

He shook his head. 'It was fine, we got a cab.'

'What was the weather like?'

He glanced self-consciously at his pale hands. 'Not brilliant, to be honest. Quite cloudy.'

'That's so weird.' Lara looked puzzled. 'Because every time I looked on the internet it said hot and sunny.'

Don flushed and adjusted his tie, playing for time. She allowed the awkward silence to lengthen.

Finally he said, 'Oh God. You know, don't you?'

Slowly, Marple-ishly, Lara nodded. 'Yes, Don. I do.'

'I can't believe it. She said you would.'

'She was right.'

He half-smiled. 'Actually, she called you a witch.'

'Charming. I wasn't stalking her, you know. All I did was bump into her at the Rec.'

Don was visibly taken aback. 'Hang on, what? Who are you talking about?'

Lara blinked. 'Why? Who are *you* talking about?'

His eyebrows were up. 'You bumped into Wilhelmina?'

'Yes! At the firework display! That's how I knew you weren't staying with her in Portugal. But I still thought that's where you'd gone . . . until now.' Lara looked pointedly at his untanned face and hands. 'Except I still don't understand why you'd need to lie about it. I mean, I was chatting to Nettie on the phone last night and she said you'd told *her* how much you were looking forward to . . . to . . . going on holiday . . .' her voice faltered and trailed off as she saw Don's expression change, 'to . . . the Algarve. Oh God, I get it now! This is like one of those dreams where nothing makes sense and everything gets weirder and weirder! You weren't abroad, were you? You've actually been staying in Keswick with Nettie! But why would you keep it a secret?' She clapped her hands to her face like Kevin in *Home Alone* and let out a shriek of realisation. 'Oh my GIDDY AUNT, I don't believe it!'

Because Don might as well be holding up a banner, his face was such a complete giveaway.

Although as a rule, her aunt was the least giddy person on the planet.

'I love Nettie,' he said simply. 'And she loves me.'

'Am I dreaming?'

'Wait.' Crossing the shop, Don locked the door and put up the CLOSED sign. He twisted his manicured hands together and took a deep breath. 'I fell in love with her at first sight. Nothing like this has ever happened to me before. I'm so happy I could burst. Every time I think of her it just feels like Christmas Day!'

Could she say it? 'OK . . . I mean, no offence,' Lara stammered, 'but the two of you are so . . . *different*.'

'I know! Isn't it crazy? But it feels so right. She's just the most amazing woman. She's everything I've ever wanted.' He shook his head in wonderment. 'And all this time I never knew. All these years I thought I should be going for a woman who was just like me . . . fussy, takes care of herself, elegant and well-groomed.'

'Like Wilhelmina,' said Lara.

'Exactly. When all along I needed the exact opposite. No wonder it never felt right before.'

Now that he was explaining it to her, everything was beginning to fall into place. With her complete lack of vanity, her can-do attitude and blunt no-nonsense manner, Nettie was the absolute antithesis of all the Wilhelminas Don had ever known. As a slightly effeminate but heterosexual man, it made a bizarre kind of sense that he should be drawn to a heterosexual but somewhat masculine female.

And, of course, vice versa.

'We always thought there might be something going on between her and Fred Milton.'

'I know, she told me you did. She thought that was hilarious.' Don smiled fondly at the memory. 'But no, he's not her type at all.' Glowing with pride, as if he could still hardly believe it himself, he added, 'Because guess what? Her type is me!'

Lara made them both a cup of tea. At this time on a Tuesday morning no customers were hammering on the locked door demanding to be let in.

'Did you like Keswick then?'

355

'Loved it. Stunning place.' Don blew on his tea, took a sip, then said bashfully, 'Mind you, anywhere would be good that had Nettie in it.'

He was like a teenager in the grip of a thrilling new crush. It was so sweet. Apart from one major drawback . . .

'So you'll take it in turns visiting each other, will you?' Lara secretly wondered how that would work out; having found driving too stressful to handle, Don had sold his car months ago. And if pootling around Bath reduced him to jelly, heaven knows how he'd cope with five hours on the M5.

'OK, sit down and listen. I wasn't planning on telling you this just yet, but I didn't know it was all going to come out so soon. And no giving me a lecture either.' His spiky hair quivered like a hedgehog's as he shook his head. 'I know what it sounds like, but it's what we both want.'

'Go on.'

'This last week has been the best of my entire life. And it's been stress-free. I feel twenty years younger,' said Don, 'and twenty times happier.' He exhaled heavily. 'I don't know how you're going to feel about this, but Nettie's asked me and I've said yes. I'm moving up there and we're going to live together. For the good of my health. And my heart. Because we've found each other, me and Nettie, and we can't bear not to be together, and who knows how long we've got left?'

Lara's mouth was dry. How could she argue with that? On the one hand it was all wonderfully romantic.

On the other hand, it rather sounded as if she was about to be out of a job.

She hugged Don. 'It's fantastic news. I'm so happy for you. And you're three years younger than Nettie, so that makes you her toyboy, which is extra cool!'

'I know.' He beamed.

'So it all started on that Sunday when you came over to lunch. If I hadn't invited you, the two of you would never have met.' Yay, that gave her such a feeling of power. Realising something else, Lara exclaimed, 'And then you bonded at your neighbours' party when you got up and sang all the karaoke together!'

Don hesitated, drank some more tea, then carefully put down his cup. 'Are you going to be shocked if I tell you we didn't go to the party?'

'But you said . . . *oh.*' Lara closed her mouth. Wow, they really hadn't hung about. Hastily changing the subject, she gestured around the shop. 'So you'll be putting your house on the market, selling this place . . .'

'Actually, I'm going to let the house for now. We thought students wouldn't mind the noise from next door. And I'm not selling the shop,' he went on, causing her heart to leap into her throat. 'I was hoping you'd run it and we'd take on someone to help you . . . *arggh*! Get off me, woman, it's like being smothered by a Labrador . . .'

'Sorry!' Grinning, Lara let him go. 'Got a bit overexcited there. And relieved. I thought you were going to tell me I was out of a job.'

'Darling, you're joking. You have to keep the business going, bring in the money.' He spread his arms and burst joyfully into Abba-style song: 'Money Money Money!'

Were there two people with more wildly differing tastes in music? But he was so *happy.* Lara said, 'When will you be leaving?'

'Soon!'

'Oh God, I'm going to miss you so much. But we'll still see you.' She wiped away a soppy tear. 'This is so brilliant.'

'Isn't it just? And Nettie won't let me eat rubbish, you know.

357

She's the most amazing cook. You won't believe all the healthy food I've had this week.'

'Actually I would,' said Lara.

'I feel better already. My blood pressure's down. And guess what?' Don patted his stomach with pride. 'I've lost four pounds!'

It had been another blissful evening at Ray and Bonnie's house, complete with fish pie and sticky toffee pudding. Leaving them in the living room arguing over which TV programme to watch, Evie was filling the dishwasher when she heard Joel coming into the kitchen.

Her heart quickened; it was definitely him. The sound of his footsteps on the flagstoned floor was unmistakable. Then she jumped as his hands came to rest on her waist.

'Careful,' Joel murmured, 'you almost dropped that cup.'

'And if I did, I suppose it would be my fault. Pass me those bowls, would you?'

'Yes, ma'am. Anything you say.' But as he gave them to her he managed to brush against her hip, by no means accidentally. As the weeks had passed, so the levels of flirtation between them had increased. But this time she was the one setting the pace. Evie had discovered the thrill of being in control and it was a heady experience.

'Listen to that.' She grimaced as the downpour outside reached the next level; freezing rain had turned to hail and was now rattling against the windows.

'Hey, no problem. I can drop you home.'

They pulled into Arlington Road twenty minutes later. In the darkness, with the engine still running, Joel turned and idly lifted a stray strand of hair away from her face. 'OK, can I just say something? This is killing me.'

'What's killing you?' *As if she didn't know.*

'Being here, with you. The two of us together. Not being allowed to do what I want to do . . .'

This, *this* was the moment to open the passenger door and jump out of the car. Nature, intervening, produced another torrent of hail so ferocious it bounced off the bonnet like gunfire. The noise was deafening.

'Evie. How many more times do I have to tell you I'm sorry?' His voice was low and genuinely regretful. It was also playing havoc with her hormones. Without meaning to, she gave a shuddery sigh.

'A hundred? A thousand? Because that's fine,' Joel went on. 'Just say the word and I'll do it. As many times as you like.'

Evie shook her head, glad he couldn't read her mind. He was still stroking her neck and it had been ages since anyone had done that. Basically, physical contact of any kind had been pretty thin on the ground for the past few months. And she was only human . . .

'Your hair smells fantastic, by the way.'

'It's Head and Shoulders,' said Evie.

Joel laughed. 'And that's why I love you.'

She didn't reply. All around them, the hail continued to hammer down.

'Look,' Joel said finally, 'it's only ten o'clock, not even late. Come back to mine for a coffee and a chat. Give it an hour and all this will have stopped. I'll drive you home then.'

There was direct access from his garage into his flat. It was a definite plus point.

Having hesitated, Evie heard herself say, 'OK, that sounds sensible.'

Well, her hair did get dreadfully frizzy when it was wet.

359

Chapter 50

It was almost midnight and Joel had been right; the torrential rain and hail had fizzled out, leaving only an eerie stillness and wet roads. Not that she could see it from here but when a car drove past you could hear the liquid swoosh of tyres on tarmac.

A voice in her ear murmured, 'Falling asleep?'

Evie opened her eyes. 'Nearly.'

'Lightweight.' He ran his fingers playfully over her ribcage, his bare legs nudging hers beneath the rumpled duvet.

'Hey, I'm out of practice. It's been a while.'

Joel began dropping kisses along the curve of her collarbone. 'Tell me about it.'

'Oh, come on, don't even say that. You've slept with other girls since we broke up.'

He raised his head, his blond hair falling into his eyes as he regarded her intently. 'You'd think so, wouldn't you? No reason not to. But I haven't.'

'I don't believe you,' said Evie.

'I suppose there's no reason why you should. But it's the truth. I've learned my lesson,' Joel said simply. 'I only wanted you, no one else.'

She shook her head. 'Still don't believe you.'

'I know you don't. So why else would I say it if it wasn't true?'

Did that make sense? Kind of. Evie checked her watch and said, 'It's late. I need to get home.'

'You don't have to leave.'

'I do.'

'Stay.' Joel touched her face. 'Please.'

She could feel herself weakening. It was cold outside. Here in his bed it was deliciously warm. She'd missed physical contact as much as she'd missed sex itself. And when Joel was being this irresistible, it was hard to say no.

'Can you get me my bag? It's in the living room.'

He jumped out of bed, returning seconds later with her handbag. Evie checked her emergency toothbrush was in there, then took out her phone and called Lara's number.

'Hi, it's me. Just to let you know I'm staying over at Ray and Bonnie's tonight. Early start at work tomorrow . . .'

Thirty seconds later she hung up. There, done. Lara had taken the excuse at face value and the white lie had made saying it all the more exciting. For once she was the one being a little bit naughty, doing what was fun rather than what was right.

'You just told a fib,' Joel playfully admonished.

'She'd have nagged me if I hadn't. Actually, I told two,' said Evie. 'I don't have an early start tomorrow.'

'Very glad to hear it.' He broke into a slow, complicit smile and pulled her closer. 'Because I'm telling you now, you're going to have a *very* late night tonight.'

Joel dropped her around the corner from his parents' house on his way to work the next morning. More subterfuge, but Bonnie would be uncontrollable if she knew what had happened.

'Come here.' He kissed her once, twice, then once more for luck. 'I love you. Can I see you tonight?'

Evie shook her head. 'We've got the Massinghams' party, remember? The one your mum was talking about, with the dance troupe and the conjurors. I won't be able to get away before eleven.'

'Damn. How about after that?'

He looked so crestfallen, her heart melted. 'Listen, we've had two hours' sleep. Three at most. We're both going to be shattered by this evening. Let's leave it for tonight.'

Joel pulled a sad face. 'OK. How about tomorrow then?'

Evie nodded, distracted by a bus trundling past; a bunch of schoolboys were mooning through the windows. That's what happened when you drank cans of Red Bull before school.

'Hello?' Joel waved his hands in front of her face. 'Tomorrow?'

'Hmm? Oh, sorry.' Her brain was fizzing, in a state of confusion. Having sex again had been lovely; after all these months, of course it had. But she needed to sort out how she truly felt about the person she'd just had the lovely sex with. Evie gave herself a mental shake. 'Yes, tomorrow. I'll give you a call.'

The party was being held at the Massinghams' sprawling country pile ten miles outside Bath, to celebrate their daughter's birthday.

If there was a more spoiled seventeen-year-old within a hundred-mile radius, Evie really didn't want to meet her. She was quite wishing she hadn't had to meet this one. Foxie Massingham, stroppy, charmless and accustomed to having her every whim catered for, had already thrown tantrums about her hair, false eyelashes, the caterers, the conjurors and her boyfriend's outfit. And the party hadn't even started yet.

'Marvin's wearing a green suit,' she ranted at her mother. 'He

362

looks like a *dork*. Mummy, make him go home and change into something less embarrassing.'

Which was ironic, seeing as Foxie was wearing fluorescent yellow micro shorts, silver thigh-high boots and a silver-fringed bikini top complete with sewn-on fairy lights that flashed on and off.

'Oh, baby, he can't do that, it's too late now.' Foxie's devoted mother said apologetically to Marvin, 'Don't worry, she'll calm down. You know how highly strung she is.'

'Not strung highly enough if you ask me,' muttered Marvin as he passed Evie in the doorway where she was pinning up more fairy lights.

Oh dear, he wasn't looking happy at all.

An hour later Foxie deemed it time to open her presents.

Her mum wrung her hands. 'But I thought we were going to do it during the party, baby. That was the plan.'

'I don't want to wait. I need to know what I've got. Daddy, bring them through now.'

Evie, watching from the other end of the room, saw Foxie accept as her due a diamond pendant, practically an entire shopful of designer clothes, three pairs of Louboutins, and – oh yes, *of course* – the keys to a brand new Volkswagen Golf.

Then Marvin gave her a small, nicely wrapped box and she opened it, her face falling as she unfolded the tissue paper and lifted out the bracelet inside.

'Is it real gold?' Foxie's lip curled as she scrutinised it.

'Well, no . . .'

'Is it real anything? I mean, these stones.' She prodded at them with a turquoise acrylic nail. 'What are they meant to be?'

'So you don't like it,' Marvin said evenly.

'I thought you were going to get me something nice.'

363

'It was all the money I had. I'm a carpenter,' said Marvin, 'not a millionaire. I *told* you I couldn't afford much and you said it didn't matter.'

'I didn't mean it though!' Foxie's voice rose. 'Jeez! I thought you'd get me something better than *this*.'

Evie winced at the expression on Marvin's face. Even Foxie's adoring parents were looking embarrassed.

'Fine,' Marvin said eventually. He took a step back, shook his head, then turned and walked away. 'Have a great night.'

'Wait! Where are you going?'

'Home.'

'No you're not! You come back,' shrieked Foxie.

'Find yourself a Premiership footballer. You'll be happier. *He* might not be,' Marvin added not quite under his breath.

Evie flattened herself against the wall as Foxie raced after him. There was a brief undignified tussle in the doorway, during which Foxie bellowed, 'But you can't go, it's my party!'

'I am going. I've had enough.' Marvin's voice was flat with resignation. 'You've changed, you never used to be like this.' He peeled her fingers off his arms. 'OK, I'm out of here. For good.'

And he left, precipitating the most almighty meltdown from his erstwhile girlfriend. It was six o'clock and the guests were due to start arriving in an hour. Foxie, evidently never having got her comeuppance before, screamed and sobbed at her parents while Evie and the rest of the hired help looked on. Marvin had gone and he'd switched his phone off. Foxie howled, 'Right, that's it, the party's cancelled.'

'Oh, Flora, no, don't say that,' her father protested.

'I just *did* say it. And for fuck's sake stop calling me Flora! We're not having a party and it's going to be ALL MARVIN'S FAULT.' As she yelled the words Foxie rubbed her hands over her face, deliberately smudging her make-up in all directions until she looked like a deranged clown. Then she started yanking at her elaborately arranged hair, ripping out the blond extensions. Snatching up the bracelet Marvin had given her, she bent it in half until it snapped then flung the pieces wildly across the room.

'Baby, come on now, calm down.' Her mother made a tentative approach, shrinking back as Foxie turned on her.

'Jesus Christ, Mother, what part of NO PARTY don't you understand?' Eyes blazing out from the smears of black shadow and half-off false lashes, Foxie snarled, 'It's cancelled, it's not happening. It's *OFF*.'

Evie left the Massinghams at nine o'clock. Following Foxie's refusal to change her mind, the poor parents had been forced to meet each of the arriving guests in turn and explain to them that the party was no more. Foxie had stormed off to her room. The caterers, the conjurors and the DJ packed up their equipment and Evie took down the decorations. Calling a taxi once it was all done, she was interrupted by the DJ carrying a couple of amps out to his purple van. 'Arlington Road, did you say? Don't worry about a cab, I'll drop you off. It's on my way.'

'Really? Brilliant, thanks so much.' Not so brilliant for the taxi company but great for her.

'Don't go getting any ideas, mind.' The DJ, who was scrawny and in no danger of being mistaken for a hunk, warned, 'That wasn't a chat-up line. I'm married.'

On the way back to Bath, Evie heard the story of how Dave – the DJ – had met and married his wife and, ten years on, how happy they still were. By the time they reached the outskirts of the city, she'd made up her mind about what to do.

'Actually, don't worry about Arlington Road.' As they headed along the A4 she saw the sign for the right turn to Bannerdown looming up at them out of the darkness. 'Could you drop me here instead?'

There came a time when you just knew something was right and there was no longer any point trying to deny it.

Chapter 51

The lights were on in the flat. Joel was at home. Which was lucky, seeing as she'd tried to call him but his phone was switched off.

Anyway, she was here now. About to press the intercom, Evie stepped back as the front door opened and the bearded man from the top flat emerged. Recognising her, he held the door open and let her in on the way out.

'Who is it?' called Joel a few seconds after she knocked on his door on the second floor.

Evie knew him too well; assuming it could only be one of the other residents, he would open the door anyway. She waited and sure enough heard the lock turn.

'Oh.' Joel looked as if he'd just run headlong into an electric fence. 'What's this? I thought you were working.'

In that moment she knew.

'The party was cancelled. I thought I'd surprise you.'

'Brilliant! I was just on my way out! Give me two minutes and I'll meet you downstairs . . . we'll go for a drink and you can tell me what happened.'

Evie struggled to keep a straight face. He was wearing a dark blue towelling robe. 'Can't I come in?'

'Seriously, I'd be embarrassed. The place is a tip, the cleaner didn't bother to turn up . . .'

'Didn't she? But that's OK, I can give you a hand with the tidying up!'

'No, no, I couldn't let you do that.' Joel shook his head, winced with pain and pressed the flat of his hand against his abdomen. 'Look, to be honest I haven't been feeling too well . . .'

'Oh no, poor you,' Evie exclaimed. 'I tell you what, why don't I go home and leave you in peace? Maybe you'll feel better tomorrow.'

His expression cleared. 'That makes sense. It's probably just one of those twenty-four-hour bugs. Yes, let's do that.'

'OK.' Evie nodded in agreement. 'And then we won't have to deal with that embarrassing situation where you've got someone else here but you're trying really hard to hide it.'

'I . . . I . . .'

'Don't know what to say?' suggested Evie. 'Can't work out how to wriggle out of this? I know, it's an awkward one.' She paused. 'Oh well, never mind. If it's any comfort, the reason I came over was to tell you we weren't going to be getting back together. So no need to feel too guilty. In a way, this is probably a good thing to happen. At least now I know I made the right decision.'

'Oh shit.' Joel closed his eyes briefly. 'I'm so sorry. I didn't mean this to happen.'

'I know. You never do. Who is she, by the way? Anyone I know?'

He avoided her gaze. Which meant yes. Evie said, 'It doesn't matter, I'm not planning on bursting into tears.'

'All the same, I'd rather not say.'

'Have you been seeing her for long? Is it one of the girls from

368

the wine bar?' Evie watched his reaction. 'Does she know you had sex with me last night?'

Joel flinched, just slightly, and mouthed *No* whilst shaking his head. Evidently having been eavesdropping from the bedroom, Emily Morris promptly appeared in the hallway behind him; tall, blonde and bare-legged, she'd at least had the decency to throw on a dress.

'Are you serious? You and Joel?' She was hyperventilating with indignation. 'You two slept together *last night*?'

'I know,' said Evie. 'Shocking, isn't it?'

'But . . . but . . . you bastard!' Outraged, Emily confronted Joel. 'You told me she'd begged you for sex and you turned her down! You told me I was the only one!'

'Brace yourself. This is pretty earth-shattering.' Evie almost felt sorry for her. 'He lied.'

This time she did have to call a taxi to take her home. Thankfully the driver wasn't a chatty one. Evie sat in the back and knew she'd made the right decision. The realisation had struck her at lunchtime, in the centre of Bath, just after she'd picked up a coffee and a sandwich from Caffè Nero. Waiting for a gap in the traffic in order to race across Milsom Street, her stomach had disappeared as she recognised the white van slowing in front of her.

The next moment she saw Ethan behind the wheel, indicating with a raised finger that she should cross in front of him. Then, belatedly realising it was her, he broke into a smile and turned the hand gesture into a tentative wave. Terrified she might start to blush, Evie pretended she hadn't seen him and hurried across the street in front of the van. Reaching the other side she heard him buzz down the window and call out, 'Evie!'

Don't turn, don't react, just keep on walking as if you haven't noticed . . . you can't hear him, you can't hear him . . .

But once she'd reached Queen Square, Evie sank down on to a wooden bench and discovered she was trembling. Ethan McEnery had inadvertently revealed his true colours; he'd turned out not to be the man she'd thought he was. But she still hadn't been able to forget the way he'd made her feel before she'd found that out. He may lack Joel's looks and glamour but being with him had just felt so . . . right. It had been like unexpectedly stumbling upon the missing piece of jigsaw you'd been searching for for years.

That was the sensation she hadn't been able to dismiss. It was also what had made her mind up about Joel. OK, so maybe neither of them was the right man for her but there had to be someone else out there capable of making her feel complete.

Also, capable of *not* being charming on the surface but rotten underneath.

The taxi reached Arlington Road. Letting herself into the house, Evie found Lara in the kitchen with Jacqueline Cumiskey from next door. There was an almost empty bottle of red on the table between them.

'Hey, you're early. Come and sit down.' Lara waved her over, pulling out another chair. 'There's plenty more wine. Jacqueline popped round to ask if we'd sponsor her; she's doing a parachute jump for charity.'

'Hey, that's brilliant. Definitely.' Evie fetched herself a glass.

Jacqueline beamed. 'Ah, thanks.'

'She came over two hours ago,' said Lara. 'We've been sitting here yakking ever since. About men, mainly.'

'And pedicures,' said Jacqueline.

'And mascara.'

'And holidays.'

370

'And leaping out of planes with only a flimsy bit of material to keep you alive, and what happens if you crash into a bird on the way down. But mainly,' Lara concluded, 'we've been yakking about men.'

Jacqueline shook her head. 'They're a mystery.'

'You're telling me.' Lara opened another bottle of Rioja.

'I slept with Joel last night,' said Evie.

Lara's eyes widened. 'Are you serious?'

'Just to remind myself what it was like. For fun, really. He kept saying he wanted us to get back together.'

'Blimey,' said Lara. 'And?'

'It was fun! But he thought it meant we were a couple again, and I didn't want that. I went over there this evening to tell him,' Evie went on, 'and guess what? He was in bed with another woman.'

'Bastard!' Lara was indignant on her behalf. 'Are you upset?'

'No, I'm glad. I did the right thing.' It felt fantastic to say it. Evie felt her whole body relax.

'Joel.' Jacqueline was frowning. 'Is he the one I gave a lift home a while back? When he was drunk and you couldn't get hold of a taxi?'

'That's the one,' Evie agreed. 'Basically, he's never going to change. He just doesn't know how not to flirt.'

Jacqueline's dark eyes were bright, her cheeks flushed. 'He did it with me that day. Made quite a pass, actually. Told me I was the most beautiful girl he'd ever seen and begged me to go with him into his flat. I *didn't*,' she added hastily. 'But, you know, he was incredibly charming and persuasive. I did get the impression it was the kind of thing he probably did rather a lot.'

Was this how a bird would feel, upon being unexpectedly released from a cage? Evie sat back and smiled. 'I think you're probably right.'

Chapter 52

'Cheers,' said Flynn. 'This is more like it, don't you think?'

'Absolutely. More like what?' Lara raised her glass of champagne so he could clink his own against it.

His smile was playful. 'You and me, out together. No more funny business with me trying to win you over and you forever turning me down. All that stupid stuff's behind us now. We can just relax, have fun and be friends. It's great. I love it.' He did another celebratory glass clink. 'Here's to us. And a brilliant Christmas.'

He actually meant it.

'Us,' said Lara. 'And Christmas.'

Be careful what you wish for . . .

It was the first week in December, Thursday evening and frosty outside. The city's famous Christmas market was in full swing, wooden chalets lining the cobbled streets around the illuminated abbey. Lights and decorations danced in the trees and the air was filled with the scents of mince pies, spiced cakes and mulled wine. Carols were playing and school children were singing, revelling in the festive atmosphere. Enchanted by the scenes, tourists were recording them on their video cameras for posterity.

Sitting inside the bar gazing out at the bustling crowds was a lot warmer. After two hours of concentrated shopping, Lara was ready for the break. It had been Flynn's idea that they should go together to buy presents for Gigi.

'It's my first year,' he'd explained. 'I want to get it right. You have to tell me if I try to buy something you know she'd hate.'

Which made sense, and also meant they wouldn't end up getting Gigi the same things. But what Lara hadn't counted on was being expected to act as personal shopping adviser when it came to other people's presents too.

Specifically, his new girlfriend Annabel.

But to object would have seemed churlish, so she'd been forced to go along with it like a good sport. When Flynn had finished choosing a pair of brown leather boots for Gigi in Russell and Bromley, he'd turned his attention to the crystal-embellished spiky-heeled shoes. 'OK, this is where you can help me out.' He held up two different styles. 'Which would Annabel prefer?'

They were both stunning, obviously. Lara, who had never owned a pair of shoes from Russell and Bromley, quelled the urge to suggest Annabel might like a nice pair of sheepskin slippers instead and said truthfully, 'The ones with the bows on the back.'

And Flynn had bought the amazing shoes for Annabel. Having done his homework, he knew she was a size three. *Imagine, a three.*

The various bags of shopping were now stacked up beneath their table. Once he'd started, he hadn't hung around. Gigi would be thrilled when she saw what he'd bought her for Christmas, as would Annabel. Flynn wasn't afraid to spend a bit of money and Lara hadn't tried to stop him; it was his to spend as he liked. Although having to try on the butter-soft honey-beige suede coat by Armani had been a low point. Having ascertained that, yes, it *would* look fantastic on Annabel, Flynn had helped her out of the size fourteen and told the sales assistant he'd like to buy one in a size eight.

Anyway, never mind that now. Here they were, Gigi's parents, drinking champagne like actual grown-ups and enjoying a break in their Christmas shopping trip. Anyone watching them might assume they were a couple, which just went to show. Appearances could be deceptive.

'I can't wait, I can't even believe I'm saying it, but this is actually going to be the best Christmas ever!'

The voice was familiar but not instantly recognisable. Casting a surreptitious sidelong glance at the two women at the next table, Lara winced as she realised who it belonged to. Oh help, Betsy Barrowman, the sweet but deluded woman who thought she had the best husband in the world *and* a near-flawless four-carat diamond on her finger.

'You look better.' Betsy's friend was speaking now. 'Happier. How's the cottage coming along?'

'All done! It's completely gorgeous. Remember how Melvyn would never let me have a dog? Well, I'm getting one next week. And a camper van! It's always been a dream of mine to travel around the coast of Britain and you know what Melvyn was like; obviously he wasn't interested in having anything to do with *that*. So as soon as the weather brightens up in the spring, that's going to be next on our list. Me and Mum, setting off together on a big adventure. Like Thelma and Louise with sensible shoes, and Tupperware boxes for our sandwiches.'

'Are you OK?' said Flynn.

'Sshh.' Lara shook her head at him and mouthed, '*I'm listening*.' Mimicking her, Flynn mouthed back, '*I know*.'

374

But honestly, it was all she could do not to fall off her chair. Trying to make sense of what Betsy Barrowman was saying was scrambling her brain. Then Betsy raised her left hand and Lara saw that it was bare. No wedding ring, no stonking great gemstone-masquerading-as-a-diamond. Had her husband died? But if he had, would she be sounding this overjoyed? It was a puzzle and no mistake—

'Excuse me, are you eavesdropping?'

Whoops, it was Betsy's companion, sounding curious rather than outraged. Lara said, 'Sorry, no . . . well, maybe a bit. I just recognised your friend, that's all, and couldn't help overhearing—'

'Oh yes, I remember you! Temple's the jewellers on York Street,' Betsy exclaimed. 'You work with Don Temple. He's such a lovely man, isn't he?'

'He is.' Was there a subtle way of saying this? Probably not. 'I noticed you weren't wearing your ring,' Lara ventured.

'Aha, well spotted.' Betsy waggled her naked left hand. 'Ring gone, husband gone, marriage over. Thank goodness!'

'Really? Wow.'

The convivial Christmassy atmosphere, together with the wine, had evidently loosened Betsy Barrowman's inhibitions. Leaning towards Lara and Flynn she said, 'Melvyn was having an affair! With some awful creature who's had her lips pumped up like bicycle tyres! And do you know, the moment I found out I was just *so* relieved, wasn't I, Mary? Because at last I had an actual reason to get out of the marriage!'

'Well, that's brilliant. Good for you.' Lara exhaled; Betsy wasn't the only one to be relieved. 'When you came into the shop, from the way you were talking about him, you seemed so . . . happy together.'

'Ha, that's called putting on a brave face, keeping a stiff upper lip, pretending everything's fine. After so many years you just get used to doing it.'

'Melvyn was a bully,' her friend Mary chimed in. 'He'd sapped all her confidence. None of us ever liked him,'

'So what happened to the ring?' Lara nodded at Betsy's hand.

'Well, it belonged to his family really. One of those heirlooms that gets passed down through the generations. And obviously I didn't want to wear it any more anyway. Luckily though, my brother's a solicitor, so when we were working out the settlement, he said if Melvyn was taking the ring back, I should have the Bentley Continental.'

'Gosh.' Could she tell her? Would it be OK to tell Betsy now? Surely it was—

'I know!' Betsy's eyes were dancing. 'And for some reason this made Melvyn furious. I mean, the Bentley was his pride and joy, he paid it far more attention than he ever did me. But my brother insisted it was only fair. So you can imagine Melvyn was even *more* furious a couple of weeks later when he found out I'd sold his precious car.' She beamed and sat back, utterly unrepentant.

Mary said with pride, 'She's a new woman, you wouldn't believe the difference in her. It's like a caterpillar wrapping itself up in a cocoon then the cocoon breaks open and out bursts a butterfly.'

'That's such a fantastic story,' said Lara. 'I'm so happy for you.' *Could she tell her now? Yes, she was going to do it.* 'In fact—'

'Hang on, there's more. So Melvyn must be head over heels in lust with this new floozy of his, because the next thing we knew, he'd given her the ring to wear.' Betsy shook her head in amused disbelief. 'He was introducing his new girlfriend to all our friends and she was flaunting it. The engagement ring I'd worn for thirty-six years! My God, it was practically still *warm*.'

'Awful,' Lara murmured, waiting for her chance to leap in.

'And then we come to the best bit,' Betsy continued. 'The floozy took her gorgeous new ring along to a jewellers in Chippenham to have it valued, and guess what?' She paused, saw the look on Lara's face and said, 'Right, you knew. I thought you probably did, from the way you kept talking about it.'

'I'm sorry. I wanted to tell you at the time. Don told me I mustn't. I felt terrible about it.'

'Ha, not half as terrible as Melvyn did when his lovely new fiancée got home and gave him what for. She wrecked the house, told him he was a lying bastard, threw a five-litre can of magnolia gloss over his new car and told him he was rubbish in bed. Rather loudly,' Betsy's eyebrows rose, 'by all accounts.'

'I heard every word,' Mary chimed in with satisfaction. 'I live next door.'

'Comes in handy,' Betsy added mischievously. 'I'm getting all the gossip. Anyway, so that was it, she packed up and moved on. Turns out it wasn't the love story of the century after all. According to his friends, my husband's now devastated and wishing he had his frumpy old wife back.'

'Which isn't going to happen.' Mary gave her arm a loyal squeeze. 'You're never going back to that life. You're over him.'

And since Betsy's friend was supportive but not necessarily diplomatic, Lara added, 'And you're definitely not frumpy.'

Flynn had sat back and kept out of the conversation but Lara had been acutely aware of his gaze upon her. When they'd finished their drinks and it was time to leave, he gathered up the bags and said, 'Ready for some more shopping?'

They said their goodbyes to Betsy and Mary, then made their way back outside. The temperature had dropped another couple of degrees.

'Where next?' Lara could feel her nose turning pink with cold and just knew something like that would never happen to Annabel.

'I was thinking about an iPod Touch for Gigi. Would that be good?'

'The new kind? She'd be thrilled.'

As they made their way towards the Apple store, a man selling bunches of fresh mistletoe called out cheerily, 'Now here's a lovely couple! You'll buy some mistletoe, won't you?'

'We're not a couple,' said Lara.

'Ah, but this is special stuff.' The street vendor grinned at her. 'That's the thing about mistletoe, it can make magic happen.'

As he spoke, he spread his hands and waggled his fingers to demonstrate the potential magical properties. Lara's heart did a flip and she shook her head. 'It'll be dead by Christmas.'

'Don't be so grumpy.' Flynn was taking his wallet out. 'Just ignore her. I'll have a bunch.'

The mistletoe was stuffed into a big plastic bag. Money changed hands. 'Good luck,' the street vendor told Flynn: 'You're a brave chap.'

'It's OK.' Flynn's tone was conspiratorial. 'I'm saving it for someone else.'

Ouch. Thanks for pointing that out.

'The berries are all going to fall off,' Lara said as they moved away. 'You know that, don't you?'

Flynn stopped walking. 'Look, I've finally met someone I really like,' he said patiently. 'And Gigi likes her too. I'd have thought you'd want me to be happy.'

'I do. Oh God, I'm sorry, I sound like the Grinch.' Her emotions churned up, Lara told herself she was being ridiculous. 'Ignore me. It's just when you hear all these stories . . . Betsy being treated like rubbish by that awful husband of hers, and the things Joel

378

got up to behind Evie's back . . . well, it's enough to make you Grinchy about men. And, you know, getting married.'

'But we're not all like that,' said Flynn. 'And there are happy marriages too. Sometimes you meet the right person and the two of you don't break up. It has been known to happen.' As he spoke, he was looking past her into the window of a jeweller's shop. Lara shivered, observing the direction of his gaze; was he checking out the engagement rings or the bracelets?

'Is Annabel the right person?' It was the equivalent of prodding a wobbly tooth; she didn't want to know the answer but felt a compulsion to ask.

'It's early days.' Clouds of condensation accompanied the words. 'But fingers crossed, she definitely could be.'

OK, get a grip, you knew this would happen sooner or later. And to give Annabel her due, she did seem charming. 'Well, that's . . . great.' Lara concentrated her attention on the seductively spotlit contents of the shop window and waited until she was in control once more, then pressed a finger to the glass. 'And I bet she'd really like that watch.'

Chapter 53

Happy endings might be thin on the ground but sometimes the most unlikely couples were capable of catching you by surprise.

'Thank goodness you're *here*,' Lara exclaimed, pulling open the front door of Nettie's house and flinging her arms around Harry. 'I've been feeling like the world's greenest gooseberry! Don and Nettie, honestly, they're like a pair of teenagers.'

'Don't say that,' Nettie protested, emerging from the kitchen. 'It's not true. Hello, pet, how are you? Fancy a nice cup of tea and some fruit cake?'

'Later,' said Lara before Harry could open his mouth to reply. 'We're going to leave you in peace for a bit. I need to see the hills properly, make sure my favourite places are all still there. We'll be back in a while.'

Harry drove, then parked and they made their way to the viewing point Lara loved most and had visited hundreds of times over the years. They sat together on a rock and listened to the silence, broken only by the sound of birds wheeling overhead. The air was cold and clear, and below them Derwentwater shone like smoked glass. The sky was white, the tops of the familiar hills dusted with snow. It was all as it should be and Lara felt her shoulders relax, the tension seeping from her body as she savoured the sense of peace.

This morning she had driven Don and a carful of belongings up from Bath. He had rented out his house and put most of his things into storage. Tonight she would head back down the M6 without him. Seriously, who would ever have predicted this?

Harry had been watching her enjoy the view. Finally, having given her enough time to drink it in, he said, 'Are they really behaving like teenagers?'

'Not on the outside. They aren't snogging and groping and twanging each other's knickers. But on the inside . . . yes, that's exactly how they're feeling.' Lara leaned against him, rubbing her cold hands together because, as ever, it hadn't occurred to her to bring gloves. 'It's really sweet. You'll have to keep me updated with how they're getting on.'

'I will.' As ever, Harry had brought a spare pair. He dug in his pockets and passed them over. 'Anyway, how're things with you?'

He felt her shrug. 'Great. Gigi's happy. I'm going to be in charge of the shop, which is brilliant. Flynn's still seeing Annabel . . .'

'And? How do you feel about that?' Although Harry could already guess.

'If she was horrible I wouldn't be thrilled. But she isn't,' sighed Lara. 'She's really nice and Gigi loves her. So what can I say? It was bound to happen at some stage.' She cuddled up closer and Harry put an arm around her to keep her warm. 'Anyway, enough about me. Business still booming, I hear.'

'It is.' Harry nodded. The Enjay effect was still in full flow, although it might start to dry up soon; there was a distinct possibility that by spring his fifteen minutes of fame would be over.

In a way it would be a relief.

'So what was it you wanted to tell me?' said Lara.

It was easier like this, sitting side by side, surrounded by hills and gazing out over the water. Harry cleared his throat. 'Well, I know I've always been a bit slow off the mark, but the thing is, I've kind of realised I . . . I prefer men.'

There, he'd said it. He watched Lara's profile as the words sank in. Finally she turned to look at him.

'You're gay?'

Harry nodded.

'Wow. What d'you mean, you've kind of realised? How long have you known?'

'Not long. A few months. I thought I *might* be.' He tilted his head from side to side. 'But like I said, I was a bit slow figuring it out. It was all so confusing. I think some people just grow up knowing this stuff from the word go.' Harry shrugged. 'But I swear to God it wasn't like that for me. I just . . . *didn't.*'

'Oh, Harry.' Lara squeezed his arm. 'But you've decided now? You're definitely sure?'

He nodded. 'Yes.'

'Well, that does explain things.' She was smiling slightly.

Harry nodded in agreement, because this was their secret. 'I'm sorry. But I honestly didn't know. When we got married I loved you and I loved Gigi. I wanted to help and I thought maybe we could make it work.'

'I know, me too. And you don't have to apologise. It's just nice to know there was a good reason why it didn't.' She turned and gave him a kiss on the cheek.

Harry was touched; at the time he knew their sadly inadequate sex life had hurt her feelings. She'd taken his lack of interest in her personally, had assumed she was to blame. Poor Lara, she'd been a stunning young bride with a husband who wasn't physically interested in her; no wonder her confidence had taken such a knock.

'It was my fault,' he reassured her. 'All mine. Not yours.'

'It's nobody's fault. You're gay,' Lara broke into a grin, 'not a mass murderer. So what's brought all this on, anyway? Have you met someone? You must have done. Ooh,' her eyes widened, 'this is exciting! Who is it? Do I know him?'

Lying to Lara didn't fill him with joy but this time Harry knew he had no other choice. A promise was a promise, it was a secret he'd vowed to take to his grave and that was what he would do.

'You don't know him. And it's over now anyway. Don't worry, I'm not heartbroken,' Harry added as Lara's forehead creased with concern. 'But while it lasted it was perfect. And it made me realise what I want from life. So that's . . . pretty fantastic.'

'Oh, Harry, I'm so happy for you. So is it a secret, or are you going to go public?'

'I'm going to do it. Out and proud,' said Harry. 'I've decided.'

'Good for you. You can be a role model. A few people might be a bit funny about it.'

He knew what she meant. Some of the old hill farmers weren't exactly twenty-first century in their opinions. 'Never mind them.'

'What about Moira?'

'She'll be fine. She's seeing someone else now. His name's Bernard,' said Harry, 'and he runs a vegan guest house in Buttermere. You should see them, they're just perfect for each other.'

'Sweet. Like Nettie always says, there's a lid for every pot. Well, that's good,' said Lara before another thought struck her. 'Oh my God, I know who *is* going to be shocked when you tell him.' She pulled a face. 'Enjay.'

Harry nodded slowly. 'I know, I spoke to him yesterday. He was.'

'Oh no. What did he say?' Prepared to leap to Harry's defence, Lara said fiercely, 'Was he vile?'

'No, no.' Out of everyone, Harry knew he could trust Lara to keep such a potentially explosive secret, but he still couldn't do it.

'Are you sure? Because it wouldn't surprise me if he said something mean. And he's such a *lech*.' Lara pawed her hands in imitation. 'All the endless groping and flirting . . . total woman-isers like that can be *so* homophobic.'

'Well, he isn't. He was fine about it.' Harry managed to keep his voice steady. 'But obviously he doesn't want it to impact on his career. Some of his fans might make comments. So we've agreed he's going to put up a message on his website saying he's just heard my news and he wishes me all the best for the future, but that I'm not scheduled to appear in any future episodes blah blah blah.'

Lara's lip curled. 'So basically he doesn't want any more to do with you. Charming.'

'It's OK.' Harry shrugged. 'It's his world, his career. I can understand that.'

'Well, you're a nicer person than I am.' She gave him another squeeze. 'But then we already knew that.'

'Enjay's all right. I owe him a lot.' How much, she'd never know. 'Look what he's done for the business.'

'Hmm, and I bet that's it from now on.' Lara did a *pfsh* of derision. 'You won't see him in any more Flying Ducks shirts.'

'Maybe not. But it doesn't matter.' Harry pointed out a curlew wheeling high in the sky above them; it was time to get off the subject. No one else in the world but Enjay and himself would ever know about their brief but perfect relationship. Nothing long-term could ever have come of it, they'd both known that, and certainly no one would ever believe such an unlikely pairing could have happened in the first place, but for as long as it had lasted, it had been life-changing.

They'd been five secret and magical days he would never forget.

Chapter 54

A trip to an amateur show being put on at a small local theatre wasn't Evie's idea of a top night out, but Bonnie had been given two tickets and had begged her to come along.

'Oh please, Ray's said no and I don't want to go on my own. It'll be fun,' she'd said in her optimistic Bonnie-type way. 'You might love it!'

The chances of that were slim, but the tickets had come from a regular customer whose son was directing the play in question. Bonnie couldn't duck out and Evie hadn't had the heart to say no.

And you never knew, it might not be as bad as they'd thought.

Anyway, the theatre was filling up fast, which was a good sign. Imagine having to sit there surrounded by empty seats whilst the poor actors performed to an audience in single figures.

'These seats are quite comfortable,' Bonnie leaned over and whispered in her ear. 'If it turns out to be really boring we can always have a doze. Nobody would notice once all the lights are turned off.'

Now where had she heard that voice before? Try as she might, Evie was unable to place it. The actress playing the part of

Maria was wearing oversized factory overalls and her blonde hair was bundled into a cap. But she definitely knew her from somewhere . . . it was driving her mad not being able to figure out the connection. Did she work on the tills at the local supermarket . . . ?

Then another actor strode on to the stage and roared, 'What's all this about you having to go home?'

Evie almost leapt out of her seat as if she'd been electrocuted. *Oh God, oh God, OH MY GOD* . . .

'But, sir, eet eez my children, zey are sick . . .'

'I don't care how ill they are!' Maria's boss shook his head. 'I don't want to hear about your bloody kids!'

'Oh, but p-please, I need to b-be wiz zem.' Maria was wringing her hands in agitation.

'Not my problem.'

'But zey are too szmall . . . Anya eez only four . . . I do *anyzing* . . .'

Evie gazed transfixed at the actors on the stage. This was unbelievable. And everyone else in the audience was just sitting watching the play, *as if nothing out of the ordinary had just happened.*

'Listen to me, we've already been there.' The factory owner dismissed Maria's protests. 'The only thing I want from you is a proper day's work. If you can't manage that, I'll find someone else who can.'

'Goodness, look at that, I've just realised who it is.' Tapping Evie's elbow and pointing at the stage, Bonnie murmured excitedly, 'Do you recognise him? It's Ethan from the Ellison Hotel, the one I set you up with on that date!'

The play had been very loosely based on *A Christmas Carol*. Ethan's character had turned out to be not so bad in the end.

When the dusty blue curtains closed then swung open again to allow the cast to take their bows, the audience rose to their feet and applauded wildly, possibly because most of them were friends or relatives of the cast and crew.

Evie clapped too, light-hearted with emotion and just praying she wasn't about to make a fool of herself and pass out − imagine the embarrassment of having to be lifted over the seats and carted out of the theatre. God, but it was such a weird sensation, and her knees were *wibbling* . . .

Finally the cheers and applause died down and the young director raised his hands for silence.

'Thank you all so much for your wonderful support, it means the world to us. Now, we hope you won't all rush off. Drinks will be served in the bar, and my mum's made enough sausage rolls to keep all of us going until Christmas.'

'Oh how lovely. Actually, I'm quite peckish,' said Bonnie. 'What d'you think, darling? Shall we stay for a bit?'

Evie swallowed; her mouth was dry and her knees were still clacking like maracas. 'Yes, let's.'

The cast had changed out of their stage costumes and were having their photos taken for the local paper at the other end of the bar. Evie, keeping her distance and clutching her drink, watched as Ethan posed along with the rest of them.

The next minute she froze as he glanced up and spotted her. The impulse to hurriedly turn away and pretend she hadn't seen him was as strong as ever − old habits die hard − but this time she forced herself to return his gaze and smile. Except she seemed to have *forgotten* how to smile; her lips were stretching into a weird unnatural grimace. Oh no, this was ridiculous, and now she appeared to be stuck like that . . .

'These sausage rolls are fantastic,' Bonnie enthused, spilling flakes of pastry down the front of her pink cardigan. 'Darling, you must try one.'

Because if there was anything more terrifying than a frozen grimace, Evie acknowledged, it was one liberally accessorised with pastry crumbs.

Although her courage was threatening to fail her now anyway. She wasn't at all sure she was brave enough to approach Ethan. And he was busy laughing and joking with the photographer, no longer even looking in her direction.

The next minute, as soon as Bonnie had moved away to chat to the director's sausage-roll-making mother, Ethan appeared in front of her. 'Hello.'

'Hi.' Evie concentrated on breathing in and out. She could manage that, surely? He smelled wonderful. It seemed unbelievable that she could remember every single line and angle of his face.

'Enjoy the play?'

'Yes, I did.'

'Were you smiling at me just now, while I was over there?'

She nodded. 'Trying to. Sorry, made a bit of a hash of it.'

'Did you see me the other week when you were crossing Milsom Street?'

'Umm . . .'

'You remember,' Ethan prompted. 'That time you pretended not to see me.'

Evie grimaced. 'Ah. Sorry again.'

'OK, can I ask you a very personal question?' He stood in front of her, clearly mystified. 'What went wrong? Because not being able to figure it out has been driving me mad. I thought we had a great evening together. As far as I was concerned it was the perfect date. Maybe I shouldn't be saying this, but I really liked you. I mean, *really* liked you—'

'So you decided not to call me,' Evie blurted out. It was no good, she may as well be honest; it had been driving her mad too. 'You didn't get in touch and I couldn't believe it. I felt like such a fool because I'd actually thought you would!'

'Oh my God, seriously? I don't believe it!' Ethan shook his head in despair. 'Hang on, but then I *did* see you again, at that party at the hotel, and you ignored me. You were dancing with that other guy . . . and then when I phoned you the next day he was there and you told me not to bother calling you again. So after that, what else could I do? You'd found someone else. I'd missed my chance. And let me tell you, I gave my sister hell about that.' He paused. 'Are you still seeing him?'

'Harry? No, I never was. Hang on, what's your sister got to do with this?'

'You mean my brilliant sister, the relationship expert?' Ethan's tone was wry. 'I liked you, rememeber? I had to make sure I didn't mess things up. So I called and asked her advice, explained that I really needed to get this right. I wanted to phone you first thing the next morning to fix another date, and she told me I mustn't.'

'Oh. Why not?'

He raked his fingers through already raked-up hair. 'She said I'd look like a complete loser, that nothing puts a girl off faster than when some new bloke acts too keen. If you met my sister you'd understand.' Ethan looked resigned. 'Her views are very strong. She insisted you'd lose all respect for me. She also said calling you the next morning would be *pukey*.'

'OK. Just so you know,' said Evie, 'I would have loved it if you'd phoned. It would have saved all that awful *waiting*.'

'Right, that's it. My sister's getting *no* Christmas presents this year. Her advice is officially rubbish.'

Evie said good-naturedly, 'We all make mistakes.'

'Hmm.' Ethan was less forgiving. 'Some bigger than others.'

The chambermaid who'd played the part of Maria came over. 'Sorry to interrupt. Ethan, can I just say thanks for offering me a lift back to the hotel but I won't need one now. Some of us are going out to a club.'

No trace of an eastern European accent, needless to say. *Because she'd been acting.*

'That's fine,' said Ethan. 'Have fun.'

'We will. You're welcome to come along too, if you like.'

'To a club? Me?' He shook his head. 'Far too old. But thanks anyway.'

'And don't worry.' The girl grinned at him. 'I'll try not to be late in the morning.'

When she'd gone, Ethan said, 'That's Lizzie, it's her fault I'm here. She was the one who dragged me along to the drama group in the first place.' Misreading the expression on Evie's face, he added, 'Don't worry, nothing like that, Lizzie just works for me. She's one of the chambermaids at the hotel.'

Time for an explanation of her own. Feeling almost weightless with relief, Evie smiled and said, 'I know.'

Chapter 55

Lara was busy in the shop on Wednesday afternoon when Flynn called her.

'What's happening with Gigi?' he said without preamble. 'I let her have the morning off for Christmas shopping and she was meant to be back here at work by one o'clock. But there's no sign of her, she hasn't called me and she's not answering her phone.'

'I don't know. Did she drive to Bristol? Maybe she's caught up in traffic.'

'Well, it's not bloody good enough. We're rushed off our feet here and she hasn't even bothered to get in touch.' He sounded exasperated. 'I've got an appointment in Cheltenham with a buyer and I can't even leave the shop.'

'Look, she wouldn't do it on purpose,' said Lara. 'If Gigi's late there'll be a good reason for it. There's probably been an accident on the M4 and she's stuck in a mile-long jam with no signal on her phone. Anyway, there's nothing I can do about it now. I'm busy too. She'll be with you as soon as she can.'

'Great.' Flynn heaved a sigh of annoyance and hung up.

'Happy Christmas to you too,' said Lara.

By five thirty, though, she'd tried calling Gigi several times and still not been able to get through. Anxiety began to gnaw at Lara's stomach; this was no longer normal. Closing up the shop and abandoning her planned trip to the supermarket, she headed straight home instead.

The moment she opened the front door, Lara knew something was wrong. Gigi's handbag was still hanging over the chair where she'd left it last night.

'Gigi? Where are you?' Lara's heart clattered with fear as she hurriedly checked the kitchen and living room, flinging doors wide and finding the rooms empty. Then she was racing up the staircase, dry-mouthed with fear, almost too afraid to enter the bedroom . . .

There was a sound like a kitten mewing as she pushed open the door. And there was Gigi lying in bed, her hair drenched in sweat, her face waxen and contorted with pain.

'Oh, Mum,' she croaked, terror in her eyes. 'Help me, I think I'm going to die.'

Lara was standing in a corner of the waiting room when Flynn burst into A&E.

'Where is she? What's happening?'

'The doctors are examining her now, then she's going down to theatre. I wanted to stay with her but they made me wait out here.' Lara's teeth were chattering with shock. 'Her appendix burst. She has peritonitis. Another couple of hours, they said, and it might have been too late.'

'God, she was just there at home on her own . . . it doesn't bear thinking about. And to happen so fast . . .'

'She went to bed early last night with a bit of a stomach ache, but we both thought it was just period pains. I didn't disturb her this morning because she hates being woken early when she doesn't have to get up for work.' Lara couldn't look at him; she'd been racked with guilt since getting home and discovering Gigi in such a state. 'She was in a lot of pain after I left the house, so she tried to sleep it off. Then it got unbearable – the doctor said that would be when the appendix burst – and she realised she couldn't get out of bed.'

'Where was her phone?'

'On charge, downstairs.' Lara felt responsible for that too; fed up with the mobile beep-beeping at night to signal each incoming text, she had told Gigi not to keep it in her bedroom.

'So she was lying there for hours, unable to move.' Flynn's eyes were boring into her, she could feel them. 'She could hear me ringing her but couldn't reach the phone.'

'Yes, all right, we know that now.' Was there anything in the world more horrendous than discovering your child was seriously ill and it was all your fault? The mental image of Gigi, burning up and rigid with pain, would stay with her for ever.

'Look I was just—'

'Don't keep on about it, OK?' Lara turned away; he couldn't begin to understand how she felt. She was Gigi's mother and the reason they were here now. Flinching as Flynn put a hand on her shoulder, she shrugged it off. If he was kind to her, the guilt would become too much to bear and she might break down.

'Hello, are you Gigi's parents?' Another doctor approached them, calm and authoritative behind doctorly wire-rimmed spectacles. 'Let me explain what's happening. Gigi's condition is deteriorating, so we're taking her straight into theatre. You can see her for a few moments before she goes down. Just to warn you, her pulse is thready so she's receiving oxygen and we've put up a drip. I'm afraid she's very unwell but we'll be doing the best we can . . .'

★   ★   ★

394

The nightclub was dark, it was noisy and it was crowded. It wasn't Harry's natural milieu at all, but he was here and he was going to tolerate it. Well, for the next hour at least.

This was all part of his New Life. He had to put himself into situations he would previously have found uncomfortable. When you were gay, it became necessary to meet other gay men, and since there didn't appear to be any local clubs for gay birdwatchers or gay poetry enthusiasts – none that he'd been able to track down, anyway – venturing into a place like this was the only remaining option.

Even if the drinks were ludicrously expensive and the music was already giving him a headache.

God, this felt weird though. Embarrassing. Sitting alone on a bar stool in a club in Carlisle, aware of being given practised once-overs by other men but having to pretend you hadn't noticed.

Then the music changed and Harry straightened up. Finally, something he recognised. His gaze shifted to the supersized TV screen behind the bar where the videos accompanying the music were shown. And there he was, Enjay, wearing a white suit and matching fedora, holding centre stage while half a dozen practically naked girls swayed and gyrated around him.

Harry's heart beat faster as he watched the video. 'What The Girls Want' was Enjay's new single, just out this week. On the screen he was dancing, simultaneously trailing languid fingers over the girls' bodies and flirting with the camera.

'What the girls want is me me me . . . want me to choose ya, gotta shake ya booty . . .'

'The song's not bad,' said the barman, making Harry jump. 'But the singer's a prat.'

'Not really my kind of music,' said Harry. 'I'm more into classical.'

The barman flashed him an easy smile, as if this didn't come as too much of a surprise. 'Each to his own. First time here?'

Was this a chat-up line? Was the barman straight or gay? Oh dear, he was rubbish at this; as he and Enjay had managed to prove to each other, they were both massively lacking in the gaydar department.

'First time.' Harry nodded, feeling rather too hot. Looking around, he belatedly discovered that no one else in the club appeared to be wearing a sweater.

'Great. Well, we're a friendly lot. So just relax, you'll be fine.'

Was *that* a chat-up line? Or was he simply being friendly? Flustered, Harry turned away from the bar and pretended to be scanning the dance floor for someone he knew. The next moment he almost fell off his stool because over there on the other side of the club *was* someone he knew.

It took a few moments to remember he didn't have to hide. It was fine, it didn't matter that he'd just been spotted by tall blond Duncan who worked in his local garden centre and who, coincidentally, had also driven the twenty-odd miles from Keswick to Carlisle in order to be here tonight . . .

Ah.

'Hello.' Duncan had crossed the dance floor to greet him.

'Hello,' said Harry when they'd both briefly wondered what to do and ended up shaking hands. Were his own palms as clammy as Duncan's?

'I didn't know you were . . . you know . . .' Duncan's tilted head indicated their surroundings.

'I know, not really my thing. To be honest I'd prefer a cup of tea and a few biscuits in front of the TV.'

'I meant . . . the kind of place this is. For people who are . . .' For an instant fear flared in his eyes, as if maybe Harry had just happened to wander in unawares.

'Oh God, sorry, you mean gay.' Harry nodded vigorously. 'Not used to this yet. All a bit confusing. Yes, I am, I definitely am. But I didn't know you were.'

Duncan hesitated. 'Nobody else knows. Well, apart from my mum. So please don't say anything. I nearly dived under the table when I first saw you.'

'I nearly tried to hide behind my bar stool,' said Harry. 'Which definitely wouldn't have worked.'

'Anyway. We're here, we've seen each other now. Are you . . . out then?'

'Of course I'm— *oh*.' Harry broke off, realising he didn't mean 'out of the house for the evening'. This new terminology was something else he'd have to get used to. 'Yes,' he amended, 'I'm out. I told all my staff last week.'

'You did?' Duncan looked envious. 'How did they react?'

'They were great.' Warmed by the memory of Morag and Betty's response, Harry said, 'They told me they should have guessed, that I was far too nice to be straight.'

'Good. That's good.' Duncan nodded, then took a deep breath. 'Look, no offence, but just in case you were wondering, you're not my kind of guy. I go for big muscly types. Nothing personal.'

'No problem.' Harry relaxed; he wasn't remotely attracted to Duncan either. 'I'm not really sure yet what my type is. But I'm here, I'm making a start.'

'No hurry,' said Duncan.

'None at all. I can just take my time. Actually, I think I'm starting to like this club.' Harry felt himself relax some more. 'It feels kind of like . . . being on holiday.'

'I know what you mean. Me too.' Duncan nodded happily in agreement. 'In the best place in the world.'

Chapter 56

Lara and Flynn occupied chairs on either side of the hospital bed. Between them, Gigi lay sleeping. Last night the ruptured appendix had been removed but they weren't out of the woods yet. Her abdominal cavity had been flooded with bacteria; now they just had to pray the intravenously administered antibiotics would be up to the task of defeating them.

So far they weren't. Gigi had a raging temperature and was still intermittently moaning with pain in her sleep. She was as white as the sheet covering her. Just seeing her so clearly unwell tore Lara in half; when you were used to someone bouncing around and never being ill, it was a terrifying scenario.

All my fault, too.

Flynn pushed back his plastic chair and said, 'I'm going outside for a bit. Won't be long.'

Lara nodded; it was eight in the morning. 'You can leave if you want.'

'Why would I want to leave?'

'Well, you'll need to get to work.'

Flynn gave her an odd look. 'Are you going to work?'

Oh for God's sake. 'No, of course not!'

'Why not?'

'Are you serious? I'm not leaving Gigi!'

'Because she's your daughter?' He paused, his gaze boring into her. 'Guess what? She's mine too.'

He left the ward and Lara watched him go. If it was possible to feel any worse than she already did, she was feeling it now. And Flynn was right; she'd assumed he wasn't as devastated as she was by what had happened.

'Sorry,' Lara murmured when he returned fifteen minutes later.

He nodded without replying, then sat back down and resumed holding Gigi's left hand.

'It's just that I've always been used to being the only one.'

'I know.' To her relief he didn't add, And whose fault was *that*? 'But you aren't the only one any more. I'm here now.'

More guilt, almost more than she could bear. Covertly watching as Flynn leaned forward and brushed a strand of hair off Gigi's waxen cheek, Lara noted the strain in his eyes, the dark shadows beneath them, the tension on his stubbled jaw. It had been a sleepless night for them both.

He loves her just as much as I do. Please God, just make the antibiotics work and let Gigi get through this.

Then she jumped as Gigi's head moved and she cleared her throat. Without opening her eyes she croaked, 'Are you both still here?'

'Yes.' Flynn gave her fingers a squeeze. 'I am.'

A lump formed in Lara's own throat. Ambushed by love she said, 'Me too, sweetheart.'

'Good. I'm glad. But could you please stop bickering?' whispered Gigi.

★　　★　　★

By mid-afternoon Gigi's eyes were open and the colour was slowly returning to her cheeks. She was still sore and uncomfortable but her condition had improved enough to have her fretting about the state of her hair. Which was evidently *gross*.

'No, you *can't* wash it yet,' said Lara. Teenagers, honestly.

'Urgh, it's like string.'

Flynn said helpfully, 'How about if I borrow a razor? We could shave it all off.'

'Ha ha.' Her mouth dry, Gigi took a sip of water from the plastic cup he was holding for her. A dribble of water ran down her chin and Lara leapt forward with a tissue.

'Thanks.' Gigi smiled briefly then turned and smiled again at Flynn. 'Thanks. You know, you two could do me a favour if you want.'

'No problem, fire away,' said Flynn.

'Go ahead,' said Lara. 'What is it?'

'You could move your chairs so you're both sitting on the same side of the bed. It would really make things a lot easier, instead of me having to keep going from side to side like I'm watching a tennis match.'

Three days later Evie visited the ward, bringing treats and toiletries and the just-out Christmas edition of Gigi's favourite gossip magazine.

'Thanks.' Gigi greeted her with a kiss, then raised her eyebrows at the well-thumbed corners. 'Have you been reading this?'

'I had to. Harry called the house to let us know there was a bit about him in it, so I rushed out and bought a copy. Oh, and these are from Bonnie and Ray.' Evie opened a bag and pulled out a pair of light-up Elton John spectacles.

'Cool!' Putting them on and posing like a celebrity while

they flashed on and off, Gigi said, 'What does it say about Harry?'

'Found it.' Lara had been riffling through the pages. Reading aloud, she said, 'Ooh dear, looks like a parting of the ways for the Odd Couple. Just a few weeks ago, Harry Wells and EnjaySeven were best pals, but now that everyone's favourite nerd has announced he's gay, ladies' man Enjay is severing all contact.

'"I'm totally surprised to hear this," Enjay announced yesterday. "I had no idea. Anyhow, filming in the UK is over. Nothing against Harry, he's a good guy, but we now have even less in common than I thought. I doubt I'll be seeing him again." Whoa, Enjay, Harry's only gay, he doesn't have rabies. It's not catching, we promise!'

'What a git.' Gigi pushed the flashing spectacles to the top of her head and said crossly, 'Poor Harry.'

'And there's a photo of Enjay with his new girlfriend.' Lara held up the magazine so they could all see. 'Apparently they're spending Christmas together at his villa in Antigua. You have to admit, she is stunning. Then again, he wouldn't go for an ugly one, would he?'

'He's such a lech though.' Her lip curling, Gigi said, 'He's never going to stick with one girl. Give it a few weeks and he'll have found someone even prettier.' She paused. 'Speaking of pretty girls, wait till you see what Annabel gave me this afternoon. Mum, can you get it out of the cabinet? I can't reach.'

'Annabel was here?' Lara didn't like the way this made her feel. Not content with bagging Flynn, did Annabel have stepmotherly designs on Gigi too? There was being nice and then there was being downright ingratiating.

'Isn't it amazing? I've never owned anything so beautiful in my life!'

'Mm.' Lara held up the purply-grey silk negligee, shimmering like iridescent suede beneath the unforgiving fluorescent strip light.

'And guess where it's from? Harvey Nichols!' Gigi's eyes were like saucers. 'Can you imagine? Annabel finished a twenty-four-hour shift this morning and went straight down to Cabot Circus to buy it for me. She said it gets so hot here on the wards you don't always want a fluffy dressing gown.'

Feeling ashamed, Lara said, 'It's gorgeous.' Oh good grief, Harvey Nichols. *What on earth had it cost?*

'Mum, we were talking about Christmas Day. I said she could always come to our house for lunch if she wanted.'

'You did?' It came out quite high-pitched. That wasn't what she wanted *at all*. Her brain recoiling from the prospect, Lara said, 'I thought it was, you know, just going to be *us*.'

'I know, but Annabel has to work on Christmas Eve and on Boxing Day . . . and it would be nice for Dad to have her there.'

Oh God, she was officially a mean person and her daughter was a lovely warm generous one. Lara felt ashamed of herself. Carefully folding the silk robe back up and returning it to the bedside cabinet she said, 'Well, if she doesn't have anywhere else to go . . .'

'She's doing really well,' the doctor told them on the fifth post-operative day. 'No signs of septicaemia, thank goodness. Everything's looking nice and clean. And the scar's healing nicely. I think we can take this drip down now.'

'Excellent.' Gigi beamed up at him. 'How soon can I go home?'

'Let's just keep an eye on you for the next couple of days.' The doctor closed her notes. 'But I'm sure you'll be out of here by Christmas.'

'Trust me, I'll be out of here if I have to crawl on my hands and knees,' said Gigi. 'No offence, but I'm not missing Christmas at home for anything. Are you single or married?'

He smiled at her bluntness. 'Actually, I'm single. Why?'

'Nothing. Just wondered.'

'What did you say that for?' Lara gave her a nudge when the doctor had left the ward.

'He's about your age, he's quite good-looking, maybe we could invite him to lunch on Christmas Day.'

'*What?*'

'To even things up a bit,' Gigi explained. 'Just a thought.'

'Well, don't think. And don't you dare invite him!'

'But he might be lonely, and it would really help you—'

'Stop it. I don't need that kind of help.' Lara held up her hand to halt Gigi in her tracks. 'No, no, *no*.'

Chapter 57

'It's leaning over to the left,' Gigi pronounced. 'Over a bit . . . over a bit . . . over a bit more . . . *oh*. Now it's leaning to the right.'

'It's a good job you're an invalid,' said Flynn.

Through the branches of the Norway spruce they were struggling to put up, Lara saw his eyes glittering with amusement. Turning to Gigi, she said, 'Otherwise you'd be leaning to the right too.'

'I'm giving you constructive criticism.' From her position on the sofa, queen of all she surveyed, Gigi said, 'I just want everything to be perfect.'

It was December the twenty-third and she had been discharged from hospital this afternoon. Before bringing her home, Lara and Flynn had gone out and bought the tree Lara had been too superstitious to buy before. New decorations had been added to the old favourites. Not allowed to join in, Gigi had spent the last three hours playing Christmas songs whilst orchestrating operations from the sofa. Strings of fairy lights were artfully intertwined with swathes of ivy from the garden and draped around doorways, cards were strung up on red ribbon and the poinsettias had been accessorised with silver bows. All they had to do now was decorate the tree.

'It looks brilliant,' Gigi sighed happily when it was finished. 'Our first family Christmas together in Bath. That tree smells amazing.'

From the CD player came the first chords of 'Fairytale Of New York' by the Pogues and Kirsty MacColl. The song brought back powerful memories for Lara, of herself and Flynn bawling along to it as teenagers. Did he remember that too?

'Here.' Flynn, who had to drive back to his flat, poured more Prosecco into Lara's glass.

'Thanks.' It had been such a happy evening, the two of them working together to get everything ready in time. And the house not only looked perfect, it felt . . . joyful. Her eyes prickling unexpectedly at the memory of those unhappy Christmases after her mother had died, Lara blinked and took a glug of the icy fizz.

'Are you OK?' Flynn was watching her.

She nodded. 'Just glad we're all . . . here.'

'I knew there was something missing,' Gigi declared. 'We don't have any mistletoe!'

'They didn't have any left,' said Flynn. 'All sold out.'

'You bought that huge bunch at the market,' Lara innocently reminded him.

He gave her an equally innocent look. 'Oh, *that* mistletoe? All the berries dropped off.'

'Scumbag.' *Would he remember?*

His mouth twitched. 'Maggot,' murmured Flynn.

That was it, their jokey exchange from twenty years ago. *He hadn't forgotten.* The knowledge gave her an inner glow.

'What are you two whispering about?' Gigi demanded.

'Nothing.' He checked his watch. 'Damn, is that the time? I really have to go.'

'Mustn't be late.' From the sofa, Gigi held out her arms for a goodbye hug. 'Thanks for helping Mum with all this. Say hi to Annabel from me.'

'Don't worry, I will.'

Lara turned towards the tree and adjusted one of the glass angels, the secret thrill of their shared joke abruptly negated by all the love in the room for Annabel.

It didn't take much, these days, to demolish a warm glow.

By midnight the two of them had finished watching the Christmas edition of *Never Mind the Buzzcocks*. They'd also managed, impressively, to demolish an entire box of mince pies.

Because Gigi was unable to reach her feet – as a result of the surgery rather than heroic mince pie consumption – Lara had given her a pedicure and painted her toenails a festive shade of Opi red. Now, with her bare legs still draped across Lara's lap, Gigi said, 'Have you bought all my presents yet?'

'Nearly.' Somehow, between the hospital visits and working at the shop she had managed to cram in the necessary frantic bursts of shopping. 'Why? Have you thought of something else you want?'

A pause. 'No, nothing new. I just wondered.'

'Well, go on, tell me.' Lara gave her knee a double tap. 'What does that mean, nothing new?'

Gigi shrugged and gazed at her toes. 'Just . . . the present I wanted more than anything, I can't have. It's OK, I know that. It's just a shame, that's all.'

For a moment Lara thought she was talking about a once-in-a-lifetime holiday or a car. Then she saw the look Gigi was giving her and understood.

'Yes, that would have been the best present of all,' Gigi went on. 'You and Dad getting together. But you wouldn't do it, and now it's too late.'

Too late. Those were the words that had been haunting Lara for weeks. She reached over and brushed a couple of mince-pie crumbs from the front of Gigi's pyjama top. 'I've told you before, it was the sensible thing to do. You know that.'

'You thought it was the sensible thing to do. But, Mum, what if you were wrong?'

The only lights in the room came from the flickering, lit-up Christmas tree and the candles clustered in front of the fireplace. Gigi's grey eyes, with the candle flames reflected in them, were huge and questioning.

'I did it for *you*.' Just saying the words made Lara's throat ache.

'But I didn't want you to do it for me.'

'That's why you're the child and I'm the parent. Sometimes we have to do something because we know it's for the best.'

'I still think you're wrong,' said Gigi. 'I know how much you like him. And he definitely liked you. Until Annabel came along.'

Liked. In the past tense.

'Well, it's done now.'

'And I feel as if it's all my fault. If it wasn't for me, you and Dad would be together now, because there wouldn't be any reason for you not to be. And the two of you could be, like, a million per cent happy. For ever. But you wouldn't let it happen, so now he's found someone else and you're miserable and on your own.'

Ouch.

'I am not miserable! Don't say that! I've got you, haven't I?' Lara gave Gigi's arm a squeeze. 'Everything's fine.'

Gigi rested her head against her shoulder and said in a small voice, 'Yes, but you can't say you're a million per cent happy. Can I ask you something?'

'You know you can.'

'Do you ever feel a bit jealous of Annabel?'

Lara hesitated. 'No.'

'Mum, be honest. You must, sometimes. Just admit it.'

'OK. Sometimes.' She'd always done her best not to lie to her daughter. 'Not that it changes anything, but I suppose I do. A bit.' She raised a warning eyebrow. 'But that's just between us. No need to go blabbing it around.'

Gigi lifted her head and gazed up at her. 'Wouldn't dream of it.'

Two brilliant things and one amusing one happened on Christmas Eve.

First, Gigi called Lara at the jewellers and said, 'Dad just phoned. Annabel has to work a double shift on Christmas Day so she won't be coming over to us after all.'

Yesssss!

Aloud, Lara said, 'Oh dear, poor Annabel, that's a shame. Can't be much fun having to work on Christmas Day.'

'Apparently she doesn't mind. Oh, and there's someone else here who'd like a word with you.'

'Who?'

'Hang on, I'll pass you over.' There was a clunk and a clatter, then Don said cheerily, 'I hope you're looking after that shop for me.'

'Yay, you're here already! Fantastic!'

'It was starting to snow up there so we set out first thing, before it could stop us getting down. Nettie drove like a . . . well, like she always does.'

'I want to see you,' Lara exclaimed. 'I might close up early.'

'You will not.' Don sounded appalled. 'Are you mad? It's

408

Christmas Eve. Men who've left everything till the last minute will be *desperate* this afternoon. You can close at six and not a minute before.'

'Honestly,' said Lara. 'Do you nag Nettie like this?'

He burst out laughing. 'Good grief, no! Wouldn't dare!'

'Thank *God* you're still open.' Bursting into the shop at twenty to six, Joel did a double-take when he saw Lara. 'Oh, hello, I'd forgotten you worked here.' He flashed her a harassed but still dazzling smile. 'How are you? Good?'

'I'm great,' said Lara. 'How can I help you?'

'I need some Christmas presents. Left it a bit late.' He was already scanning the contents of the glass cabinets, sliding past the more expensive items and coming to rest on the silver bangles. 'They're nice. Do girls like that kind of thing?'

Lara nodded. 'So long as you don't go for the skinny cheap ones.' She paused. 'The bangles, I mean. Not the girls.'

He grinned and she unlocked the cabinet. Within thirty seconds he'd decided on the style he wanted.

'That one. Do you do gift-wrapping?'

'We do.' Precisely for all those men who couldn't be bothered to wrap their partner's presents themselves.

'Brilliant.' Relieved, Joel took a credit card from his wallet. 'Can I have three?'

Chapter 58

Then at last it was Christmas morning. And Lara was in tears.

'I knew this would happen,' said Nettie with an air of long-suffering.

Lara wiped her eyes. Listening to *The Snowman* always had this effect on her. But usually she wasn't wearing mascara.

'And I'm the one chopping onions,' Nettie marvelled.

'You said you wanted to make the stuffing.' Lara, who had been tasked with wrapping bacon around tiny sausages, pushed up her sleeves. 'I could have bought ready-made.'

'Mine's miles better and you know it.' Nettie smiled at Don as he came into the kitchen with a bottle of cava.

'She's right.' He popped the cork and topped up their glasses. 'This lady's the best cook in the world.'

And he was looking very well on it. In only a matter of weeks, good home cooking and no junk food whatsoever had trimmed a stone off Don. His eyes were brighter, there was colour in his cheeks and he was happier and healthier than Lara had ever seen him look before.

'*Brrrr*, it's freezing out there.' Back from her visit to Joel's parents, Evie came bursting into the kitchen. She would never become their daughter-in-law, but Ray and Bonnie had accepted that now and still loved her anyway. She had an extra glow about her too, these days. She and Ethan were a wonderful match for each other; sometimes you could just tell that a relationship was meant to last. Lara was thrilled for her, and glad they were taking things steadily. Evie was staying here for lunch at around two, whilst Ethan socialised with his guests at the Ellison, then later she would join him at the hotel.

'Ooh, thanks,' Evie exclaimed, accepting a glass of cava from Don.

'. . . Walking in a winter wonderland,' Don sang, admiring the view from the kitchen window. Last night a thin layer of snow had come to rest on Bath, with clear skies and sub-zero temperatures conspiring to cover it up with a sparkling topcoat of frost. Now the sky was blue and the sun had come out but the air outside was still so cold nothing was melting.

'Yay, Dad's here!' Her ears attuned to the sound of his car, Gigi invalid-hobbled across the hall and waited in the open doorway for Flynn to make his way up the path. 'Hello, Happy Christmas!' She let out a squeal of delight as he reached her. 'I just realised I've never said Happy Christmas to my dad before!'

Lara, watching from the kitchen window, swallowed the lump in her throat. That was her fault too. Flynn was loaded down with bags of presents but he stopped and put them down on the snow-dusted gravel in order to wrap his arms around Gigi. From here she could no longer make out what was being said, but the bond between them was unmistakable.

They loved each other.

It also looked as if he was determined to play catch-up and shower his daughter with eighteen years' worth of presents.

The next minute they appeared in the kitchen. Flynn greeted

411

everyone, rubbing his cold hands together and looking so outdoorsy and handsome that Lara's stomach did that familiar giddy dolphin dive with an extra swoop for Christmas. He was wearing a dark red lambswool sweater over a white shirt and charcoal wool trousers. He also smelled amazing. When it was her turn he said, 'Hey, Happy Christmas,' and gave her a kiss on the cheek, less than an inch from her mouth.

Less than an inch. Imagine if she'd sneakily turned her head at just the right moment . . .

But no. Be sensible. Instead she said, 'You too. How many presents have you bought Gigi?'

Flynn shrugged, unabashed. 'Probably too many. Don't tell me off.'

'Poor Annabel, having to work.'

'I know. Can I ask you something?'

Lara's pulse quickened. The last time someone had uttered those words to her, it had been Gigi wanting to know if she was jealous of Annabel. Warily she said, 'What?'

Flynn reached out and touched her cheeks. 'Why have you got mascara all over here, here and here?'

Bugger. And no one had bothered to tell her.

'Sorry, *The Snowman* made me cry.'

'Where is he, out in the back garden?' Amused, Flynn said, 'Want me to go and rip his carrot nose off?'

'Come on, put everything down, we're all going through to the living room.' Gigi reappeared next to them, her eyes shining. 'Time to open the presents!'

Gigi had been spoiled, the living-room carpet was awash with wrapping paper and Flynn was the proud new owner of a computer mouse mat with a photo of his daughter on it.

'In case I forget what you look like.' He grinned at her, because she'd also given him tea towels printed with images of herself as well as a photo in a black lacquered frame of the two of them together.

Lara was embarrassed. Terrified at the prospect of being caught out not buying Flynn a Christmas present, she had got him a midnight-blue Oswald Boateng shirt. Whilst it was good that he'd been really pleased with it, he hadn't offered her anything in return, which meant she was now left feeling *more* awkward than if she'd not bothered in the first place.

Then Gigi reached for the last two presents under the tree, resplendent in black and silver striped wrapping paper.

'Those are for your mum,' Flynn told her.

Lara exhaled with relief; there was nothing more mortifying than one-sided giving. Except he'd got her two, which meant she now owed him one. OK, don't worry about it for the moment. Also, how *exciting* . . .

'You need to tell her now,' Gigi said matter-of-factly.

Flynn shook his head. 'Let's do the presents first.'

'Dad, no way, trust me.'

He looked discomfited. 'But—'

'That wouldn't work,' Gigi interrupted before he could protest. 'Do it now.'

What was going on? Lara could hear Don, Nettie and Evie out in the kitchen, singing along to 'White Christmas' on the radio. She watched as Gigi and Flynn exchanged a long mean-ingful look. Finally Gigi said, 'If you don't tell her, I will.'

'Tell me *what*?' But in that split second she knew why Flynn was so reluctant to break what was clearly pretty momentous news. Oh God, and of course Gigi knew because he would already have discussed it with her. Inwardly trembling, Lara said,

'Let me guess, it's about Annabel.' She hoped her voice didn't sound as weird and echoey as it felt; if she hadn't already been sitting, her legs might have wobbled and given way. 'You've got engaged . . .'

This was what Gigi had been preparing her for the other night, letting her know she'd missed her chance.

'Yes,' said Flynn. He paused and shook his head. 'Well, no. I mean, yes, it's about Annabel . . .'

'Honestly, you're hopeless. Forget it,' Gigi interrupted when he faltered once more. 'I'll do it myself. OK, now listen.' She turned to address Lara. 'Back in October, Dad met Annabel at the wine-tasting we told you about. They got chatting afterwards and she told him she was dreading a works dinner where she was expected to take a boyfriend along with her, because she didn't have one.'

Flynn joined in. 'Then she said jokily, "Unless you'd like to do the honours." And it was on a night when I was free, so I said I would. Just to help her out.'

Lara wondered how much longer she was going to have to keep the this-is-so-interesting expression fixed to her face.

'So he did,' Gigi announced with relish.

'Lovely! Isn't that romantic?' Lara's valiant smile was starting to make her cheeks ache.

'And then he asked Annabel to return the favour.'

'Right.' Bemused, Lara said to Flynn, 'What, you needed to take a partner along to some event?' Really, could they get the story told and finished? The last thing she wanted to hear was every last nauseating detail.

'I did. At Aqua,' said Flynn.

'Oh.' *Bloody sodding Aqua.* 'So that's why it's your favourite restaurant.'

'Mum.' Gigi rolled her eyes. 'Sometimes you're quite clever.

414

And other times you're just amazingly, *incredibly* thick.' She hauled herself to her feet and looked at Flynn. 'OK, my work here is done. She's all yours now. Good luck.'

The door closed behind her and then it was just the two of them in the living room. Flynn raked his hair back from his forehead and said slowly, 'Annabel isn't my girlfriend. She never was. It was Gigi's idea, she said maybe it would do the trick, make you change your mind about . . . you know, *us.*'

This was so much the opposite of what she'd been bracing herself to hear, Lara struggled to take the words in. It was like being six years old again, giddy with excitement on Christmas Eve as she put carrots and mince pies out ready for Santa and his reindeer. Until her father had whispered in her ear, 'Santa isn't real, you know. He's just made up. I'm the one who has to pay for your presents.'

It was a moment she'd never shared with anyone. Even when her mum had carried on gaily chatting about Father Christmas and Rudolph, Lara had instinctively known her mother would be upset if she told her what she knew.

The memory had risen up from nowhere, a disorientating revelation that at the time had rocked her six-year-old world. Lara blinked; Flynn's words might have the ability to rock but there was one all-important difference now. This time he was telling her something she did want to hear.

'I asked Gigi what she wanted for Christmas,' Flynn went on.

'So did I.' Her skin was zinging, the air in the room crackling with electricity. Or did it only feel that way?

'I'm guessing she gave us both the same answer.' He paused, watching her. 'Well, anyway, there you go. Now you know the truth.'

'But . . . you took me shopping to help you choose presents for Annabel.'

415

'And I took them straight back to the shops the next day. That was Gigi's idea too, to make you jealous.' Another pause. 'Did it work?'

Go on. Be honest.

'Yes,' Lara said simply. 'It did, it really did.'

'Well, that's a good start. She said it would. I wasn't so sure.'

It was still a struggle; one minute she'd been expecting an engagement announcement, the next she was being told that Annabel didn't exist . . . well, she still existed but not in a girl-friendy way. 'Can I ask something else? What about the silk dressing gown from Harvey Nicks?'

'It wasn't from Annabel. Or Harvey Nichols. We ordered it off Amazon, express delivery.' Flynn smiled. 'It only cost fifty pounds. Why, would you like one too?'

Actually, she probably would. Fifty pounds was a complete bargain for something that looked as if it had come from Harvey Nicks.

'So basically, this was quite a complicated plan,' said Lara.

'Sometimes you need a complicated plan. God knows, none of the other ones worked.'

'Oh? And what were they?'

'Telling you I liked you,' He started counting on his fingers. 'Trying to seduce you. Telling you I no longer *wanted* to seduce you . . .'

Lara bit her lip at the memory of the last one, which had definitely made her feel a bit panicky.

'And this is the last resort,' said Flynn. 'It's up to you now. You know how I feel. You know what Gigi wants. And there are never going to be any rock-solid guarantees, but I really think we could be happy together for the rest of our lives and it would be a bloody tragedy if we didn't even give it a try. So, yes or no?'

416

Yes or no? Yes or no? He was the father of her child and she'd never stopped loving him, not for a minute. She'd spent these last months saying no and convincing herself it was for the best.

But what if she'd been wrong?

Rising to her feet – God, her knees were jiddering – Lara took a clumsy couple of steps forward and said, 'Yes, please.'

Chapter 59

How long had he been kissing her? All Lara knew was that the singers in the kitchen had been warbling along to 'A Winter's Tale' and now they were all bellowing out Greg Lake's 'I Believe In Father Christmas'. Whether there'd been other songs in between was anybody's guess.

'Now listen to me.' Flynn drew back at last and gazed into her eyes. 'I love you, more than you'll ever know.' He held her face between his hands. 'This is going to work, do you believe that?'

Lara nodded, blinking back tears. It was such a relief to be able to relax and stop fighting every animal instinct in her body. 'Yes, I do.'

'Good.'

'And I love you too.' She needed to say it, needed him to hear it. It was the truth.

'Guess what?' said Flynn, his thumbs stroking her cheeks. 'This is all I wanted for Christmas . . .'

'Brilliant. Lucky I kept the receipt for that shirt, then.'

Amused, he indicated the parcels under the tree. 'Your presents are still there. Want to open them now?'

'Are they good ones?'

'I think you'll like them,' said Flynn.

Of course she liked them; hadn't she practically chosen them herself? The light-as-a-feather, swingy suede coat from Armani and the perfect black stilettos with crystal bows on the heels. They looked amazing and fitted like a dream.

'You took a risk,' said Lara. 'I thought you were buying them for someone else. I might have chosen horrible stuff on purpose.'

'But I knew you wouldn't. You're not that type of person. That's why I love you.'

'Is that the only reason?'

'If I put my mind to it, I'm sure I could think of a few more.'

Lara kissed him again, then said, 'That crew in the kitchen will be wondering what's going on.'

'You're right. We should probably tell them.'

The door burst open and Gigi cried, 'No need, we were listening! This is so *brilliant* . . .'

Behind her, Evie said, 'And about time too.'

By one o'clock all the food had been prepared and was either in the oven or on the hob.

'If you two want to head off,' said Nettie, 'now would be the best time to do it.'

'Head off? What for?' Lara wasn't missing lunch for anything.

'We'll be dishing up at two.' Nettie wiped her hands on a tea towel and tapped the watch on her wrist. 'So you'll have an hour.'

'Great.' Flynn had already reached for his car keys. 'That's plenty of time.'

'Hang on, I don't have a clue what's going on here.' Her face burning, Lara feigned ignorance; if he'd asked Nettie to give them an hour so he could whisk her back to his flat for mad passionate sex, she would just *die* of embarrassment.

419

I mean, OK, it would be seriously long overdue mad passionate sex, but still. Talk about inappropriate.

'Ha!' Gigi was pointing gleefully at her. 'Look at Mum's face! I know what she's thinking.'

'It's not that.' Flynn was holding the caramel suede coat out, ready for Lara to slide her arms into the sleeves. 'There's something I want to show you.'

Hmm, she'd heard *that* line before.

'It's another present.' Gigi was clearly in on the surprise. 'Well, kind of. No designer labels though, this time.' She pointed to Lara's feet. 'And you won't want to be wearing those heels.'

Never before had driving through central Bath been so effortless. The normally clogged streets were virtually empty, all the shops closed. The silence was surreal.

'Are you going to tell me where we're headed?'

'No, you'll just have to wait. Be patient.' Flynn glanced sideways at her and said good-naturedly, 'See how much you like it, for a change.'

Great waves of happiness kept washing over her; Lara simply couldn't keep the stupid smile off her face. 'If a thing's worth waiting for, it's worth . . . waiting for. OK, that's not quite right, but I know what I mean.'

'Eighteen years. Actually, nineteen years now,' he amended. 'That's a pretty long wait.'

'I'm worth it.'

Flynn's mouth twitched. 'So am I.'

The city was looking stunning; the sky was palest blue and the snow sparkled like crystallised sugar in the bright sunlight. When she saw where Flynn was stopping the car, Lara realised why Gigi had insisted on her changing out of stilettos into low-heeled boots.

Royal Victoria Park, open every day of the year, was also emptier than usual, although they did pass the occasional family and dog-walker along the way. Much as she wanted to admire the beauty of the frost-laden trees, Lara found herself endlessly distracted by the sight of her hand clasped in Flynn's. It looked and felt so right. Just being here, her arm pressed against his, the blissful physical proximity, filled her with pure joy. She'd learned her lesson; life was here to be lived and risks needed to be taken. It was the only way.

'Not far to go now,' said Flynn as they climbed a slope and took a left turn.

This wasn't where James had collapsed and died. Thankful for that, Lara gave his hand a squeeze. Finally they rounded a bend in the path and Flynn said, 'Here we are.'

They'd reached a small clearing ringed by shrubs and trees. In the centre stood a wooden bench, its slats covered with a light powdering of snow. Allowing him to draw her towards it, Lara watched as he used his free hand to wipe frost from the brass plaque on the bench's backrest.

Engraved on it were the words 'Barbara and James. In loving memory.'

Flynn's arm was around her. Lara leaned against him, her head resting on his chest, and gazed at the plaque until the names blurred.

'That's perfect. Thank you so much. They're here for ever now.'

'I know.' He gave her a squeeze and dropped a kiss on top of her head.

It felt fantastic; how could she ever tire of that happening?

Gazing up at him, Lara said, 'What would you have done if we hadn't got back together?'

'I'd have sneaked back here in the dead of night with a screwdriver and taken the plaque off. Or hired a van and driven off with the whole bench, then burned it.' He broke into a smile and shook his head. 'No, this wasn't a bribe; it's not part of the deal. I wanted to do it anyway.'

'I love it.' Lara surveyed the clearing. 'I wonder if my mum and James were ever here, actually right here on this spot?'

'Oh, I'm sure they were,' said Flynn.

Where was he taking her now? She stayed at his side as he led her away from the bench and towards the trees in front of it. He paused at the edge of the clearing and pointed to the trunk of an old silver birch, its overhanging branches iced with snow.

'Oh . . .' breathed Lara, transfixed by what was carved into the silver-grey bark. There it was, the slightly lopsided heart painstakingly created by James almost forty years ago, enclosing the initials BC and JA. Shaking her head, she said, 'I can't believe you found it. I spent ages looking.' She'd come here to the park a couple of times following James's death, but with fifty-seven acres to search, had been defeated.

'I'd love to lie and take the credit.' Flynn watched her reach up and slowly trace the initials with her index finger. 'But I can't. I asked one of the gardeners employed by the council's parks department. He didn't know, but he put me in touch with another gardener who told me there was an old guy called Billy who's retired now, but worked here for forty years.' He paused, then went on, 'So I spoke to Billy and he knew at once which tree it was. But he couldn't describe the location very well, so I went to fetch him and brought him along in his wheelchair to show me.'

'Where did you fetch him from?'

'He lives in Manchester now.'

Unbelievably touched by the lengths he'd gone to, Lara said, 'And here it is.'

'And here it is.' Flynn nodded in agreement. 'Your final present.' He gazed up at the spreading web of branches overhead, fifty feet high and every bit as wide. 'Sorry I didn't wrap it for you.'

'That's OK. It's the best present I've ever had.' Lara pulled him to her and kissed him. 'I definitely won't be taking this one back to the shop.'

'You won't be returning me either.' His mouth as warm as his hands, Flynn smiled as he murmured, 'You're stuck with me now. For good.'

'At last! Honestly, I don't know what took you so long,' said Lara.